Jane G. Austin

The shadow of Moloch Mountain

Jane G. Austin

The shadow of Moloch Mountain

ISBN/EAN: 9783743338371

Manufactured in Europe, USA, Canada, Australia, Japa

Cover: Foto ©Andreas Hilbeck / pixelio.de

Manufactured and distributed by brebook publishing software
(www.brebook.com)

Jane G. Austin

The shadow of Moloch Mountain

THE

SHADOW

OF

MOLOCH MOUNTAIN.

BY

JANE G. AUSTIN,

AUTHOR OF "CIPHER," ETC.

NEW-YORK:

SHELDON & COMPANY.

1870.

THE SHADOW OF MOLOCH MOUNTAIN.

CHAPTER I.

"MORE THAN KIN AND LESS THAN KIND."

NEAR the town and seaport of Milvorhaven, stood, some years ago, an old farm house known as the Brewster Place.

The Brewster Place.

The house itself might have been copied as a type of rural architecture in the New England of fifty years ago, with its low, red walls; its roof sweeping downward at the back until it touched the ground; its huge chimney-stack occupying nearly half the area of the house; its unhewn "door-rock" and primitive elm-shaded well; its lilac and syringa bushes, and the fine, short turf crowding close to the low sills. A pleasant house, although somewhat lonely, set as it was in the midst of low sand-hills and dwarfed pine forest, with no hint of neighborhood in sight, unless it was to be inferred from the narrow wheel-track winding away from the door and losing itself in the blue-green shadow of the wood. A pleasant house, and a good farm, as farms went in the township of Milvorhaven; and yet, as Peleg Brewster, driving his span of stout grays from the barn to the house, cast a gloomy look over his possessions, he muttered with a bitter curse: "I wish the devil had the farm—and me too, for that matter."

At the door of the farm-house stood a woman about thirty years old, whom one might call pretty at the first glance, qualifying the opinion as he chose, after noting with a second look the cunning and sensual lines about the red mouth, the false light in the greenish-blue eyes, the depression of the forehead, and the firmness of the lower jaw. This woman was Semantha Brewster, second wife of the black-browed farmer who, sitting in the wagon at the gate, sternly asked of her:

"Well, where is Ruth ?"

"Getting ready, but as ugly as sin about it," said the woman sulkily.

"Tell her to make haste, or I'll come and fetch her in a hurry," ordered her husband

and the woman disappeared within the house.

Peleg Brewster, still sitting at the gate, watched the door for a moment, and then suffered his eyes to wander on, over the low, round hills, over the dense pine wood, past the scattered houses, set here and there upon their lonely farms, until far on the horizon-line he caught the glint of the sea, bright beneath the morning sun.

It was the same view that had met his eyes ever since he first opened them forty years before; and yet, to-day, he looked upon it as a stranger might, noting with curious interest the zigzag line of the half-cleared wood, where he had gone chestnuting so long ago that half these trees had sprung since then, the broken chain of hills beyond, the gap where they parted to let Milvor Branch bring its bright waters to the sea, and, finally, the fields and pastures, green with aftermath, of his own domain. Over all these swept the gloomy gaze, softening and saddening as it went, until, with a sudden movement, Peleg Brewster turned and looked intently toward a rising ground behind his house, where, within an enclosure of evergreen-trees, lay a little burial-place dotted with white gravestones.

"If Mary had lived!" muttered he, and leaning an elbow upon his knee, rested his chin in his hand, and set his haggard gaze straight before him.

"Forty years boy and man, and now I'm going. The same roof shan't cover us——"

The figure of a man crossing the road in front of his horses' heads broke the line of that set gaze, and it altered to an expression of concentrated rage.

"Hallo, there! Joe—Joe Brewster, I say! Come here," called he, sitting upright, and clenching the hand a moment before hanging supinely from his knee.

The man thus addressed paused, hesitated a moment, and then came slouching down the road, until, standing near, but not within reach of the wagon, he raised his eyes as far as the other's breast, then dropped them again, and asked in a low voice:

"Well, Peleg, what is it?"

Peleg Brewster did not immediately reply, but in the look he fixed upon the other's face burned such concentrated scorn and wrath such utter loathing and contempt, that the glance could not fail but reach the consciousness of its object with a sting words might have failed

to convey. Shifting uneasily from foot to foot, and moistening his white lips before he spoke, the new-comer asked again:

"Did you want to say any thing more, Peleg? I'm just a going."

"The same father and the same mother owned us, and I wonder why I don't take this gun and shoot you in your tracks," said Peleg, half turning toward a rifle lying behind him in the wagon. His brother glanced apprehensively in the same direction, but made no reply. Peleg still regarded him in silence, and within the house was heard the soft and silky voice of Semantha, calling:

"Come, Ruthie, aren't you ready yet?"

The sound seemed to rouse her husband from the gloomy reverie into which he was falling, and he hurriedly said:

"What I have to tell you, Joe Brewster, is this: I am going to the 'haven this morning, and to Milvor this afternoon; and before I come home, I'll sell this place, and every hoof and every stick upon it, and I'll make a will that shall put the price of my home out of your reach, and out of hers—yes, and out of the child's too, that you, between you, have made near as big a devil as yourselves. And when that's over, I'm going—no matter where. Where I never shall see or hear of the man I called my brother, or the woman I called my wife, or the girl that was Mary Brewster's daughter. Curse you, curse you all, I say, and may——"

He shut his teeth firmly over the next words, and though the tempest of passion shook him like a leaf, and though his writhing lips grew white, and his very eyes blanched in their agony, the imprecation remained unspoken.

Oh! well for you, Peleg Brewster—well for you before the night fell, that those words were never said, that you fought the fight and conquered!

Wiping the great drops from his forehead, he said more calmly than he had yet spoken:

"Take whatever belongs to you, Joe, and keep the farm-money which I gave you last week, but begone from here before I come home; mind that, or I won't answer for what I may do. Begone from here by five o'clock this afternoon, as you value your life. To-morrow, I shall take Semanthy to her mother's, and in another day I shall be gone myself."

He spoke the last words more to himself

than to his brother, and again his haggard eyes wandered over field and wood, and distant ocean-view, with the strange, sad gaze of one who looks with new eyes upon the dear spot he leaves forever.

Joe, stealing a glance upward, caught the softened expression of his brother's face, and, after a moment's hesitation, asked deprecatingly:

"Why can't you let me try to explain a little?"

"Explain!" interposed the other fiercely. "Do you think I need any explanations? Do you take me for a fool? Be off, I tell you! Don't wait till the devil gets uppermost in me, or——"

A savage glance filled up the sentence, and without waiting for another, Joe Brewster turned and made the best of his speed toward the shelter of the grove whence he had emerged. At the same moment, Mrs. Brewster appeared at the door, followed by a girl of about twelve years of age, meanly dressed, tall and gaunt, and with her face as nearly hidden as possible beneath a large cape-bonnet made of striped print. Between them, these two carried a small round trunk, covered with horse-hair, which they placed in the back of the wagon. The girl then came forward to the step, but her father, without looking round, and with a backward motion of the hand, repulsed her, saying shortly:

"Get in behind, and sit on the trunk; I don't want you here."

And as Ruth silently obeyed, he continued still, without looking round:

"Semanthy, you can put up every thing in the house that you brought to it, and whatever else you've any claim to; but see that you don't touch a thing that was Mary's—mind you that! To-morrow morning, you'll go home to your mother, and if she wants to know why you've come, I'll tell her."

Still, without looking round, he gathered up the reins and drove away—away from the house where he had been born, where he had lived ten happy years with the wife whose white head-stone now looked farewell from the far hill-side—from the home which, to his mind, had of a sudden grown less a home than the narrow bound beside that dead wife where he had always thought to be laid.

Away from home, and the memories of forty peaceful years, drove Peleg Brewster, and the rustling shadows of the pine-wood received him and hid him, and threw themselves an impassable, if impalpable, barrier between him and that home forever.

CHAPTER II.

MARSTON'S CHOICE.

FOLLOWING the waters of Milvor Branch ten miles back from "The Haven," as Milvor folk loved to call their little seaport, one finds their source in the confluence of two or three merry little brooks near the foot of Moloch Mountain. Each one of these brooks is a beauty in its way, and as full of character as most beauties are not; but the loveliest, the most piquant, and utterly fascinating of them all is the tricksy watercourse known as the Millbrook. As the name implies, the little stream has been utilized, or rather practicalized; for let no man deny that beauty is also use, and that to be is to be utilized; but it chanced one day that Millbrook, dancing along in her usual heedless fashion, found a barrier across her path, and after a little pause of indignant astonishment, gathered her forces and leaped it. The fall was not high, and rather enjoying it than otherwise, the brook, hurrying on, next encountered a large wooden wheel, which, as she dashed through and by, began to revolve—slowly at first, then faster, snatching up masses of the bright water, scattering them in the sunshine, and letting them fall again into the sparkling torrent, like a giant baby playing with his mother's diamonds.

"Ha! ha!" laughed the brook. "This is fun—now, isn't it?" and slipping by the wheel, she danced out into the sunlight again, all dimpled with laughter and babbling with fun, as she held her course to the rendezvous where she and her sisters were to join forces and rechristen themselves Milvor Branch.

And from that day to this, Millbrook tumbles over the dam and through the wheel—not because she can't help it—oh! no; but because it is so capital a joke, and really such an amusing little variety to the old routine; and always when she reäppears, it is with a whirl and a slide, and babbling and dimpling all over with fun, and a new joy in sunshine and liberty. But one cannot expect human nature to go to school to the brooks, or if he does, he will probably be disappointed.

Just where Millbrook, yet unconscious of what life means, comes rioting down the side of Moloch Mountain, and, making a sudden fantastic twist, crosses the path ascending that eminence, two lovers lingered to watch the setting of the sun whose rising had seen Peleg Brewster sitting before his farm-house door, and bidding good-by to the familiar scenes and memories of a lifetime.

Two lovers, and yet as unloverlike as a six-months' married couple, with whom the honeymoon is over, and the serene sun of marriage not yet risen; for Marston Brent, leaning against a tree-boll, with his arms folded, his heavy jaw set, and his black brows drawn low over his moody eyes, looked more like a Brutus than a Romeo; and Beatrice Wansted, spite of her yellow hair and soft hazel eyes, had more of Kate than Juliet in her present mien.

Was it an odd chance, a presentiment, or a cause working out its own effect, that had led the girl's dead mother to call her Beatrice? One thing was certain, that when Alice Wansted returned a poor widow to her father's house, the only relic of her brief magnificence that she brought with her was an exquisite copy of the Cenci, done by a young Italian artist whom Arthur Wansted had fancied to patronize during the winter in Rome that had opened a new life to his young wife, and ended in his own death. So, the poor young widow, creeping home to the quiet country fireside where she had been born, brought hardly more than this exquisite picture, her broken heart, and the unborn child whom, with one of the few faint breaths drawn between its birth and her own death, she named Beatrice. The desire was heeded, as dying people's wishes occasionally are, and the little girl, developing, year by year, into rarer beauty, developed too so striking a resemblance to the pictured face she best loved to contemplate, that the country-folk who visited at the old house could not be persuaded but that the picture was a likeness of Mrs. Wansted, although her husband and the artist might, perhaps, have given it the untoward name now borne by the child. Even the expression, the melancholy beseeching, mingled with an indomitable resolution, "the stern, yet piteous look," that tells the story of Beatrice Cenci to-day, from Guido's canvas, as it spoke from her living lineaments two hundred years ago, was to be found, latent as yet, perhaps, in this young girl's face. There, too, the sensitive and exquisite lines that told of a heart to love till death; a pride that would hide that love beneath the ruin of a life; passion, resolution, and over all an invincible purity and refinement.

Just now, however, that fair face expressed no more than vexation and astonishment, as, looking up in her lover's face, Beatrice quietly asked:

"You don't mean to refuse my uncle's offer, do you?"

"Why, yes, Beatrice; I have just explained to you that I should do so, and why."

"What folly!" ejaculated the young lady pettishly. "He said himself that before ten years were out, you might be an equal partner with himself, and meantime would be sure of a handsome salary."

Marston Brent raised his dark head a trifle higher, and said quietly:

"I prefer to be my own master even for ten years."

"And you prefer to become a miserable—what shall I call your future occupation?—wood-chopper, perhaps, to becoming a merchant prince?" asked Beatrice bitingly.

"I prefer the woods to the cities, nature to trade—yes," replied her lover.

"And your own will to my wishes?"

"My own judgment to your fancies."

"Fancy! No; it is something more than fancy that makes my taste and my pride, my whole nature indeed, revolt from the life you propose to me, especially when we see the way so fairly opened to another."

"But, Beatrice, don't you perceive that what you wish is to sacrifice my pride to yours? It is not a very amiable quality, to be sure, but as I have unfortunately as large a share as yourself, you must allow me to consult it a little; and to become a clerk in your uncle's counting-house would injure my pride far more severely than the mode of life at which you sneer could injure yours."

Miss Wansted plucked a handful of leaves from the alder beside her, and cast them into the stream with a scornful air, but otherwise made no reply.

Marston Brent looked down at her with the half-angry, half-loving air of a man at once vexed and charmed with his antagonist, and throwing himself upon the sward beside her, seized her hand, saying good-humoredly:

"Come, Trix, don't be unreasonable. Wait until I set my plans once more before you, and see if I cannot make you look at them through my eyes. When the news of my father's death reached me, you know, I was on my way home from the West, and had been for some weeks visiting Mills in his logging camp, and you have no idea of the sport we found——"

"You told me all that," interposed Miss Wansted, just a little scornfully.

"Excuse me. I remember that I did. I will try not to weary you more than I can avoid. Mills had just decided, as I left, to return to the city and resume his former business, and was anxious that I should purchase his claim, including the bark-mill, tannery, and all the logging shanties and tools, offering them at a bargain. I had no money then; but now, after settling my father's affairs, I find myself master of very nearly the whole sum Mills demanded, and shall no doubt be able to make easy terms with him for the remainder. Then, Beatrice, the rest depends upon my own strength, energy, and ambition, and I hope it is not boasting in me to say, I have no fear of failing in either of the three."

He raised his eyes with a proud smile to those of his betrothed, but found there no answering expression. No marble could have been colder than Miss Wansted's face as she inquired:

"And do you propose to take me to one of the 'shanties,' as you call them, and have me cook the pork and potatoes for you and your wood-choppers?"

Brent bit his lip, flushing redly the while, but answered patiently:

"I told you—did I not?—that I am meaning in the spring to build a pretty cottage beside the river, and ask you to furnish it to suit your own taste. Could not you be happy in such a home with me, Beatrice, though it might be many a mile from city or watering-place?"

The girl was silent, and he continued with a simple pathos in his voice, the more touching from contrast with the rugged strength and energy of his former tone:

"Only have faith and patience, Trix, and I promise that you shall be a rich woman before you are twenty years older—perhaps before ten years. Only give me time and the heart to work, knowing that I am working for you, and I can do any thing."

"In twenty years, I shall be forty years old, and half my life will have been spent in a wilderness. How shall I be fitted for the society I may then have an opportunity of enjoying?" asked Beatrice sullenly. "Not that I would refuse to consent even to this," added

she presently in a softened tone, " if you had no other prospect or hope. But to contrast with this dreary future, here is my uncle's letter, offering you a position in one of the first mercantile houses in the city, and with such prospects as he himself says not one young man in a hundred can command. It is downright folly and perversity for you to refuse, and I will never consent. Give up the woods, or give up——"

"Stop, Beatrice! Don't say that, and don't let us become excited or ill-tempered," said Marston, dropping the hand he had held until now, and sitting upright. Had Beatrice glanced then at his face, and read there the nature she had never yet learned to know, the whole course of her life might have been changed by the brief lesson; but she only tore at the alder-leaves in her hand, and set her lips more firmly together.

"The time has come," said Marston very patiently, " to you and me that must come to all people who try to make their two lives run in one channel. One of us must yield a decided wish, opinion, and plan to the other. Now, Trix, in choosing the occupation and whole character of my future life, of my man-work in the world, it cannot be doubted that my own capacities, tastes, and ideas of independence should be the first things to be consulted, nor can it be doubted that these are better known to me than they can be to you. I have chosen, and I am very sure that I have chosen rightly. More than that," and he paused a moment, then went on full voiced, " I shall not alter my decision; but though I cannot give up my manhood to please you, Beatrice, there is hardly any thing else I would not do; and I need not tell you again that your love is the sweetest and dearest thing in life to me, and that to call you wife has been for months the fondest hope I have ever known. Darling, do not fear that you shall suffer want or care in our forest-home, or that any ill shall reach you other than those——"

"Stop, if you please, Mr. Brent," said a clear, cold voice; and Marston, raising his honest eyes to those of his mistress, felt an involuntary thrill of admiration, for never had Beatrice Wansted looked so beautiful as now, with her hazel eyes wide and bright, her creamy cheek lightly flushed, and her mouth curved with pride and scorn.

"You have given your decision," said she slowly, " now hear mine: I will never follow you to the wigwam you offer. I will never marry you if you persist in your refusal to accept my uncle's offer. Choose this moment between your will—and me."

With an involuntary motion, Marston grasped her wrist, and bent his head until their eyes confronted: in his a sudden anguish, in hers a scornful assurance—in each an indomitable will. He was the first to speak:

"Beatrice, be careful. You know that I love you, heart and soul, and with every fibre of my whole body. You know that to part from you in this way would be like dragging that heart and body asunder. But you do not know, you cannot know, that to go back from my pledged word, my solemn purpose, would be worse. Beatrice, I cannot; I tell you I cannot yield to you. For God's sake, show in this moment that you have a woman's softer nature, and save both our lives from wreck."

She looked him steadily in the face, marked with a sort of wonder the terrible emotion that in one moment had drawn and blanched it until it might have been the picture of a malefactor expiring under torture, and then she slowly repeated:

"Choose between your own will and me."

"Not now. Let us go home and wait a little—wait perhaps until I have been away a year, and then I will come and ask you again. You shall be free as air in the mean time—only you will let me come and ask again when the year is over, and the little cottage built?"

His deep voice pleaded now like that of a little child, and the tears stood in his dark eyes as he sought hers, which for a moment had turned aside.

"Do you mean by let us wait that perhaps by morning you may change your mind? Of course, after a year, you could not," said Beatrice coldly.

"My God! Have I not told you that I cannot change? Ask the rocks, the trees, the water to change, but not me. It is not in me anywhere. It can never be," burst out Marston in a tone of desperate agony.

"Then we part this moment, and forever," said Beatrice, the whole passion of her nature flaring up through the icy mask she had assumed. "If you cannot and will not yield to me in this, neither will I yield to you. I will not wait; no, not one hour, one moment. I will never see you, never speak to you, or, if I can help it, breathe the same air with you

again. You have made me love you, and now you wish to make a slave of me through that love. You are hard, and selfish, and obstinate, and I am well released from you."

She rose to her feet; he too, and holding her by the shoulders, looked into her face, his own white and set.

"Beatrice," said he slowly, "you are spoiling both our lives. Have a care, for you will suffer too. I will not take your answer now; I will write to you from Wahtahree."

He was turning away, but she caught him passionately by the hand. He turned and met the fiery devil in her eyes with a look of unmoved determination.

"Stop!" cried she, "stop and hear me! If you write to me, I will return your letter unopened; if you try to see me, I will order you from my doors; if you send me a message, I will not listen to it; if you leave me now, you leave me forever—forever. Marston Brent, though you come but to-morrow to lay yourself with the world's wealth at my feet. Now choose, and for the last time—your own will or my love."

A moment, another, and another went by, and still he stood looking into her white face and burning eyes, with a solemn earnestness conquering the pain and the bitterness that had so wrung his soul. At last he said:

"Beatrice, swear before God that what you say you mean."

The girl lifted her palm to heaven. Marston caught it in his own, and a sudden terror sprung into his eyes as he cried:

"Oh! think once more. Remember how I love you, remember that the long future lies before us, and that your next words make or mar it forever. Wait one moment, think one moment."

But Beatrice, tearing away her hand, lifted it again to heaven, and said slowly:

"I swear before God that what I have just said I mean and will do. Now choose, Marston Brent."

"I choose—liberty," said he, and without another word, they parted, going by different paths, down the mountain-side which they had climbed, his arm about her waist, her hand locked in his.

CHAPTER III.
THE OLD GARRISON.

THE autumn twilight was deepening into night as Beatrice Wansted reached her home, and paused, before pushing open the swinging gate, to look at it with a strange distaste.

"How can I go in and sit down as if nothing had happened? How can I smile, and talk, and live day after day? How long will it be before I break out into raving madness, crazed by the cold monotony of such a life—such a life for me?"

So whispering, she leaned upon the mossy fence, and stared at the old house with such distasteful interest as a trappist, newly hidden but not divorced from the world, might feel for the spot where he is bid to dig his future grave.

And yet the Old Garrison, as Milvor called it, was no uncheerful dwelling, albeit venerable and quaint as its origin promised. More than two hundred years ago—not fifty after Beatrice Cenci had expiated upon the scaffold her most righteous crime—a party of Puritans, straying from the settlement about Plymouth Bay, had urged their skiff up Milvor Branch, and at its head had diverged into Millbrook, following the bright course of its waters, until, not far from the mouth, they curved in a sudden bend about a pretty knoll surrounded by rich meadow-land. Here they halted, and here one of the party, Peleg Barstow by name, decided to remain; and being a godly and just man, bestowed such treasure of beads, gunpowder, cloth, and, it may be, less innocent wares, upon the Indian owners, as induced them to affix their signs-manual to a deed, yet extant in the old house, by which they made over to Peleg Barstow and his heirs forever all right and title to knoll, meadows, upland, brook, and the herring which crowded its merry waters, forever and a day.

But—alas! that we should say it—not fifty years later, Peleg and his sons found themselves obliged to fortify their dwelling against the invasion of these same savage allies, now become their cruel enemies; and so successfully did they strengthen its defences that the women and children for miles around flocked to them for shelter, and the house received the name it has since retained, and is still known as the Old Garrison.

But to the few rooms of the original house with their walls three feet in thickness, and their leaden casements with tiny diamond-shaped panes, came to be added, by successive generations of Barstows, additions of such style and size as suited the wants or the taste of the builders, so that the house stood final-ly a sort of hieroglyphic genealogy of the race, and Beatrice Wansted might have read, had she been so minded, the story of her ancestors in the motley architecture of the home they had bequeathed her.

But Time has power over none but his own dominion, and though the work of old Peleg Barstow's hands had well-nigh mingled with the dust that had once been flesh and bones of that sturdy old Puritan, the knoll and the brook, and human nature remained much as they had been in his day; and this his fair descendant stood contemplating her home in the gray twilight, with far less thought of the past it represented, than of her own future, linked it might be to those crumbling walls—it might be to far different scenes.

"But never," whispered Beatrice again, as she softly swung open the gate, "never to be passed at your side, or beneath your feet, Marston Brent—never—never!"

She murmured the words again and again, the bitter refrain of a dreary song, as she lingered up the narrow path whose box-borders, brushed by her garments, gave out a faint, melancholy perfume, a perfume of night and autumn, of dead memories and hopes, and life slowly lapsing into death, and then decay and nothingness.

Fine ladies have their fancies, and in after years it was noted as one of Miss Wansted's whims to detest the sight or smell of box-plants.

Near the door she paused, and stood looking in at the unshuttered window, with the same half-loathing interest that had held her at the garden-gate.

She saw a room low and large, its ceiling divided by two heavy beams crossing each other in the centre. Other beams stood sentry in the corners, and ran like a low bench around the side of the room. To one of these a descendant of Peleg Barstow, crazed through religious fanaticism, had been chained by his family, and then had dragged out the twenty weary years lying between such strange imprisonment and death. The scar worn by his chain still stared from the heavy beam—a character, and a significant one, in the hieroglyphic history unconsciously left behind by the successive occupants of the Old Garrison.

At one end of the room yawned a fireplace so wide that the bright copper andirons, with their load of three-foot maple logs, were quite at one end of it, while at the other end and in the back of the chimney was the door of a great brick oven, and below it a bench where Beatrice, a little rebellious imp, had often been set to recover from the effects of too long a ramble in the winter woods, or an involuntary immersion in the icy waters of the brook.

In one of the deep recesses of the windows lay an enormous tortoise-shell cat, her fore paws curled under her breast, her yellow eyes half closed, and winking slowly at the fire. Beyond her in the corner stood a clock, reaching from floor to ceiling, sedate and grave, in spite of the glittering brass ornaments which it wore as meekly as an old lady wears the gold beads she retains from habit, although the vanities of youth have long been laid aside.

Above the high mantle-shelf was fastened the head and branching antlers of a deer, and as the firelight rose and fell, its shadow, changing in every fantastic fashion, danced upon the ceiling—now spreading to its farthest limit, in semblance of a tangled arabesque, now shrinking to such narrow limits and so defined a shape that it might have been the ghost of the murdered stag peering down into the room and demanding restitution of his stolen honors.

All alone in his deep arm-chair, before the fire, sat an old man—a man so old that his hair, long and thick and soft, had not one dark thread left in its creamy masses; that his face was not lined, but grained with wrinkles; that his toothless jaws met in a straight, deep line, hiding in great measure the expression of the mouth; and his form was bowed and trembling, even as he sat motionless before the fire. His eyes, shrewd and kindly, even through the dimness of age, were fixed upon the blaze, and his white and shapely hands were folded meditatively upon his knee. A charming picture of serene old age, but Beatrice regarded it with a shiver.

"Ninety-four years old!" murmured she, "and I but twenty. If I should live till then!"

She moaned impatiently, and twisted her fingers within each other in a gesture of fierce protest.

A door opened in the back of the room, and two women entered—one of them nearly as old as the dreamer before the fire, the other perhaps fifty years younger, but claiming neither the beauty of youth nor age; for while losing the bloom of one, she had not yet acquired the serenity of the other; and with her tall and angular figure, sharp features, abundant red hair, and quick gray eyes, contrasted unfavorably enough with the placid patriarch and his cheery, active wife.

Beatrice looked at her, and made a little mutinous gesture, full of defiant expression.

"And to live with Aunt Rachel all my days, or until I come to be just like her!" muttered she; and slowly raising the latch, she passed through a square passage into the room where the family were collected. All looked up at her entrance, and saluted her variously.

"Well, daughter," said the old man. "So you have finished your wanderings for one day more. Night brings the stray lambs home, but they go out with the sun again."

"You shouldn't linger out in the night-dews so, child," chimed in his wife. "It's dreadful unwholesome to breathe the air at this time of day. I declare, you're as pale as a ghost—and no wonder. Sit to the fire and heat the soles of your feet. Won't you drink a little balm-tea if I make it for you? It's proper good with sugar in it; or you can have some tansy if you like it better."

"Just look at that dress round the bottom, and then your skirt, Beatrice! Where *have* you been trailing them? I can tell you, miss, if you had the washing or the starching or the ironing to do, you wouldn't be quite so careless of your things. You put them on clean this afternoon, didn't you? And where is Marston?"

Beatrice stooped and kissed the hand her grandfather held out to detain her, smiled coaxingly at her grandmother, while she said:

"Please not any balm-tea, grandma. I will be good without it." And to her aunt: "I have been on Moloch Mountain, and I did put the dress and skirt on clean, and I do not know where Mr. Brent is at this moment."

Then she passed on to her own little chair in the farther corner of the fireplace, and pushing it deeper into the shadow, sat down, and obediently dried her feet and garments, drenched with the heavy dew.

CHAPTER IV.
WHAT THE RUSHES HID.

HEART-WOUNDS, while they sink deeper and last longer in a woman's nature, convey more instant agony to the firm fibre and powerful organization of the man. So, while Beatrice Wansted went quietly home, and stopped at the gate to speculate upon her future—preparing herself, as it were, for the slow death of many a lingering year—her lover rushed from her presence, dazed, blind, mad with agony, his tortured heart consenting to no future, incredulous of any relief, present or to come, feeling only that his hope had failed him, his motive was gone, that earth had lost its savor and life its salt.

Up to the last moment, even until he heard her sternly call God to witness her words, he had hoped that Beatrice would repent, and since, as he had naïvely asserted, it was impossible for him to retract his decision, that she herself would yield to him, especially in this matter, where, as he still told himself, his own convictions should be final in both their minds.

But now that she had decided against him, and had so solemnly sealed her determination, Marston's own ideas of truth and honor, his reverence for the woman whom he adored, would have withheld him from one word of argument or entreaty, had she remained forever in his presence. She had taken her resolution, and he his. Hers, sealed by a solemn oath, was to him irrevocable; his, simply spoken, quite as much so. All was over between them, over forever; and even while ready to dash his life out against this self-created barrier, it never occurred to Marston Brent to try to scale it.

Wandering whither he knew not, moonrise found him near the foot of the mountain and in its densest shadow. The wood-path he had been unconsciously pursuing ended in the secluded road skirting the base of the mountain, and leading from Milvor to Milvorhaven. Beside this road, at the point of intersection, lay a sluggish pool, product of the mountain drainage retained in a natural hollow; and, leaning upon the broken roadside-fence, the young man stood staring into the shadow of the willows and alder-bushes that had sprung up around it. Hardly had he taken this position when the sound of coming footsteps broke upon the silence, and the figure of a stout lad, dressed in farmer's costume, appeared coming round the turn of the road.

With a gesture of annoyance, Brent would have plunged again into the covert of the wood, but the new-comer had already seen him and called cheerily:

"Good-evening, Mr. Brent. I was just going to your house, but meeting you will save me the two-mile walk, and after digging potatoes all day, I'm willing enough to lose it."

Marston Brent, staring steadily in the young man's face, answered him never a word; and he, rather embarrassed and yet sturdily self-possessed, went on:

"You know you were talking to me about going into York State with you to learn lumbering; and the more I think of it, the more I think it will suit, and I've pretty much made up my mind to try. The terms we talked of the other day suit me well enough; and anyway, I know you'll do the fair thing by me, and I'd as lief have your word as a lawyer's writing; but I can't leave Barstow's before next week. When was you calculating on going?"

"To-morrow morning," said Brent hoarsely.

The boy whistled in dismay.

"Why, I thought you said the last of the week, or the first of next. I can't leave to-morrow morning, nohow. Mr. Barstow has hired a man, but he isn't coming till Saturday, and —— to be sure Jabez Minot would come and do the chores night and morning till then—and to-day is Tuesday. But I want to go to the haven and haul my money out of the savings-bank; and, no, sir, I don't see as I could go anyway to-morrow morning, but I can come alone, and if you will give me the directions, I will. I suppose you'd as lief pay my fare next week as this?"

He waited for an answer, but Brent, his elbows on the railing, his face buried in his hands, had forgotten his presence.

The lad looked at him keenly.

"Do you feel bad anyway, Mr. Brent?" asked he, touching him on the shoulder.

Brent started and raised his haggard face. "What do you want?" asked he fiercely.

"I asked if you were sick or anything. I thought you seemed to feel bad," said the boy, still fixing his keen eyes upon the other's face, and silently deciding that neither intoxication nor illness had produced the ghastly change he saw.

"Sick? Oh! no, there's nothing the matter, Paul. A little tired with walking, that's all. You say you are going with me to Wahtahree. I shall start in the morning, before light perhaps. I am going to drive my horse and wagon to Bloom, where I have sold it, and take the cars there. You can come to my house to-night and start with me, if you like. There, I won't keep you from your preparations."

He turned away with a gesture of dismissal. The boy looked intently at him a moment, and then walked slowly away without audible reply, although to himself he muttered:

"I'll think over it a bit first, I reckon. More than that, I'll ask Miss Trix. She'll know what's up." He looked round at the turn of the road. Brent had already forgotten his presence, and leaning his folded arms upon the rail, was again staring into the dark shadow of the willows, his white face showing ghastly and spectral against the black background.

So he stood when, an hour later, the moon, climbing the crest of Moloch Mountain, glanced athwart its shadow, and thrusting aside with slender, trembling finger-rays the leaves of willow and alder, peered down upon the surface of the pool.

The black waters, sullen and irresponsive, gave back no dimpling smile like that with which Millbrook all night long received and returned the kisses of the moon; but as the rays, growing momently more vertical, plunged deeper and deeper into the leafy cavern above the pool, a strange horror and mystery gathered from its depths, and lay waiting till those accusing fingers should reach and pluck it forth. From the pendent leaves, whose whisper had told the story over and over to the shuddering night; from the gnarled and writhing roots, showing above the water like the muscles of a tortured Titan; from the blotched, unwholesome palms of the hand-like leaves, held up in dismay by the foul weeds rooted beneath the tide; from the tangled grasses, floating like the hair of a drowned woman upon its surface; from the faint mist gathering in the dark recesses of the wood, and creeping out to peer at the beholder, and see how he should bear it; from the inarticulate murmurs and whispers of the night—from these, and all these, gathered the horror and the mystery the moon had come to look at, and, as they gathered, drew Marston Brent within their circle and held him there.

In vain did he struggle to arise and flee. In vain did he seek to throw off the mysterious chain binding body and soul to the moment he felt approaching. In vain even did he try to fix his thoughts upon his own misery, and the proud heartlessness of his mistress.

Vainly, vainly. Moment by moment, the slowly-creeping horror mastered all. Thought, memory, consciousness, will, life itself, fell, one by one, within its grasp, and all were concentrated in a nameless horror, a breathless expectancy of what must come.

Slowly the moon crept on; slowly and surely the relentless fingers stole deeper and deeper into the shadow—searching, groping always

"A white, white face, with wide open black eyes."

for what they had come to seek, until in the blackest recess of the covert they found it, and with one shuddering flash seized and held it.

A white, white face, with wide open black eyes staring horribly at the sky; thick dark hair, with which the waters, moved by a little shivering breeze, toyed in ghastly fondness; shrunken lips, showing the teeth strongly clenched beneath; a dim figure half hidden among the gnarled roots; a hand awfully outstretched, as in dumb appeal—such was the aspect, such the form of the slowly gathering mystery and terror—such the secret that the sullen pool had vainly tried to hide—such the secret plucked from its recesses by the resistless grasp of light and truth.

Marston Brent, staring incredulously at the awful thing below him, watched while one feature, then another, took form, vainly trying the while to doubt the evidence of his own senses, vainly arguing that it was but the flickering light, the changing shadows, his own disturbed imagination, that had formed this ghastly image from the creeping mists of the pool, and that he should see it presently waver and change to some other if not less hideous form. But still as he gazed, the white face and staring eyeballs grew more distinct and personal ; the figure assumed more unmistakably human proportions ; the stiff white hand seemed to beckon more and more imperiously to him for aid and vengeance.

Slowly and with effort, he drew himself to a standing posture, and looked stealthily about him, half expecting to find the familiar scene changed by sudden glamourie to one of those wild regions where the soul, wandering forlorn, lapses from horror to horror, and wastes itself in vague and unfruitful efforts to escape an unknown evil.

But the mild autumn night lay serene and beautiful about him. The moon, now riding high in heaven, looked calmly down, content in having brought human consciousness to human ill, and willing to leave the sequel to the sure hand of justice.

Far down in the valley twinkled the lights of the village with cheerful intimation of home and companionship within reach. A solitary farm-dog drowsily bayed the moon, and the clock of the little church struck the hour of ten.

It was these familiar sights and sounds, more than any conscious effort of the will, that restored to Marston Brent the self-possession he so seldom lost ; and to-night more from the shattering blow, dealt by the hand of the woman he loved, at all the plan and hope of his life, than from any weakness of organization or undue susceptibility to the marvellous.

Standing with his back to the pool for a few minutes, and forcing himself to note the objects about him, the young man found both his physical and mental excitement toned rapidly down to a condition in which he could once more exercise will and purpose, reässuming as it were the reins of his own imagination, and checking it to its ordinary sober pace.

Then he turned, and, parting with his arms the drooping limbs, gazed steadfastly into the pool, satisfied himself that the drowned body of a man actually lay there, and that he could not reach it from the bank, and then, throwing off his upper garments, stepped quietly into the black waters, which curdled and seethed about his limbs as if eager to draw them within their corrupting grasp.

Reaching the body, the young man stooped to examine the face more closely, but failed to recognize it, and after a moment of hesitation placed his hands beneath the arms of the corpse, and, wading back to the shore, drew it after him. His utmost strength, however, no more than sufficed to place it upon the bank, for the body was that of a stalwart man, and the heavy clothes were saturated with water.

" Lie there, then," muttered Brent, arranging the limbs as decently as he could, " while I go for help."

He stood a moment, gazing down at the face of the dead man, in whose rigid lines and staring eyeballs was to be read nor liking nor disliking, assent or refusal, and then turned away.

But with his feet upon the highway, he paused, turning now this way, now that—this, leading toward his own home, two miles away, and inhabited only by a stupid serving-woman ; that, by which he should reach in ten minutes the house of Deacon Barstow, the house that for the last two months had been to him more than home, but now——

" I must, but I need not see her," muttered he at last ; and striking down the road in the same direction taken by the boy called Paul, he soon stood before the Old Garrison, and half unconsciously noted, as he pushed open the gate, the picturesque effect of the weather-beaten house, with its drooping woodbine-wreaths, the dewy knoll and shining brook, with the moonlight lying over all like the silvery veil covering, but not concealing, the charms of an Eastern bride.

The blaze in the great fireplace had died away to a dull glow, and the arm-chairs of the old man and his wife were vacant. A glancing light in the rooms at the back of the house showed Aunt Rachel thriftily preparing for the morrow, and convincing herself that the house was secure from intrusion. One figure alone remained in the great east-room, as it was called—the graceful figure of a girl crouching upon the floor, her golden head laid upon the beam where, a hundred years before, the gibbering maniac had lain to moan away his life, her hands tightly clasped across her eyes.

A piteous sight, and a cruel one to Marston Brent, who, gazing, felt the great grief at his heart rise again above the horror of the last hour, and turn him sick and faint with its extremity of anguish.

Had there been anger, pique, or jealousy in that heart, that moment must have crushed it out, and Beatrice Wansted had seen her lover at her feet; but in the grand, simple nature of the man, each added pang, each fresh proof of intensest love but added another line to the barrier between him and the woman whose word was to be held by him as truth too solemn for even a thought of doubt.

"She called God to witness that she would never yield, and I will never ask her; nor if I were coward enough to do what I know wrong to please her, would she accept the lying sacrifice."

So groaned he between clenched teeth, and turned away.

At the window of his little chamber sat Paul Freeman, his chin resting on the sill, his eyes vacantly gazing at the moon. Not looking at her, however, but using the luminous surface as a tablet upon which fancy painted pictures of the future, as brilliant and beautiful, and, alas! as far away, as that fair moon herself.

"Paul! Paul, I say!"

The boy started, and looking down, answered quietly:

"Yes, sir. Do you want me?"

"Yes; come down as quickly as you can, and make no noise."

Paul disappeared from the window, and the next minute slid back the bolt of the kitchen-door and stepped out into the moonlight.

"Is Miss Rachel still up?" asked Brent.

"I guess so. She's the last one mostly."

"Call her quietly."

But the feline ears of Aunt Rachel had already caught the slight disturbance, and as Paul turned to enter the door, she stood upon the threshold inquiring:

"Is that you, Marston?"

"Yes, Aunt Rachel, and I want some help."

"Well, I'm ready."

In a dozen words, Marston Brent told his errand, and asked hospitality for the poor,

homeless effigy of a man lying stark and forlorn upon the margin of Blackbriar Pool.

In one strong, brief sentence, Miss Rachel bid him to bring it without delay, promising to be ready when it should arrive. Then when the men had departed, she turned into the east-room. Beatrice rose, with a coldly careless mask drawn so suddenly over the anguish of her face as to but half conceal it. Her aunt glanced keenly at her, and said bluntly:

"Come, Trix, you must rouse up. There's a man drowned, and they are bringing him here."

"A man!"

All the blood in the girl's veins flew to her heart with a cruel pang, and then back to her brain, sending her reeling against the wall.

Had she murdered the man for whose pleasure she would have died in torture? Had she indeed "ruined his life" here and hereafter? But she only gasped again:

"A man!"

Miss Rachel's keen gray eyes fixed themselves steadily upon her niece's face.

"Yes," said she coldly. "And the man is not Marston Brent. He is no such fool as that."

CHAPTER V.

THE FIRST SUSPICION.

"It's Peleg Brewster," said Paul, kneeling beside the corpse and peering into the sodden face. "Peleg Brewster," repeated he, rising and looking at Brent, who was staring abstractedly into the pool.

"Yes, I never knew him, though I remember the name," said he, rousing himself with an effort. "Well, let us get the body upon the stretcher."

With laborious effort, the ghastly burden was arranged, and the litter raised between the two men. Through the rustling wood, and along the quiet road, between hedges of goldenrod and asters, they carried it, until coming to the farm-house, they laid it upon the bed prepared by Rachel Barstow's active care, and left it in the hands of the doctor hastily summoned by Nancy, Miss Barstow's maid.

"Quite dead hours ago, but not by drowning," mysteriously pronounced the healing oracle, after a prolonged examination.

"What then?" asked Miss Rachel bluntly.

"He was killed by a shot fired from behind,

and passing through the heart, and out at the other side. It is a pity it is lost."

"Pity what is lost?"

"The bullet. It would help to convict the murderer," said the doctor gravely.

"He was murdered then?" asked Brent, aghast.

"Men do not shoot themselves in the back," replied the physician dryly.

"Who could have done it? Had the man enemies?" pursued Marston, upon whose mind the satirical hint at his own obtuseness made no more impression than a drop of vinegar upon the coat of a Newfoundland dog.

"That is a question for the coroner and his jury. You will have to attend, Mr. Brent."

"I shall not be here. I leave early in the morning for the West."

"I am afraid you will have to postpone your journey for a day at least. You are the principal witness in this matter," said the doctor gravely; and the young man turned away with an uncontrollable gesture of impatience.

The doctor's eyes followed him, and he asked: "Did Mr. Brent know Brewster at all? Had he ever any dealings with him?"

"No, he hadn't, Dr. Bliss. There's no use in thinking about that," said Miss Rachel, somewhat sternly; and the two pairs of keen eyes met and read each other. At last the doctor said:

"Then I won't think about it, Miss Rachel. I have no doubt you are right."

"And I have no doubt that sugar is sweet, or ice is cold, or the sun bright, or water wet," rejoined Miss Rachel with asperity. "And after you have proved me wrong in all these, we'll talk about the other matter."

The doctor shook his head, with a smile at once respectful and tolerant, saying the while:

"Very positive and very warm, as usual. You don't change as the years go on, Miss Rachel."

"No, I don't change," said Rachel Barstow briefly; and they both remembered the day—now twenty years by-gone—when she first had said those words to Wyman Bliss.

The woman's hard face softened, and, after a little while, she said, toying nervously with her apron-string:

"My friends must take me as I am, Wyman. Hard, and narrow, and obstinate, and cross-tempered. I cannot change."

"But you won't let them take you, as they would be glad to do, good and bad together,"
said the doctor significantly; and Miss Rachel, freezing suddenly, replied:

"If you have got through with the body, Dr. Bliss, I will call Nancy to help lay it out."

"By no means, Miss Rachel, by no means. It must not be touched in any way until the coroner has seen it. We will lock the door of this room if you please, and leave every thing just as it is until the morning. I will take all the necessary steps toward making the matter known to the authorities, if you like."

"Thank you—I wish you would. Father is old now, and we try to keep him as quiet as we can," said Miss Barstow wearily. And with a few words of farewell, the doctor rode away, saying to himself, as he turned into the road:

"A great pity, my dear—a great pity for us both."

Marston Brent meantime was striding home across the moonlit fields, having left the Old Garrison without seeing Beatrice, or even hearing her name. Beside him walked Paul Freeman, whom an uneasy and excited mood had debarred from sleep or rest.

Nearly a mile had been passed, and neither had spoken, when Paul suddenly asked:

"Would they hang a woman if she killed a man, Mr. Brent?"

"Of course they would if she was convicted," said Brent.

Another silence—again broken by Paul:

"Well, it was the best thing that could have happened to him."

"That's weak as water, Paul. A man should never want to die because things go wrong, and he is miserable. Rather let him live, and live it through, and live it down. Work, my boy—that's the salvation of a sick heart."

He threw back his shoulders, opening his broad chest, and looking up to the sky as he spoke. Already the strong vitality of his nature was gathering to assuage the wound which at first had seemed so hopeless of cure.

Paul stared at him a moment, then said: "Peleg Brewster had work enough to do; but that didn't hinder this."

"No," replied Brent vaguely; and then: "You knew him it seems?"

"He brought me up. His first wife was like a mother to me. She was a real good woman," blurted the boy.

"And why did you say that death was the best thing that could have happened to him?"

"He was so unhappy at home. You see,

sir, his wife died, and in a little while he married again, and the second woman was just as far below the mark as the other one was above. She led him a dog's life, and, what was worst, set his child and him against each other, till it seemed as if the house couldn't hold the three of them. Then Joe came to live with them, and I quit."

"Who was Joe?"

"Joe Brewster, brother to Peleg, and the same for a man that Semanthy was for a woman—only he was a coward, and she wouldn't have been scared by Old Nick and all his host."

"And what happened then?"

"Why, it happened that, from quarrelling, they come to fighting; and one day, Peleg struck Semanthy in the face, and sent her up against the wall. Lord, sir! Did you ever see a cat that mad that she'd fly at the biggest dog that ever was, and beat him too? Then you've seen Semanthy Brewster as she leaned up against the wall and looked at Peleg and smiled. Yes, sir, smiled; and I hope I'll never see another smile like that."

"When did this happen?" asked Brent, after a little while.

"About a year ago—just before I left there."

"And how have they gone on since?"

"From bad to worse. I've been once in a while to see Ruth."

"Who is that?"

"The child of the first wife, and, to be sure, the only child, for Semanthy never had any. She's thirteen now."

"And what sort of girl?"

"It would be hard saying, sir. Five years ago, when her mother died, there wasn't a nicer little girl nor a likelier anywhere round. She was always shy and quiet to strangers, but with her mother she'd come out and show for what she was. Semanthy set out to ruin her, and she's done it."

"How, and why?"

"Why, because Peleg was fond of her, and Semanthy meant to rule the roast herself; and how, it would be hard to tell unless you seen it. She made Ruth feel that her father wasn't satisfied with her, and didn't think her equal to other folks, and she made her think he talked against her mother—which I don't believe he ever did, for I know how he set by her; and then she made Peleg think Ruth was sulky and lazy, and told lies, and spoke disrespectful of him behind his back. And so she

kept at work, now this side, and now that, till she'd got a good wide wedge drove in between them, as ought to be like the bark and the wood, and then there was no healing the wound. I haven't seen any of them for a month or more; but Miss Rachel was telling me that Ruth was going out to service, she heard. I don't know if she's gone, but I hope so."

"Poor child! How old did you say?"

"Thirteen. Just three years younger than me," said Paul; and then the two walked on in silence until they came upon the little farmhouse bequeathed to Marston Brent by his father, lately dead.

Here they paused, and the elder said: "I shall not get away to-morrow, Paul; and if you can finish your business here, we may leave together the next morning. I shall drive from this house to Bloom, and you can go with me if you choose."

"Yes, sir, I should like to. I'll be on hand," said Paul, but with so marked a change from the joyous alacrity he had shown in first speaking of the matter, that Brent turned to look at him curiously by the light of the setting moon.

"Not falling back already, are you, boy?"

"No, sir; not a mite of it. I ain't given to backing down. But I was thinking of Ruth Brewster—poor little Ruthie. I wish I knew what she'll do."

And bidding good-night, or rather good-morning, the boy thrust his hands deep in his pockets and strode thoughtfully away.

CHAPTER VI.
THE CORONER'S VERDICT.

SEMANTHA BREWSTER, wife of the deceased, being duly summoned and sworn, suddenly scandalized all judicial propriety by exclaiming, without waiting to be questioned:

"It was Ruth did it!"

"What!" exclaimed the coroner, not more startled at the idea than at the mode of conveying it.

"It was Ruth that killed him," repeated Semantha doggedly; and before the horrified silence that fell upon the company could be broken by question or exclamation, she went on:

"There was bad blood between them. She was jealous of me because I was in her mother's shoes, and he set by me, same as a man had ought to by his wife, and so there was trouble between them. Finally, the night before it happened, he got real mad at her, and said he'd take her off to live with a woman over to Milvor that he'd spoke to about taking her, and she up and declared she wouldn't go. They had an awful time about it, and I heard Ruth stamping about her room pretty much all night. But yesterday morning he tackled up, and made me pack all her things in a trunk, and took her off with him. He had his rifle in the back of the wagon, going to get it fixed over to Milvor, and he made her sit over there on her trunk, because he was so provoked with her he couldn't bear to have her on the seat alongside of him. So then, I expect, when they got into the woods, she up and shot him."

"Could she use a rifle?" asked the coroner, still too much astonished to notice the informality of these proceedings.

"I guess you'd think so if you'd seen her, as I have, shooting at a mark down in the meadow, along with him, when they was good together. She'd hit it as well as any man, almost," said Semantha coolly.

"Well—but—where is the child now?" stammered the coroner.

"There, again," rejoined Semantha, triumphantly; "she's run off; and what would she do that for if she didn't feel she'd done what she hadn't ought to?"

"Now, Mrs. Brewster, this isn't the way to give evidence. You are to begin at the beginning, and tell all that you know of your husband's leaving home, and what followed relating to it; but do not give any opinions or arguments, or accuse any body of any thing. Go on, if you please."

And the coroner, feeling that he had vindicated the judicial dignity, and restored things to their true position, leaned back in his chair, and listened complacently.

Mrs. Brewster, thus adjured, began with her story, and repeated it substantially as before, contriving, with small feminine tact, to suggest the suspicions of Ruth, no longer openly expressed.

When she had finished, Joachim Brewster, brother of the deceased, was summoned, and gave his evidence so closely, to the same effect as that of Semantha, that the coroner shrewdly inquired, as he finished:

"Did you and Mrs. Brewster talk over together what you'd say to-day?"

"No, we didn't. It's because both stories are true that they fay in so well together," said Joachim, a little anxiously.

"Was any body else in or about the house that morning?" pursued the coroner.

"No, we don't keep any help. Peleg and me carried on the farm, and Semantha and Ruth did the work in the house. There was nobody else about."

"Very well; you can sit down now. Call Marston Brent."

And Marston Brent, being summoned, deposed to finding the dead body of Peleg Brewster in the water called Blackbriar Pool, and bringing it up the previous evening to the house of Deacon Barstow, where it now lay. He also spoke of searching for and finding traces the next morning of the heavy wagon and span of horses driven by the deceased, and following them down the road to a sudden turn, where the wagon lay broken, with one horse still attached, and the other lying dead not far off. The rifle and the little girl's trunk had been thrown out by the upsetting of the wagon, and lay in the road beside it. The rifle had been discharged, and he had found no trace of the child. So ended this important evidence, and at its close the coroner solemnly asked:

"What is your own opinion, Mr. Brent, formed upon these circumstances, of the manner in which the deceased came to his death?"

"My opinion is, sir, that the shot which killed him was fired from behind, while the wagon was passing through the thick clump of trees shading Blackbriar Pool; that the explosion frightened the horses, who swerved so much as to throw Brewster from the wagon into the water where I found him, and that then they continued down the road as far as the turn, where they upset."

"And do you think it possible that a girl of thirteen could have fired the shot which killed this man?" continued the coroner, relying more than he would have confessed upon the opinions of the man before him.

"Certainly, it is possible," replied Marston Brent reluctantly.

"And if the wagon tipped enough to throw out her father's body, it is not likely the child would have remained in it?"

"No, especially sitting upon a trunk in the back of the wagon."

"And if she had been thrown into the pool or upon its banks, you would have found her or her body?"

"Certainly. I waded over nearly the whole pool when I took the body of the deceased from it, and I have been all about there this morning."

"Alone?"

"No; Paul Freeman was with me."

"That will do, Mr. Brent. Summon Paul Freeman."

But Paul Freeman, however summoned, was not to be found, and the latest intelligence to be gathered concerning him was Miss Rachel Barstow's statement, that about an hour before the inquest she had seen him going upstairs to his own bedroom. He was not there now, however, nor were any of his belongings, from which Miss Rachel inferred that he had gone to carry them to Mr. Brent's house, whence he was to start for the West early the next morning.

A messenger was immediately dispatched in search of the truant witness, while the examination of those present went on; but in a brief half hour he returned with the report that Paul Freeman had not been seen at Mr. Brent's house, or at any other upon the road there, and the inquest was perforce brought to a close without his testimony, which, indeed, was only expected to corroborate that of Marston Brent.

The consultation of the jury was long and animated—a natural incredulity and horror in every mind arguing against the verdict plainly suggested by the evidence. Slowly and reluctantly, however, man by man yielded his wishes to his convictions, and when at last the little audience was readmitted, it was to hear that, in the opinion of this jury, "the deceased came to his death by a shot fired from his own rifle by Ruth Brewster, his daughter," and a warrant for the apprehension of the said Ruth was obtained upon the spot, and placed in the hands of the County Sheriff, then present.

"It's no more that child did it than I!" exclaimed Aunt Rachel, bringing one fist down into the palm of the other hand. "I say it, and I'll stick to it."

"I wish I could say so too; but I've heard too much of the way she and Peleg would go on together. They were run in the same mould, and when their temper was up, I wouldn't have stood in the way not for a good deal. I had a hard time of it with that child, the dear knows," said Semantha, with the corner of her shawl to her eyes.

"I don't believe any such story. I knew Mary Brewster as well as I know my own sister; and I'm not going to believe her child could be brought to all that in two years' time, even by the worst of management," rejoined Aunt Rachel significantly, and with no answer except an oblique gleam from her beryl-tinted eyes, Semantha left the house.

CHAPTER VII.
CRYSTALS.

THE shadow of Moloch lay over all his western valley, and only his topmost pines caught the red light of the summer dawn, when Marston Brent, alone and sorrowful, came to bid good-by to the Old Garrison House and its sleeping inmates. Avoiding the creaking gate, he climbed the little paling, and stole softly through the garden-walks, smiling sadly as he brushed by the bachelor's-buttons, with whose blossoms Beatrice had sometimes merrily decked his coat, and bitterly as he stood beside the plot of pansies whose bed he had himself fashioned into the shape of a great heart, and planted in its centre his own and her initials.

"Heart's-ease!" murmured he. "Yes, for her and me!" And with the smile which such men use instead of tears, he gathered some of the flowers and held them a moment to his lips, then flung them down.

"Heart's-ease is sweet, but it does not last," said Marston Brent; and so bid good-by to the old garden where they two had lingered through so many blissful hours.

Then he passed on through the grove and the meadow to the brook-side, where he had planted the weeping willow, and fashioned a seat beneath it—a seat just wide enough for two, as he said that day, and now he sat down upon it alone—alone forever, as he told himself in bitter iteration; and plucking the long branches that swept his face, he bound them mockingly about his arm, then flung them indignantly aside, and started to his feet.

"No willow for me!" said he aloud. "Or if I must have it, I'll make a staff of it."

And taking out his knife, he cut a stout shoot from one of the principal branches of the tree, and trimmed it to a walking-stick, careful that all the twigs and leaves he cut away should fall into the stream, instead of littering the grass about the seat. The day before, under the same impulse, he had plucked away the weeds from the grave where his mother lay ten years buried ; but this sorrow was harder to bear than that.

As he turned from the brook-side, he found Beatrice close behind him, her eyes dim, her face wan, her drooping figure full of pathos and of appeal.

He took her hands in his, and looked at her long and sorrowfully.

"It is hard for you, too, poor darling," said he.

At the Brook-side.

And at the loving word, her tears burst the bonds she had laid upon them, and she sank upon the little seat, sobbing without restraint

He looked at her tenderly, pitifully, but did not offer to approach her, did not dream of returning upon the path wherein he had set his feet.

Presently she looked up.

"I knew you were here, Marston. I saw you in the garden. Look !"

And she held up the pansies he had kissed and thrown away.

"You will keep them, Beatrice ?"

"Always. But, O Marston ! must you, will you ?"

"What, Beatrice ?"

"Must you go ?"

"You know I must."

"Is it quite, quite impossible for you to yield to my wishes ?"

A slight frown changed the expression of patient sadness upon his face.

"I am sorry you asked me that, Beatrice. Is my word of so little account with you ?"

"And yet you suffer !" murmured Beatrice.

"More than you can know, or I can tell."

"But that is not firmness, that is ——"

"What ?"

"Obstinacy, fanaticism. You sacrifice yourself and—yes, and me, rather than give up an idea."

"Beatrice, do you remember, in the chemical experiments that amused us last winter, watching the crystals form ? Could those crystals have been persuaded to change themselves back into their component parts ? And just so, as it seems to me, a conviction should form itself in a man's mind, and there remain in its integrity through time and circumstances, and the tears of the woman that he loves, and the passion of his own heart, beat against it without ceasing. It may be fanaticism, dear, it may be obstinacy, but it is I as God made me, and as I shall live and die."

"Well, then," cried the woman, driven to her last extremity, and throwing to the winds all considerations but the one standing closest to her heart. "Well, then, if you will not yield, Marston Brent, I will. I am not made of these cold, hard crystals, but of warm flesh and blood, thank God ! I give up my opposition to the life you propose. I consent that you should go to Wahtahree, and I will follow ——"

"Stop, Beatrice. Do not finish that sentence, do not make that offer, for I——O Beatrice ! how can I accept it ?"

The color slowly left her face, the light faded from her eyes, and she stood staring at him, her lips parted for that next word whose utterance he had forbidden.

Brent went on, no less moved than she, yet very firm :

"How can I accept it, Beatrice, when twelve hours ago you deliberately resolved and vowed, and called God to witness the oath, that you would never consent to the entreaty I urged upon you, would never follow me to Wahtahree as my wife, would never yield to the plan you had formed for me to that I had formed for myself ? Dear love, if I should allow you to perjure yourself to-day, you would despise yourself and me to-morrow ; and whatever else befalls, I would save you from the careless pang of self-contempt. Words may be but air, but honor turns them to claims that may not be broken. Say that I am right, Beatrice, for, O child! my burden is very hard to bear."

And snatching at her hands, he held them close, turning upon her the while a face of such white agony as might look up from the rack whose utmost power may extort a groan, but no recantation.

Her eyes met his, steadily enough now, and coldly too.

"Thank you, Marston Brent," said she; "you have saved me from a great folly and a great mortification. Good-by."

"Good-by like this, Beatrice, after all that has come and gone between us two!"

"Good-by," repeated she; and drawing her hands from his icy grasp, she walked steadily up the path and disappeared in the wood, nor once turned to look behind her.

Brent watched until the last flutter of her dress was lost among the leaves, then cast one slow, loving glance on all about him, reverently raised his hat, murmuring:

"God bless and guard my darling, and all about her!"

And taking the willow staff from the place where it had fallen, went his way.

CHAPTER VIII.
EXODUS.

ARRIVED at his own house, Brent found his housekeeper impatiently awaiting him. She was an old woman, and had lived in the family so many years as to have acquired many privileges.

"Why, where have you been, Mr. Brent?" began she as Marston entered the house. "Here I've had breakfast ready this hour past, and that boy's been hanging round asking after you every five minutes."

"Paul Freeman?"

"Yes. Have you forgot all about telling me to fix him up a bed last night, and get breakfast for him this morning? How do they do up to Barstow's?"

"If breakfast is ready, we will have it, Zilpah, and the sooner the better. I did not see you last night, or I should have told you that I sold the place yesterday to a man at Milverhaven, who will be over to-day, I suppose, to take possession. The furniture and everything in the house I give to you, to do as you

please with. You can either have an auction and sell it all off, or carry it to your brother's."

"Well, now, Marston, I declare if that a'n't real generous! That's your mother all over again. Oh! she was the givingest creatur' that ever walked, and you're as like her as two peas. Not but what your father was an obleeging man too, but his folks was always a little near—dreadful fore-handed and nice-feeling, but a leetle close. Your mother was a Winship, and they was different. But do tell, Marston, do you mean all the stuff, every mite of it, a free gift right out?"

"A free gift, Zilpah, and much good may it do you," said Marston, smiling sadly at the old creature's incredulity; and then he turned to greet Paul as he entered the house, and the three sat down to break their bread together in patriarchal simplicity.

"You don't eat, Marston. I made them pancakes on purpose for you—you was always so fond of them. Don't you rec'lect how you used to come slying round, when you was a boy, going out to work with your father in the field, and tease me to have pancakes for supper?"

"And you always humored me, Zilpah," said Marston, taking one of the pancakes upon his plate.

"Always when I could, and so did your mother—and your father too, for that matter. Oh! we was a happy and a u-nited family in them days; and now the heads of it lays in the grave, and the strength of it is going away forever; and nobody but me, the poorest and the weakest of all, is left, and that won't be for long. When you come back for your wife, Marston, there won't be no old woman to wish you joy, nor to go along to your new home and tend your babies. O dear! O dear! I wish't I was dead too along of her."

And Zilpah, throwing her apron over her head, rocked to and fro, in the abandonment of age and grief.

Marston rose in much emotion.

"Zilpah, do you want to go with me?" asked he suddenly. "And can you go now—immediately? My home will be no better than a hut, and we may suffer many hardships; but if you will go, you shall, for you are the only creature alive who will mourn my absence."

"Do you mean that, Marston Brent?" asked Zilpah, raising her poor old tear-stained face with the quick appreciation of a love-quarrel innocent in her sex.

"I mean it, Zilpah."

"Then I'll go as quick as say it; for your mother was like a sister to me when I was in trouble, and she shan't have it to say in Heaven that I turned my back on her boy when other folks treated him bad. I'll go with you—but how about the stuff?"

"We will stop at your brother's, on our way to Bloom, and ask him to come and move every thing over to his house. Then you can write directions about selling what you do not care to keep. I suppose you know pretty well what is in the house."

"Every stick, and thread, and pin, and scrap," said Zilpah complacently; and starting from her chair with new alacrity, she began setting the house in order, and preparing herself for departure. Such good speed did she make, assisted by Paul, whose good fairy had endowed him with the gift of "handiness," so much more valuable than the purse of Fortunatus, that in another hour she locked the door of the house behind her, thrust the key into its time-honored hiding-place beneath the steps of the door, and climbed to her seat in the wagon beside Brent, who watched her proceedings with a vacant eye.

Paul disposed himself behind, among the various packages with which Zilpah had encumbered the march, and sat biting his nails, and casting uneasy glances at Brent, as if anxious to speak to him, yet not quite seeing his opportunity.

When, however, Zilpah, having reached her brother's house, insisted upon dismounting and holding a private interview with her sister-in-law upon the subject of her household stuff, Paul stepped across the seat and said, not without embarrassment:

"I was wanting to speak with you, Mr. Brent."

"Well, Paul, what is it?"

"Have you any objection to my taking my little brother along with us, sir? I will pay his car-fare, and all the costs there will be to it; and when we get there he can do chores round the house enough to pay his board. He won't charge any thing of course, and I don't think he'll be any trouble."

"But where is your brother now, and why did not you speak of this before?" asked Marston, in some surprise, both at the matter and the manner of his new retainer's speech.

"He's at Bloom, sir. I told him to meet us at the depot, and I didn't have a chance to speak before."

"I never knew you had a brother, Paul. Where has he lived all this time?"

"With a farmer's family, sir. I never said much about him," said Paul, a little uneasily.

"Well, I don't know as I object, if you choose to take charge of him and his expenses. How old a boy is he?"

"About a dozen years old, sir."

"Strong and active?"

"Well, not very, sir, but he can do light jobs round the house. He isn't very rugged, to be sure."

"Well, he may come along. I shall have quite a family by the time I reach Wahtahree."

And Marston smiled a little cynically as he fancied Beatrice presiding over such a family.

Zilpah, reluctantly torn from her parting gossip, was at last reëstablished in the wagon, and Marston, hurrying his patient horse a little, drove into Bloom, and leaving his charge at the station, went to transact a little last business at the office of his agent. When he returned, he found an addition to the party in the person of a small, delicate lad, whose pale face, downcast eyes, and slender hands promised little in the way of profitable labor, but at the same time appealed not unsuccessfully to Brent's softened feelings.

"You don't look very well, my boy," said he, kindly patting him upon the shoulder. "What is your name?"

"His name is Willy, sir, and he is feeling a little poorly just now, but he'll be better pretty soon. I guess we'll go out and see if the cars are coming, sir."

"Very well; I will take tickets for the whole party, and we will settle some other time," said Marston, noticing Paul's haste and confusion with some surprise, but attributing them to a country boy's nervousness in commencing his first journey.

"Marston—Mr. Brent, I should say," interposed Zilpah at this moment. "Be we going to take that other boy along too?"

"Yes. He is Paul's brother, and Paul is anxious to keep him under his own eye," said Marston absently.

"Lor! A boy like that keeping any one under his own eye," sniffed Zilpah contemptuously. "I reckon I'll keep a couple of eyes on both of 'em, till I see what they be, anyway."

Marston made no reply except a smile as he moved away, and a few minutes later the train arrived, swept up the waiting passengers, and bore them away to new scenes and strange experiences.

_____

CHAPTER IX.

A NEW BEGINNING.

"Six of damsons, six of green-gages, and a dozen rare-ripes—and, to my mind, there's no peach like a rare-ripe for a preserve.

" _Mowers knee-deep in greenest grass._"

There, that will do for to-day," said Aunt Rachel complacently, tying down the cork of her last bottle of rareripes, for these were not the days or the meridian of " air-tight cans ;" and had such innovations been suggested to Aunt Rachel she would probably have snubbed them as " new-fangled " and " too notional" for her.

" Now, Nancy," continued she, " I am going round to open the slide into the best china-closet, and you can pass the bottles in. Mind you don't drop them."

" I won't drop 'em. They do look proper nice to be sure, and I guess the doctor'll think more than ever of our plums when he eats 'em this way," replied Nancy, rubbing her hands dry upon her tow apron, and eyeing the jars of sweetmeats appreciatively.

" Lor! who cares what the doctor thinks?"

demanded Miss Rachel, bustling out of the room, and through the long entry whose open door framed a lovely little picture of mowers knee-deep in greenest grass, while Millbrook sparkled by, and Moloch rose dark and grand against the summer sky. But Miss Rachel's eye was not artistic, and her heart was just now filled with visions of sweetmeats, with, perhaps, one little suggestion of Doctor Bliss crowded down in the corner, as the old masters were apt to introduce the reigning pope among a crowd of saints and angels. So, without heeding the lovely " bit" framed by her front door, Miss Rachel hurried by and threw open the door of the parlor, a room sacred to cleanliness, order, and decorum, but upon the threshold she stopped dismayed.

The heavy inside shutters were all closed except the upper half of one, through which streamed a flood of noonday light, falling full upon the picture of the Cenci taken from the wall and placed upon a chair. In the deep window-seat, with the light just glancing over her red-gold hair as it passed on to light the one stray curl creeping from beneath the white turban of the pictured head, sat Beatrice, her hands folded listlessly upon her lap, her eyes fixed upon the painting. She neither moved nor looked round to notice the advent of her aunt, who, after a moment's wondering gaze, exclaimed ;

" Good gracious, Beatrice, what _have_ you got the room fixed up this style for?"

" I wanted to see this picture, Aunt Rachel, and it hung in a bad light," said the girl wearily.

" See that picture ! Well, I should say you'd had a chance in the course of twenty years ! Didn't you ever notice it before ?"

" She was killed—beheaded, was she not ?" asked Beatrice, unheeding the little sarcasm.

" Yes, I believe so. I forget about it just now ; but I think that is what your mother said."

" And she looked just so calm and serene when they came to lead her out to die, they say," pursued Beatrice in the same dreamy way.

" Who says ? She died a hundred or more years ago in Italy, or somewhere out there, and who is to say how she looked or how she felt ? I value the picture more for its likeness to your mother than for itself. It does look a sight like her if the hair was fixed differently, and it had a common sort of dress on," said

Aunt Rachel, gazing thoughtfully at the painting.

"And like me too, does it not?" asked Beatrice, looking at her aunt a little anxiously.

"Well, yes, it does—though why it should look like you and your mother too, I don't see," said Miss Rachel with emphasis.

"Why? Did not we look alike? I always supposed we did," exclaimed Beatrice in a tone of dismay.

"'Looks are nothing; behavior's every thing.'" quoted Miss Rachel. "And when you come to behavior, you and your mother are as near alike as cream and red pepper—just about. Alice was the sweetest, prettiest, patientest woman that ever trod—never wanting any thing she ought not to have; never thwarting people that tried to do her good; never answering back or saying pert, saucy things to her elders and betters, or fretting because she wasn't the queen and Pope of Rome."

"And I am all that she was not," interposed Beatrice, half inquiringly, half pleadingly, as she looked up into her aunt's face, which softened as she met that look.

"Well, I don't say that," replied she, smoothing down her brown-linen apron, and pleating the string between her fingers. "You have your good points and your bad ones, like the rest of us, I suppose, Trix, but you're not like your mother—more like your great-aunt there in the corner, though you don't look like her."

"Tell me about her. I never heard any thing but her name, and that she married a nobleman," said Beatrice, opening the other front shutter, and looking with some curiosity at a picture hanging upon the opposite wall.

It was the portrait of a woman in her ripest bloom, with clear gray eyes, red lips, at once full and firm, a low forehead, with blue-black hair rolled high above it, a rich, sunny complexion, and a square white chin. Will, strength, and passion marked this face for their own; and gazing at it, Beatrice felt an answering chord thrill through her own heart.

"Tell me about her, Aunt Rachel," said she softly.

"Why, you must have heard about her from grandfather. He was always fond of telling about her till he got so silent lately. Her name was Miriam Barstow, and she lived here in the Old Garrison with her father and brothers, in the time of the Indian troubles,

more than a hundred years ago, I suppose; and once, when the men-folks were all away, and a party of savages came to plunder and burn the house—for they spited it, you see, because it had sheltered the folks they were after so many times—she saw them coming, and barred the doors and windows, and parleyed with them out of one of the upper casements. They tried to shoot her with their arrows—and there's the stone head of one buried in the side of the window now, there in my chamber—and then they set out to burn the house down. She warned them off once or twice, but they didn't mind, and then she took down her father's musket and shot the head man dead in his tracks. He fell, so I've heard, right across the door-stone, and his blood made that dark streak you can see there now; for blood never washes out, especially if it's shed in anger, and his hasn't."

"And what became of her then, Aunt Rachel?" asked Beatrice with kindling eyes.

"Why, the Indians ran away, I believe, and the men-folks came hurrying home to see what was the matter; and here she was as cool as you please, not scared a bit. After that she married an English lord that came over here and travelled round to see the country. She was pleased enough, so they say, for she was as proud and haughty as she was smart; and after she got to England she sent home this picture to let her folks see how fine she dressed, I expect. Don't you see, she's got on a velvet gown, and those are diamonds round her neck and in her ears. She was Lady Daventry then, all over."

"But she would have taken off velvet and diamonds and defended her father's house against the Indians again, if it had come in her way to do so, and done it as coolly and as well as she did while she wore linsey-woolsey and tow-cloth here at home," said Beatrice proudly. "And she would have gone to her death as haughtily as Beatrice did serenely to hers. She would have defied Death, as Beatrice conquered him."

"Well, I haven't any more time to waste on pictures or talk, and I should hope you hadn't either," said Aunt Rachel, coming back to real life rather crossly. "Here's your uncle coming to tea, and this room all up in arms, and grandma's new cap not done."

"I will see to both, and every thing else you mentioned this morning; and, Aunt Rachel, I am going to try to be more patient and better tempered after this—only please don't say any thing to me about Marston Brent, for he and I are——"

The girl had her arms about her aunt's neck now, while all the golden curls went dropping down that withered maiden's bosom, as if searching there for tender memories and sympathies responsive to the desolation of that pathetic cry.

Miss Rachel smoothed the bright hair and kissed the drooping head. Then she softly said:

"I'm sorry, Trix, and I'll be careful not to say any thing. But it's the way of the world, child; most all of us get disappointed once. Sometimes we get over it, and sometimes that's the end of every thing. I guess you'll get over it, dearie, you're so young and so pretty. Your old auntie didn't."

"Were you disappointed, auntie?" asked Beatrice, startled even through her grief by that rare confidence.

"Yes, child. You see I thought it was me he wanted, and it was Alice all the time; but they never knew, and he made her a real good husband, and she died and I had to live on. But—well then! I never said so much to mother nor any one, and though I always thought the doctor mistrusted how it was, he never said any thing. 'The heart knoweth its own bitterness;' though there isn't any bitterness left to it now, whatever there was once, and sometimes it sort of eases off the pain to know that other folks have felt just as bad or worse, and got over it. I'm not afraid of your saying any thing as if you knew it, Trix, and I'm not sorry I told you."

"You need not be sorry, Aunt Rachel, and I never loved you or respected you in all my life so much as I do now," said Trix, pressing her ripe lips to the withered ones that trembled as much as they.

"I shouldn't wonder if we got along better after this, Beatrice," said the elder softly; and then the two embraced once more and separated, each already anxious to hide her emotion from the other.

"Now, you put this room to rights, won't you? and if you've a mind to bring in some flowers out of the garden, I don't care—only mind and don't let the water go over on the table, and pick up every mite of litter as fast as it makes," said Aunt Rachel, going into the closet and opening the slide to the front

kitchen, where stood the preserve-jars and Nancy.

"Well! I didn't know as you was ever coming," exclaimed the latter somewhat indignantly. "I might have had the sauce-kettle scoured inside and out by this time if I'd known you'd be so long."

"Why, you haven't been standing and waiting all this time, Nancy Beals!" exclaimed her mistress in the same tone. "I should have thought common-sense, if you'd got any, would have told you to go about your work till you heard me open the slide. Do give me the jars now, and be done with it."

Beatrice meantime, smiling a little at the unwonted permission to "litter the front room with a parcel of flowers," as her aunt generally described the operation, took a basket and scissors and went out to the garden, but as her eyes fell upon the pansy-bed, as her garments brushed the borders of the box and drew forth their heavy perfume, she faltered and turned toward the house, but at the end of three steps turned again.

"Miriam Barstow was not afraid to take the life of her enemy, and Beatrice Cenci was not afraid to lay down her own life, and I—I am afraid of the sight of a bed of pansies and the smell of a box-border," muttered she scornfully, and then went on without a pause. The basket filled, she set it in the shade of a great clump of lilacs, and passing swiftly through the garden and the grove, she reached the seat beneath the willow, looked at it, passed on until she stood upon the edge of the brook, returned and seated herself.

"Here I first saw Marston Brent," said she aloud in a hard, mechanical voice. "Here I urged him to resign his resolution for the sake of my love, and when he refused I offered to give up my own, and to break my solemn vow, and to follow him to the wilderness as his wife. This I offered, and he—*refused!* Yes, and he said he did it to save me from self-contempt. What does a man think of a woman whom he must save from herself in that way? Good-by, Marston Brent."

She set her lips over that last phrase, as her ancestress may have done over the dead body of her enemy, and then she rose and went slowly back to the house, dressed her flower-vases, finished the simple decoration of the room, and then crossing the hall to the east-room, where the old people sat, one at either side of the little blaze—pleasant even in summer to their chill blood—she took the unfinished cap and sat herself down to make it close by her grandfather's chair.

"Tell me about Miriam Barstow, grandpapa," said she; and the kind old man told the story once again, as she had already heard it, and at the end smoothed the fair head beside him, saying:

"I am glad you will never have to shoot Indians, daughter. Your lines are cast in pleasanter places than that poor girl's."

"No, I shall never have to shoot Indians, grandpapa," said Beatrice, bending over her work.

CHAPTER X.
UNCLE ISRAEL.

No railway had as yet invaded the quiet of Milvor woods and fields, no steamboat had desecrated the waters of Milvorhaven, and such communication as was held by inhabitants of either with the outer world was carried on by means of a stage-coach visiting them semi-weekly, and a packet sloop making its passage when wind, weather, and the humor of the skipper's wife allowed.

The day whose morning we have noted was one of those made memorable by the arrival of the stage, and punctually at five o'clock it appeared, rattling down the hill, across the little bridge and round the corner, until, with a superfluous whirl and flourish in honor of its freight, it paused at the gate of the Old Garrison House, whose inmates awaited it at the open door.

"Here's all your folks waiting to see you," said Aaron Bunce, the driver, swinging himself off his box and opening the door, while a sympathetic smile opened a cleft in his red face wide enough to display an ample set of ivory.

"So I see, Aaron, so I see," replied a handsome middle-aged gentleman, slowly descending from the coach, and putting a hand in his pocket, while the smile upon the driver's rubicund face widened expectantly. And while Mr. Israel Barstow pays his passage-money, and adds, according to his gracious wont, a *buona-mano* for the benefit of his old friend and playmate, Aaron Bunce, we have time to notice that he is a man of about fifty years old, handsomely and soberly attired, although his watch-chain is of the heaviest, and the *solitaire* diamond fastening his black cravat is of the costliest.

For the rest, Israel Barstow is the oldest and now only son of the old man watching his arrival from the open door; is a bachelor, and a very prosperous merchant in the China trade, a circumstance memorized to the inhabitants of the Old Garrison House by the periodical arrival of chests of tea, boxes containing blue-printed china jars of preserved ginger, bamboo, limes, sugar-cane, and a curious compound called chow-chow sweetmeat; dress-patterns of silk, handkerchiefs, shawls, toys of carved ivory, pictures upon rice-paper, monstrously drawn and gorgeously colored; an occasional bit of furniture or china, and all the other odd or useful presents abounding among the fortunate friends of oriental traders. Nor can it be denied that Mr. Israel Barstow's visits to his paternal home were hailed with all the more pleasure and interest from the circumstance of his never coming empty-handed, or failing to bring some especial gift to each member of the family carefully adapted to the especial taste of the individual—a style of gift-making contrasting favorably with the practice of those persons who offer presents as Timothy, Lord Dexter did punctuation — namely: in the lump, to be distributed according to taste.

But Mr. Barstow is already upon the doorstep, with his mother's arms around his neck, and her withered lips pressed to his. Then came the warm hand-pressure and the blessing of his father; then an angular embrace from Miss Rachel; and then, by way of *bonne bouche*, a frank kiss from the fresh, ripe mouth of Beatrice.

"Glad to see you looking so well, friends, every one of you. Father, you are as hearty as I am, for any thing that I can see; and as for mother, I expect her to dance at my wedding yet—unless, to be sure, Rachel gets the start of me. How's the doctor, Rachel? And as for that monkey, Trix——where is she?"

"Never mind just now, brother," interposed Miss Rachel, a little nervously. "Let me take your bag and show you upstairs."

"Show me upstairs, Shell! Why, I carried you up and down those very stairs before you could walk alone. You are grown amazingly ceremonious, it seems to me."

"No; but I want to speak to you a minute before you see Beatrice, if you please, Israel," insisted Miss Rachel; and her brother, with a shade of alarm upon his florid face, suffered himself to be led away to the guest-chamber.

pride of Miss Rachel's heart, with its neat canton matting, its bed, and window-furniture of white linen, embroidered by some Penelope of an ancestress in huge bouquets of flowers, dwarf-trees, and wonderful birds, decked in Joseph coats of many-colored silks; its high-backed carved chairs, black mahogany clothes-press and chest of drawers; its spider-legged dressing-table and light stand, and the great easy-chair, covered with silk patchwork of Rachel's own composition—each article resting solidly upon the carved eagle-claw feet so charming to *virtuosi* in antique furniture, and perfect in all its ornaments.

Over the fireplace hung a piece of embroid-ery, framed and glazed, depicting, in glowing colors, the death of Absalom, who hung pend-ant from an oak whose acorns were consider-ably larger than his own head, while Joab dismounted from a horse smaller than the dog who followed him, attacked his master's son with a lance longer than the oak was tall. Beyond a division-line composed of harps and crowns, set one above another, was shown King David sitting upon his throne, with a sceptre like Magog's mace at his feet, and both his royal hands clutched in a mass of hair which the most admiring courtier must have confessed needed thinning; while Bathsheba the fair stood beside him, a head and shoul-ders taller than her lord, and with two large tears wrought in white floss streaming down the most hideous face that ever haunted a Christmas-supper dream.

Upon the mantleshelf below this prodigy stood a pair of Chinese josses grinning fiend-ishly at each other in mockery of the Biblical memorial above, and between them lay a rosary of carved ivory, whose use or intent Miss Rachel understood as little as she did the worship of the josses, or the droll mixture of religious faiths thus placed in juxtaposition.

"Well, what is the matter with Trix?" de-manded Mr. Barstow, as his sister followed him into the room and closed the door.

"Nothing, Israel; only she has broken off with Marston Brent, and, of course, it's a sore subject, and she would rather not have it spoken of. So I thought I would tell you, lest you should hurt her feelings without knowing it."

"Of course, of course. But what is it? What's the matter? He hasn't treated her badly, has he?" asked Mr. Barstow, growing very red in the face.

"Oh! no. At least, I know he couldn't have; but Beatrice has never said a word about it, except just that it was broken off and all over, and he has gone out West."

"He has, has he? Why, I thought——but it is just as well. Broken off, have they? Sho! I thought Trix was all settled, and just the same as married; but, after all she might do better. Brent was a good fellow, but she is a girl to shine among a thousand. I'll have her to spend the winter with me, Shell. I'll take her home Monday, if you'll get her ready. It is just the change she wants, and it'll brighten up my old house there amaz-ingly."

Miss Rachel stood aghast.

"Carry her right off Monday!" exclaimed she.

"Yes; why not? I suppose her stockings are mended and night-caps washed, aren't they? And if she needs a new gown, she can buy it after she gets there. It will be amuse-ment for her."

"But, brother—why, who will take care of the child?"

"Child! She was twenty last birthday, I know, for there are twenty stones in the ruby bracelet I sent her; and as for care, why, I shall look out for her, of course; and then there is Mrs. Grey."

"Your housekeeper?'

"Yes. And as nice a woman as ever trod."

"But is she suitable—does she go out to parties and the theatre, and such places? You know Beatrice ought not to go alone, and you won't want to be following her round all the time," said Aunt Rachel, whose ideas of social propriety had not all been learned in Milvor.

"Well—yes, there is something in that, I suppose. How much more fuss there is about a girl than a boy!" said Uncle Israel rather testily, as he rubbed the somewhat scanty hair from his forehead, and looked reproach-fully at his sister, who looked meekly back at him.

"Mrs. Grey don't go into company, does she?" inquired Miss Rachel presently.

"No, no, of course she don't—that is, not into the sort of company Trix will frequent. I suppose I could find some lady——why, there's Jane Charlton!"

And Mr. Barstow's face lighted with an Eu-reka glow, as he stopped opposite to Miss Rachel, his large handkerchief suspended from his hand, and his hair in a state of frightful confusion.

"June Charlton!" echoed Miss Rachel.

"Yes; my friend Chappelleford's niece, you know. Now, Shell, don't tell me you don't remember Chappelleford, who came down here with me last year—no, two years ago—and took such an interest in the Old Garrison."

"Oh! yes; that old gentleman who cut a piece out of the sitting-room wainscot to see the logs behind it," said Aunt Rachel rather acrimoniously.

"Well, I told him he might if he didn't believe that it was a log-house originally; and I suppose he didn't believe it, that being a good deal his way, and so—— But all that is neither here nor there," said Mr. Barstow, resuming, with a slight air of vexation, the interrupted use of his handkerchief. "All that is neither here nor there, but what I am coming to is: Chappelleford has a niece, a young widow—somewhere about thirty, I should say—who has boarded with him for the last year at the Grandare House, and who is about the most charming woman you ever laid eyes on, Miss Shell. I'll get her to come and make me a visit, and go out with Beatrice. So, there, now."

"And she is a clever, nice woman, isn't she? For you know, brother, Beatrice is new to the world, and a great deal depends upon the first start."

"Clever and nice! Ha! ha!" laughed Mr. Israel Barstow, rubbing his hands together. "Well, I don't believe, Shell, that any one ever put those words to June Charlton's name before, and you would laugh at yourself if you should see her once—only just see her, you know."

"Why, brother?" asked Miss Rachel, a little hurt.

"Why because she's splendid, gorgeous, bewitching—I don't know what—but not clever—that is, not the way you use clever, Shell; and as for nice—why, I shouldn't call the sun nice, should you?"

Miss Rachel looked very thoughtful, and made no reply.

"And now," continued her brother presently, "run away, like a good girl, while I change my clothes, and then I will come down to tea. Can Paul bring up my trunk, do you think? It is a little one this time."

"Paul has gone West with Marston Brent, but there is a man here doing his work until

we can get some one, and he will, or Nancy will."

"No, no; not Nancy. If your man is away, I'll fetch it up myself. No woman ever lugs trunks or blacks boots for Israel Barstow, nor will while he has the use of his own arms and legs," said the sturdy bachelor; and Miss Rachel hastened from the room just as her brother laid violent hands upon the lappets of his coat.

CHAPTER XI.
SEMANTHA'S TEARS.

IF Miss Rachel had secretly hoped, or perhaps feared, that the hidden sorrow of her niece's heart would prevent her from accepting an invitation which must leave the Old Garrison House so lonely, she was disappointed, for Beatrice hardly hesitated a moment before assuring her uncle that she should come to him with the greatest pleasure, and could be quite ready at the end of the four days he proposed remaining at home.

"And you won't miss the old folks, though they'll be dull enough without you, lambie," said the grandmother, putting her shaking arm about the stately young figure, and looking lovingly up in the pale face half turned from her gaze.

"Indeed, I shall miss you, grandmamma, and I would never think of going if—if—I felt that I could stay at home."

"Can't stay at home! What does the child mean? Do you suppose we can't support you, Beatrice? I had to go out to work when I was a girl, but you haven't any such call, I'm sure."

"Oh! no, grandmamma, I never thought of such a thing," replied the girl, laughing in spite of herself. "But I feel as if I must have a change. That is all."

"Growing unsteady? Why, Trixie, that's something new for you," began the grandmother, in a tone of gentle reproof; but the tremulous voice of her husband interposed:

"Don't urge the child too much, mother. These young things have their own secrets, and have a right to keep them. Our child won't go wrong, it isn't in her nature; and though the lamb stray from the fold for a while, the Good Shepherd has her in His charge, and will lead her gently home at last. Come here, little one."

And Beatrice, kneeling at the feet of the good old man, his hand upon her head, his blessing falling like a mantle about her, wept tears that left a healing behind them, and soothed as nothing yet had done the agony of that fresh wound so jealously hidden in her heart of hearts.

"She'd better go away for a while, wife," said the grandfather, when the old couple were again alone. "Don't say a word to prevent it, or to make her feel that we shall miss her too much."

"No, I won't; but I wish there was time for me to knit her another set of lamb's-wool under-vests before she goes. Folks that are out of spirits and cry are always dreadful chilly; but I'll send them after her if she stays all winter. I always thought, if Alice had worn lamb's-wool, we might have saved her."

Deacon Barstow raised his mild eyes to his wife's face with a quaint smile, but made no reply; and while she fell into a fit of musing, he resumed the volume of Fenelon, which he preferred to all reading, except that of the great quarto Bible always lying upon the stand at his elbow.

"What is all this dreadful story about Peleg Brewster and his little girl, Rachel?" asked Mr. Israel Barstow, soon after his return home; and Miss Rachel, nothing loth to expatiate upon the story to a new listener, proceeded to narrate it with all the horrible details, and giving the coroner's verdict at the end as the solution most generally received of the mystery that to her mind still hung about the murder.

Israel Barstow listened attentively. The murdered man had been his schoolmate and playfellow in those long-past days when the prosperous merchant still lay concealed in the sturdy country boy, predominant in the republic of the district school, not through his father's wealth or position, but his own powers of combination and command. His wife also, Ruth's mother, appeared among the memories of those early days as a fair, gentle child, grateful to the Deacon's sturdy son for such small benefits as a coast upon his sled, a share of his liberal lunch, or permission to harvest the chestnuts beneath his father's trees.

"Yes—Mary Williams—I remember her very well," said Mr. Barstow, softly drumming on the window-pane, as he listened to his sister's story, while his thoughts went swiftly back to those years so far behind him now, and touched upon many a half-forgotten memory.

And Peleg was a fine fellow too—a thought hasty in his temper, and a little dangerous at times, but a fine, brave fellow always. Yes, we were boys together; but it is a great many years ago now, a great many years."

"Not so very many, Israel. You're not an old man now," said his sister, a little jealous for the brother whom she admired and loved, far more than she ever showed, even to him.

"But Joe was younger, and I don't remember him so well," pursued Israel. "My impression is, however, that we didn't like him very well. He was a bit of a sneak, if I remember."

"He isn't very much thought of, nor Semanthy either," said Miss Barstow, breathing upon the spot dimmed by her brother's finger-tips, and rubbing it bright with her apron.

"Semanthy? I don't remember her," said Israel.

"No, I guess you never knew her. When Mary Brewster was taken sick, or rather after she got too feeble to do her work, Peleg got Semanthy Whitredge to help her, and finally to do all the work. She belongs to a family over at the 'haven, and I rather think they are poor sort of people anyway. Then, after Mary died, Semanthy stayed on, and after a while Peleg married her. She isn't very well spoken of."

"I think I shall go and have a talk with Joe Brewster. I want to hear more about poor Peleg, and what grounds they have for accusing that child," said Israel at length; and Miss Rachel, after a moment's hesitation, replied:

"Well, I believe I will go too."

The next afternoon accordingly, as brother and sister returned from an excursion to Milvorhaven, where they had dined with some family friends, Israel turned the horse into the sandy by-road leading past the Brewster place, and presently checked him at the very spot where Peleg Brewster had sat a week before, and unconsciously looked his last upon the familiar scenes of his boyhood.

Following the simple country fashion, the visitors entered the open door without the ceremony of knocking, and passed into a small entry with a door opening at either hand, and a square staircase filling the middle space.

"Knock on that door, Israel—I believe it is the sitting-room," said Miss Rachel audibly; and as she spoke, both visitors were startled by the apparition of a white face peering at them from over the banister, and a sound of hurrying footsteps and hastily closing doors in the room at their left hand.

"Is Mrs. Brewster at home?" asked Miss Rachel, throwing the question at random up the stairs; but the face had been withdrawn as soon as seen, and no reply followed.

"Knock, Israel!" said his sister; and while Mr. Barstow obeyed, Miss Rachel glanced out at the door.

"See there!" whispered she, laying her

" *The figure of a man beside a high stone wall.* "

hand upon her brother's arm, and pointing to a field at the corner of the house. Mr. Barstow looked, and distinguished the figure of a man crouching beside a high stone wall, and pursuing its line toward the woods.

"It is Joe Brewster, and he was in that room and heard us when we came in, and he's running away," whispered Miss Rachel with emphasis; but before her brother could reply the door at their right suddenly opened, and the crafty face of Semantha appeared in the opening.

"Oh! excuse me, Miss Barstow," said she, after a moment of apparent surprise; "I was out behind the house looking after my bleach-

ing, and I did not know that any one was here. Have you waited long?"

"Not very. Are you all alone in the house?" asked Miss Rachel, fixing her severe gray eyes upon the false and faltering green orbs of the other.

"Yes. Joachim he's been away since noon, I rather guess he's over at the 'haven; and there's no one but us two left of the family now, you know. Won't you come in?" asked Semantha, reluctantly opening the door a little wider.

"Thank you. We'll stop a few moments. This is my brother, Mr. Barstow, Mrs. Brewster. He used to know Peleg and his first wife very well when they were all young."

"Happy to make your acquaintance, Mr. Barstow," said Semantha, in the stereotyped phrase of Milvor introductions, and extending a clammy hand, which Israel somewhat reluctantly enfolded in his large, warm grasp.

"Sit down, won't you? How's your folks, Miss Rachel?" continued the hostess, putting forward two wooden rocking-chairs fitted with feather cushions in patchwork covers.

"Very well, I thank you. Are you going to stay here alone?" asked Miss Rachel, seating herself with an air of reserve.

"Yes, I suppose so. Joachim calculates to stay and carry on the farm."

"You and he alone?"

"Why, yes; I don't seem to see any other way," said Semantha, nervously stooping to pick some threads from the not over-clean floor. "I don't know what folks will say."

"I suppose they'll say a good deal; but when anybody's doing just what's right, I don't know that they need ask what folks say," replied Rachel significantly.

"No, I suppose not," replied Semantha, turning very red; and then followed an awkward pause, broken by Israel:

"I was very much shocked at hearing of my friend Peleg's death, and especially at the manner of it, Mrs. Brewster," said he kindly.

"Yes, every one was, I expect," replied Semantha, with her apron at her eyes. "He was a good man, a real nice man, and he and me were dreadful fond of each other always. And then, as you say, Mr. Barstow, it makes it so much harder to bear when we think that it was his own child did it——"

"*I* don't think his own child did it, and I didn't understand my brother to say that he thought so either," interposed Miss Rachel with considerable emphasis.

"Why, the coroner said so, and he'd ought to know," disconsolately replied the widow.

"Coroners may know, and they may not know; but there's One that does know, and, for my part, I'm not going to doubt that some time or other He'll bring this and every other hidden sin to light. And when that day comes, I don't believe it will be Mary Brewster's child that will be found guilty of Peleg Brewster's murder," replied Rachel with emphasis.

"Well, I'm sure I hope not; but if she didn't, I don't know who did do it," said Semantha, wiping her eyes, and looking first at the one and then at the other of her guests.

"What sort of disposition had the little girl? Her mother, I remember, was very mild," asked Israel in a conciliatory tone.

"Well, sir, I don't want to say any harm of the child, for her father was a good man to me always, but since you ask it, I must own that of all the deceitful pieces that ever stepped, Ruth Brewster was the deceitfulest. She was so smooth and soft when any one was here that you'd think butter wouldn't melt in her mouth, and then when we were alone, if she got mad, it was enough to make any one's blood run cold to hear the way she'd talk. To say she threatened to poison me is no more than a beginning——"

"And it had better be an ending too, for I don't believe a word of it, and I don't want to hear any more," said Miss Rachel, rising and pulling her shawl vehemently about her. "I've seen that child, and I'm not a fool; and I knew her mother and her father too, and I'm not a fool. Come, Israel."

"Softly, Rachel," interposed Israel. "You have no right to speak in this manner to Mrs. Brewster. We cannot suppose that any person suff'ring under the affliction that has overtaken her could tell other than the truth, or would slander the character of even a child who is not here to defend herself. Mrs. Brewster, I am very sorry to hear such an account of your step-daughter; but if it is not too painful a subject, will you be so good as to tell me what motive could have led her to commit so frightful a deed?"

"Clear ugliness of temper," replied Semantha with decision. "She and her father didn't live happily together, and he had

threatened more than once to put her out to service. At last they had a quarrel worse than any that came before, and he took her off that morning, and told her in my hearing that she never should touch a cent of his money, or a stitch of her mother's clothes, or come under his roof again till she had turned a square corner, and was a different girl from what she had been. He talked pretty ha'sh, and she didn't say much; but there was a look in her eye that made my flesh creep on my bones. Then they set off, and he, without thinking, I suppose, put his loaded rifle right down beside the trunk where she was sitting, and I suppose when they got away from houses and out in the woods there, she thought nobody would see, and——"

"Israel Barstow, if you're a mind to stay here any longer, you may stay alone. I wish you good-afternoon, Mrs. Brewster; and the next time you peek over your banisters and see me in your front entry, I'll believe any story you're a mind to tell me."

And Miss Rachel, urged far beyond her wont by the indignation and disgust rising in her bosom, marched grandly from the house, and climbed into the chaise without assistance.

"You don't believe I'm a liar and a slanderer, Mr. Barstow?" whispered Semantha, rising and approaching her remaining guest, one hand covering her eyes and the other outstretched in farewell. "When a woman is poor and alone in the world, and them that should stand up for her and take care of her is dead and gone, there's enough that'll turn against her, and trample her into the dirt; but Israel Barstow isn't one of that sort—I know it, and I'll always say it."

"Thank you. No, I never want to add to any body's trouble, I'm sure. I am sorry Rachel spoke so harshly; but she's a woman of strong feelings, and she was very fond of Peleg's first wife; but she should not have hurt your feelings so; and—there, there, don't cry, now don't, and if you would not be affronted——"

And the successful merchant, to whom experience had thoroughly taught the power of money, whether as a consoler or a mediator, laid a bank note of considerable value upon the table, and then hastily joined his sister, who preserved a grim silence during nearly the entire journey home.

CHAPTER XII.
ZENOBIA AND DIOGENES.

"How are you, James? All right at home?" asked Mr. Barstow of the respectable-looking coachman who stood ready to meet the travellers in the station at the terminus of their journey.

"All right, sir. We got your orders by telegraph day before yesterday," said James, assuming his master's bag and shawl, and respectfully touching his hat to Miss Wansted, who followed her uncle down the steps of the car.

"Well, let us get home as fast as possible. I hope Mrs. Grey won't keep us waiting for dinner," said uncle Israel, a little impatiently; and in a few moments Beatrice found herself seated in a luxurious carriage, and rolling rapidly through the lighted streets.

"It seems a little close here, after the country, does it not?" asked Mr. Barstow, letting down the windows with a jerk. "We must have a run down to the sea-shore after you have fairly established yourself in Midas-avenue. By the way, you have never seen my new house; I was still at the Grandare when you visited us three years ago."

"Yes, sir," said Beatrice wearily.

"And that was before Chappelleford brought his niece from the South, was it not?"

"I think he had gone for her then. I never saw Mr. Chappelleford."

"Not when he was at the Old Garrison?"

"No, sir. I was still at school."

"Oh! yes; I remember. Well, I have invited him and June to dine with us to-night, and particularly asked them to be at the house to receive us. I thought it would seem more cheerful for you, my dear, to find the house full."

"Thank you, uncle," said Beatrice, inwardly longing to creep away somewhere, and hide from the glare, the bustle, the introductions, and the effort before her.

"You will be great friends with June, as soon as you get to know her," pursued Mr. Barstow complacently, "and we will take her to the beach with us. She was longing to leave town the last time I saw her; but Chappelleford never stirs from the neighborhood of the libraries and museums among which he lives; and June has no money of her own, poor girl. Her husband died a bankrupt, or worse."

"Is her name really June?" asked Beatrice, feeling that she must say something.

"Oh! no. It is Juanita, and people generally call her Nita; but I fancied to pronounce the first syllable as it is spelled, and make June of it. It is the same name as Jennie, Mrs. Charlton says—that is, Juan is John, and Juana is Jane, and Juanita is Jennie. Her mother was a Spanish woman from Cuba, who married Vezey Chappelleford's younger brother in New-Orleans, and June lived there until three years ago; so her blood is more tropical than arctic, and her temper also; but she and I always get on together admirably."

"And I dare say she and I will also," said Beatrice, smiling a little at the lesson in philology administered by her uncle, and beginning to feel a dawning interest in this tropical June-bird, whose praises her uncle so persistently sung.

But the carriage-wheels already woke the echoes of Midas-avenue, and presently stopped mid-way down that aristocratic thoroughfare, before a house large enough and handsome enough to have served as the residence of an ambassador, or to have crushed its *parvenu* owner into insignificance had he been a man less single-hearted and unpretentious than Israel Barstow, who, opening his carriage-door himself, stepped gayly out, and tendered a hand to his niece, saying:

"Here we are at home, Trixie, and home you must feel it to be, for there isn't the first thing in it which is not yours as much as mine."

"Thank you, uncle," said Beatrice quietly; and in stepping from the carriage, she cast one comprehensive glance at the house and locality, feeling that the panacea for a wounded spirit thus offered her was one not to be despised.

At the door stood Mrs. Grey, a pale, placid matron, with faded brown hair neatly folded under a cap, faded blue eyes, habitually downcast, and a faded smile upon her faded lips. She dressed always in black silk or stuff gowns, and wore clear-starched white muslin aprons, and ruffles about her hands.

Mr. Barstow shook hands heartily with his housekeeper and introduced his niece.

"This is Miss Wansted, or Miss Beatrice, if you prefer it, Mrs. Grey, and she has travelled sixty miles since breakfast, and would like her dinner. I am very sure, I suppose, though, she wants to wash her hands first, and I am sure I do mine. You have a room ready for her?"

3

"Certainly, sir. Shall I show you up-stairs, Miss Wansted?"

"Thank you, Mrs. Grey."

And Beatrice meekly followed the housekeeper through a hall and up a staircase, wrought and furnished in the luxurious fashion of the day, to an apartment upon the second floor, whose magnificence was its only fault.

"Mr. Barstow wrote me word that these were to be your rooms, Miss Wansted," said the housekeeper, opening two rooms at the further side of the sleeping-chamber. "This is the dressing-room, and this the sitting-room, with another door into the hall. I hope you will find them comfortably arranged, though Mr. Barstow said that you would re-furnish them to suit yourself as soon as you were settled. Shall I send a maid to help you change your dress, Miss?"

"No, thank you. If you will let some one bring up my trunks, I will do all the rest. Is Mrs. Charlton here, Mrs. Grey?"

"Yes, Miss, she arrived about half an hour ago, and is in the drawing-room waiting for you."

"Thank you. Won't you call me Miss Beatrice instead of Miss Wansted, as my uncle said?" asked Beatrice with a smile; and the housekeeper replied less formally than she had yet spoken:

"Thank you, Miss Beatrice, it does sound more home-like, and I hope you will make up your mind to stay with us a good long while. Now I will send up the trunks, and dinner will be ready at eight."

Half an hour later, Beatrice, whose hands were as quick as her head, came from her chamber refreshed in body and mind, and dressed with a quiet simplicity sure at least not to offend, although a critical beholder might feel that more elegant attire would better suit her patrician style of beauty.

The drawing-room door stood open, and Beatrice, while descending the stairs, assured herself that the room was occupied, and that her uncle was not of the company. A shy impulse prompted her to retreat, and wait for the protection of his presence before entering; and she had actually stolen up several stairs, when a reactionary pride arrested her steps, and, turning, she went steadily down, and into the drawing-room without pause or hesitation. The struggle, however, had brought a deeper color to her cheek, and lent a certain haughty self-possession to her bearing, so easily to be mistaken for the *aplomb* of a woman of the world, that none but the keenest observers would have recognized it as the defiant self-assertion of inexperienced pride.

Vezey Chappelleford *was* the keenest of observers, and he at once came forward to meet the young girl whom he had already catalogued as "Barstow's rustic *protégée*."

"Miss Wansted, allow me to claim a sort of collateral acquaintanceship with the kinswoman of my old friend, and to present my niece, Mrs. Charlton. Nita, Miss Wansted and you have much to do in settling the etiquette of welcome, since both are, in a manner, hostess for this evening. By to-morrow, Miss Wansted will have fairly assumed the sceptre."

"I am but too happy to take my place as guest upon the instant," replied Mrs. Charlton, in a voice peculiarly rich and mellow in its modulations, and subdued in its tone. Beatrice, while murmuring some commonplace reply, noted the voice, and examined its possessor with a glance of feminine comprehensiveness.

She found a woman framed upon the heroic scale, but with a figure of admirable proportions, with a head which might have been regal had it not been languid in its pose; a face of dark, sultry beauty, with a life's experience beneath the drooping eyelids, and in the curve of the passionate lips, and with a manner of perfect polish and indolent grace.

"Cleopatra!" thought Beatrice, as her slight fingers lay within the firm, satiny touch of Mrs. Charlton's large white hand.

"No; Zenobia," said she again, as the other led her to a seat, and placing herself beside her with the air of one receiving rather than conferring a favor, asked some courteous questions of her journey.

While she replied, Mr. Barstow entered the room, and as he welcomed his guests, Beatrice looked at Mr. Chappelleford as she had at his niece, and following the same bad habit he had indulged toward her, mentally bestowed upon him the *sobriquet* of Diogenes. Nor could that famous cynic have possessed a more dome-like brow, stronger lineaments, or determined reticence of manner. With the majority of mankind, Vezey Chappelleford lived on terms of mutual intolerance; among *savans* he was known as a man of profound and varied erudition; to Israel Barstow, who never disputed the most untenable of his theories, or interfered in the remotest manner with his pursuits, he was a good humored patron, although the merchant's daily income far outweighed the philosopher's yearly annuity; to children he was a simple-hearted playmate; to women, a courteous misogynist; to Juanita Charlton a puzzle without a key.

"Sorry to have kept you waiting, friends, and to have left you to introduce yourselves to each other," said the host, shaking hands with every body. "But in my dressing-room I found that fellow Rowley—my head clerk, you know, Chappelleford—and he had been waiting an hour, and would have waited until to-morrow morning if I had not attended to him; so I had to sit down and listen and answer, and sign, seal, and deliver, just as he ordered. A shocking tyrant, that fellow."

"Poor Rowley! I wish I had imagination enough to fancy his crossing a *t*, or dotting an *i*, without your especial permission, or your amazed indignation should he do so," said Chappelleford with a cynical smile.

"Well, well, some people tyrannize by humble appeals, as well as others by downright bullying," replied Mr. Barstow, reddening a little at finding himself unmasked.

"Yes, that is the usual style of feminine tyranny; is it not, Miss Wansted?" asked Chappelleford, offering his arm to Beatrice as dinner was announced.

"The disguise would not be of much use where it is convicted beforehand," replied she, with a merry glance into the keen eyes bent upon her; and the cynic replied with a smile whose beauty always took the beholder by surprise.

"You are right, young lady; most disguises are like the shirt of Nessus, and he who assumes them finds himself ruined within them."

"'Honesty is the best policy' is as true now as it ever was, and that's as true as the sun," remarked Mr. Barstow, who had caught the last remark while seating himself at the foot of the dinner-table.

"No need to look in books of reference for that motto," growled Chappelleford in reply, "It is unmistakably English: none but a nation of shopkeepers could have originated it, or needed it."

"Pitching into trade again?" laughed the host with perfect good-nature, while his niece raised her eyes indignantly. "Have some turtle and a glass of Madeira, and consider that, without trade, you must have begun your dinner with clam-chowder and cider, and finished it with hickory nuts and currant-wine."

"After which, we have only to consider whether Madeira or manhood, callipash or constitution, is more important to a nation, and the question is settled," said the philosopher, sipping his glass of wine with a relish, and glancing quizzically at Miss Wansted's flushed face.

"Do you really think trade dishonorable, Mr. Chappelleford?" inquired she, meeting the glance.

"Did you ever read Mill on Political Economy, Miss Wansted?" replied the philosopher."

"No, sir."

"Nor I, and Heaven send that we never may. Is my friend Miss Barstow quite well, and has she forgiven my rat-like invasion of her wainscot, in search of truth?"

"Did you take a lantern to aid your search for it?" asked Beatrice, her irritation outweighing her discretion for the moment; but her low voice was drowned by her uncle's burly tones, and the allusion was unheard.

CHAPTER XIII.
REIN, GRAHAME, AND LAFORET.

"AND now," said Mr. Barstow, as with his niece and their guests they sat in the dimly-lighted drawing-room, while the music of the songs without words Mrs. Charlton had been playing died dreamily away—"and, now, June, this little girl and I want to know when you are coming to take care of us. You made no answer to my letter asking you to spend the fall and winter here."

"I thought to tell you better when we met how much pleasure I should take in accepting the invitation, and now I find it impossible to tell you," said Mrs. Charlton, looking significantly toward Beatrice, and then upward into her host's face.

"You like her then?" asked he in a pleased tone.

"So much. I am afraid I shall love her," sighed Mrs. Charlton, idly striking minor chords with her left hand, while the right lay, a white, glittering wonder, upon her lap.

"Why do you say afraid? I hope you will love her, and she you," replied Mr. Barstow bluntly.

"No, oh! no. I wish never to love, never to hate, never to care for any created thing. The only joy is calm," murmured Juanita; and honest Israel Barstow looked puzzled and disturbed.

"You got that from Chappelleford, but it is a cold, dismal sort of philosophy—not fit for a woman at all events," said he. "Why, to my mind, a woman ought to be all love and enthusiasm, more so than any man; we go to them for just that sort of thing."

"And find it generally, I don't doubt. There, at all events."

And Mrs. Charlton again looked admiringly at Beatrice, who was listenin with a face of animated interest to Mr. Chappelleford's description of Eastern scenery.

"Yes, Beatrice is enthusiastic enough, and loving enough too, poor child," said Mr. Barstow with a sigh; and Mrs. Charlton, although she wondered, did not ask him what he meant.

"Then you will come and stay with us?" said the merchant presently; and Juanita, with a gracious smile, replied:

"Thank you very much. It will give me the greatest pleasure to do so."

"That's right. You had better remain tonight, and I will send for your traps."

"Thank you. But you have little idea of the commotion of a feminine change of residence," replied Mrs. Charlton with a languid smile. "I have oceans of preparations to make; but if you will kindly send for me tomorrow about noon, I will try to be ready."

"Certainly; the carriage shall go for you at twelve o'clock, and I will amuse Trix myself until then. I don't want her to get homesick, you know."

"Certainly not;" and Mrs. Charlton, sweeping her drowsy eyes once more upon Beatrice, decided that she had prospered ill in some love affair, and that Mr. Barstow had brought her home with him to break up the train of painful association.

"And asked me here as *dame du compagnie*," thought she. "Well, I shall earn my daily plover, if not in the sweat of my brow, in the strain of my endurance, and I like carriages better than horse-cars."

So the next day, Mrs. Charlton and Mrs. Charlton's luggage arrived in Midas-avenue, and when Mr. Barstow came home to dinner, he found two beautiful, well-dressed, and well-bred women ready to receive and entertain him, and to make for him a home in his hitherto somewhat dreary palace.

"This is the pleasantest thing I have seen to-day. This is what a man likes to look forward to while he is bustling about on 'change, or bullying other men in his or their counting-rooms," said he, throwing himself luxuriously into an arm-chair after dinner, and contemplating the two young women—seated, the one at her needle-work, the other at the piano.

"And now, my dears," pursued he, "I have been all day settling affairs at the office, so that I might be spared for a while, and to-morrow, if you say so, we will turn our backs upon the town, and go the sea-shore, the mountains, the prairies, or even across the water, if you will be satisfied with a peep and good-by, for I cannot leave home for more than a month or six weeks. What do you say?"

"Which does Miss Wansted prefer of all these delightful visions?" asked Mrs. Charlton, smiling at Beatrice.

"Oh! the sea by all means, if I am to choose; but which do you and my uncle like best?"

"I wouldn't give a copper to choose. They are all new to me; for since I left Milvor, I have lived here in the city, boy and man, until I feel strange anywhere else. I have never cared to take a play-time before, since I had the means of giving myself one," said Mr. Barstow honestly; and Mrs. Charlton added with a smile:

"It is the meeting of extremes, for I have travelled so much, and seen so many varieties of scenery, that I do not care at all which way I turn when I leave home."

"Then it shall be to the sea-shore, and we will go to-morrow, if you say so."

"I shall be ready, uncle," said Beatrice, with feverish eagerness; and Juanita quietly decided:

"It is a fresh wound, and stings keenly. Poor fool! By and by, she can lay her finger upon the scar and smile at its memories."

A few days later found Mr. Barstow and his "family," as he liked to call the beautiful women under his charge, established at one of the loveliest points upon the New-England coast, and entering with avidity into the life about them. The place was crowded, and both Mrs. Charlton and Mr. Barstow found many acquaintances—she among the gayest, and he among the soberest of the crowd.

Beatrice knew no one, and cared to know no one—contenting herself with nature, and continually stealing away to sit upon the rocks by the shore, or weary herself to exhaustion in mountain scrambles, and woodland walks.

"This will not do; she might as well have stayed in Milvor," said Uncle Israel confidentially to Juanita one day, when his wilful niece had quietly disappeared from a projected bowling party. "June, we must keep her among people, make her merry, teach her to flirt as these other girls do—any thing to take up her mind. The truth is, you see, the poor child has met with a disappointment; I don't know much about it myself, and I never should speak of it to her; but she needs to change the scene inside her mind, as well as outside her body. Now, you can do that, if any one can, I am sure."

"Yes, I can do that," said Mrs. Charlton, with one of her smiles of languid power. And that evening she introduced Rein, the artist; Grahame, the author; and Laforét, the invincible of the *salons*, to her charge, having previously dropped a quiet word into the ear of each.

"Have you ever dreamed of such a head for a study?" asked she of Rein; and while he looked, she murmured to Grahame:

"There is a story there. See if you can find it out." And to Laforét:

"She is to come out this winter, and will make a sensation. I will introduce you before the world finds her out."

So these three men, the nucleus of "society" at Dream Harbor, devoted themselves, each in his own interest, to the rising star, and left her no longer a hope of solitude or quiet. Did she wander to the sea-shore or the mountains? Rein quietly attended her, and begged leave to sketch her as a sea-nymph, a dryad, an urchin, a saint, as every possible form of beauty and inspiration. Did she listlessly dream away the long summer hours, her thoughts wandering, she knew not where? Grahame was beside her, softly leading the talk to personal experiences, to sympathy, to the forgotten dreams, the impossible visions of youth. Or did she seek refuge in the crowd, who so ready as Laforét to ask her to dance, to propose croquet, with himself as her partner, to

idle at her side, and affect an intimacy Beatrice hardly took the trouble to deny.

"Why do these people haunt me so? I do not want them or try to make myself agreeable to them," asked she of Mrs. Charlton once when she had perforce spent the whole day in company with Messieurs Rein, Grahame, Laforét, and their friends.

"Because, my dear, these persons are society, and society claims you as a fresh young victim, and sends out its high priests to capture you. Haven't you a taste for martyrdom? If not, you had better cultivate one, since it is your fate."

"Does society mean martyrdom, then?" asked the novice.

"As long as you persist in egotism," replied the teacher. "Go with the stream, and you will swim easily and pleasantly; set your face against it, and attempt some new method of overcoming the inevitable, and you will be in every one's way, and every one in yours, and will finally be overwhelmed and drowned."

"But with what stream am I to swim?" asked Beatrice wearily. "I do not care for Mr. Rein's ideas of art—they seem to me conventional and hackneyed. Mr. Grahame's favorite literature is too sentimental for my taste, and Mr. Laforét's gossip is a weariness to the flesh. Am I to force myself to sympathize with my antipathies?"

Mrs. Charlton raised a warning hand.

"To answer the end of your question first, my dear, let me warn you against that style of thing: antitheses, syllogisms, argument, metaphysics, are all topics *défendre* to a *débutante*. They are the weapons of maturity, of waning beauty, and it is as unfair and unbecoming for your use as rouge or pearl-powder, antimony or belladonna."

"Who uses antimony and belladonna?" asked Beatrice, yielding to a small side-current of feminine curiosity.

"Secrets of the prison-house," gayly replied Juanita. "I won't even tell you their uses; but again I warn you against the deep waters which are as yet bad style for you. Freshness, *naïveté*, universal interest in all persons, all pursuits not too heavy for you, all topics of the day—this is your *rôle*. You have a taste for repartee—indulge it sparingly and mildly. The reputation of a satirist, or even of a wit, is as fatal to a young beauty as that of a *bas bleu*. All this will come in time; but meanwhile accept Rein's teachings in art,

Grahame's in literature, and Laforêt's in society. They are all fools, but they are the world's mouthpieces, and their jargon is its Shibboleth. Learn it, for it as necessary as French in the circle you are entering."

"Thank you," said Beatrice sadly. "Perhaps I had better have stayed at Milvor."

"Not at all, dear. You would have died there—perished of——"

"What?" inquired the girl, flushing like the morning.

"Of egotism," coolly replied Juanita. "You were quite too important to yourself there—to other persons also, no doubt; but to yourself fatally. In the world, we soon learn that our own experience is every one's experience, that our original ideas are hackneyed, and our life hurts are other people's callous scars. It is a good school."

"You indulge in the philosophies you deny me," said Beatrice, smiling bitterly.

"My dear, I am thirty-three years old, and at sixteen I had seen more of the world than you at twenty. Do not revenge yourself by disliking me, for I like you better than any one I have met in a dozen years."

"Do you? Thank you," hesitated Beatrice. "I do not dislike you indeed, but I dislike your theories and your world more than I can tell."

"You will come to adopt both as your own, my poor child. Good-night."

"Good-night. I am so sorry to seem ungrateful," said the girl; but her new friend only smiled a little, and went without reply.

CHAPTER XIV.
A FRIEND.

THE next day had been appointed for an excursion up the mountain, but the advent in the morning of a rival base-ball club, challenged some days before by the champions of that noble game resident at Dream Harbor, broke up all other excursions, and filled the public mind with visions of blue or scarlet banners, badges, dresses, prizes, and preparations. Even the dogs of the respective houses, and sheep of the field where the match was to be played, were decorated with ribbons of the rival colors, and one enthusiastic young lady was heard to propose that a couple of calves grazing in an adjacent paddock should be adorned, the one in blue and the other in red ribbons, and turned loose among the combatants; but this notion was for some reason

hastily suppressed, and the young lady detailed to the manufacture of paper caps for the players, each one with a bow of ribbon upon its pointed top.

Beatrice, who cared not at all for base-ball, and a great deal for mountains, watched these preparations with rather petulant disdain, and finally, by condescending to a little coaxing, persuaded her uncle to resume the idea of the excursion, confining the party to their two selves; for Mrs. Charlton was already the centre of an eager throng, each claiming her as a partisan, and making her umpire upon various questions of dress, usage, and propriety.

"Of course I must side with the red, for I have not a scrap of blue anything in my possession; and scarlet is the only color I wear. See, I assume my badge."

And winding an Indian scarf about her head, she became at once a sultana, a Zobeide, a picture, an "Admirable of the Red," as a very young man, still in his Sophomore year, remarked with the air of saying a good thing.

"She can spare us, uncle, and of course it is proper if you go with me," urged Beatrice. And the matter was arranged with but slight opposition from Mrs. Charlton, who enjoyed the position she affected to disdain, and had little thought to bestow upon her charge.

"There! This is real pleasure," sighed Beatrice, as near the crest of the mountain they halted their panting horses, and turned to look behind them. The day was perfect, with so rare an atmosphere that the most distant summits lay faintly purple against the tender blue of the sky, and the gleam of waters, leaving the farthest shores within the reach of human vision, became distinctly visible. Tempering the glow of the summer noon, great white clouds floated now and again across the fathomless blue depths of heaven, their shadows falling upon sea and land, mountains and valleys, like God's gift of sleep; far out at sea the flash of white sails showed the course of craft else hidden in the distance, and still beyond them, ocean and heaven hid their marriage kiss behind a veil of dazzling light, tempting and impenetrable to mortal vision.

"Yes, it is a fine view," said Mr. Barstow, adjusting his double eye-glass upon his nose. "Now, I wonder which of those peaks is Kahtadin," pursued he, scanning the horizon, "and Mount Washington. They told me at the house that I could see them both to-day. Washington is one hundred and seventy miles from here, and it is seldom that it is visible; but to-day is so clear. Now, where should you look for it, Beatrice?"

"I do not know, uncle, I am sure. I suppose the people up here can tell you," said Beatrice dreamily. "But don't you think it just as pleasant to look at the landscape as if you were the first person who ever saw it, and it was all your own, as to know the names that other people have given to every thing, and be told that this is Goose Pond, and the other is Bear Mountain, or Burnt Porcupine Island?"

"Eh? Well; but if things have names, why it is by the names you know them, and talk

"*The little inn at the summit of the mountain.*"

about them. If I send to Canton for a cargo of the tea that I like best, my agent would think I was a fool, and would write back to ask me its name. Don't you see?"

"But," persisted Beatrice, "you don't send for the mountains to come to you—you go to the mountains, and when you are with them, the names make but little difference to you or to them."

"And when you go away, and want to talk about them to your friends, what then?"

asked Mr. Barstow; and Beatrice, laughing, said:

"Your common-sense is too much for me, Uncle Israel. Let us drive on, and find a guide and a guide-book."

Half an hour brought them to the little inn at the summit of the mountain, and while Mr. Barstow ordered dinner and awaited its announcement in a comfortable rocking-chair, with a bottle of London stout and a stand of capital cigars at his elbow, his niece strolled out upon the rocks, perversely determined to make her first acquaintance with the scene, alone and unaided by "guide or guide-book."

Out of sight of the house, and yet within hearing of a summons, she paused, and seating herself upon a boulder, kindly fashioned by nature into semblance of a chair, with back and footstool, she drew a full, free breath.

"Alone at last," murmured she, and leaning her face upon her hands, she gave way to the tears that had lain, as it seemed to her, for weeks, a crushing and intolerable weight upon brain and heart.

"Is any thing the matter with thee, friend?" said a low voice behind her; and hastily looking up, Beatrice saw a woman of middle age, dressed in the sober livery of the Quakers, but carrying within her uncomely head-gear a face so sweet, so calm, and withal so strong, that no fashion could disguise or disfigure it.

"I do not wish to intrude upon thee," continued the stranger, as Beatrice hesitated how to reply to her. "But as I came softly over the rocks, I heard the sound of thy grief, and thought I possibly might be of use. Is thee hurt in any way?"

"Oh! no—thank you. I was thinking of other scenes, and absent friends. I thought I was quite alone," stammered Beatrice; and then fearing to have seemed rude and ungracious, was suddenly silent.

"May I sit beside thee for a moment or two? This is the finest outlook I have found," said the stranger, quietly seating herself, while Beatrice, half vexed, half attracted to that lovely face and reässuring voice, sat still, without reply.

"I have been all day upon the mountain," continued the new-comer, "and am not yet tired. It is a grand thing for us who live in cities to see how much larger the world is than we are taught to remember. Does thee live in a city?"

"Sometimes I visit them."

"I live always in Pennapolis. My name is Mary Askew; what is thine?"

"Wansted—Beatrice Wansted," replied the young lady, with a half smile at this direct questioning.

"And did thee ever come nearer to understanding creation than here?" asked Mary Askew, pointing to the grand panorama at their feet.

"I—I have hardly looked yet," faltered Beatrice.

"Why?" demanded the Friend, fixing her

"A rude log-cabin in the forest."

clear, truth-compelling eyes upon those of the young girl.

"Because, I was thinking ——"

"Because thee was looking inside instead of out; because thee was thinking of Beatrice Wansted instead of God and His works, and that was where thee was short-sighted. Does thee know, Beatrice, why God made these mountains and lonely places, and puts it into our hearts to run away from our daily lives and seek out the solitudes, when we are sorely tried? I think it is that we may see at one look the immensity of creation, and remember how small a part of it our finger-hurts must be."

"But if an insect is crushed to death, it does not cure it to know that the earth moves on," cried Beatrice bitterly.

"Thee is not an insect, Beatrice. Thee has a soul higher than the mountains, deeper than the ocean, wider than the sky. The grief of to-day, keen though it may be, will not outlast even thy mortal life, and after that comes eternity. That word, it seems to me, dwarfs all else."

Beatrice, weeping no more, turned and gazed into the face of her companion with absorbing interest.

"But if the same soul exists after death, how can you tell that the same troubles will not cling to it?" asked she.

"The troubles of this world belong to this world: thee may so use them that they will warp and deface thy soul even after it has left them behind, if thee chooses, or thee may make of them stepping-stones to a peace and joy that ripen the soul for eternal bliss as no prosperity ever ripens it," said the Friend, in a voice so full of meaning that Beatrice remembered Aunt Rachel's words: "Most all of us get disappointed once," and asked herself if the sweet content upon Mary Askew's brow had been won from a stepping-stone of sorrow such as now filled her own heart.

"Thee should look at that ocean and that sky for the meaning of my words; not in my face. I do but speak to thee as the spirit moves me, and the translation is in thy own heart," said the Friend quietly; and just then the clear notes of a horn blown at the house-door recalled the two to a warning of daily needs and waiting friends.

"I hope to see more of thee, Beatrice Wansted," said the elder, as they walked together to the house; and Beatrice, a little shyly, answered:

"You are very kind, and I should be glad to know you better."

CHAPTER XV.

IN THE WOODS

"THERE, Zilpah, this is home—the best that I have to offer, at any rate. Are you sorry you came?"

So spoke Marston Brent, throwing open the door of a rude log cabin buried in the heart of a hemlock forest, many miles from any town, village, or even hamlet, and connected with the haunts of man only by the capricious highway of the Sachawissa, loveliest and most unreliable of rivers. From the Ford, as the highest point of sloop navigation upon this stream is called, Brent had transported his family and his chattels in two stout wagons drawn by oxen, who now stood panting before the log-house in the waning of a September day.

"Well, I don't know as I be," said Zilpah cautiously, and pausing to look well about her before she made reply. "Looks kind o' woodsy, don't it?"

"Yes; that we must expect in a logging-camp; but the trees just about the house are cut away, you see," said Marston, with an effort at cheerful speech.

"Hm! That was so's to get something to make the house of, I expect," replied Zilpah coolly. "It's a reg'lar log-cabin, a'n't it?"

"Yes; I told you it was."

"I know it, Mr. Brent, I know it, I a'n't complaining — don't you think it; only it looks kind o' cur'us to any one that's always lived amongst folks; now don't it?"

"I suppose so," said Marston, smiling, as he remembered the seclusion of Milvor, where Zilpah had been born and bred; and then he added gayly:

"Well, we must make company for each other, Zilpah. Come into the house, won't you? And, Richard, you must explain matters a little as to where we are to get fuel, water, and such matters. You know we are new to this way of life."

Richard, a veteran logger, who, having spent the previous winter at Wahtahree, in the employ of Mr. Mills, had been selected as the fittest cicerone of the new proprietor, came forward at the summons, saying with a grin:

"As for fuel, Cap'n, why there's enough of that all about. I should say; and as for water, there's a spring right down there, and the boys might fetch some in this bucket when the cattle have done eating their meal out'n it. There's a first-rate cook-stove in the shanty, and I'll get the pork-barrel unloaded right away. I expect she knows how to fry pork and bile potaters, don't she? That's logger's fare, mostly."

"I guess I know as much as that, young man, and I know better than to get water for folks and feed critters in the same bucket. Paul Freeman, you get a pail out of Mr. Brent's goods. There's one there that won't pizen, as I expect," said Zilpah, with so much dignity that Brent was fain to turn away to hide a smile, and Richard grinned from ear to ear as he led the way into the cabin, or shanty, as the building would be styled in forest parlance.

This consisted of two rooms and a closet upon the lower floor, and a loft above, furnished with wooden boxes or bunks filled with hay, in which the wood cutters were expected to sleep. The outer room, into which opened the principal door, was furnished with a long table extending down the middle, with a bench at either side, all of evident home manufacture, and more solid than elegant; two or three stools, and a smaller movable table, set in front of the wide, open fireplace. This was the dining and sitting room of the family, while the smaller one behind it served as kitchen and scullery. The closet was set apart as Zilpah's bedroom, and Richard, Paul and his brother, and the lumbermen, when they should arrive, were quartered in the loft. For his own use, Brent reserved a small room in an adjacent building designed as a store-house, and thither had his personal belongings transported as they were unloaded.

Such articles of household gear as Zilpah declared indispensable, Brent had purchased at their last stopping place, and the list had finally lengthened so far that the great ox-wagon engaged to transport them had almost proved insufficient, and the old housekeeper, watching her master's face during the process of loading, expected every moment to see some precious article discarded, or some favorite scheme upset by loss of its material elements. But Brent, like other men of his large, strong nature, was ever over-indulgent to the weak and helpless under his control, and although Richard grumbled, and his assistant teamster swore, Zilpah was not mulcted of pot or pan, bread-tray, clothes-horse, or rubbing-board, and Brent arranged all difficulties by hiring a second yoke of oxen to accompany them to the end of their journey.

These, her household gods, the old woman now received at the hands of Paul, who was unloading the wagon, and arranged them upon the shelves, hooks, and walls of her new home with much satisfaction.

"There, now, that looks something like!" exclaimed she, as Brent returned to the shanty, after superintending the ordering of his own room. "Look at here, Mr. Marston, and see my tin-shelf. Don't that seem most like Milvor over again? Recollect our coffee-pot to home? Wa'n't it the moral of this'n?"

"I should think so. Yes, they look very home-like and housewifely, Zilpah. But what!—a warming-pan!"

"Well, yes, Mr. Marston," replied the old woman, a little sheepishly; "you see a warming-pan is dreadful handy in case of sickness; and there's no knowing what might happen to any of us, away off here in the woods, away from doctors so."

"But where did you get it?" asked Brent, suppressing a smile.

"Why, don't you remember, while I was trading with that tinman, you and he went off to look at some kind of ox-tackle he'd been getting up, and whilst you were gone, I sort o' prowled round in the back-shop and peeked into the cellar-way and the loft—not for no harm, only to see what sort o' things he'd got stowed away; and then I see this warming-pan, and it looked so sort o' home-like—you see, my folks had one when I was a small girl, and I rec'lect my mother warming my bed over when I'd got a bad cold—and so I thought you wouldn't care, Marston, and I just tucked it into the things that was sot off for us, and didn't say nothing about it."

"But did the man know it? There was no such item in the bill," said Marston, taking a note-book from his pocket, and selecting a paper to which the man of stoves had affixed not only his name, but several of the black "thumb marks" which our illiterate ancestors used in place of signatures.

"No, it is not in the bill," added Brent severely, as he refolded the document.

"Oh! well, dearie, if it isn't, it's no fault of your'n," said Zilpah in some confusion, and making a great rattling among her pots and pans. "He might have seed it if he'd looked, I'm sure. It a'n't a thing I could hide in my pocket."

"But the articles were all noted down as they were selected, and the shopman put them into the wagon while his master made out the bill. You have stolen this warming-pan, Zilpah, and under cover of my name too," exclaimed Brent indignantly.

Whereupon, Zilpah, dropping the tin basin and dipper from her hands, threw her apron over her head and broke into violent weeping, mingled with protestations of immaculate innocence and wounded feeling at such unde-

served suspicion from one whom she had regarded all the same as her own boy."

Brent looked on for a moment in the helpless and absurd way in which a man always contemplates a weeping woman whom circumstances or her own will do not permit of his taking in his arms and kissing, and then he strode out of the house, and stood vacantly staring at the gloomy autumnal prospect.

And this, he thought, was his home and his life. These petty and sordid cares within the house were to be his relief from the exhaustive labor without, from which he did not shrink. No companionship, no sympathy, no contact with a gentle and more delicate organization to soothe away the asperities of his daily life.

"Beatrice was right," muttered he at last. "It is no place for her. I am glad she did not come."

But the idea of regretting his own choice, of reconsidering a decision deliberately made, never crossed the mind of this man, whose nature, ardent and impressionable as heated lava, like hardened lava retained forever the impressions so made. Nor was it in him to devote many moments to repining, or, indeed, to reverie of any sort; and before Zilpah, cautiously peeping from her kitchen to ascertain his whereabouts, had hidden the obnoxious warming-pan in her own bedroom, Brent had thrown off his coat and was helping his man to move some of the heavier articles of their load, and to stable the oxen, and the horse he had provided for his personal use. He was still engaged in this manner when a timid voice at his elbow pronounced his name. He turned and found the boy Willy watching him attentively.

"Well, my little man, what is it?" asked he good-naturedly.

"Zilpah sent me to tell you that supper is ready," said the child.

"I will come. And how do you like the woods and our fine log house, Willy?"

"Very much indeed, sir. Do people ever come here?" asked the child, glancing timidly around him.

"People? No, indeed," replied Brent with a short laugh. "Except my gang of lumbermen, who will be along next week, I suppose we may not see a human being before the spring. We are pretty well 'out of humanity's reach,' as poor Selkirk has it. You won't be lonesome, will you?"

"Oh! no, sir. I am very glad indeed that people won't come," said the boy, raising his large dark eyes to Brent's face with an expression of confidence and reliance that went to his heart.

"I don't think any body would hurt you if they did come, Willy," said he kindly. "Not if I was about, at any rate."

"I know it, sir, and I should like to keep where you are all the time if I could."

"What, stay with me rather than Paul?" asked Brent laughing, and a little surprised.

"Yes, sir. You are the biggest, and besides, you are the master here. Richard says you are the boss, and that the boss can do any thing he likes in a logging camp, and every one has to mind him, or else he can almost murder them."

Brent laughed aloud.

"Richard would make a despotism of our encampment, and a tyrant of me," said he. "And so you want to keep where I am, do you, my boy?"

"Yes, sir," said Willy, looking once more about him before he entered the house.

CHAPTER XVI.
BRENT BECOMES A LAW-BREAKER.

THE meal of fried pork, boiled potatoes, hard bread, bannocks of Indian meal, and coffee without milk, was set upon the long table, already noted, in the large room of the shanty. Tablecloth, napkins, silver were all dispensed with, and even the coarse earthern plates and cups produced from among Zilpah's purchases were an innovation upon the severe custom of the woods, which sanctioned only tin and iron as table equipage.

Brent had from the first decided to live with his men, and as his men, laboring with them, eating with them, resting with them, reserving to himself only the privilege of a separate sleeping-room, somewhat more fastidiously, though hardly more luxuriantly, appointed than their own. He now sat down at the head of his homely table, and glancing from its meagre appointments to the faces at either hand, said simply:

"Welcome, friends, to our first meal together, and may God make us all duly thankful for this and his other gifts."

"I don't know how you're a going to drink your coffee without no milk in it, Mr. Brent. It a'n't what you're used to," said Zilpah querulously, as she filled and passed the cups.

"We will have a cow next week, Zilpah, and, meantime, if we cannot drink coffee without milk, there is plenty of cold water," said Brent cheerily.

"I never see no milk in a logging-camp, nor no cow neither, nor yet sugar," said Richard, reaching rather contemptuously for the sugar-basin. "Where I've been, they always bile merlasses with the coffee. Merlasses is first-rate with fried pork too."

"Molasses with fried pork!" cried Zilpah indignantly.

"Jus' so. Didn't you ever eat none?" asked Richard over the edge of his cup.

"No; nor I don't never mean to."

"No more I wouldn't if I didn't want to; but I'd like some, if you've got it hand, and the boss ha'n't no objection."

"Not the least," said Brent smiling; and Zilpah, with a snort of indignation, produced and filled a japanned molasses-cup, which Richard nearly emptied upon his plate, following the usual habit of his class, to whom instinct teaches the lesson of science, that the carbon necessary to feed the fire constantly formed by fierce labor and exposure is to be found in heavy sweets and concentrated oils, or, as they embody them, in molasses and pork-fat.

Brent, silently revolving this idea in his mind, finished his repast, and rising from the table with the rest, was about to leave the house, when Zilpah touched him upon the arm, and mysteriously beckoned him into her own room.

Brent followed, a little apprehensive of a scene, and rapidly resolving to set the old woman's mind at rest upon the vexed question of the warming-pan by promising to pay for it the first time he should have occasion to send to the town. But Zilpah's conscience was not of the peremptory and persistent sort that will let neither its possessor nor accuser rest, and so long as her felonious possession remained snugly ensconced in the corner, behind a black bombazine petticoat, Zilpah was very willing to appear to forget it.

Her present subject of conversation was of a different nature, and she heralded it with the inquiry:

"There a'n't no sleeping-room except this and your'n, and the loft where the men sleep, is there?"

"No. What is wanted of more?" asked Brent in some surprise.

"Well, I don't know. Where was you calculating that Willy would sleep?"

"Why, with his brother, I suppose."

"I shouldn't hardly love to have 'em do that way, seems to me," suggested Zilpah mysteriously.

"Why not, in Heaven's name?" demanded Brent, rather irritated at his housekeeper's diplomatic reserve.

"Well, you see, Mr. Brent, I don't know nothing about it, but I kind o' mistrust that it a'n't all just as it appears with these boys."

"Do tell me what you mean, Zilpah, without any more mysteries. What is wrong with the boys?"

"Well, *I* didn't never hear that Paul Freeman had any brother. He was took out of the poor-house, and his mother was a traveller that died there, and nobody knows who his father was; so where's his brother going to come from, I'd like to know?"

"Are you sure of this, Zilpah?" demanded Brent, whose anger was always stirred by deception, even of the most trivial description.

"Sartain sure, Mr. Marston; and more than all that, I've my suspicions that the boy a'n't no boy at all."

"Which boy? What *do* you mean, Zilpah?"

"Why, Willy. I don't believe he's any kin to Paul Freeman, and, what's more, I don't believe he's a boy. He's a gal, unless I miss my guess, and his name's Ruth Brewster."

"What, the girl who killed her father? Peleg Brewster's daughter?" demanded Brent in horror.

"Sho! Who's going to believe Semanthy Brewster's stories about any one she spites?" demanded Zilpah in high disdain. "Who killed Peleg Brewster a'n't for me to say; but you take my word for it, that young one that you call Willy is Ruth Brewster.'

"That is soon proved," said Brent, striding from the room, in spite of Zilpah's efforts to detain him.

Paul Freeman was not in sight from the door of the shanty, but Willy, crouching upon the doorstep, was making play with Blunder, Richard's ugly little terrier.

"Come here, child," said Brent, laying a heavy hand upon his shoulder.

At sound of that stern voice, and touch of that determined hand, the child started to his

feet, and raised a pale and terror-stricken face to that bent so severely upon him.

"Oh! what is it, Mr. Brent?" exclaimed he, visibly trembling in every limb.

"Nothing to alarm you if you have done no wrong," replied Brent gravely. "Come with me—I wish to talk with you a little."

And much to the disappointment of Zilpah, who had expected to make a third in the conversation, he led the child into the store-house, and shut the door.

Alone with him, the young man seated himself, and fixed his eyes keenly upon the terror-stricken face of the supposititious boy.

"Child," said he, "I can forgive almost any offence against myself, but I cannot forgive a lie, for that is an offence against God. Will you remember this?"

"Yes, sir."

"And will you answer me some questions fully and freely?"

"Yes.'

"I do not force you to it, remember. If you prefer, you may leave here to-morrow with the man who drives the oxen back, and go wherever you please. In that case, I shall ask you nothing; but if you stay, I shall expect you to give a full account of yourself. As you said, hardly an hour ago, I am the master of this place, and I want thoroughly understood the position of each member of my family. Will you be silent and leave me, or will you stay and speak?'

The child hesitated for a moment, and then, trembling all over, but resolutely raising his eyes to Brent's, answered:

"I will stay and answer you."

"Fully and truly?"

"Yes, sir."

"Then tell me your real name?"

"Ruth Brewster.'

"The daughter of Peleg Brewster, of Milvor?"

"Yes, sir."

"And how came you here, in this disguise?"

"I met Paul, and I was—I was feeling very bad, and he said he could get me away, and take care of me; and he took me to Bloom, and bought me these clothes, and then I came with you to this place."

"I must settle that part of the deception with Paul, I perceive," said Brent; and then, laying a hand upon the girl's shoulder, and fixing his eyes yet more keenly upon her face, he asked:

" Ruth, why are you hiding from the relatives and friends to whom you belong? Why did you wish to be disguised, and to escape from Milvor?"

" I cannot tell you, sir. Oh! I can't bear to think about it!"

And the nervous trembling of the slender figure increased to such a pitiable extent that Brent could not in humanity pursue his interrogatory in the same tone in which he had begun it. Rising, he placed the young girl in his own chair, offered her some water to drink, and said kindly, although coldly :

" Do not be so distressed. I have no intention of harming you ; but I must know the truth, or I cannot let you remain here. Now tell me, Ruth, do you know of what you stand accused at home?"

" They think I did it, don't they?" whispered the child, her very lips blanched to a deadly whiteness.

" Did what?"

" Killed father."

" Yes, Ruth, they say so. It is a terrible question to ask of a child, but it is my duty to ask it. Did you do it?"

But instead of replying, Ruth slipped from her chair to the floor, cowering there in a little trembling heap, and hiding her face upon her lap, while she burst into a fit of hysterical weeping.

Brent looked at her in pity and dismay, for he could not reconcile this excessive agitation with the innocence in which he wished to believe.

" Ruth," said he at last, " won't you speak to me ? Say that you are innocent of this horrible crime, and I will not ask you another question ; for I am very, very sorry for you, child."

" Oh! don't, don't. I can't tell you anything about it. I dursn't," gasped the child, crouching still closer to the floor.

" Dare not! What are you afraid of, Ruth? Is it of me?"

" No, sir, not of you."

" Of whom then?"

" I can't tell, but I dursn't say a single word to any body."

" Cannot you even tell me that you are innocent of your father's murder?" asked Brent, in a voice of deep regret. " For on that turns our whole future re'ation. If you can truthfully deny that one accusation, you shall stay with me, and I will protect you. If you can-

not, Ruth, you must leave Wahtahree to-morrow."

" O Mr. Brent! Leave you and Paul? Where in all the world can I go?" asked the child in sudden terror ; and drawing herself nearer to Brent, she clung about his knees, her wet face imploringly raised to his. Inexpressibly moved, the young man took her in his arms, and seated her beside him. Then with his arm still about her he said in a voice of tenderest entreaty :

" Little Ruth, have faith in me. Whatever alarms you so terribly forget it now, and only remember that I have power to protect you, and make your life a safe and happy one. But you must trust me, child. I do not ask you to break any promise, for even a bad promise must be kept, unless the hand of God Himself breaks it ; but surely you can assure me that you are innocent of the awful crime charged upon you. That is all I ask."

The child, no longer weeping, hid her face for a moment in her hands, as if communing with herself ; then raised it, clear and luminous with the truth, to meet Brent's tender but penetrating look.

" I promised, and I said I hoped God would strike me dead if I broke the promise, that I never would say a single word about it anyway. So can I?"

Brent sadly shook his head.

" No, child, you cannot."

" But, Mr. Brent, look at me," and the child, slipping from her chair to the floor, stood upright before him, her slender figure straightened, her small pale face uplifted, her dark eyes clear and fearless. " Look at me, please, sir, and if you think I could have killed my dear, dear father, the only one I had left to me in all the world—O Mr. Brent! if you think I killed him, let me go away—not to morrow, but now, this very minute. Let me go out into the woods, and I don't care what becomes of me till I die."

And Brent laid his two hands upon her shoulders, looked deep into her steadfast eyes, and said :

" No, Ruth, I do not believe that you did it, and although your oath of silence must not be broken, I will believe the testimony of your eyes against all the world. Nor will I ever ask you another question upon this matter. Rest content, and as happy as you may, little Ruth, for I will take you safely upon my own shoulders."

"I won't be afraid any more, then," said Ruth quietly; and Brent smiled at the unconscious flattery.

CHAPTER XVII.
SMARTNESS AND HONOR.

But with Paul Freeman, the master of Wahtahree dealt less lightly.

"How am I to trust you again?" asked he of him. "You have thoroughly deceived me—you have trapped me into connivance with you in shielding an accused criminal from the law—you have lied to me, for you said the child was your brother!"

"No, sir!" interposed Paul; "I never said

"How am I to trust you again?"

downright that it was my brother, and I never said that I had a brother at all."

"Prevarication!" exclaimed Brent contemptuously—"it is worse than lying, because more cowardly. That defence is the very worst you could have selected."

"Well, then, sir," replied Paul, throwing up his head a little haughtily, "since you think so bad of me, you had better let me go at once. I am sure I don't want to stop with a man that a'n't going to believe a word I say, or trust me about his work. I think I did just what was right by Ruth—placed as she was, and if you don't, why, sir, we'd better part, and the sooner the better."

"If you think so, you had better go," replied Brent coldly.

"Well, I will. Ruthie and I will go along with the men to-morrow."

"You may, if you see fit—Ruth remains here."

"What, sir! you don't mean to keep her away from me!" exclaimed Paul in a tone of angry incredulity.

"I am going to keep her. You are free to go or stay," repeated Brent calmly.

"Why, sir, what good is she to you; and what do you care for her? Maybe you think of sending her back to Milvor to be tried for murder."

"What if I do, Paul Freeman? She is under the ban of the law, and perhaps that is my duty."

The boy clenched his fists, and shut his teeth hard together, looked at Brent, and made no reply.

The latter returned the look with one of calm superiority for a moment, and then slowly said:

"The matter is in my hands completely, you see, lad; and although I have no intention of sending the child back to Milvor, and do not believe her guilty of her father's murder, you are none the less a law-breaker yourself in bringing her away, and she one in coming. I shall not send her back to Milvor, but neither shall I permit her to leave this place with you. I will keep her under my own eye."

"I don't want to be impudent, Mr. Brent, but isn't it law-breaking for you to keep her just as much as it was for me to take her?" asked Paul shrewdly.

The question was one which had already risen with troublesome persistency in Brent's own mind, and he answered it from the lips of another, as he had answered it to himself:

"Here, in the woods, I have a right to take the law in some measure into my own hands. I must decide for myself many questions which, elsewhere, would be decided for me."

Paul Freeman stared for a moment, considered the question, and then said heartily:

"Well, that's so, sir; and though you won't trust me, I'll trust you—not only on your account, for that a'n't much, but on her account, which is a good deal. I'll stop with you, if you'll have me, and I'll let her stop too—

though, of course, I could take her away from here as easy as I could from Milvor, if I set out to do it. I'm a Yankee boy, sir, and they're smart, they are."

"I was a Yankee boy myself once," coolly replied Brent; "but I find that truth and honor are as effective weapons, in the long run, as all the boasted 'smartness' of our countrymen. If I have judged her rightly, Ruth Brewster is of my way of thinking. Let us see."

And Brent, who had seen the child from the window where he stood, opened the door and called her in. She came quickly, but timidly. Brent took her hand, and looked her steadily in the face.

"Ruth," said he, "you feel the importance of a promise, and you can keep one through all temptation to break it. So much I know of you. Now will you make me a promise?"

Ruth glanced aside at Paul, upward at Brent, colored slightly, and said:

"I can't give up Paul, sir."

"I do not ask you to give him up. The promise I speak of is, that you will not leave this place, either alone or with any one else, without my knowledge and consent. Will you sacredly promise this?"

"Yes, sir, I will." And with instinctive gesture, the child placed her slender, pale hand in that of Marston Brent, and looked confidingly into his face.

"Thank you, Ruth—that will do," said Brent kindly. "Please to wait for me a moment outside the door."

Ruth obeyed, and when they were alone, the master calmly said:

"The child's honor is my sufficient guarantee against any amount of 'smartness' on your part, Paul; and now we will lay aside all weapons, and meet on the common ground of interest in Ruth, and a mutual duty to each other. Work with me instead of against me, and we shall both fare the better. Is it a bargain, my lad?"

"It's a bargain, sir," said the boy, putting his hand into that cordially outstretched toward him; and as he walked slowly away into the hemlock forest, Paul Freeman thought:

"'Honor and truth better than smartness?' Let me see. Why not try to join them altogether? I don't see but what they'd fay in well enough."

Brent, meantime, took Ruth by the hand, and led her to Zilpah.

"Here is a little girl who wants some clothes," said he gayly. "How are we to get them for her?"

"Good land! You don't say so, do you now?" exclaimed the wily dame, apparently overwhelmed with astonishment. "A gal! And what's your name, dear?"

"Ruth," replied the child timidly.

"Ruth Freeman, instead of Willy Freeman! Now, do tell! And so you wanted to steal off along of Paul, and thought you'd pass for his brother instead of his sister, 'cause you knew we couldn't think of taking a little gal along, when we might like a boy well enough. There, there, you needn't say a word. I understand all about it, and I'll tell the men, so's they needn't wonder. But how will you make out for clothes?"

"I guess Paul has got mine along with his. He said he'd bring them," said Ruth shyly.

"Did? Well, that will make it all handy: and when Mr. Brent sends to town, he can get some factory cotton and gingham, and I'll make you up another suit or so, and that'll be all you'll need; and then you can help round the house. On the whole, I'm glad you a'n't a boy."

"Well, is it all settled?" asked Brent, who had retired a little from the feminine discussion of clothes, and who now returned.

"Yes—all settled," replied Zilpah hastily; and the young man asked no further questions.

CHAPTER XVIII.

AN EASTERN SPICE.

"THAT is all, Fanny; you may go and order James to drive round to the door. Now, Beatrice, please look at yourself in the full-length mirror, and say that you approve my taste."

Miss Wansted rose from the low chair in which she had submitted, during the last hour, to the hands of her hair-dresser and ladies'-maid, and obediently placed herself in front of the mirror. Confronting her in its depths she saw a regal figure, clothed in soft, lustreless white silk—the hem, open neck, and short sleeves of the dress ornamented with embroidery of gold wrought in a classic pattern; while the arms, the white throat, and the bands of brown-gold hair were encircled with chains of antique cameos, set in dead Etruscan gold—Vezey Chappelleford's almost priceless gift to his constant entertainer, Israel Barstow, and transferred by him to his niece.

From this simple, severely classic, and yet magnificent toilet, shone a face more incontestably beautiful than that Marston Brent had seen reflected beside his own in the mountain-pool, where Millbrook pauses in her descent of Moloch—more beautiful, because more thoughtful, more assured—bearing traces of a deeper life and larger experience.

"Well, what do you think?" demanded Mrs. Charlton, a little impatiently.

"Why, that I ought to be named Lucia, or Claudia, or Veronica, at the least. If Lord Macaulay were to suddenly drop in upon our transatlantic gathering, he would suspect me of intriguing for a Lay of Ancient Rome in my especial honor," said Beatrice laughing.

"He would probably lay his ancient Rome aside, and devote himself to youthful Columbia in your person, my dear. Confess now that face, figure, manner, and costume harmonize admirably in the picture you seem so satisfied to contemplate, and I am so delighted to claim as my own production."

But Beatrice was spared a reply she might have found difficult to render both truthful and modest, by the entrance of a servant with a bouquet.

"For Miss Wansted, with Mr. Laforét's compliments," said he, presenting it.

Mrs. Charlton eagerly examined it; then laid it somewhat contemptuously upon the dressing-table.

"Roses, camellias, fuchsias, salvia, heath—every thing in the hot-house—and all bundled together without design or sentiment. You must not touch it, Beatrice, under penalty of spoiling your entire toilet."

"Poor Mr. Laforét!" smiled Beatrice, rather languidly.

"I hardly think you should carry a bouquet at all," continued Juanita thoughtfully. "I do not know what would suit that dress."

The door again swung open to admit Thomas, carrying, with imperturbable face, another bouquet upon his salver, and saying, in precisely the same tone he had used before:

"For Miss Wansted, with the compliments of a friend."

"A friend! What friend, I wonder," exclaimed Beatrice, while Mrs. Charlton examined the offering with a very different look from that she had bestowed upon its predecessor.

"Now that is almost a miracle. I could not have selected it better myself. Nothing but a spike of tuberoses and a handful of Parma violets in this *porte-bouquet* of Venetian filagree. Thoroughly Italian, if not precisely Roman. Now, this is admirable."

"But who is the friend? I do not like accepting or carrying anonymous *porte-bouquets*, although I cannot object to the flowers," said Beatrice a little anxiously.

"Nonsense, my dear," quietly replied her chaperone. "If almost any gentleman had offered the bauble in person, or over his own name, you must have refused it, of course; but dropping from Heaven, as it does, you must accept it as a gift of Heaven—or, to suit your ideas to your dress, as a gift of the gods."

"Well, then, as a gift of the gods. And now are we ready? How nicely you are looking yourself, Juanita. I have been so selfish, and so—tired, I believe, that I have not looked at you until now."

"I do very well," said Mrs. Charlton carelessly, as she cast one comprehensive glance at her own toilet of wine-colored velvet, rich black lace, and the garnets which blazed like red-hot coals upon her white, satiny neck and arms, and among the abundant folds of her blue-black hair.

"Yes, I do well enough for an old woman. Come, here are your handkerchief, your gloves, and this fan, dear, which I should like to give you. I have had it for some time, but never carried it—white silk embroidered with gold—almost in the same pattern as your dress, you see."

"Admirable! How very kind of you, Juanita. You think too much of me, and too little of yourself," said Beatrice, with a flush of self-reproach; and then the two beautiful women went together down the stairs, and were escorted to their carriage by Mr. Barstow, who sat smoking in his library with his friend Chappelleford.

"Good by, dears," said he, as they seated themselves with all the pleasant flutter of silken skirts, perfumed handkerchiefs, laces, bouquets, jewels, wraps, that attend such embarkations. "Have a nice time, and we will look in before you come home."

Half an hour later, Beatrice was the centre of a crowd of courtiers, and bearing herself right royally among them. Not even the rivals, who enviously watched the assumed ease

and grace of her every movement, and noted
the manner so nicely balanced between dignity and archness, could find a flaw in either,
or could suggest a possible improvement in
person, dress, or bearing; nor could the most
critical observer detect in the style of this, the
latest "queen of society," any trace of the
country breeding she never thought of concealing, unless in a certain freshness and vitality always remarked, and always celebrated
by Miss Wansted's admirers. She was not
without her weapons either, and could defend
herself upon occasion, as when Laforét, leading her to the head of a set of Lancers, murmured reproachfully:

"My poor flowers were not worthy to be
carried to-night, then?"

"Ah! Mr. Laforét, I have a quarrel with
you upon that subject! Which of my ill-
wishers, what woman selected that bouquet
for you to send me?"

"Ill-wishers! Woman! I beg your pardon for echoing your words, and also for my
stupidity, but what *do* you mean?" asked the
unfortunate Laforét in great bewilderment.

"Why they were so magnificent, so rich
and varied in their colors, so conspicuous in
their brilliancy, so altogether admirable in
every way, that they would have utterly anni-
hilated the wearer. She would have become
merely the woman carrying that bouquet.
Now, what but feminine malice could have
suggested such a mode of smothering me in
honey? Confess, Mr. Laforét—tell me her
name."

And Beatrice, flashing a bewildering smile
into her partner's face, turned to balance at
the corner with Rein, the artist, who seized
the occasion to murmur:

"If you would only sit to me in that
dress!"

"I will lend it you with the greatest pleasure," replied Beatrice, returning to her partner, who began:

"No; but really were the flowers so unbecoming?"

"The flowers were magnificent. It was I
who was not equal to the occasion. Forward
with me, please."

And Mr. Laforét finished the Lancers in a
state of mind equally balanced between doubt
and delight.

"But if I might ask, who gave you th
flowers you carry?" inquired he, escorting his
partner to her seat.

"It would be an odd question for you to ask,
or me to answer; but if you should ask, and I
should be indulgent enough to answer, I could
only say what was said to me: they are from
a friend."

"That means any one among a hundred
men," said Laforét.

"One among a hundred? One among a
thousand, if he were really a friend," returned
Beatrice with a smile more bitter than gay,
and a little gesture of dismissal.

"Miss Wansted, allow me to present Mr
Monckton, a gentleman who can give you the
latest news of the anthropophagi and King
Theodore," said the hostess, pausing with a
gentleman in front of Beatrice.

Murmuring the conventional answer, she
looked up, and met the regards of a pair of
alert brown eyes set in a thin and deeply
bronzed face, whose claim to beauty was one
to be considered before determining.

"May I sit down, Miss Wansted? I am so
accustomed to making myself comfortable
whenever I have the opportunity."

"Certainly; although, from what Mrs. Wes-
ley says of the direction of your travels, I
should not imagine comfort to have been your
principal object," said Beatrice, quietly removing her skirts from an ottoman beside her
chair.

"No. But like most of the good things I
have obtained in this world, it has often come
to me while I was looking for something
else. For instance, I came here to-night because I thought I must, and—I have been
introduced to you."

"I thought persons who travelled learned
new things," remarked Beatrice very sweetly.

Mr. Monckton colored a little, then laughed.

"Really, Miss Wansted, I know it is rude to
be personal, but you must allow me to say I
had no idea that you would do that sort of
thing," said he.

"What sort of thing, please?"

"The sarcastic and humiliating sort of
thing—the discovering so quickly, and telling me so frankly, that I was talking like a
fool."

"Not at all. I only meant that you talked
as if you supposed me one."

"I shall never again suppose you one."

"Again?" repeated Beatrice, with a smile of
quiet malice.

"Now, really, Miss Wansted! But I have
been so long out of society—the society of

ladies, at least—that a good deal must be pardoned. I have forgotten the usages of the *beau monde*, you perceive."

"And I have never learned them; so let us lay aside all thought of them, and talk like human beings uncorrupted by this *beau monde* of which you speak. Have you really travelled in the East?"

"From Alexandria to the Vale of Kashmeer, and from Jaffa to Jerusalem and the plains of Palestine," said Monckton, smiling frankly.

"And will you please tell me all about it?"

"All?"

"Oh! yes; for where could you stop when once you had begun?"

"And will you give me time to tell all?"

"Begin, please."

"Shall I tell you then, while we watch these dancers and listen to this charming music, of a nautch that I attended in Delhi, when the eldest son of Rajah Ahmed Defter Singh was married to the daughter of the Baboo Ali Raj Malimoo?"

"Pray do. But remember, please, that I have read the *Arabian Nights* and also the *Thousand and One Days*."

"I will quote neither, but tell you the truth *pur et simple*. I was in Delhi ——"

"Miss Wansted, I believe I have your promise for this quadrille," said a young gentleman, bowing before the lady, whose smile of acquiescence was, to say the least, a little forced.

"It is the German, and will last all the evening," said she apologetically, as she rose from Mr. Monckton's side.

"And my poor nautch story? May I come and tell it you to-morrow?"

"Thank you," said Beatrice, a little doubtfully.

"I think my old friend, Mr. Barstow, will not close his door in my face. *Au revoir*," said Monckton smiling.

And Beatrice, her doubt resolved, answered gayly:

"*Au revoir* then."

CHAPTER XIX

THE BEDOUIN IN THE DESERT.

WITH the morrow came Mr. Monckton, and Beatrice, somewhat to her own surprise, found herself interested in his coming.

"You will see him, June, will you not?"

asked she of Mrs. Charlton, who was doing Sultana in a cashmere wrapper, with her slippered feet curled under her, upon the lounge in Miss Wansted's sitting-room.

"Must I? For whom did he ask, Thomas?"

"He is with Mr. Barstow, ma'am, and Mr. Barstow told me to speak to the ladies."

"Oh! well; if your uncle is down-stairs, there is no need of my going—and really I am so comfortable. Tell him, please, Trix, that I am used up with last evening's gayeties—that is, if he inquires." And Mrs. Charlton, with a luxurious sigh, sank back among her cushions, as Beatrice, with a little smile upon her lips, went down-stairs, and glided into the drawing-room with the stately and yet graceful motion characteristic of her.

Monckton stood, hat and cane in hand, looking at a picture upon the wall. It was an odd bit, the freak of some dreamy artist, starving with cold in his barren garret, perhaps, and mocking the sufferings of his body with the illimitable fancies of his soul. At least, that was the theory Beatrice had framed about this sketch, and for the sake of the theory, had asked her uncle to buy it.

An immense level plain—Sahara perhaps—stretching away in such admirable perspective that the eye returned from seeking the vanishing-point, weary and strained—a coppery sky arching the yellow sand, with no cloud upon it except the faint white wreaths so expressive of intense heat—the last faint breath of earth, as they seem, sent up in an expiring prayer to heaven.

In the midst of this plain, a fallen camel, lying with outstretched neck, gaping mouth, and staring eyeballs, the limbs slightly convulsed in dying agony, and standing upon his prostrate body a solitary Arab, shading his eyes with his hand, and searching the horizon for the help that we read in the whole tone of the piece was not to come.

One long shadow of man and beast stretched far toward the West, and faded into the sands by fine gradations of color.

That was all; and yet Miss Wansted had gazed for an hour at that picture, and turned away unsatisfied.

"Good-morning, Mr. Monckton," said she now. "Do you remember the scene?"

"I beg your pardon—good-morning," said the traveller, cordially extending his hand. "Yes, I remember the scene."

"You remember it!"

"Yes, or rather I remember as much of it as human eye ever saw."

"Oh! what do you mean? Pray tell me all about it."

And Beatrice, with a look of excited interest, rare enough upon her statuesque features, sank into a seat, and motioned her guest to another, her eyes continuing the eager inquiry of her lips.

Monckton smiled, well pleased.

"It is a fortunate chance for me to have noticed this picture this morning, since it gives me an opportunity of gratifying you," said he, so simply that the words rang true, and not with the hollow tinkle of flattery.

"It was three years ago," pursued the traveler, "that I, journeying from Cairo to Damascus, chose to pursue the old desert route, and in the old desert fashion; for to my mind, this invasion of the Orient by steam, and this erection of railway stations and free-lunch booths within the shadow of the Pyramids, and under the very eyes of the Sphinx, is a sacrilege likely enough to bring back old Cheops to avenge it; and one looks to see each grain of sand become a dusky warrior, armed with bow and spear, and hungry for the slaughter. At any rate, I preferred the camels and the caravan, and so did Floyd, a young artist whom I found hanging about Cairo, full of fancies and inspiration, and singularly empty of every thing else. Finding that he was eager to get to Damascus, and utterly devoid of means, I offered him an opportunity, and we set out."

"How grateful he must have felt to you!" said Beatrice softly, while her shining eyes spoke sweet applause of the generous deed. But Monckton laughed.

"Grateful!" echoed he. "Pardon me, Miss Wansted, but that remark speaks better for your heart than your experience. No man is grateful for having what he fancies his rights offered him as an alms, and I saved myself from Floyd's enmity only by asking him to come along as a protector and reliable companion, for I had no white man with me then. As for the camels and provisions, they were already engaged, and his presence made no difference, which view of the case he obligingly accepted, and consented to oblige me.

"Four days out of Cairo, Floyd and I, indulging in an eccentric tour around an oasis, missed our company just at nightfall, and were forced to encamp upon the sand. Early in the morning, we remounted, and just before falling in with our men, we came upon that scene—with a difference, for the poor Bedouin lay with his head upon his camel's neck, as dead as he. The camel, we noticed, had been wounded in the leg, probably in some desert fray, and had been unable to bring his master to the journey's end before both were exhausted and fell, almost within sight of harbor. Floyd seemed very much impressed, and lingered longer than I liked, examining now the group, now the surrounding scene, with a dreamy look in his eyes that I was sure meant picture. At last he got out his sketch-book, and in half a dozen strokes caught the spirit of the whole thing. Just then our fellows came up; they had missed us in the dark, and were now retracing their steps to look for us. They made very light of their fallen countryman, and even refused to bury him, saying—as I suppose truly—that if they did take the trouble, the wind or the jackals would undo their labor before another day. So we rode on, and left them as they lay.

"A year later, a package reached me in Rome charged with so much expressage that it nearly ruined me. Within was this picture, and a note from Floyd, who said that he sent it me as a remembrance of our pleasant journey across the desert. Of course I knew that it meant camel hire and hard biscuit; but if it soothed his feelings to put it in the way he did, it could not injure mine to accept both his picture and his definition of its meaning, as I did. Having no provision for picture transportation, however, I gave it soon after to a man who seemed to fancy it excessively, but who has, it appears, parted with it for filthy lucre. Do you know where Mr. Barstow found it?"

"At an auction sale of paintings in New York. He asked Mrs. Charlton and me to go and look at them, and mark in the catalogue what we should like. I selected this," said Beatrice, looking with a new interest at the desert scene.

"But," resumed she presently, feeling a little nervously that Mr. Monckton's eyes were as earnestly fixed upon her face as hers upon the picture—"but I wonder that you did not keep it for yourself."

"What should I do with it?"

"Bring it home with you when you came."

Monckton smiled sadly.

"Miss Wansted, you speak in a language I

cannot understand. I have no home. I have never known one. My childhood was passed at school, my youth at foreign colleges; my manhood has been as nomadic and as ignorant of the sweet influences of home as that of the Bedouin, whose death may but foreshadow mine."

And as the traveller fixed his eyes upon the picture, a softness rarely seen in those piercing orbs crossed their depths, and lent a strange charm to the thin, brown face most persons found so hard and unemotional.

The next moment he turned sharply, and met the full, pitying gaze of those other eyes whose hazel beauty he had already confessed.

"You are very good, Miss Wansted," said he, answering the unspoken sympathy of that look. "But I should beg your pardon for my bad taste. This is but another proof of what I told you last night, that I have become a mere uncivilized savage, unfit for society, and unworthy of the patience you have vouchsafed me."

"Last night I proposed that we should drop the *beau monde*, and talk like simply a man and woman," said Beatrice softly.

Monckton shot a keen glance at her face. He found it slightly flushed, smiling, and guileless as water, and he leaned toward it eagerly.

"Miss Wansted you tempt me strangely," said he.

"In what manner?" asked Beatrice, smiling still.

"To believe in you, to feel again that human faith and interest which I had thought dried out of my life forever. Miss Wansted, if this is folly, if it is unconventional, inadmissible perhaps, you should blame yourself. You bid me with those candid eyes to be natural, to speak from the heart out, and I speak as I have not spoken for years, as I thought never to speak again. Do you pardon me?"

"For what? Obedience?" asked Beatrice, the subtle smile of power in her eyes.

"Yes," said Monckton, steadily regarding her. "I have been for many years out of the artificial and hollow world we call society, but I do not think I have lost the power of discriminating between a fresh and ardent nature, as yet uncorrupted and untrammelled by that world, and—a finished coquette."

"Is it so difficult to distinguish between the two?" asked Beatrice.

"More difficult than to determine between

a gem of the Palais Royal and a genuine diamond," said Monckton. "And yet I am sure that I am not mistaken."

"And if you are not?" asked Beatrice.

"If I am not, I should dare to hope that I might once more possess a friend; that sympathy and confidence and the honest speech of heart to heart were not yet dead-letter phrases for me, and that one spot of earth, one human being, might become to me of more importance than another. Miss Wansted, it is for you to rebuke, if you will, this last and wildest folly of a life outwardly prosperous, and inwardly blank and desolate as that Sahara. Do you find my presumption something too monstrous for reproof?"

"Why should I, Mr. Monckton? I urged you to throw aside the idea of etiquette, and speak to me as honest man to honest woman. You have done so, and I thank you. After that, if you find my sympathy in the homeless and friendless life you describe of any value, it is yours; if you care to try whether that sympathy and our mutual liking can become a friendship, I will help you; and if it is so, you will be no better pleased than I, for I too am lonely, and sometimes heart-sick, and I too need a friend."

Her voice softened and faltered upon the last words, and Monckton looked at her as shrewdly and more kindly than Juanita Charlton had done in first espying her heart-wound. Past masters both, in this world's lore, they had both found it quickly enough, and viewed it, the one with the indulgent and delicate pity of man for woman, the other with the scornful and inquisitive pity of woman for woman.

"Then, Heaven helping us, we two are to become friends," said Monckton, rising and offering his hand.

"Yes," replied Beatrice, laying hers in it with a confiding smile.

CHAPTER XX.

A DINNER-PARTY.

MR. CHAPPELLEFORD was not in a good-humor—in fact, he was in a very bad one, and developed it in so many and such decided forms, that even his patient friend, Israel Barstow, was nearly out of patience with him, and Miss Wansted entirely so. As for Mr. Monckton, who made the fifth at Mr. Barstow's little dinner-party, he received the attacks, covert or open, of his fellow-guest much as he would have done those of an ill-conditioned family dog—as something to be courteously tolerated on account of its proprietors, so long as it remained in their presence; but with a reserved right upon the part of the sufferer in favor of vengeance at the earliest possible opportunity.

Mrs. Charlton, the remaining guest, looked on with an air of impartial and cynical amusement at her uncle's ill-humor, her host's uneasiness, Beatrice's indignation, and Mr. Monckton's patient endurance.

"So, Livingstone has turned up all right," said Mr. Barstow, casting about for a remark adapted to the tone of his company, and not likely to provoke discussion.

"Who's Livingstone?" inquired Mr. Chappelleford, in a tone of contemptuous indifference.

"Livingstone! why—ah—why, of course you know whom I mean," stammered the host, already doubtful of his own authenticity.

"There was a person of that name who went peddling beads and calico-aprons among the negroes—do you refer to him?"

"Why, he's the great African traveller of course—every one acknowledges that, don't they?" insisted Mr. Barstow, growing a little warm.

"Great! Well, I don't know. Little men might find him so," replied the cynic.

"The title of the great African traveller should, I think, be given rather to Speke, for he has solved the question of centuries as to the source of the Nile, and penetrated farther than any man before him into the interior of Africa," said Monckton quietly.

"Solved the question of the source of the Nile? So have a dozen adventurers before him, and so will a dozen after, Mr. Monckton. Who is to say that this Lake Victoria N'yanza is more stationary or reliable than other African water-holes and rain-puddles? The Nile may rise there to-day and somewhere else to-morrow, and probably does, even granting—which is a great deal to grant—that this man—Paddleford, Livingstone, Speke—whatever his name is—has been there at all, or knows anything about the matter. As for penetrating into the interior of Africa, what does that amount to? The negroes away from the coast wear bones in their noses, and those on the coast wear oyster-shells; the first breech themselves with cocoa-cloth, and the last with kelp-leaves: what difference does it make to us which is which? Of course one sees why

this insatiate trader risked his life, and those of the fools who accompanied him, by his explorations. The remoter the savage from civilization, the more value he attaches to beads, and the more gold-dust he is willing to pay for them."

"But then it makes us, who are so civilized, and none of us at all like savages, appreciate our own advantages so much the more highly, to hear of these poor, ignorant, rude creatures, who know no better than to talk and behave as they do," said Beatrice, whose burning cheeks and sparkling eyes strongly belied the unconscious and naïve tone she attempted.

Mr. Chappelleford shot a keen glance in her direction from beneath the gray pent-house of his brows.

"I read a pretty story that would please a young lady, I should think, in one of these African books," said he. "The story of a male humming-bird attacked and nearly demolished by a bigger bird, when, just as the humming-bird was about to succumb, his mate, who had watched the contest from her nest, dashed down into the face and eyes of the intruder and beat him off—by sheer audacity, as you may say."

"Audacious courage may be admired, but audacious insolence ——" began Beatrice; but her trembling voice was covered by Mrs. Charlton's full, round tones:

"That reminds me, Mr. Barstow, of the loveliest thing I ever saw. It was a humming-bird worn as an ornament to the hair by a lady at Mrs. Lee's, last night, and composed entirely of gems. You never saw anything so magnificent, and I resolved to tell you of it, because you admire jewels so much."

"Yes, I do, and I should like, of all things, to see this one. Do you suppose another is to be found for sale?"

"Oh! dear, no. This was Parisian, and, I presume, made to order. It must have cost a fortune," said Mrs. Charlton, glancing at the faces of her companions, and wondering whether the diversion had been effectual.

"I wish you would write as good a description of it as possible for me," said Mr. Barstow thoughtfully.

Mrs. Charlton laughed.

"Oh! I could not let Beatrice wear it if you had it made," said she; "it would be entirely inharmonious with her style; and, you know, she is in my hands this year."

"Æsop has a fable of a fox, who took charge of a farmer's poultry-yard, and, strange to say, found his own advantage in the position," remarked Mr. Chappelleford.

Juanita softly laughed and turned to Monckton.

"You must have seen some splendid jewels in the East, Mr. Monckton," said she, inquiringly.

"Yes; I was just thinking of a set of turquoise shown me at Delhi. They would have suited Miss Wansted admirably."

"I have seen turquoise from Delhi of remarkable beauty. How were these set?" asked Mrs. Charlton.

"Very elegantly with pearls. There was a crescent for the hair, a chain of stars for the throat, and bracelets with pendent ornaments of gold in various Oriental devices. They were very handsome."

"I should think so. Now, Mr. Barstow, where is your express for Delhi?" asked Juanita, with a little laugh.

"I wish I knew how to send there, and I would do it in a minute," said the merchant, smiling meaningly upon his niece, whose cheeks were slowly regaining their natural color.

Mr. Monckton unclosed his lips as if to speak, shut them again, and smiled a little. Mrs. Charlton, whose neighbor he was, also smiled and whispered:

"You have them, and will offer them to——"

"My *fiancée*," murmured the traveller in reply; and Juanita looked thoughtfully at Beatrice.

"The jewels of India are no more than traditions now," said Chappelleford dreamily. "When one reads of Shah Jehan's peacock throne, six feet long and four broad, one solid block of gold, surmounted by a canopy supported upon twelve pillars, all of the same metal, and all inlaid with the most marvellous of Oriental gems, while at the back stood the golden peacocks, their fans blazing with jewels worth a monarch's ransom, and remembers that this was but an item—an adjunct of the Mogul's imperial state—then we look with somewhat of impatience upon the trinkets of the modern Chandee Chok."

"Is that story about the throne literally true, Chappelleford?" asked Mr. Barstow breathlessly.

"It is as literal as Israel Barstow himself." replied the philosopher.

"And what might such a thing be worth in money? Do any of your books tell that?"

"Oh! yes. It was seen by one Tavernier, a jeweller, who visited Delhi, in the way of trade, and who estimated it professionally at a sum about equivalent to thirty millions of dollars. It was made by a Frenchman, too, one Austin, of Bordeaux—a fellow who, obliged to leave his country to save his neck, took refuge in the domain of the Grand Mogul, and turned his talents to account by decorating the imperial palace. The ceiling of the throne-chamber, also his handiwork, was of gold and silver filagree, and round the cornice ran an inscription, in golden letters, to this effect:

'If there be a paradise on earth, it is here—it is here!'

That was what Shah Jehan had to say for himself, and he had hardly seen the golden lie put in its place, when his four rebellious sons clapped him into prison in the fortress of Agra, and kept him there until he died. It took ten years to kill him, however, and he kept some of his best jewels until the last. Aurungzebe, the third son and successful usurper, used to send polite messages to his papa, inquiring the state of his health, and asking if he had not better give up the care and responsibility of those jewels to his affectionate son and successor. Old Shah Jehan answered in the same strain until he got tired of it, and then he sent word that he should never give up the jewels while he lived, and that if any attempt was made to take them by force, he would pound them to atoms with a big hammer, which he kept in readiness. After that they let him alone."

"But what became of the peacock throne, and where is it now?" asked Mr. Barstow.

"About a century after Shah Jehan's deposition," said the scholar, leaning his elbow upon the table, and shading his eyes with his hand, "Nadur Shah, a Persian soldier-king, invaded India, conquered Delhi, and murdered Mohammad Shah, the emperor of the day, in spite of the most abject submission and the most piteous entreaties on the part of that unhappy prince. Then he gave up the city of Delhi to his soldiers for rapine and pillage, without restraint, and the historians say that the aqueduct through the middle of the Chandee Chok, or principal street of Delhi, ran red with the blood of her slaughtered inhabitants. Six weeks later, Nadur Shah returned home, carrying with him the peacock throne, all the imperial jewels, and a countless treasure beside. That was the death-blow of the Mogul

THE SHADOW OF MOLOCH MOUNTAIN.

empire; and next came the English, ready, ghoul-like, to devour the poor remains of the dead sovereignty."

"Was it not Shah Jehan who built the Taj at Agra, of which you were telling me the other night?" asked Beatrice, over whose mood a story exercised as modifying an influence as over that of Schariar himself; nor was this circumstance unknown to Mr. Chappelleford, who now answered courteously:

"Yes, in honor of his wife, Moomtaz-ee-Mahal, the ornament of the Harem, and niece of the more celebrated Noor-Mahal, wife of Jehangeer."

"I saw the Taj while I was in India, and it is really a marvellous structure. Shah Jehan himself is buried there, they tell me," said Monckton.

"Yes; after he was dead, his son did not know what else to do with him, and so tucked him in beside poor Moomtaz, who thought, I suppose, that she might at least have her tomb to herself; but Aurungzebe was of an economical turn of mind, in all but his own pleasures, and by making room for papa in the Taj, he gave him a magnificent mausoleum, without its costing the reigning sovereign a single rupee. Shrewd fellow, Aurungzebe," said the philosopher, obeying the signal to rise from the table.

CHAPTER XXI.

THE AMULET.

"STEP into the library a moment, if you please, Miss Wansted," said Mr. Chappelleford, as, dinner over, the guests went up-stairs together. "I brought that proof-engraving of which I was speaking to show to you, and left it in here. Will you look at it?"

"Certainly," said Beatrice, still a little coldly. "But why not take it into the drawing-room, and let our friends see it also?"

"Because I brought it for you, and not for your 'friends,' as you call them."

"I said our friends," replied Beatrice smiling.

"None for me, thank you," replied the philosopher. "It is some years since I indulged in that delusion."

"What—of friendship?"

"Exactly. It is one of the dreams of youth, and as impossible to retain as your milk-teeth. There, is not that a fine head?"

"Admirable. But about friendship—I wish you would not say such things," said Beatrice, only glancing at the engraving, and fixing her wistful eyes upon the shrewd, sad face of the philosopher.

"Why do you wish so?"

"Because you know so much, and are so often right when we differ, that it terrifies me to have you assert what I cannot bear to believe true."

"Then you have a particular fancy for this particular delusion?" asked Mr. Chappelleford, not unkindly.

"Fancy! I consider friendship one of the holiest and sweetest of realities, and it is because I do not wish to have my faith disturbed that I dread to hear you speak of it."

"Like the man falling asleep at low-water mark, who begs his companions not to disturb his nap."

"But even if friendship is a dream, it will not hurt me to believe in it. There is no approaching destruction like that threatening the sleeper you speak of," pleaded Beatrice.

"Which is worse, destruction of your body or destruction of your interest in keeping it alive?" asked Chappelleford. "Believe in a man, and after he has deceived you, or after you have proved him a fool, you despise or hate all men on his account. Avoid friendship, that you may continue to care for mankind. If you wish to value the species, don't examine specimens—familiarity breeds contempt.'"

"O Mr. Chappelleford! yours is a very dreary faith!" exclaimed Beatrice bitterly.

"My dear young lady, when you come to my time of life, it will be yours as well. I remember the period when I too believed in all these pretty toys of friendship, confidence, mutual reliance, and the rest, and the waking from my dream was like the revivification of a drowned man, who is roused from the sweet visions that are death to the keen torture that is life."

"And what comes afterward?" asked Beatrice slowly.

"Indifference," replied the philosopher drearily. "Things take the place of men, theories of sentiment, speculations of passion. You become an observer instead of an actor—a thinker instead of a puppet."

"And then do you become happy?" asked

the young girl slowly wringing her hands together

"Happy!" echoed the philosopher scornfully. "What is the need of that? Content yourself with your position as an atom in creation, and do not expect the universe to be delayed, or its eternal order to be disturbed, because you do not like travelling so fast, or because some other atom becomes divided from you. Nothing is more puerile than this outcry for happiness in which young persons constantly indulge. Make yourself happy, if you choose, with what you have, or, if you prefer, go unhappy, but expect nothing better than what chances to befall you, for you will not get it. And, after all, happiness is principally a question of digestion, and your best friend is a pill-box."

"I do not like you in this mood, Mr. Chappelleford, and I am going to the drawing-room," said Beatrice, turning toward the door.

The cynic smiled grimly, and followed her across the hall. In the open doorway of the drawing-room he suddenly laid a hand upon her arm, and drew her slightly back.

"Look!" whispered he. "There are two of the friends whom you trust the most, and who have no secrets from you, as you fancy."

Half startled, half indignant, Beatrice followed the direction of his eyes, and saw Mrs. Charlton standing with Mr. Monckton in the recess of a bay-window at the farther end of the room. She, with her face buried in her hands, appeared to be weeping bitterly, and he, stooping toward her, was talking in a low voice, full, as the accents betrayed, of tender meaning. As Beatrice looked, he extended his hand with something in it toward the weeping woman, who seized and kissed it passionately. Then she made some request, in a voice broken with sobs, and Monckton, leaning over her, clasped the bauble he held about her neck. Seizing it in both hands, Juanita kissed it again and again, while Monckton leaned caressingly over her.

"No secrets from you, you know," whispered Mr. Chappelleford mockingly.

And Beatrice angrily replied:

"At least you shall not make a spy of me," and walked openly into the room.

As she approached the window, Monckton came forward, and with a skilful remark, drew her to the piano where lay some new music, while Juanita made her escape through a door at the farther end of the room. Beatrice understood the manœuvre, and smiled sadly. For a moment she considered within herself, and then fixing her eyes upon Monckton's face, quietly asked:

"Of what were you and Juanita talking when I came in?"

"Oh! nothing much. I was speaking of Venice, I believe," said the traveller; and Beatrice turned away from him without a word.

In a few moments, Mrs. Charlton reëntered the room, smiling and calm as usual; and Beatrice, sitting in a shaded corner of the sofa, a fire-screen before her eyes, looked on in silent amazement while she placed herself at the piano, selected one of the new pieces offered by Mr. Monckton, and played it through with a faultless brilliancy, proving the closest attention and real interest in the subject before her.

Mr. Chappelleford, who, instead of returning to the library with his host, as was his usual fashion, had followed Beatrice into the drawing-room, now took a seat upon the sofa beside her.

"This cannel-coal makes a very pretty fire," remarked he; but Beatrice did not hear him.

"You were telling me that you wanted a new study yesterday," said he again. "You seem to have found one. How do you like it?"

The girl turned her eyes upon him, dark and piteous with anguish.

"Do not mock me," said she pleadingly. "Can it be that those two have deceived me?"

"In what?"

"Why, they both seemed so open and so trustful with me. He said I was his friend and knew all his life; and she—she always spoke of him as a stranger. And now what does it mean?"

"Poor child, my warning was too late," said the philosopher pitifully. "You have trusted, and you have been deceived—that is all—only the old story once more. I do not know the precise meaning of what we saw, but I do know that Juanita Charlton is a coquette, trained and practised from her earliest youth. I know that she has risked her own reputation and the happiness of others in more than one folly, and I know that she sincerely wishes to marry any one with money and position to render her independent of me; for which desire

I do not blame her in the least. As for Mr. Monckton, I only know that he is—a man."

"But when I spoke to him just now he told me—— I am sure it could not have been true," murmured Beatrice.

"It was what you should have expected. Your question was a piece of Quixotic daring. Not one man in a thousand could or should have answered you truly."

"What! you defend a lie?"

"For Mr. Monckton in that situation—yes. It was a necessary part of his system."

"What is that system?" asked Beatrice faintly.

"The system of polite, social intercourse," replied the philosopher.

"What would you have done in his place?"

"I cannot imagine myself in his place; but had I been, I suppose I should have told you I did not choose to answer your question. That would have been bearish and brutal, and that isn't Mr. Monckton's manner of doing things."

"But why not the truth?"

"What! that I was making love to another woman! Pardon me, Miss Wanstel, but you suggest a stupidity."

"Better that than a lie."

"That depends upon who has the choice to make," said the philosopher, rising and strolling toward the piano, where he began to speak to his niece in so confidential a tone that Mr. Monckton withdrew, and after a little uneasy wandering, seated himself near Beatrice, who met his attempts at conversation with cold reserve—only tempered by remembrance of her position as hostess. Monckton felt it, and determined to bring the matter to an issue.

"You are offended with me in some manner. What is it?" asked he. "Remember that we are friends."

"How long since we became friends—that is, since I told you that I considered you one?" asked Beatrice.

"Nearly four months—four very happy months to me," said Monckton earnestly.

"Well, in all that four months I have never deceived you in a single point. There are passages in my life which I have not told you, because I tell them to no one; but every thing that has occurred to me since you knew me, I have told you with perfect unreserve, and I have never answered one of your questions with less than entire truth. Do you believe this?"

"I believe it most fully, Beatrice."

"And can you say as much upon your part?" asked Beatrice, fixing her eyes keenly upon him.

Monckton hesitated.

"Do your ideas of friendship demand as much as this?" asked he.

"Yes; every thing or nothing," replied Beatrice.

"There is only one relation of life in which that can be expected," said Monckton, in a still lower voice than that he had already used.

"No relation is to me more sacred than a professed and accepted friendship—no relation demands stricter honor or more inviolable confidence," said Beatrice severely.

"I know what you mean, Beatrice," said Monckton, after a silent but obvious struggle; "and I cannot clear myself at present from your imputation of insincerity. I confess that I told you an untruth just now, when you asked me, in Mr. Chappelleford's hearing, of what I had been talking with Mrs. Charlton; but my reply was a mere form, as I wished you to perceive. I could not answer you, and I could not leave you unanswered. I was obliged to speak, and I replied as a lady does who sends word that she is not at home when she means she cannot see company. Nor can I very clearly explain myself, nor——"

"It is quite unnecessary that you should do so at all, Mr. Monckton. You confess to having told me one untruth this evening; and although you defend your course in some remarkable manner, I am not enough of a sophist to follow you. Let us drop the subject at once and forever; and I will now wish you good-evening, and leave you to complete your explanation to Mrs. Charlton, who will probably understand it better than I can."

"Before retiring, please to receive my adieux, as I am on the point of leaving. Good-evening, Miss Wanstel, and may our next interview find you less severely and more reasonably inclined. Good-evening, Mrs. Charlton—Mr. Chappelleford. May I trouble you, Mrs. Charlton, to say good-evening for me to Mr. Barstow?"

And with a formal bow to every one, he was gone; and Beatrice, honestly indignant though she felt, was yet conscious of a heavy pain at her heart in feeling that he had gone in anger.

Mr. Chappelleford soon took his leave; and the two women, left alone together, eyed each other in the manner of familiar friends between whom lies an unspoken secret. Suddenly Juanita approached the sofa, where Beatrice still sat, and crouching upon the hassock at her feet, held up by its chain the glittering toy hanging about her neck.

"See what Mr. Monckton gave me just now. It is an Eastern amulet, and was sent to me by a friend whom Mr. Monckton met abroad," said she.

"And he has never given it to you until to-night?" asked Beatrice incredulously.

"No, he could not. I cannot tell you about it just now."

"There is no need, Juanita. It is no affair

The Amulet.

of mine; and these answers of form, as Mr. Monckton calls them, are very distasteful to me. You need not have tried to explain at all." And Beatrice, her heart full of bitterness and her eyes of tears, rose, and hastily left the room.

Mrs. Charlton rose also, and replacing the amulet in her bosom, muttered:

"Poor child!—poor, jealous baby—striking at the hand that tries to soothe you. I am sure it was very good of me to try to explain, and no fault if she would not listen; and yet I am sorry to break off that friendship. But, O

my heart! my heart! what are all these childish troubles to your great anguish? Now, at least, I can be alone."

And with hurried, yet trembling steps, Juanita fled to her own chamber, and locked herself into it alone.

CHAPTER XXII.
A LETTER FROM AUNT RACHEL.

"My Dear Niece Beatrice: It is a long time since we heard anything from you, and I trust that both you and brother Israel are in good health and prospered in your undertakings. We are all in the enjoyment of our usual health, except your grandmother, who has an attack of rheumatism, from standing at the porch-door talking to Jacob, our hired man, about the new calf. This calf is the daughter of Polly, the red and white heifer that you liked so well and dressed with a garland of wild flowers, which she pulled off and eat up. That was last Independence-day, you remember, and you got mostly blue flowers, because you said, she must be red, blue, and white. The new calf is very pretty, and we think of raising it; but we shall not name it until you come home, as you may have a choice in the matter. Grandfather is very well, considering, and often speaks of you. He says he wants to see you very much, and hopes you will not have grown out of knowledge. He forgets, being old, that you are grown up already, and will not change outwardly any more until you begin to grow old, which I suppose will not be yet.

"Nancy is well, I suppose, but she tires me very much through forgetting what I tell her. Yesterday she set a flat dish under the churn-stand, pulled out the plug and let the buttermilk run, and then forgot to stop it until it had flashed out of the dish all over the floor. Then she forgets to make grandma's farina for breakfast until I go out and do it, and that disturbs grandma very much. But we all have our trials, and I know these are not as great as those some are called to bear.

"There is no news in Milvor, except that Joachim Brewster and Semanthy Brewster are married, which many of us think a burning shame—not but what it is better than some other ways of living which I will not allude to. Last month they found the bones of poor little Ruthie in Black Briar Pool, with the remains of her dress and shoes still on her. The body had drifted under the bank where it shelves over, and lay hid among the weeds. It was Joachim found it, going fishing, and a good many knew the piece of calico clinging to the poor arm-bones. It all seems straight enough, and they had a funeral, and a coroner's inquest, and it was put down in the town records that it was Ruth Brewster that died; but somehow my mind misgives me that it is not all exactly right. I am sure I do not know how it can be wrong, but I would not trust Semanthy Brewster with a dish of apple-parings if I was particular the pig should get them; and as for Joachim, he never had much force anyway, and I guess she trains him round pretty much as she has a mind to.

"I do not know of any more news, my dear niece, except some that I suppose will surprise you a good deal—and that is, that I have concluded to be married to Wyman Bliss, and we shall have the wedding next fourth of March, the same day that the new President begins to live in the White House, and it seems a sort of date to start from. I hope, my dear niece, that you will not feel that I am doing any thing unbecoming in a maiden lady who is no longer young; but it seemed to me as good as any thing that could be done, for your grandfather is getting so old it seems as if there ought to be some other man round the house, and Wyman, being a doctor, makes it real comfortable in case of sudden sickness or any thing happening unexpectedly.

"Grandfather and grandmother seem very well pleased with the arrangement, and grandfather is going to give up the farm to us—which, I suppose, means to me, for the doctor has his hands full with his profession—as is no wonder when you consider that there is not so good a doctor in the country. But though we take the farm now, you need not be afraid, my dear niece, that you are to be cheated out of your rights, or Israel either, as I shall explain to him when I see him, which I hope will be soon, for neither Wyman nor I would do any thing unfair or try to get the upper hand, especially when you know, Trix, that you've always been like a child—I will not say to me, being a maiden lady, but in the house, and we all take an interest in you just as we always did. I have begun to get ready somewhat, but I should be glad of a little of your taste about my new gown—I refer to the one I shall be married in, and also to know whether I had better wear a bonnet; for as for flowers on my head, or a veil, or any such nonsense, I must say I should not consider it respectable. Also, grandmamma would like a new blonde cap, she says, and perhaps you will buy the material for her. Also for the dress, for which I enclose the money, twenty dollars. It is a large sum for one dress, but I want it good and handsome, and something that will be serviceable. I should say a cinnamon brown bearing on a chocolate would be a good color, but perhaps a gray would be better. For service, I should prefer a black silk, but I suppose that would not be considered proper for a bride—that is, for a person going to be married.

"But, above all things, my dear Trix, I want to see you. We shall have a quilting-bee here all day Thursday of next week, and I wish you could make it so as to be at home. To-day is Tuesday; so that gives you ten days to say good-by in, and to buy the lace for grandmother and the other that I mentioned.

"Give my love to your uncle, and, if you please, you can mention what I say.

"Your affectionate aunt,
"RACHEL M. BARSTOW."

With this letter in her hand, and a smile upon her lips, Beatrice sought her uncle in his dressing-room, and tapping gently at the door, was bidden to enter. Obeying, she started back in some surprise—hardly recognizing her relative beneath the mask of soap-suds with which his manly visage was adorned.

"The deuce! Is it you, Trix? I thought it was the fellow with my boots. But come in, little girl—come in, if you're not afraid to. I'm almost through dressing, and then I must hurry off down-town; so you might as well say what you have to say here as anywhere. You'd like a little money, eh? See how sharp your old uncle is at guessing."

"No, indeed, uncle; I have not half spent what you gave me last time. You are so generous I never have the opportunity to ask for money. I came this time to give you some news."

"What! you're not going to be married?" asked Mr. Barstow, turning from the glass, razor in hand, and contemplating his niece with comic dismay.

"Oh! no, uncle, I have no thoughts of it; but I will read you Aunt Rachel's letter, and then you will know all about it."

"Rachel! The old folks aren't dead! No—you wouldn't look so smiling. Well, there! I am a fool to keep guessing, when, if I hold my tongue, I shall know all about it; so, go ahead, Trix."

And Mr. Barstow effectually sealed his own lips with a fresh brushful of lather, while his niece, perching herself upon the edge of the writing-table which adorned the merchant's dressing-room, read the letter through without interruption. As she finished, Mr. Barstow's face issued from the napkin, which finished his tonsorial operations, rubicund, smiling, and smooth as a new-shaven lawn.

"The jolly old sister going to get married at last!" exclaimed he. "Well, if that isn't the last dodge! And Wyman Bliss, too! Why, I knew him when he was a boy, and he's always been hanging round after Rachel ever since. Well, we must go to the wedding, and have a rousing good time, and we'll make them some presents. What do you say to a dinner-service of plate with the coat-of-arms, and all just as we have here at home?"

"I am afraid they would never use it, uncle," replied Beatrice gently. "But there are a great many things that would be delightful to give them. Aunt Rachel has sent to me to buy her wedding-dress, you know——"

"And sent twenty dollars to pay for it! Ha, ha!" laughed Mr. Barstow. "Why, a first-rate silk gown, fit for a—' a person that is going to be married'—ha, ha!—would cost a hundred, wouldn't it?"

"The silk itself would cost about fifty, and the trimming as much as any one chose to give," said Trix.

"Well, you go down-town and pick out the very best and handsomest silk in the shops, and the nicest sort of trimming to go with it, and mind there's plenty of it—both gown and trimming—and send the bills to me; or had you rather have the cost in hand?"

"A little of both, please, uncle. I may have

to look about for trimmings, and go to new places."

"Very well; here is a check for two hundred dollars; and when that is gone, just drive down to the office, and send up for me, or if I am out, for Rowley. As for credit, you can use that at discretion. And while you are about it, Trix, you might as well get yourself and June new dresses for the wedding—something handsome, but not showy enough to make the good Milvor folks feel ashamed of their own rig. That wouldn't be good manners, you know."

"No, indeed, uncle; and for my own part, I do not need a single thing; I have a great plenty of dresses for a year to come. But, uncle, do you think Mrs. Charlton had better go to the wedding?"

"Why, she's one of ourselves, isn't she?" demanded Mr. Barstow, in considerable surprise. "I supposed of course she would go."

Beatrice, folding and creasing the corner of the envelope she held in her hand, made no reply.

Mr. Barstow looked at her a moment in much perplexity, whisked an atom of dust from his coat-sleeve, and then asked:

"Don't you want her, Trix?"

"To tell the truth, uncle, I think she would be rather out of place at Milvor, and I do not believe Aunt Rachel would enjoy seeing her."

"Oh! well, that alters the case. Very likely Rachel might feel a little troubled about the country ways and homely fashions of the Old Garrison House——"

"Uncle Israel! you don't suppose I meant that there was any thing to be ashamed of in our dear old home? I am sure I wish every one was as honest, and truthful, and reliable as Aunt Rachel, or that other people's ways were half as good as the country ways and homely fashions of the Old Garrison House. No matter who goes to Aunt Rachel's wedding, there will not be a better woman there than herself."

If Mr. Barstow had been surprised before, he was now actually petrified, and stood staring at his niece, who never, in the whole course of her life, had spoken so vehemently in his presence before.

Beatrice, looking up, met his eyes, and her own filled with tears of shame. Springing suddenly from her seat, she threw her arms about his neck.

"Oh! forgive me, Uncle Israel! I was

very, very wrong to speak so to you, but I—I am not well, I believe—I am hardly myself. It will do me good to go home and be quiet for a while. Let me go to-day."

"Not to-day, dearie, or to-morrow, but as soon as we can make you suitably ready," said Uncle Israel, tenderly smoothing the bright hair straying over his breast, while his honest face never lost its look of wonder and concern. "Yes, little girl, you shall go and stay until after the wedding; but then, you know, you are to come home for good and all. This is home, remember."

"Thank you, dear, dear uncle."

"Thank you for nothing, you mean. Don't you know that I can't get on without you, you monkey? And as for asking June to the wedding, I believe you are right. She would be a little out of place, and it might be uncomfortable all round. She can stay with her uncle at the Grandare while we are away, eh?"

"Just as you please, uncle," murmured Beatrice.

"Then that's settled; and now give me a kiss and let me go, and you take the carriage and go buy the wedding-finery."

CHAPTER XXIII.

WEDDING-FINERY.

"AND now, Aunt Rachel," said Beatrice, the morning after her arrival in Milvor; "now let us have a little fire in your chamber, and I will show you my shopping."

"Dear me, child, I'm in no hurry whatever about that. Miss Billings isn't coming until Friday to cut my dresses, and it will be time enough then."

"Now, Aunt Rachel, that is clear, sheer nonsense! You want to make me believe that you have no curiosity even about your wedding-dress, and I shan't believe a word of it. Of course you want to see it, and I want to show it, and I am not going to hurry about it either; so I shall just go and make the fire myself, and then call you up."

With which declaration, Miss Wansted, her brilliant robes exchanged for one of gray linsey-woolsey, with a bit of blue ribbon and the plainest of linen collars at the neck, and a pair of cuffs to match at the wrists, ran out of the room, and was presently seen picking up chips in the wood-yard.

"Dear creetur," murmured her grandmother —"not the leastest mite of difference, for all the silk gowns and fal-lals Israel has given her, and all the attention the young fellers have been paying her. I was dreadful afraid she'd be set up in her own conceit, and not think so much of our humble ways; but there isn't any thing of that, as I can see."

"You're too modest, wife," replied the deacon, glancing at her over the top of his Fenelon. "I don't know why our grand-daughter should be either daunted or too much astonished by the ways of people richer maybe, but no better, I hope, than those she has always lived among."

"Well, that's true enough, too, father," assented the old lady, straightening herself a

Picking up chips in the wood-yard.

little. "The Barstows are as good as anybody——"

"So long as they behave as well," interposed her husband, with a quiet smile behind his book; and Mrs. Barstow rather doubtfully assented to the qualified self-glorification.

Beatrice, meanwhile, had filled her pretty black silk apron with long ringlets of pine shavings, cones of the fragrant fir-tree, splinters and clean white chips from the heart of the beech and buttonwood logs lying cleft in the wood-yard, and some dry branches lopped from the tops of the pine trees, whose straight trunks lay side by side, ready to be hauled to the saw-mill; for the deacon burned his own wood, and had some to sell to his neighbors beside.

"Will you please bring in an armful of wood, Jacob? Up into Miss Rachel's room, if you please," said the young lady, bestowing a gracious smile upon the sinewy, wiry, and most unlovely Yankee who at present replaced Paul Freeman at the Old Garrison House.

"Oh! yes, I'll fetch in as much as you want. Kind o' chilly this morning, a'n't it?"

"Somewhat more than chilly, I think, Jacob," said the young lady, glancing rather ruefully at the snowy landscape; "it looks like midwinter yet."

"Not if you know how midwinter had ought to look," bluntly replied Jacob. "See them great white clouds banking up in the south? You don't never see none of them in December or January, do you? And then see how sort of rotten the snow breaks away when I pull a stick out o' the pile. There'll be a change o' weather 'fore long, and I mistrust it'll be rain. Declare for 't, I guess I'd better go into the woods to-day, and leave this 'ere chopping for a time when I can't do nothing else. Wonder what the deacon 'd say?"

And Jacob, straightening himself with a huge armful of wood, drew his right shirt-sleeve across his nose and looked inquiringly at the sky.

"You had better go into the sitting room and speak to grandfather," said Beatrice smiling; "and if you do go to the woods, I should like to go with you. I have not seen the woods this whole winter."

"Well, you can if you're a mind to, and I suppose you'll be for riding home on the load, so I'll carry along a buffalo for you to set on," replied Jacob, with composure; and Beatrice, thanking him as politely as she ever thanked Messrs. Laforêt et Cie for less genuine courtesies, ran into the house and up-stairs with her light burden, soberly followed by Jacob with his wood.

"Shan't I build the fire for you, ma'am?" asked he, clumping carefully across the carpet, and leaving a cake of half melted snow at every footfall.

"No, thank you, Jacob; I know how very well myself. You had better speak to grandpapa; and if you are going to the woods, send me word by Nancy. You won't start just this minute, will you?"

"No ma'am; I suppose I must chop up some kin'lin'-stuff for Nancy's oven, or she'll be in my hair. They're going to bake to-day."

"Well, I shall be ready in half an hour," said Beatrice rather breathlessly, for the large log she was adjusting at the back of the fire-place required all her strength. Jacob watched her movements admiringly for a moment, and then clumping out as carefully as he had clumped in, went down-stairs muttering:

"A smart gal that, and as pretty as a pieter'."

The back-log adjusted, Beatrice pushed the andirons close up against it, selected a solid white-oak fore-stick to lay across them, filled the interval between back and fore-stick with small wood crowned with some of the dry pine-twigs and cones, and then made a little heap of shavings, chips, and twigs underneath.

"There," said she, looking at the completed edifice; "grandpapa couldn't have done it better himself."

Then she lighted a match, touched it to the shavings, and seated à l'Orientale upon the hearth-rug, watched, with well-satisfied gaze, the flame as it devoured the shavings, then caught upon the pine-twigs, and creeping upward through the lattice-work of more solid fuel, leaped hungrily upon the dried pine-needles and fir-cones at the top, and feeding upon them, grew strong enough to attack the heavier sticks between the two.

"How lovely!" whispered Beatrice, selecting half a dozen cones from the heap of kindling, and placing them so artistically among the sticks as to lead the flames from step to step through the whole pyre; and then warming her red-tipped fingers at the growing blaze, she watched admiringly the play of the flames, and remembered one of Mr. Chappelleford's whimsical theories, to the effect that every wood, in process of combustion, produces a flame shaped like the leaf of its own tree, and she tried to distinguish the pointed needles of the pine, the sinuated leaves of the oak, and the five-fingered palms of the buttonwood, in the rustling river of flame that now poured up the chimney. But try as she might, the flame-leaves only reminded her of the fantastic and airy forms of the trees that grow in fairy-land; and after a while, Beatrice, desisting from the effort, sat gazing dreamily into the fire, and thinking her own thoughts, or perhaps those of Cornelius Agrippa, who tells us through a modern poet:

"As the Spirits of Darkness be stronger in the dark, so Good Spirits, which be Angels of Light, are augmented not only by the Divine Light of the Sun, but also by our common Wood Fire; and as the Celestial Fire drives away dark spirits, so also this, our Fire of Wood, doth the same."

From this reverie she was startled by the voice of Aunt Rachel.

"Well, I declare, Beatrice, you're just the same careless girl you used to be—picking up chips in that black silk apron, all trimmed off with lace and beads and fal-lals, and all but new, I dare say. And then those French slippers right out in the snow, and silk stockings! Well, Beatrice, you may laugh, but it is no better than tempting Providence, and I don't suppose you'll say you mean to do that."

"Why, aunty, what do you think Providence could be tempted to do to me? Don't you believe Providence means our Father in Heaven, who only wishes to make us happy and well?" asked the girl, without removing her eyes from the blaze, where, perhaps, she had found the creed which filled Aunt Rachel's good Calvinistic heart with dismay.

"Beatrice Wansted!" exclaimed she, "don't tell me that you're going to turn Free-thinker and Radical, and all that. You've been to hear Parker, I know you have!"

"Why, Aunty Barstow! you cruel, cruel dear, to go and call your little Trix a Free-thinker! Aren't you horribly ashamed of yourself?" And the girl, jumping up, threw her arms about her aunt's neck with a laugh and a kiss, whirled her sacrilegiously round the room, and finally seated her in a great wooden rocking-chair in front of the fire, while she herself fell upon her knees before the great trunk which she had caused to be placed in her aunt's room instead of her own.

"Well, I believe I was wrong, and that you are changed in some things, Trix," said Miss Rachel meditatively.

"How, aunty?" asked Beatrice, bending over the open trunk to hide a smile.

"Why, you seem to have got a way of sliding off from things you don't want to talk about, and that once you'd have got provoked over," said Miss Barstow, and Beatrice bent still lower into the trunk.

"There, aunty, there is a new dress for

Nancy," said she suddenly, as she drew out a piece of woollen stuff, and laid it upon her aunt's lap.

"For Nancy, child?"

"Yes, aunty. Uncle Israel gave me some money to spend for wedding-finery, he said, and I thought I would get Nancy a dress out of it."

"Why, it's too good. Merino, isn't it?"

"Yes, I thought it was not best to get silk for her, although I could have bought it for the same price as the thibet."

"Silk indeed! I should think not!" exclaimed Miss Barstow. "I don't desire to see any one in my kitchen dressed out in silks or satins. That is a pretty color; what do you call it?"

"Bismarck-brown, aunty. It is very fashionable."

"Just about the color I thought of for that dress I asked you to get me. Where is that?"

And a tinge of red rose to Miss Rachel's withered cheek as she thus betrayed her secret impatience.

Beatrice took a huge parcel, carefully enveloped in tissue-paper, from the trunk, and laying it upon the bed, proceeded very deliberately to unpin it, while she said:

"Now, Aunt Rachel, there is a good deal to say upon the subject of that dress. In the first place, cinnamon-brown, or chocolate, or even Bismarck, are not the colors for a wedding-dress; and you know you want to look as a bride should—now, don't you?"

"Bride! At my time of life! Pho! child."

And the reflection of the blaze or something else glowed in a very becoming crimson upon Miss Rachel's cheeks and lips, and danced brightly in her eyes.

"Time of life, indeed! No one would take you for a day over thirty to see you now, aunty. But about the dress. I don't think Miss Billings is quite so good a dressmaker as we have in town, although she is a very nice old lady; and, besides, you have so much to do, you know. So the amount of the whole is, that Uncle Israel told me to get a dress, and have it made up and trimmed, as his present to you, and here it is."

With which summary introduction, Beatrice, a little flushed herself—for what woman is quite iron-clad against the cunningly-feathered arrows of the genius of Dress?—unfolded and shook out upon the bed the folds of a moire silk, tinted like the soft gray clouds that float so lovingly across the blue of a June sky. The dress was fashioned in a quiet modification of the style of the day, and was doubtfully pronounced by the modiste who wrought under Miss Wansted's directions—"Very, very plain indeed, although of splendid material."

Miss Barstow's verdict was different:

"Why, Beatrice—Beatrice Wansted!" exclaimed she, holding up both hands, and staring at the shining folds of moire with a look divided between awe and admiration.

"It is fit for Eugeny with her crown on!"

"I hope it will fit you even better, aunty dear; and that the day when you first wear it will make you happier than any queen," said Beatrice, kissing her aunt with dewy eyes.

"And here," continued she, bringing forth a carton tied across with blue ribbons, "here is a little present from me to go with the dress." And with dexterous fingers she drew forth and adjusted upon the silk a collar, sleeves, and head-dress of fine Mechlin lace ornamented with knots of blue ribbon.

"Blue ribbons for me, 'Trix?" exclaimed Miss Barstow feebly.

"Yes, aunty, they make such a lovely contrast with the pearl gray of the dress, and you know you must not be married all in gray. You asked me about a bonnet, or a veil, and so I thought perhaps you would fancy this head-dress, which has, you see, a sort of veil hanging at the back, and for other occasions you can alter it a little, or take off the veil."

"That dress cost a great deal more than twenty dollars, Beatrice?" said Miss Barstow severely; and her niece could not restrain a little laugh.

"It isn't pretty to ask the price of a present, you know, dearie," said she; "and I thought perhaps you would like to spend the twenty dollars in something for grandmamma: so I bought this nice black silk for her to wear at the wedding, and this cap to go with it. But Uncle Israel rather scolded me for doing it, because he said it was not business-like to spend the money sent us for a certain purpose in another way. So if you would prefer the money, I have it all ready; or if you would like to make the present to grandmamma, you can do that."

"I should like to make the present to grandmamma, and you were a very thoughtful, good girl to think of it," said Miss Rachel, well pleased, as Beatrice had foreseen that she would be.

"And what will you wear yourself?" pursued she, glancing at the nearly-emptied trunk.

"Oh! I brought down two dresses, and you must tell me which you like best," said Beatrice carelessly; and produced from the depths of the box a mauve silk, and one of sky-blue, both of them fresh and handsome.

"Two silk gowns at once, Beatrice!" exclaimed her aunt reprovingly. "I am afraid your uncle is teaching you extravagance and a love of dress."

"Oh! no, aunty; but we went out so much, I had to have a variety, you know," said Beatrice apologetically; and while her aunt still examined the dresses with disapproving admiration, Nancy opened the door to say:

"Jacob wants to know if you're going into the woods with him, Beatrice. He's 'most ready."

"Say Miss Beatrice, Nancy," suggested her mistress sharply; "and don't wait with your oven cooling. I heard you taking out the fire ten minutes ago. What about the woods, Trix?"

"Oh! I am going, certainly," said Beatrice, hastily bundling the packages back into the trunk.

"Not in that dress, Beatrice!"

"No, indeed, aunty. I saw one of my last winter's poplins in the closet of my chamber."

And Miss Wansted, disappearing before further disapproval could be spoken, presently returned, dressed in a simple short dress and a warm coat.

"See here, aunty," said she, mischievously raising her skirts high enough to show a very jaunty pair of Knickerbockers nearly meeting the tops of her high Polish boots.

"Well, I never! Why, Beatrice Wansted, if I shouldn't be ashamed!" exclaimed the spinster, turning nearly as scarlet as the obnoxious garments.

"Why, aunty! why should I be ashamed?" laughed Beatrice.

"Why, to wear those things. Almost like —really, now, they *do* remind me——"

"Of what, aunty?"

"Why, child, a gentleman's *pantaloons*," whispered Miss Barstow, the scarlet turning crimson.

"Not a bit of it, aunty! Pantaloons are tight to the leg, and tie with strings round the ankles; and what gentlemen wear are called trowsers; and these are nothing like either, and are called Knickerbockers."

"Beatrice! say limbs, and not legs; and don't talk so glibly about things no young woman should ever mention," said Miss Barstow severely.

CHAPTER XXIV.
THE CAPTAIN'S PURCHASE.

"ALL ready, Jacob?"

"Yes, ma'am, all ready," said Jacob, who was adjusting an inverted soap-box upon the middle of his ox-sled, and covering it with a warmly-lined buffalo-robe.

"There, that's for you to set on," said he, when all was ready.

"How charming! I expected to stand up and hold on to one of the stakes," laughed Beatrice, seating herself upon her extempore throne, and looking more than ever lovely, with the bright color of the frosty morning upon cheek and lip, and her eyes sparkling like sunbeams beneath the brim of the little round hat whose black plumes contrasted so charmingly with the gold-brown braids they shaded.

So dimly perceived Jacob, standing a moment beside the sled, to draw on his blue and white mittens, patriotically fringed with red, Mrs. Barstow's handiwork; but Jacob would have thought it unpardonably "sarcy" to have intimated his admiration in the most distant manner, and so went silently forward to his oxen's heads, and with a jerk and a creak the sled started, cutting its way through the softened snow with a dull, crunching sound, quite different from the crisp crackle of mid-winter drifts, or the sharp creak made by passing over a snow-road in the coldest and heaviest of frozen weather.

"Where are you cutting wood now?" asked Miss Wansted, when, after piloting his team into the road, Jacob stepped upon the sled and stood there, Colossus-like.

"I've been cutting up to the Captain's Purchase. I a'n't cutting now—I'm hauling. You wouldn't have wanted to go and see me chop all day, I reckon," said Jacob, with a laugh. "All I've got to do now is to load up and turn right round. We'll be home to dinner."

Beatrice did not reply. A sudden cloud had come over both face and mood, and she sat looking straight before her with wide, sad eyes.

The Captain's Purchase, a tract of wood

land so named in the old records, and so called to-day, although tradition has no story to tell of either captain or purchase—not so much as the name of the one, or the price of the other—the Captain's Purchase was the place where the May-flowers bloomed earliest, the lovely, pink-flushed, odorous *Epigæa repens*, which a perverse world will call trailing arbutus, and thither to gather them had she gone with Marston Brent in the sweet days that were no more.

"No more, no more forever," whispered Beatrice, her sad eyes searching field and wood and sky for a contradiction to the mournful prophecy, and finding none. And then pressing in at the door thus set ajar came trooping the memories she had believed at rest—memories of tender words, of loving looks, of sweet hopes, and half-formed plans of life, of all the joy that might have been, and now should never be. And whose fault that it should never be? "Not mine," said the girl's softened heart. "For did I not humble myself, and give up all for love of him? Did I not even ask him to let me come to him in the home he had chosen?" "And," asked Pride, "what did he say? Did he not thrust me back and refuse the love I offered him, and hold me to my word in my own despite? And is it for such a man that I am mourning now, and feeling that because he is lost, all else is valueless? O shame, shame! that any woman should so forget woman's value! If Marston Brent cared more for his own will than for me, I care more for those late leaves whirling to the ground than for Marston Brent."

And wrenching herself away from even memory of him, Beatrice turned to her companion, who, softly whistling and holding to one of the stakes of the ox-sled, viewed the rapidly clouding skies with a speculative eye.

"Going to have a change o' weather, sudden," said Jacob, perceiving that Miss Wansted was ready for conversation.

"More snow?" asked she languidly.

"I guess more like we shall have rain. The air's most too soft for snow. Rain 'll play the very old mischief with the goin', there's such a heft o' snow on the ground."

"Yes. I am afraid it would prevent my aunt's party to-morrow," said Beatrice, raising her eyes to the soft white clouds fast shutting out the blue of heaven.

"Quiltin'-bee, a'n't it?"

"Yes, I believe so."

5

"They'll come fast enough, women-folks will," said Jacob, laughing a little, and rolling his eyes quizzically upon the face of his companion. "You see they don't stir about so much as men-folks, and toward the end o' winter they get so sort o' stalled stopping in the house, that they'd go anywhere's for a change. I declare I think sometimes, if Old Nick was to give a tea-party on top of Moloch Mountain in February, he'd get as many to set down as he'd find cups and saucers for. You'll see there won't no one stop away from the bee to-morrer, rain or shine, except them as can't get their men-folks to bring 'em, and can't hitch on to no one else's team."

"Why, Jacob, it isn't a bit polite to me to make fun of women-folks," said Beatrice with dancing eyes.

"Land o' Goshen, ma'am, I don't mean you when I talk about women-folks. You're altogether different," said Jacob gravely; and, after considering the point, added:

"You see, ma'am, you've had advantages, and been round, and haven't had to buckle to't, and work for a living, same as they have; and I don't see, for my part, why a woman, if she has advantages, and improves 'em, a'n't ekil to men—some men."

"Why, yes—some men, as you say, Jacob; and, Jacob, I'm very much obliged to you for your favorable opinion, and will present you with a vote of thanks in behalf of the rest of the sisterhood; and the first woman's-rights convention that I attend I will nominate you as chairman. And now, Jacob, I want to know how much of the Captain's Purchase you have cut over this winter, and what the wood is worth a cord, and how much you have hauled to market, and how much home, and how much remains upon the ground."

"Well, that's a good many questions to answer all to once," said Jacob, scratching his head beneath his fur-cap, and glancing a little uneasily at the sparkling and satirical face upraised toward him.

"However, I'll try: I've cut well on to three acres of the Purchase, and have corded up about a hundred cord, maybe a hundred and a quarter, and ——"

"How much is that to each acre, Jacob?"

"Each acre? Well, it's about—about—why say forty cord to each acre."

"Oh! no, Jacob! A third of a hundred is not forty, and a third of a hundred and twenty-five is more than forty."

"I said about that; forty's nigh enough," said Jacob with dignity.

And Beatrice pursued her inquiries, the smile she banished from her lips dancing in her eyes:

"Well, how much is it worth a cord, Jacob?"

"Why, that's accordin' as how the wood is. First-rate hard wood, white-oak, with a sprinklin' o' walnut 's worth six dollars, and pine's worth four, and oak trash's worth two, and pine-trash's worth one."

"And if the hundred or a hundred and a quarter cords you've cut this winter are about

"Here we be at the Captain's Purchase."

equally divided into those four kinds, how much are they all worth?" asked Beatrice demurely.

But a dim suspicion that he was being unfairly dealt by entered with the question into Jacob's brain, and, after a moment's consideration, he replied dryly:

"That sum's in Greenleaf's first part, a'n't it? We'll drive round by the school-house coming home, and I'll get my little brother to do it for you."

"Thank you, Jacob; but I don't think you need your little brother to help you through,"

said Beatrice, laughing so heartily at her own expense that even the sensitive pride of the New-England yeoman, the most sensitive of all mankind, was soothed, and Jacob joined in the laugh.

"Here we be at the Captain's Purchase," said he, jumping off the sled, and throwing down some bars closing the entrance to a wood road, deep embowered in greenery when Beatrice last beheld it, and though the scene was "now changed to winter frore," it held too close a likeness to that she so well remembered to be denied at least its moment of silent recognition. So, Beatrice, her face suddenly pale and still, sat silent, fighting down those memories laid but now, and again arisen, until Jacob halted his oxen at the edge of a large clearing covered with corded piles of wood, while the ground between was strewn with limbs and leaves, and splinters and chips, as a battle-field with the smaller relics of the strife, after the bodies have been removed.

"Guess you'd better get off now, ma'am," said he very kindly, for the honest fellow had noted the sudden change in his companion's mood, and attributed it to mortification at his rebuff.

"I'm a going to turn the team in among the brush, and it'll be awful jolty, and then ag'in I've got to begin to load right away. Sorry to disturb you."

"Oh! not at all, Jacob; don't apologize," said Beatrice absently; and, accepting Jacob's offered hand, she stepped lightly to the ground, and stood looking about her, while the man arranged the box and buffalo robe close beside her.

"There, you can set right down again, and make believe you're riding," said he soothingly. "Or, if you'd rather, you can walk about a little. There a'n't much to see in the woods this time o' year, but maybe you can find some checkerberries where the snow has melted off, or maybe a squirrel-hole with some nuts in it. I'll be as quick as I can."

"Oh! don't trouble about me, Jacob," replied Beatrice, rousing herself with an effort; "I am used to the woods, and know how to amuse myself, winter or summer. I shall run about and get warm while you are loading, unless you want my help."

"Your help, ma'am! Lord love you, no," laughed Jacob, picking up his ox goad, and bawling directions to his team, Calvin and

Luther, whom the deacon had so named because he said he would make those two eminent personages draw together somehow.

Left to herself, Beatrice strolled along the road, until, having crossed the clearing, it struck into the woods at the other side, and so soon as she was out of sight, perched herself upon the stump of a monster pine, and stood like a statue upon its pedestal, admiring the scene before her, and resolutely banishing once more all thoughts but those connected with it. From her position, near the top of a high hill, she commanded the valley below, with its little frozen pond, where in summer bloomed the whitest lilies ever known, and around whose margin grow the sweet, white swamp azalia, and its rarer rose-colored sister, and as she saw the spot, Beatrice remembered the great bouquets that she had received—— No, that memory was among the forbidden, and she turned to admire, instead, the smoke-like tracery of the birch-trees fringing the border of the swamp below the chestnut wood— the chestnut wood where she had nutted many a day in those by-gone years ; and Beatrice, stepping impatiently from her pedestal, hastened on through the wood, intent only now upon escape from that army of phantoms which environed her.

She saw no longer the strange, still beauty of the winter woods, forgot to note the soft shades of color upon twig, and trunk, and clinging withered leaves, the beauty of form, hidden in summer, and now displayed so vividly, as the naked tree-tops cut the sky, and long arcades lengthened through the forest, impenetrable to the eye in summer-time. The saucy squirrel crossed her path, or stood chattering upon the branches close above her head ; the rabbit peered from his burrow, with round, startled eyes ; the partridge rose with startling whir-r-r-r from almost beneath her feet ; the fox, stealing through the coverts of the wood, peered at her from beneath sheltering twigs—but Beatrice heard not, saw not, felt only that the past was present still, and that the future held no hope of forgetfulness.

CHAPTER XXV.
THE GUEST OF THE OLD GARRISON.

"BE you ready, ma'am ? If you be, I be."

It was Jacob's voice ; and Beatrice, raising her eyes from the ground, discovered that she had returned in a circle to the point whence she had started, and was just entering the clearing when met by Jacob, who had set out to look for her.

"What! have you loaded your sled already ?" asked she, in some surprise.

"Sartain I have, and didn't work so dreadful smart, neither. Now, be you going to ride on the load ?"

"Oh! yes. That was what I came for, you know."

"Well, I've driven the steers out into the road, and fixed the buffalo on as well as I could. The box we'll leave up here till another time. Strange if we get home before the rain comes on."

"I am afraid I have kept you waiting."

"Oh! that ain't of no account if you don't mind the resk of a wetting. I am sorry we haven't got no umberill. There, set your foot right in there ; I left a kind of a step on purpose, and—there you be!—you're spry on your feet, any way, ma'am."

"All right, Jacob. This is a very nice seat, and I can see the whole country around."

"Yes, it's ekil to being on top of a stage-coach, and some folks won't never go inside if they can help it."

"I am one of those folks, Jacob. I always ride over from Bloom on the top of the coach when they will let me."

"Do! Well, I've heerd so, but I didn't know. They say they'll lay the railroad from Bloom to Milvorhaven some time, and then there won't be no stage-coach travel."

"Oh! I hope not! I hope no railway will ever come nearer to the Old Garrison House than now," said Beatrice, with energy.

"Waal now ; why not ?"

"Oh! because there are driving, growing places enough all over the country ; and Milvor is just as it has always been, and just as I should like to have it always remain. I don't want the march of improvement to trample down the quiet old ways, and slow, sleepy fashions of the place."

Jacob considered the point in silence for several moments, and then, with a comical twist of his dry face, slowly said :

"That reminds me of something I read in a book Miss Rachel loaned me a while ago. It was the History of England, I believe, and it told about a king that liked every thing just as it always was ; and so he turned a lot of folks out of their houses, and pulled up their improvements, and put the whole dees-

tric' back into wild land, as nigh as he could
get it; and had a lot of deer and varmint
turned in, and then he used to go in and hunt
them, just as folks has to in a wild country to
clear the way for a settlement. Your idee
about not letting the railroad come through
Milvor is suthin' like that king's, a'n't it?"

"No; he was a revolutionist, and I am a
conservative—two quite opposite creatures.
However, I do not imagine that my fancies or
wishes will have much effect upon the progress of civilization and the iron-horse. You
will have your railway, I don't doubt."

"Hi, Calvin! Gee, Luther! Gee! There's
a team coming up behind, and they think they
must swerve out to make room for it. I never
see critters think as quick as this yoke o'
steers—never. There! now that feller can
pass if he's handy with his horse."

The jingle of sleigh-bells, which for some
moments had been growing louder and louder as the swift horse overtook the ox-team,
suddenly ceased, and a voice close behind the
load called out pleasantly enough:

"Can I pass there, my man?"

"Yes, I reckon you can," replied Jacob,
with slightly surly independence; and Beatrice, startled at the voice, looked down from
her elevation to meet the wondering eyes of
Mr. Monckton.

"Miss Wansted!"

"Yes, Mr. Monckton, it is really I."

"You should have invited your friends to
your coronation—or rather to your enthrone-
ment."

"I am afraid Milvor would not have contained them."

"What you say sarcastically we should say
seriously; but having asserted yourself, won't
you descend and accept a share of my humble
equipage?"

"Oh! no, thank you. I don't believe in
descending when one can remain elevated.
Will you pass us?"

"Why, no, thank you, I will follow—that
is, if you will permit me to accompany you
home. I was on my way to call upon you."

"We shall be most happy, certainly. Drive
on, if you please, Jacob."

And Beatrice, not attempting to conceal her
dissatisfaction, turned her head away from the
self-invited guest, and fixed her attention upon
the oxen.

Mr. Monckton, too much a man of the world
to be discomfited, or to appear conscious of any
annoyance, entered into an animated conversation with the youth who drove him; and
nothing further passed between the lately familiar friends, until both equipages stopped in
the open space at the southern front of the
old house.

"Now, ma'am, I'll help you down," began
Jacob, pulling off his mittens, wiping his nose,
and settling his fur cap firmly upon his head.

"Permit me, Miss Wansted," interposed Mr.
Monckton.

"Thank you, but Jacob is the cavalier of
this occasion," said Beatrice, deftly placing one
foot in the interstices of the load, and resting
her little hands upon the shoulders of the
woodman, who, grasping her slender waist,
swung her lightly to the ground.

"I must congratulate Jacob both upon his
opportunities and his mode of improving them,"
laughed Mr. Monckton, meeting Beatrice, as
she regained her feet, with a hand so cordially
extended that she could not have refused it
had she tried.

"Yes, he is a capital escort. Jacob, I have
had a very nice drive and pleasant time. I
shall go with you again some time."

"Any time that suits you, ma'am. It'll always be agreeable to me," said Jacob, with
grave courtesy; and Miss Wansted led the
way to the house.

In the east room, before the brightly-blazing
fire, sat the old people, while Rachel, just appearing at the inner door, drew hastily back
at sight of a stranger.

"This is Mr. Monckton, grandfather, a
friend of Uncle Israel's; my grandfather,
Deacon Barstow, Mr. Monckton. My grandmother."

"I am glad to see any friend of my son's.
Take off your coat, sir, and sit to the fire.
Beatrice, will you please tell Jacob to put up
the gentleman's horse?"

"Thank you, sir, thank you extremely, but
I do not think it worth while to put up the
horse for the little while I have to stay," began Mr. Monckton; but Mrs. Barstow broke
in upon his excuses with voluble hospitality.

"You must stay the night, sir—of course
you must stay the night. Nobody ever comes
to Milvor for less than one night, for it would
not be worth the journey, especially in winter
time. Did you drive over from Bloom, Mr.
Monckton?"

"Yes, madam. Finding myself in this part
of the country, I thought I would run over

and see the Old Garrison House, of which I have heard so much—make the acquaintance of my friend Barstow's family, and call upon Miss Wansted."

"That's right, and I'm real glad you came," said the grandmother, glancing around to see that Beatrice had left the room before she added : "Nor I don't blame any body for wanting to see our Trix, for she's just about as nice a little girl as you'll find anywhere."

To this expression of opinion, Mr. Monckton was spared the perplexity of reply by the entrance of Miss Barstow, who, like her parents, welcomed the unexpected guest with a cordial hospitality more often found, perhaps, upon stage-routes than railroad-lines.

Mr. Monckton, well pleased, and equal to the occasion, seated himself between the patriarch and his wife ; talked ethics, politics, traditions, with the former ; parried pleasantly enough the downright questions of the latter upon his personal affairs, and repaid them with bits of gossip disguised as news. Miss Rachel, coming and going upon her household affairs, felt grateful in her heart to the guest who gave "the old folks" so pleasant an hour with so little apparent effort ; and when Mr. Monckton suddenly appealed to herself upon some question of taste, she was ready to respond with her most gracious smile.

Matters were in this prosperous condition when the sound of the dinner-bell summoned the family to the long low-ceiled room at the back of the house, once used as a kitchen, but converted by Miss Rachel into a dining-room.

"The Lord make us all truly thankful for the bounty we are about to receive," said the deacon, reverently bowing his silvered head ; and then Mr. Monckton seated himself beside Beatrice, who, somewhat paler and stiller than her wont, awaited the family in the dining-room.

"Perhaps you don't like b'iled dish, Mr. Monckton?" said Mrs. Barstow, hospitably piling her guest's plate ; "but it's our regular Wednesday dinner, and has been for fifty years. Beef and pork, and turnips, and potatoes, and cabbage, and carrots, and onions—we've had 'em all every Wednesday, the year through, for fifty years, and I suppose we shall every Wednesday—well, for as many years as we have to live."

"And may they be many," replied Monckton, receiving his loaded plate with an admiring gesture. "Oh! yes," added he, "I think this is rather our national dish, after all—inherited, to be sure, from English rural fashion ; but the English pot is never so generously filled or so often replenished as ours. I remember a story of my grandmother's, about one of her own boiled dinners. My grandfather was an ambitious sort of man, whose whole heart was given to raising immense crops, and carrying on more land than his neighbors, so that he was rather apt to neglect the smaller details of household management, and leave to my grandmother and her woman more than their share of labor. One morning, just as he was setting off for the fields with his laborers, my grandmother called him back.

"'Mr. Monckton,' said she, 'I have no wood to burn to-day. What shall I do?'

"'Oh! send Lois round to pick up some,' said the good man, making a stride toward the door.

"'But she has picked up all she can find.'

"'Then let her break up some old stuff.'

"'But she has broken up every thing already.'

"'Oh! well, then, do the next best thing—I must be off,' said the farmer ; and off he was, whistling as he went, and no doubt wondering in his heart what that next best thing would turn out to be.

"Noon came, and with it came my grandfather and his four hungry laborers. My grandmother stood in the kitchen, spinning on her great wheel, and singing a pleasant little ditty ; Lois was scouring tins in the back-room, and the cat sat purring on the hearth, before a black and fireless chimney, while the table sat in the middle of the room, spread for dinner, but with empty dishes.

"'Well, wife, here we are,' said my grandfather cheerily.

"'So I see,' replied she placidly. 'Have you had a good morning in the corn-field?'

"'Why, yes, so-so. But where is the dinner?'

"'In the pot on the door-step. Won't you see if it is done?'

"And on the door-step, to be sure, sat the great iron pot, nicely covered, but not looking particularly steamy. My grandfather raised the cover, and there lay all the ingredients of such a dinner as we have before us—every thing prepared in the nicest manner, and the pot filled with the clearest of water, and all as raw as they had ever been. My grandfather stared, and my grandmother joined another roll to the yarn upon her distaff, and began another verse of her song.

"'Why, woman, what does this mean?' began my grandfather indignantly. 'This dinner isn't cooked at all!'

"'Dear me! is it not?' asked the good wife in pretended astonishment. 'Why, it has set in the sun this four hours.'

"'Set in the sun!'

"'Yes, you told me to try the next best thing to having a fire, and I thought setting my dinner in the sun was about that.'

"My grandfather stood doubtful for a moment; but finally his sense of humor overcame his sense of injury, and he laughed aloud. Then picking up his hat, he said:

"'Come, boys, we might as well start for the woods. We shall have no dinner till we've earned it, I perceive.'

"'Won't you have some bread and cheese before you go?' asked my grandmother, generous in her victory, as women almost always are. And so she won the day."

"So that was your grandfather and grandmother, Mr. Monckton," said Mrs. Barstow, when the laugh which chorused the story was over; "and they were farmers?"

"Yes, madam, I am proud to say so."

"Then you think well of farming?"

"It was the condition of man next to Paradise, madam."

"But imposed upon man as a punishment and a curse," said the deacon dryly.

"Your grandmother was a real smart woman," pursued Mrs. Barstow opportunely. "Can't you tell us some more of her doings?"

"One more anecdote of the same sort occurs to me," said Mr. Monckton, smiling complacently.

"The cellar-stairs in the old farm-house had become broken and so unsafe that my grandmother besieged her husband, early and late, to repair them, lest some accident should happen. He always promised to do so, and always forgot to fulfil the promise. At last, one day, my grandmother fell in going down, and spilled the milk she was carrying.

"'Are you hurt?' asked my grandfather, smoking his pipe beside the fire.

"'No matter whether I am or not,' returned the angry housewife, reappearing with her empty pan. 'That is the last time I carry milk down those stairs until they are mended!'

"'Please yourself, and find the next best way to get it down,' said the husband, a little vexed at her tone.

"'I will,' said my grandmother, and was as good as her word. The next evening, my grandfather went down cellar to draw some cider.

"'What in thunder!' exclaimed he—nothing worse, I assure you, madam, for he was not a profane man. 'What in thunder is the matter here? Why, woman, your milk is all over the cellar-bottom!'

"'Is it?' replied my grandmother tranquilly. 'Well, I think that is likely enough, falling so far.'

"'Falling so far! What do you mean?'

"'Why, you know I said I shouldn't carry the milk over those broken stairs again, and you told me to try the next best way of getting it down, so I took up a board in the kitchen-floor, threw down the pans, and then strained the milk down into them.'

"The cellar-stairs were mended next day."

CHAPTER XXVI.

RECONCILIATION.

THE eight-day clock in the corner of the east room was on the stroke of ten, and the old people were already deep in their punctual slumbers. Miss Rachel, aided by Nancy, was engaged in some last preparation for the morrow, and Beatrice remained alone with Mr. Monckton for the first time since his arrival.

"Do you know why I came here to-day?" asked he, after five minutes' silence had divided his words from the gay jest he had last uttered.

"To try your adaptive powers in a new direction, perhaps."

"Why are you so bitter with me? I came because you would not see me the last time I called at your uncle's house. You have not seen me since the evening when I displeased you."

"Not displeased me so much as ——"

"Well?"

"Shocked me, disillusionized me — why should I fear to say it?—told me a lie."

"Your words are something more than cordial, Miss Wansted, and they humiliate me, as you mean that they should. Still, I thank you for speaking them, for any thing is less deadly to friendship than silent displeasure."

"Friendship?"

"Yes; you gave me yours."

"Cannot I reclaim it?"

"Not if it was true friendship. My theory is that friendship means the complete harmony of two natures—not to be discovered in a moment, or perhaps in a year of study, but once perceived, not to be disallowed without some such convulsion of being as separates soul and body. I have explained to you before how sacred and holy a thing I felt this to be, and with what incredulous joy I accepted it at your hands. Can you deprive me of this great joy? Will you try to do so?"

"Perfect friendship means perfect confidence," said Beatrice sadly. "You and Juanita deceived me into thinking you almost strangers, and I suddenly discovered you to be—I know not what—confidents, lovers, conspirators—at any rate, other than you had taught me to believe. I asked you frankly for an explanation, and you gave me ——"

"A conventional answer, which I did not expect or wish you to believe. Do you not know that one of the first principles in social ethics is to avoid betraying or forcing others to betray emotions not to be publicly dealt with?—in other words, to avoid 'scenes,' and keep the surface of matters smooth until the time arrives when they may properly be disturbed?"

"That is not sincerity."

"No; but it is good manners, and, like paper-money, as good as what it represents so long as we all agree to receive it as such. But you and I, Beatrice—if you will allow me still to call you by that name—you and I found in each other something better than conventionality, something truer than the life we both were leading; you allowed me to call you my friend, you gave me faith, and confidence, and esteem. I cannot lose those gifts without a struggle."

"But still you offer no explanation," murmured Beatrice, half ashamed of her own persistency.

"No; nor can I offer one. There is a secret between Mrs. Charlton and myself—I do not deny it; but the secret is not mine, and I cannot reveal it. I saw her after your departure, and asked her either to explain the matter to you or allow me to do so. She would consent to neither course, and I have come to you with no means of exculpation in my hand, no peace-offering of confession or explanation. I come, Beatrice, simply because I could not rest away from you, knowing you to be displeased with me."

"It has been a sorrow to me also, for our friendship was one of my most valued possessions," said Beatrice sadly.

"Do not speak of it as a thing in the past—do not withdraw it from me," pleaded Monckton. "O Beatrice! if you knew how dry and arid my life was before it felt this gracious dew, and how all good things were springing up under its influence! Beatrice, you do not know the depths and darkness of a man's heart who has no woman to make a link between him and heaven."

Never in all their intercourse had Monckton spoken with such fervor and unreserve; never before had he betrayed how much value he attached to the friendship she had granted him; and Beatrice was conscious of a thrill of pride as well as joy. She turned her eyes upon him with a shy smile.

"How can you care so much, you who have seen all the wonders of the world, for a simple girl like me?" asked she.

"No matter how, it is enough that I do," said Monckton eagerly. "Tell me, Beatrice, will you still be my friend, will you forgive me, trust me, believe in me again: or do you send me forth, the hopeless, homeless wanderer you found me?"

"And am I to trust you again as I did before, with no pretence of explanation?" asked Beatrice, arching her eyebrows and curving her lips in mock disdain.

"Yes; for that is friendship."

"Then you must promise that you will tell me no more—what do you call them?—conventional answers."

"Well, I will promise you that, and run the risk of appearing as a boor, or a lunatic escaped from Madame de Genlis's Palace of Truth, before the world," said Monckton, leaning toward Beatrice and taking her hand.

At this moment, Miss Rachel hastily opened the door, noted the condition of affairs, without appearing to look beyond the loaf of cake she carried, and, crossing the room, opened the door of a store-closet beside the fire, from whose recesses came a rich odor of spices, tea, coffee, syrup, and all the choicest treasures of the housewife.

"You must excuse my going right on as if you were not here, Mr. Monckton," said she, returning without the cake. "I hope Beatrice is entertaining you."

"Admirably, Miss Rachel," said Monckton with a smile; and Miss Rachel discovered that Beatrice had fled.

CHAPTER XXVII.

BUSY BEES.

THE morning proved Jacob a true prophet, for it broke with a steady downpour of rain, of the soft, quiet description, as little likely to change as the will of those smiling, serene women, than whom the mountains are less obstinate.

"Now, Mr. Monckton," said Aunt Rachel, as the traveller after breakfast approached the window, "you might as well consent to what you can't help. The going will be miserable to-day, and the rain will soak through that coat of yours like brown paper. Send back your sleigh to Bloom and make yourself contented here until to-morrow, when you can take the stage. We are going to have a bee to-day, and there will be some gentlemen to tea; and Beatrice, she isn't of much account for quilting, and she will keep you company through the day. You'd better stay."

"I think so too, sir, and I should be glad of some one to keep me in countenance among so many of the more powerful sex," said the deacon, with the quiet smile that always suggested a little good-humored satire in his remarks upon womankind, and reminded his hearers that the opinions formed sixty years ago were less liberal in their appreciation of the fairer half of mankind than those of to-day.

"Oh! yes, he'll stay," chimed in grandmamma. "There'll be a plenty of pretty girls here, even if we hadn't one of our own."

"And we shall be edified in watching some new proofs of universal adaptiveness," said Beatrice softly.

"How can I choose but stay with so many temptations, even if my own wishes were not too powerful to be denied?" said Monckton gayly; and Miss Rachel slipped out of the room to give the stable-lad from Bloom a substantial breakfast, and bid him make ready to depart alone.

A few hours later the bees began to arrive in spite of the continued and increasing bad weather.

"I told you how it'd be," said Jacob, as he approached the doorstep where Beatrice was lingering to enjoy the soft, moist air, while the guests she had just welcomed were piloted upstairs by Miss Rachel.

"Yes, but how will they get home again?" murmured the young lady, as Jacob took the horse by the head and began to lead him toward the barn.

"Oh! that's of no account," replied he scoffingly. "They're here, and they a'n't to home, and that's all they care for."

"How unlikely such a servant would be in England!" said Mr. Monckton, who had quietly approached the open door.

"So familiar, and yet so truly respectful," said Beatrice.

"The bees began to arrive."

"Yes. Here in New-England, a servant is merely a man who for wages consents to perform certain service for another man. He retains his self-respect, and commands the respect of his employer, and both of them tacitly confess that some day the employed may become employer, and even rise to a rank far above that of his present master. There is nothing servile, nothing presuming in this man's manners, but a servant who is born and will die a servant cannot cease to be servile without becoming presuming."

"'My country, 'tis of thee,
Sweet land of liberty,'"

sung Beatrice with a smile; and as another sleigh, heavily loaded with women, old and young, one small boy, and several umbrellas, toiled up to the door, the friends, now really friends once more, withdrew to the east room, which was to be left undisturbed for the occupancy of the old people, and whoever chose to join them.

"Maybe, Mr. Monckton, if you are not wanted at the quilting, you would like to look over some old records and curious papers saved through two hundred years in our family," said the deacon, feebly rising and unlocking the great brass-bound secretary, whose deep drawers and pigeon-holed recesses contained antiquarian wealth enough to set a whole college mad.

Mr. Monckton, who had the taste to relish and the training to appreciate these treasures, accepted the offer with a cordiality which evidently raised him in the opinion of the old man, who seldom vouchsafed such an offer to a stranger, and who valued his family treasures to their full extent.

With a smile of quiet amusement, Beatrice watched the preparations of the two convives as they seated themselves to their feast, and so soon as they were fairly engrossed, left the room and joined the throng of workers already busy in the great parlor.

"How d'y do, Beatryce? How's your health since you've been to the city?" asked Mrs. Green, the sturdy, comfortable wife of Doctor Bliss's rival in Milvor.

"Very good, thank you, Mrs. Green. Let me help you with that bar."

"Thanky. You see we thought we'd set up the best quilt in this room, because it's the parlor, and birds of a feather had oughter flock together—don't you see?"

And Mrs. Green looked round upon her coadjutors for the approving laugh, of which they did not disappoint her, it being a fortunate illustration of the law of demand and supply, that to any persons of small intellectual average a very little wit goes a great way, or even no wit at all supplies the place of that stimulant better than the genuine article.

Beatrice politely joined in the laugh, and also with more interest in the labor of raising the heavy quilting-bars upon the backs of four chairs, and securing them in the form of a hollow square by means of gimlets kept for that purpose. Next, the lining of the quilt—economically composed of a worn and faded counterpane—was sewed to the border of cloth tacked to the inner edges of the bars; then the rolls of cotton-wool were laid upon it, and a warm discussion as to the proper amount to be used went round the circle of ladies gathered about the frame like a congress of crows considering a prey fallen into their midst.

"Well, every body has their own notions; but for my part, I don't never want more than two pound of cotton in a quilt that's going to lay over me. If you get in more, it's more heft than warmth," said Mrs. Green.

"What I say is, if you're going to have a quilt, why have it, and let it be of some use. I don't think four pound of cotton a mite too much, and I haven't got a quilt in the world with less in, and one I've got for the boys' bed has got six in it."

"I should think your boys would be smashed down flat under it, Miss Williams," suggested another matron, slightly flushed with the heat of argument; and at this moment, fortunately for the harmony of her party, Miss Rachel entered the room. The question was at once referred to her, and decided with a dove-and-serpent wisdom which excited the admiration of her niece, who had become a little alarmed.

"Why, to my mind, it depends altogether on where the quilt is to be used," said Miss Rachel. "For a cold, windy room—up garret, say—I like a good thick quilt, or maybe a comforter, and if the wool is good and clean, I don't believe four or five pounds would be too heavy; but in a warm room, I think it is better to have your quilts lighter and more of them, so that you can throw them off and put them on, as you like. My mother, now, has four quilts on her bed besides the blankets, and I don't believe there is more than a pound apiece in them. So, seems to me, I wouldn't put more than two pounds in this quilt, and after we get it out, we'll tack a comforter, and put five pounds in. Then they could go on one bed together, and whoever slept there could turn one or the other off as they were a mind to."

"Yes, it's well to suit all tastes when you can; and some folks like to lie warm, and some not so warm," said an old lady soothingly. And the two pounds of cotton were laid in, with no more discussion.

The next operation was to adjust the cover or upper crust of this cotton-wool pie. This was patchwork, composed of small octagonal

squares of brightly-colored calico, alternated
with large octagons of solid colored cambrics,
and had been Miss Rachel's fancy-work during
the last month.

It now received many encomiums and a
minute examination, sweet to the vanity of
the laborious artist.

"There's a piece of your lilac calico," and
"Where did you get that rosy piece?" or
"These pretty cambrics was your morning-
gowns, Beatryce, wasn't they?" and "What
a lot of work to get them all together, and how
nice you set off the colors one against another!" were some of the ejaculations. And
Miss Rachel modestly deprecating the praise
she felt richly merited, helped to lay the
cover evenly upon the cotton, and to sew it to
the edges of the bars.

"Now, what pattern be we going to do it
in?" asked Mrs. Green, producing a ball of
hard white cord and a piece of chalk from
her pocket

"Herring-bone is about as pretty as any
way, a'n't it?" asked Mrs. Williams.

"I like di'monds, inch-square di'monds,"
said another lady positively.

"Shell-pattern is pretty," remarked one.

"Waves are prettier," suggested another.

"How do you do waves?"

"Why, lay down a small plate or a saucer,
if you want them small, and chalk round half
the edge. Just like shell-pattern, only you
do that with a teacup"

"It's pretty to have double parallel lines,
each pair about ten inches from the next, and
then waves in between each pair," said quiet
Mrs. Phelps, the minister's wife.

"Like skeins of yarn drying on a clothes-
horse," whispered Mrs. Green, who never ap-
proved any other person's suggestion, and yet
dared not openly contradict the minister's
wife, whose proposed pattern was at once
adopted by Miss Rachel.

"First we must mark out the lines," said
Mrs. Phelps, looking about her. "Mrs. Green,
will you chalk your cord, and lay it on where
you think it ought to go?"

Mrs. Green thus called to the front, graciously obeyed, and first drawing the cord
over the lump of chalk, laid it across one
side of the quilt, and held it firmly at one end,
while Mrs. Phelps drew the other tight.

"Now, Miss Rachel, you must snap it, for
the sake of the sign," said Mrs. Green ; and
Rachel, with a prim smile, took the middle of

the cord between her thumb and forefinger,
raised it a little, and let it fall with a smart
snap, striking out a line of chalk-dust.

"What is the sign?" asked Beatrice.

"Why, the one that snaps the first line on a
bed-quilt will lay under a wedding bed-quilt
first of any one in the room," said Mrs. Green
mysteriously, as she and the minister's wife
moved their chalked cord about an inch, had
a line snapped there, and then removed it ten
inches further inlaid, and chalked another pair
of parallel lines, while Mrs. Bruce, with an inverted breakfast-plate and a piece of chalk
sharpened to a crayon, proceeded to draw the
"waves" between the two.

Leaving them thus engaged, Beatrice stole
away and upstairs, where in the room overhead
she found another group of ladies similarly
employed over a "comforter," already in the
frame, and ready to be "tied" in diamonds, a
process effected by pushing a needle filled
with soft thread down through cover, cotton,
and lining, and drawing it up again nearly
in the same place, a little bunch of bright
colored wools being tied into the knot thus
formed. But in the other front chamber, the
guest-chamber, a knot of matrons, working in
secret conclave, were preparing the crowning
glory of the day—Miss Rachel herself being
rigidly excluded from the room, and Beatrice
only allowed to enter under promise of inviolable secrecy.

This was an album bed-quilt, the gift of
Miss Barstow's widest circle of Milvor acquaintance, each octagon composed by a different
person—the only point of harmony insisted
upon being the size, and a small white square
in the middle, bearing the name of the donor,
either written in indelible ink, or fairly
wrought in cross-stitch, according to her taste
or ability. Below the name was generally a
date, and frequently a couplet, either original
or selected—as :

"When this you see,
Remember me."

"The rose is red, the violet blue,
Pinks are pretty, and so are you."

"Of your dreams just when you wake,
Special notice you should take."

"Your hand and heart
Shall never part."

"I send this square to Miss Rachel,
To show that I wish her well."

"As soon as you're married, dear Miss,
You'll surely be living in bliss."

"This pretty piece of bedding
Is to grace Miss Barstow's wedding."

Beatrice gravely read these and many similar effusions, admired the taste displayed in the various squares, some of which were very pretty, and was just about to assume her place among the needle-women already busily at work, when her aunt's voice summoned her into the hall, and she obeyed, first renewing her promise of secrecy.

CHAPTER XXVIII.

STINGING BEES.

"BEATRICE, it's just struck twelve, and don't you think we'd better call 'em out to luncheon?" whispered Miss Barstow, drawing her niece into her own chamber, at the moment deserted, although the bed was piled up with outer garments, and a small baby slumbered peacefully in a basket upon the hearth.

"Why, aren't we going to have dinner pretty soon?" asked Beatrice, stooping to touch the velvety cheek of the little sleeper with her lips.

"Dinner! Why, Trix, have you forgotten? We are going to give them luncheon now, and by and by, about five o'clock, when it gets too dark to quilt, and the gentlemen come, we're going to have dinner and supper all in one."

"Oh! yes, I remember, aunty. They must have some tea with their luncheon, mustn't they? Old ladies always like tea when they are at work, I notice."

"Yes, they will have tea, and coffee, and bread, and butter, and cake, and cheese, and apple tarts," said Miss Rachel, checking off each article upon her fingers. "And I want you to carry round the cream and sugar on that little silver waiter that brother Israel gave me last New-Year's, and just see that everybody is getting enough to eat, and sort of urge them to take more, or something else, you know. Some people always say no the first time, and mean yes all the while."

"I know it, aunty. Yes, I will see that they are all properly urged. Where shall I find the salver?" asked Beatrice, smiling roguishly at her aunt's directions.

"It's in the buttery, with the silver cream-pot and sugar-bowl on it, all ready. You needn't put any napkin over the waiter, Beatrice. I am going to carry in a little hot dinner to grandpa and grandma in the east room, because they hate to be put out of their ways you know, and I suppose Mr. Monckton will

eat with them. I'm afraid he's dreadful lonesome, Beatrice."

"Not a bit, aunty. He is having the nicest time you can imagine, with grandfather and the old records. I peeped in there just now."

"I dare say you did," said Miss Rachel grimly, touching her niece's rosy cheek with her forefinger. "Well, Trix, I think he is as nice a man as I have seen for a great while. I like him ever so much."

"So do I, aunty; but don't go to building air-castles with me for Chatelaine; although it is natural enough that your thoughts should run on matrimony."

"You saucy girl——" began Miss Rachel; but Beatrice with a merry laugh was already running down stairs to look for the silver salver.

Long afterward, both she and her aunt remembered that merry laugh and that light-hearted audacity, and wondered that no shadow of the clouds sweeping across that brilliant sky should have warned them of its coming.

The luncheon was served, and Beatrice, flitting from group to group, the pretty salver, with its cream-ewer and sugar-basin, in her hand, and her face bright with cordial interest in those whose wants she supplied, presented a more attractive picture to the eyes of a reasonable man than even Beatrice in all the luxury of her gala robes, and the plenitude of her social power.

So thought at least Mr. Monckton, standing unobserved in the hall of the old house, sipping his coffee, and watching the groups in the various rooms with the attentive eye of a practiced observer. As Beatrice approached, he, wishing her to remain unconscious of his presence, lest she should lose the simple earnestness which charmed him so much in her present manner, seated himself quietly behind a group of thick-set matrons close at hand, and so became most unintentionally auditor of their conversation.

"Zilpah says she's real comfortable," pursued Zilpah's sister-in-law. "They don't have no great variety, nor no company, and it's so seldom that they any of them go out of the woods, that she hadn't had a chance to write before, since they got there; and I don't believe she'd have written now, only she wanted to tell about some things that Marston Brent gave her when he broke up here, and she left them with Samoel to sell for her, and I suppose she thought it was time to hear from them. She was always dreadful sharp after money, Zilpah was, and that's a complaint folks don't get better of as they get older."

"Marston Brent and his folks thought a sight of Zilpah," said another matron meditatively.

"Yes, and she of them. She has a lot to say about Marston in her letter. He's going to be married."

"Is? Why, who to, up there in the woods?"

"Well, a girl that's living with him someway now. Zilpah don't say much about it; only that evenings, they all sit round, and he teaches Comfort all sorts of things. Zilpah says that nobody here needn't think he's feeling any way bad about what's past and gone, for she never see a man more taken up in a girl than he is in this Comfort, and they'll be married soon."

"He's got over the breaking off with——"

"S—h! here she is," whispered another voice; and between the portly forms of the matrons, Monckton saw the glitter of the silver salver, and heard a low voice saying:

"Will you have some more sugar or cream, ladies?"

It was not five minutes since he had heard that voice so free, so sweet, so ringing with innocent mirth, and hardly his own eyes or ears could persuade him that this was the same. He stole a look at Beatrice, more careful now than before not to let her perceive him. Yes, face as well as voice had met a change so great as to be almost incredible. Those blanched cheeks—those lips, straight, hard, and colorless—those eyes, vacant, yet burning—that constrained, mechanical manner! Ah! was this the light-hearted Beatrice he had stolen away from his appointed place to admire?

And then he fell to speculating upon the sudden change. The talk of those women—it must be that; and this Marston Brent was the man she had loved, and from whom she had been separated. A lover's quarrel, which she had thought some day to reconcile, and now he loved another woman! And she, so proud, so sensitive, so—yes, she was jealous in her friendship, as their late difference proved; and still more would she be jealous in her love—not meanly jealous, not desiring to harm or wound either faithless lover or

successful rival, but disdaining a divided reign, resigning all without a struggle the moment a struggle became necessary. This was the temper of the woman whom Monckton read as easily as that morning he had read the old Saxon Bible brought from England by her ancestor.

Passing quietly behind the matrons, and out of the room, he waited in the hall until she should come out, meaning he knew not what, but to comfort her in some way. Presently she came; and even Monckton, practiced socictist as he was, stood confounded before her. The change wrought by those idle words was not more absolute than this—so different from both the other moods; and who but he, who knew the whole, could have distinguished between the girlish glee of the first and the practiced *persiflage* of the present manner?

He looked at her curiously. Yes, her eyes were bright, her lips smiling, her checks flushed, her tone gay and unconcerned, and the slight pallor about her mouth and the slighter tremor of the jesting voice were so faintly marked that no observer less acute than he could have distinguished them.

"And she could hardly forgive me for the transparent lie I told in self-defence. That is woman," said he softly to himself. Beatrice paused before him.

"Why, Mr. Monckton! A drone among the bees! Aren't you afraid of being stung to death?"

"Not while the queen-bee is my friend," said Monckton significantly, and making a show of helping himself from the salver, he detained her long enough to see that the allusion had shaken somewhat her desperate mood.

"I am glad that we were reconciled last night," said she, suffering her face to fall for one moment into an expression of such piteous suffering that all the manhood of Monckton's heart was stirred.

"So am I. I want to see you alone, when all these people are gone," said he.

"For what?"

"I will tell you then. Nothing that will trouble or annoy you—be sure of that."

"Sure? I am sure of nothing now." And with this one cry, wrung from the sharp agony of her heart by his sympathetic tone, Beatrice passed quickly on.

CHAPTER XXIX.
FEEDING THE BEES.

THE afternoon passed much as the morning—the usual conversation, varied by occasional remarks upon the weather, which continued " soft " and threatening for the homeward flight of the bees. Needles, however, flew as actively as tongues, and by five o'clock three bed-quilts, including the famous album-quilt, and four comforters lay completed upon the floor of the guest-chamber : the frames were rapidly dismembered and taken to the garret, the rooms cleared of litter, and the ladies requested to amuse themselves for half an hour, when supper would be served. Complying with this invitation, the elders, after smoothing their black silk or alpaca dresses, and adjusting their cap-ribbons, repaired in squads of two and three to the cast room, to pay their respects to the patriarchs, while the younger women, after devoting a little more time and pains to the renovation of their toilets, collected in groups, gossiping in low voices and with much-suppressed giggle, or hanging around the window to watch the arrival of the gentlemen who had been invited for the supper and evening frolic offered to the bees by way of recompense for the toils of the day.

This supper, as it was justly styled—for certainly it was neither breakfast, dinner, nor tea —was a feast such as never perhaps is spread out of New England, and, alas ! is rarely seen in these degenerate days even in that favored region. It was spread upon two extempore tables extending the length of the dining-room, and crowded upon both sides with plates; for Miss Rachel strongly condemned the inhospitable fashion of " stand-up teas," and declared that if she was to have any thing to eat, she also wished a comfortable place to eat it in, or wanting that, had rather go unfed. Upon these tables, then, were set the dishes, including an enormous round of spiced beef at either end, roasted turkeys and geese as central ornaments, and such trifles as roasted and boiled fowls, hams, tongues, headcheese, and smoked beef between. Varying these meats were plates of smoking-hot fried doughnuts, hot biscuit, brown bread, dipped toast, and short-cakes, and to succeed them upon the bill of fare came pies of every imaginable variety, cake of every hue and description, sweetmeats, pickles, cheese, custards, and fruit.

At a smaller table across the head of the room stood Miss Barstow and Beatrice, pouring cups of coffee and tea, which Nancy smilingly distributed ; while Dr. Bliss, Mr. Monckton, and a few other gentlemen, waited upon the fair guests at the tables, carving the *pièces de resistance*, and urging them upon the delicate creatures whose creed of manners peremptorily inculcated resistance to all such overtures, however much exhausted nature might crave support. This point, however, being thoroughly understood among the jocund swains of these shy Daphnes, was easily disposed of, and somewhat in this fashion :

" Have a piece of the turkey, Miss Welch ?"

" No ; I'm obliged to *you*, Mr. Snell ; I can't get through what I've got on my plate."

" You ha'n't got nothing but a piece of bread, as I see. Better have some turkey, it's first-rate."

" La ! no, I couldn't eat it if I was to take it."

" Well, if you don't, maybe it'll eat you, for one of you's got to suffer, and there it is."

" O my ! Mr. Snell, what be you doing ? Well, then, I shall leave it on my plate."

Which she did not do.

Mr. Monckton, everywhere at once, attentive to every one, rather preferring the older and less attractive of the guests to the younger and prettier ones, proved an invaluable auxiliary, and won for himself more golden opinions than have often crowned more real self-sacrifice.

The admiration excited by his fine face and polished manner among the younger ladies might, indeed, have become dangerous to the peace of their respective swains, had it not been tempered by the information, dropped early in the day by Miss Rachel, and industriously circulated ever since, to the effect that this was " Beatrice Wansted's beau," and therefore not available for any other aspirant. At a later day, Miss Barstow defended herself with considerable skill from the charge of setting a false rumor in circulation, with the remark :

" Well, if he wasn't, he ought to have been, unless my eyes deceived me when I came in with that loaf of cake."

But with all Mr. Monckton's efforts, he never lost sight or thought of the friend whose grief was to him as his own. He saw that the exertions she forced herself to make were too great to be sustained ; he was sure that presently she must fail utterly, either in muscle or nerve—must faint or burst into hysterical weeping; and he well knew how cruelly she would afterward reproach herself for either betrayal.

Watching her with ever-increasing anxiety, he saw her eyes glazing with the inward fever that burned upon her cheeks and lips—wander about the room with the appealing gaze of some timid creature trapped and doomed to death, yet seeking despairingly an impossible escape. He saw her totter and grasp at the back of a chair for support, and in the next moment he was at her side, her hand within his arm.

"One last effort—look about you and try to smile—don't fail now—remember all these people!" murmured he in her ear, supporting her as well as he could without attracting attention, and leading her rapidly from the room. In the hall she tottered, and would have fallen, but with his arm around her waist, he raised and carried her into the deserted parlor and laid her upon a sofa. The cool air and tender twilight of the place revived her, and opening her eyes, she whispered:

"Thank you. I am so glad——"

"I did not mean to let you spoil all your effort by breaking down at the last. You have done nobly."

Beatrice opened her eyes more consciously, and fixed them upon his face. Then she said half defiantly:

"Yes, I have been growing tired for some time."

Mr. Monckton bowed with a face which neither denied nor accepted the proposition, and Beatrice blushed scarlet.

"You should teach me how to say those things better," said she bitterly.

"You need first some food; then warmth and rest," replied Monckton quietly. "Go to your own room, and I will send you something to eat and drink. You have taken nothing since breakfast."

"How do you know?"

"Am I not your friend?"

"I do not like *surveillance*."

"You like nothing to-night; but after eating you will wrap yourself very warmly, and go to sleep—to oblige me."

"Why should I?"

"Because I cannot be happy unless you are at least physically comfortable—because I am your friend."

"Ah!" shivered Beatrice, as if the word had hurt her; and with a sudden, uncontrollable impulse, she laid both her hands in his, and fixed those piteous, eloquent eyes upon his face.

"My friend! Are you indeed my friend?" moaned she. "Then pray that I may die to-night."

"Beatrice! No, child, you shall not be alone through the sharpness of this agony—you could not bear it yet. Come into the other room, and sit beside that saintly old man; the peace and perfectness of his calm will soothe you, and the thought of the battles he has fought and conquered will give you strength for your own. Come."

She suffered him to raise and lead her from the room, just as the advance guard of the devastating army in the dining room appeared at the lower end of the hall, returning upon their footsteps. Monckton quickly opened the door of the east room, entered with Beatrice, and closed it behind them. The grandparents, sitting placidly at either side the fire, with a little tea-table between them, looked up and smiled.

"Miss Wansted is so much fatigued with her hospitable efforts that I persuaded her to come in and rest a little, and, if I might venture, I should suggest to Mrs. Barstow to make her drink a cup of tea."

So speaking, with the easy manner of one who knows his presence and his proposition sure to be favorably received, Mr. Monckton seated Beatrice in a comfortable chair near her grandmother, left the room in search of a cup and saucer, and brought back with them a plate containing some bits of chicken and a piece of bread.

"Now, Miss Beatrice, if you will allow me, I shall recommend as much chicken and bread as you can possibly dispose of; and to show that I really believe in my own prescription, I shall go and bring yet another plate, cup and saucer, and set you a good example. You see, Mrs. Barstow, we have been so busy in waiting upon other people that we have as yet done nothing for ourselves, and I fear this young lady is quite exhausted."

"I haven't a doubt of it," replied the old lady, with emphasis. "It was always the way with her from a child; if she got excited, or tired, or any thing, she wouldn't eat perhaps not a mouthful in a day, and then, of course, she'd break down. She isn't very rugged at the best of times, nor her mother wasn't before her. Somehow, these pretty creters don't seem to wear so well as the plain, homespun ones—like Rachel, say."

"My wife probably wishes to say, sir, that, without unnaturally giving the preference to either of her daughters, she values each for her own peculiar gifts," said the patriarch, somewhat severely; and his wife, stirring her tea, vehemently exclaimed:

"Certain, certain; that is what I meant."

"*The Bees going home.*"

Mr. Monckton, replying to both with a smile that conveyed every thing or nothing, as the receiver chose, left the room, and presently returning with his own supper, drew a chair to the table; and while eating and drinking with unfeigned relish, contrived to insist upon Beatrice's doing the same. When she would take no more, he contrived that her grandmother should suggest her reclining upon the soft, old-fashioned couch, and himself threw a shawl across her feet. Then, returning with a smile her look of gratitude, he set aside the little tea-table, and devoted himself to conversation with the deacon and his wife upon topics which he knew to be especially interesting to his silent auditor.

Thus was he still engaged when the jingle of sleigh-bells announced that the guests were about to depart; and Mr. Monckton feeling that he also owed a duty to Miss Rachel, rose to fulfil it, seeing, with quiet satisfaction, as he passed the couch, that Beatrice had fallen fast asleep.

"Ef there a'n't some hosses' legs broke 'fore we all get home, why *I* lose my guess," remarked the father of a family, standing rather discontentedly upon the doorstep, and examining the gray, watery sky, the plashy and uneven road, and the erratic movements of the sleigh just driving from the door.

"Now, look out, girls, for some fun. If you don't get upset before you reach Four Corners, it won't be my fault!" exclaimed a jolly young farmer, escorting a bevy of shrieking, exclamatory girls to the same point. And half an hour later the last guest had said good-night, and the Old Garrison returned to its usual condition of quiet and repose.

CHAPTER XXX.
BEATRICE LOSES HER FRIEND.

THE rain continued all night, and by morning the roads had become so bad that Aaron Bunce decided that the risk to his horse's legs and the integrity of his coach was greater than any hope of gain in prosecuting his usual journey, and therefore remained quietly at home. Whether Mr. Monckton would have gone with him had he driven to Bloom remains an open question; but at all events, he acquiesced very amiably in the necessity of remaining at Milvor, and divided his time through the day between fireside conversations with the old people, good humored aid to Miss Barstow, who pervaded the house like a revolution, setting right the wrongs of the past, at expense of the peace of the present, and unobtrusive watchfulness of Beatrice, who went languidly about her various duties, and alternated in her mood between fictitious gayety and undisguised depression.

In the evening twilight, he saw her steal softly into the empty parlor, and as quietly followed her.

Beatrice looked round at the opening door with obvious annoyance.

Monckton quietly approached, and seated himself upon the sofa beside her.

"I know that you came here to be alone, and that you regard my presence as an intrusion," said he. "But you will remember that

I told you yesterday, I wished to see you for a few moments alone, and this, my first opportunity, will probably be my last, as I leave Milvor early in the morning."

"We shall be very sorry to lose you," murmured Beatrice, courteous amid all the suffering she controlled so painfully.

"Thanks. You reproached me bitterly a little while ago, Beatrice, for want of candor to you, who have a right, as my intimate friend, to claim my utmost truth. Now, you will be tempted to reproach me for over-much candor, and meddling with affairs which are not for the touch of any hand save your own. Shall I speak, or may I keep silence, and yet preserve our compact of perfect sincerity?"

"Speak," whispered Beatrice, averting her head.

"Well, then, I heard that woman's words. I heard that Marston Brent, in his forest solitudes, is training to his own liking a wife to take the place of a lost love, and that this lost love is no longer regretted. Now, tell me, Beatrice—that is, if you will—was this report the blow that prostrated you so suddenly yesterday?"

"Yes."

"Then you still love this Marston Brent?"

"No."

"Forgive me if I trespass, but I wish to help you. This report may be false—very possibly it is; at any rate, before you fully credit it, allow me to go and ascertain the facts. Will you?"

"What, go to Wahtahree? It is five hundred miles from here."

"If it were five thousand, I would go, if, by going, I could set your heart at rest."

"Then friendship is something better worth than love."

"That is another question, and, besides, you overrate my offer. Travelling is my profession, and I have been quiet too long. Shall I go to Wahtahree?"

"No, not for me."

"But why do you refuse?"

"I do not wish news of Marston Brent."

"But you believe this old wives' tale, and it distresses you."

"I believe it, and I am indifferent to it."

"Indifference does not show like this."

"Mr. Monckton, your inquisition partakes of the nature of torture. You have passed the question ordinary, and reached the question extraordinary."

"You shall not discourage me by a petulance that arises from overwrought nerves. I wish to serve you, even in your own despite. Is it to be done by clearing away this cloud between you and Marston Brent?"

"No, a thousand times no. Were this story proved the most baseless fiction, you can bring us no nearer together. We are separated forever."

"By your will, or his, or circumstance?"

"Both—all—every thing. Must I tell you the whole story before you will let me rest? Six months ago, we two were compelled to settle our future paths through life; he asked me to follow his—I bid him follow mine; both refused, and so we separated, and every step since has led us farther apart. Stop, I have not told you the greatest final barrier: I, setting forth alone, would have faltered and turned back to join him; and he—he bid me hold to my determination, and respect my own word, or he should cease to respect me. What more can be said between us? The shock of hearing that he loved another woman, and already made himself happy with her, was, as you too clearly perceived, a severe one; but it is over now, and it has never for one moment meant regret—that is, not a regret that softens my resolution never to yield one half inch to any temptation such as you place before me."

"The temptation to recall yourself to his mind?"

"Yes, or to recall him to mine. All I desire is to place an impassable barrier between those days and these — to forget Marston Brent and the life we lived together—to blot out the past."

Monckton rose and paced the dusky room up and down, his arms folded, his head bent upon his breast. Beatrice, watching his lithe figure and dark face, passing and re-passing—now shrouded in the gloom filling the farther end of the apartment, now showing in the gray light near the windows—thought of that maniac ancestor of hers who, not yet mad enough to wear the fetters, whose scar she had so often traced upon the beam in the east parlor, may thus have paced the gloomy twilight rooms, fighting down the crowd of visionary enemies who, at the last, conquered him.

"I wonder if I shall go mad too," whispered she, shivering down in the corner of the great sofa.

Just then, Monckton paused before her.

"Beatrice, I have turned coward all at once, I wish to speak to you, and I dare not," said he.

"Afraid of me! Your friend, as you have liked to call me!"

"It is just because I have called you so, and because you have for that name's sake given me your confidence, and showed me the wound you hide from others—just for that reason, I dread to speak."

"What can you mean?"

"I fear lest you should call me false to my own professions, lest you should deem me a traitor, who, having the key of the treasure-casket given him, uses it to possess himself of the jewels he was sworn to guard. Beatrice, you have granted me your friendship, and from that fair height I see the Paradise of your love, and, man like, I wish to attain the best. Have you one word of hope for me?"

But Beatrice, spreading both hands before her, as to ward off a blow, could only cry:

"No, no, no! Do not say it, do not think it! Must I lose you too?"

"Beatrice, you said you desired only to place an impassable barrier between yourself and Brent, to prove to him that you have forgotten him, as he you. How could you do this more surely than by marriage?"

"No, a thousand times no. You were right, Mr. Monckton, when you feared to make this proposition to me, and I was weaker than weak to believe that any man is capable of a pure and disinterested friendship. Oh! why could not you have been content? for already I was turning to this friendship as my comfort and my refuge against utter desolation. I believed in you, and you have deceived me."

"I deceived myself as well, for until within this last four-and-twenty hours I believed as fully as yourself that my feeling was one of purest friendship. Your distress, your helplessness, your unmerited mortification changed every thing at a blow."

"And I have lost my friend, and gained nothing in his place."

"If you would accept him, you have gained a true and tender lover in his place."

"I do not want your love, Mr. Monckton—I have none to give in place of it, no room for it in my heart. I asked you for bread and water, and you offer me spices and wine."

"I have committed a great mistake, and I

felt it to be such even while yielding to the temptation," said Monckton bitterly. "And yet, God knows, Beatrice, I never intended to deceive you."

"Well, well, it is of small importance now. All is alike wearisome and disheartening. Let all pass together."

And Beatrice, with a gesture of sullen despair, turned her face toward the pillow, shutting out sight and sound, and, if she might, all memory of the world whose fair fruit had already turned to ashes upon her lips.

Monckton stood looking at her, the vast pity in his heart gradually absorbing the mortification he had endured, and even the disappointment of his love. Then he said:

"Beatrice, forget this hour. Fancy that, sleeping here in the dusky room, you have dreamed a dream, and, waking, smile and let it pass. Look upon me with the coming daylight as your firm, fast friend, steadfast for the future against even the tempting of his own heart, and true to you through all the chances of both our lives. Beatrice, will you do this?"

"How can I, how can I? How shall I forget, or, remembering, how shall I trust myself not to recall these feelings which you banish now? I should be afraid to speak or look or behave toward you with the unguarded confidence that friendship should permit. I never could be sure that you forget, I never could forget myself."

"Oh! fool that I was, and traitor—not to you alone, but to the whole tenor of my life!" exclaimed Monckton bitterly. "What had I to do with woman's love, and the tender hope and peace that make gardens in the desert of other men's lives? Have I not known it and felt it since consciousness began, and from that day to this have cheated fate by denying my heart all interest in man or woman? And now, one moment of weakness has destroyed the care of years; for, Beatrice, I shall not forget you, I shall not cease to love you while I live."

"Stay! Where are you going? What do you mean?" exclaimed Beatrice, as Monckton turned abruptly from her side.

"I am going to leave you for the moment. To-morrow, I return to the city, and from thence I go —— where the wind goes. Good-by."

"No, no, I cannot bid you good-by thus. I did not know that you felt so deeply, so bitterly——"

6

"Child, do you think a man, in the vigor of his manhood, uncloses his grasp of the one thing he prizes on earth as easily as a girl drops a withered flower? Because this love of mine is the idlest of all follies, it is none the less a real thing to me, and the heart that has never been touched until now will not heal easily over its wound."

"But wait one moment. You said but now that you would forget it, that you would return to yesterday, and be again my true, calm friend, and nothing more. If that were possible?"

"It is not. The effort would be a fresh treachery, and would end as this has done. I might hide the true feeling for months, for years perhaps, but it would always be there, and some day the volcano would burst forth afresh. I am glad your eyes were clear enough to read the proposition rightly."

"Then I have lost my friend, as before I lost my love, and now must set my face toward the end, unguided, unaided, alone."

"Hush, for God's sake, hush! You bring my selfish folly too hideously to light. Had I contented myself with friendship, you never need have uttered that lament. O Beatrice! try to forgive me, for I never can forgive myself."

He hastened from her presence, and Beatrice, alone in the darkness and the gloom, fell upon her knees crying: "God help me! God help me, for I have no other friend!"

CHAPTER XXXI.

A DISAGREEABLE SURPRISE.

THE day before the wedding, arrived Mr. Israel Barstow, and was received with sober joy by his parents, with fluttering cordiality by the bride-elect, and with a feverish eagerness by Beatrice, who, with the instinctive desire most of us have felt to hide our sorrows in a crowd, was longing to return to her city home.

Uncle Israel received all these demonstrations gratefully, and yet in a strangely preöccupied manner very different from his usual hearty fashion, and so marked that each of his friends noticed and put a different construction upon it—his father fearing that his business had become involved; his mother watching for symptoms of illness; Rachel concluding that her own marriage had reäwakened some long-past

tender memories; and Beatrice dreading lest he had learned Mr. Monckton's rejection.

But when at the stroke of nine o'clock, the old people prepared to retire, and their son dutifully rose to bid them good-night, the mystery was suddenly solved.

"Before you go, father and mother," said Mr. Israel Barstow in a strangely confused voice, "I should like to tell you something—something which I hope you will like to know, or at least not take unkindly. The fact is, that I'm going to be married too."

"You married! Why, Israel Barstow, what do you mean? What sort of a girl have you picked out at last?" exclaimed the mother; and Rachel added approvingly:

"'Better late than never;' and you're not so much older than I, Israel."

"Who is it, uncle?" asked Beatrice, with a sudden terror seizing upon her heart.

"Some one you know, and can't but like, after all the time you've been together. Mrs. Charlton, Beatrice," said Mr. Barstow, growing very red in the face, and avoiding his niece's grieved and astonished eyes.

"A Southern woman!" exclaimed the Puritan father.

"A widow!" ejaculated his wife.

"A regular fashionable!" added Miss Rachel; while Beatrice, without remark, removed her hand from her uncle's arm and turned away.

"Well, you, each of you, seem to find a separate fault, and none of you any thing pleasant to say," remarked the lover rather bitterly.

"I hope you have judged wisely for yourself, son, and I trust that your future life will be made a happy one," said the father mildly. "This is a matter in which every mature man should judge for himself. I shall be glad to see the woman you have selected as your wife whenever you see fit to bring her here; and now I will wish you a good-night."

"Of course we shall be glad to see her, and if she makes you a good wife, she shan't complain that her husband's folks don't notice her enough. Why didn't you bring her down with you this time, Israel?"

"Thank you, father and mother. I know you will like her when you see her; but I thought it would be better to come some quiet time after the wedding," said Israel, with an air of relief at having gotten over the announcement. "You see we shall not make such a parade as Rachel and the doctor are doing. We are to be married quietly in church some morning, slip away to Washington for a few weeks, and then settle down at home. Well, good-night. You're not off too, Rachel?"

"Yes, I have to help mother a little about undressing, but I will be back in a minute," said Miss Barstow; and closing the door, she left her brother alone with his niece, who for the first time in her life felt embarrassed in his presence. The constraint was mutual, but Mr. Barstow was the first to overcome it.

"Trix," said he, approaching her as she leaned upon the high back of her grandfather's chair and stared dreamily into the fire, "you seem out of spirits about something. I hope it is not because your friend is going to become your aunt."

"O Uncle Israel! don't!" exclaimed the girl with involuntary dismay.

"Don't what, child?"

"Don't speak of Mrs. Charlton as my aunt."

"But she will be. Of course your uncle's wife will be your aunt, and I don't take it kindly of you, Beatrice, to show this dislike to a step that I am sure will add so much to my happiness, as well as to that of a very charming and very lovely woman."

"Of course, uncle, I have no right to show or to feel disapproval of your action. Only I was so ——"

"Well, so what?" asked Mr. Barstow a little harshly.

"Shocked, I was going to say," murmured his niece.

"That is a strange word to use about such an affair. Pray what is there so shocking in it?"

"Do not be angry with me, uncle—I have not been well since I was here, and I am tired and nervous. Don't mind what I say at all."

And Beatrice, crossing her arms upon the chair-back, leaned her head upon them, and wondered bitterly if so desolate a creature as herself lived.

The expression of the drooping figure was more eloquent than speech, and went straight to the kindly heart of Mr. Israel Barstow, already tingling with a little remorse, as he remembered his openly avowed intention of adopting Beatrice as his daughter and heiress.

"Come, come, my little girl," said he, tenderly drawing her to his embrace, and smoothing with a familiar gesture the beautiful hair he had so often praised. "You are not to suppose this makes any change to you. My house is your house, and I shall insist upon you making a home of it; and as for money, why I fancy there will be enough for all of us, both now and by and by. Nothing will be changed from what it has been, except that you will be nearer and dearer to both of us. She told me to give her love to you, and I have a little note in my pocket that I was to hand you after you had heard the news."

"After I had been prepared," thought Beatrice, and then casting the bitter feeling resolutely behind her, she put her arms about her uncle's neck and kissed him tenderly.

"Dear Uncle Israel," said she, "unless you wish to make me feel like the most ungrateful and degraded creature in the world, never talk so to me again. Did you, could you think that I remembered money, or that I was afraid I should not have all that I ever enjoyed in your house? I do not deserve, I never have deserved your kindness, but at least I am not ungrateful."

"Nor I either, Trix, and it's I that am the debtor. But you'll come home with me, won't you, dear? The fact is, I am a little lonely after all our pleasant times, and miss you sorely. Of course, June has not been with us since you left, and the house seems dull enough."

"Certainly I will come, if you need me, uncle. Mrs. Charlton will not return until after —after you are married, I suppose."

"No, oh! no. She is terribly rigid on all points of propriety, you know."

"Yes," replied Beatrice faintly.

"We are proposing to be married quite soon—in fact, next Thursday, the day after I get home from here, and we start upon our tour the same day," said Mr. Barstow, a little nervously; "and I should be very glad to have you go with us, Trixie, but——"

"Oh! no, uncle," interposed Beatrice hastily, "that would be quite out of the question. Don't think of it!"

"Well, so June said," replied Mr. Barstow innocently. "And I suppose it might be a little odd; but then, you know, we are not very young, or very romantic, either of us, and I thought it would be pleasant—— However, if you will stay quietly in Midas Avenue with Mrs. Grey, and just overlook a little some new furnishing and decorating that is to be done in our absence, I can't tell you how much obliged I shall be. Besides, Trix, you must remember these turtle-doves here will want their nest to themselves, and we shall both of us be better out of the way than in it after to-morrow."

Beatrice did not reply. The bitter waters in which she seemed sinking closed her lips, and had she unclosed them it would be to say :

"Yes, you make your home no home for me, and in the same moment remind me that I am no longer needed or wanted in the only other home open to me."

But she did not say it, and before Mr. Barstow could pursue the subject, Miss Rachel entered, her momentary annoyance at her brother's marriage past, and her tongue voluble with questions, information, sly jests at her own and his late romance, and all the pleasant flutter natural to a bride upon her marriage eve, and a secluded woman in possession of an exciting piece of news.

CHAPTER XXXII.
MRS. CHARLTON'S SECRET.

THE next morning, after her return to town, Mr. Barstow accompanied his niece in a formal call upon Mrs. Charlton.

Beatrice, who had nervously dreaded this visit—more, however, upon Juanita's account than her own—smiled at her own tremors before the first five minutes were over. Mrs. Charlton's perfect breeding answered the exigencies of the occasion better even than sincerity, which involves emotion, and opens the way for awkward situations—edge-tools not to be handled without serious risk to the fingers of the handler. But awkwardness, absurdities, embarrassment, were unknown ingredients in any of Juanita Charlton's combinations, and this interview, apparently so natural and free from all constraint, had been the subject of her deepest thought from the moment it had been announced by Mr. Barstow's hastily-pencilled note.

Toward Beatrice her manner was precisely what it had been before they separated—kind, familiar, a little protecting and indulgent, as far removed from fondness as from formality, and with no shade of consciousness that any new relation existed or was about to exist between them. Toward Mr. Barstow she was, perhaps, a little more familiar than formerly, and there might be perceived a slight tone of

deference and of dependence upon his judgment and opinion, not to be noticed before ; and yet, as Beatrice acknowledged to herself, the keenest satirist could have found no room for a sneer, either in the manner she adopted upon her own part or the manner she permitted upon that of the mature adorer, who evidently only waited her sanction to display his passion in the most decided manner.

At the end of half an hour, Beatrice rose to take leave with a feeling blended of admiration and gratitude toward the woman whose social talent had rendered easy, and even pleasant, an interview that might have been so exceedingly disagreeable.

But, in parting, Mrs. Charlton slightly detained her future niece, while, with a smiling gesture, she intimated to her lover that he was to proceed down-stairs alone.

"I want to see you, Beatrice. I have a message for you."

"From whom ?"

"No matter just yet. Will you wait now, or call again after you set down your uncle? I will go for a little drive with you, if you will take me."

"Certainly," said Beatrice, smiling at thought of how soon carriage and horses would be Mrs. Charlton's own ; and then she hurried down-stairs, only anxious just then to part from her companion, and almost forgetting to wonder what the mysterious message could be.

"Now, Trix, you may take me down-town, if you don't dislike the drive, and then go home, or wherever you choose," said Mr. Barstow, handing his niece into the carriage with the ceremonious politeness natural to him.

"Yes, uncle, we will drive down town, certainly ; and then Mrs. Charlton asked me to come back and take her out for a little. She has something to say to me," said Beatrice, determined to become entangled in no concealments.

"Has she? Poor girl, I suppose she thinks you are not reconciled to the marriage, and she wants to explain a little. You'll be kind and gentle with her, won't you, Trix?"

"I will try, uncle," said Beatrice demurely, and almost laughed aloud at the idea of Mrs. Charlton's needing indulgence and encouragement at her hands, or feeling any desire to apologize for her course.

An hour later, Mr. Barstow's handsome carriage again stopped at the private entrance of the Grandare Hotel; and, in answer to Miss Wansted's card, Mrs. Charlton came rustling down the stairs, elegantly dressed, and with a contented smile upon her lips, presenting the picture of a fresh and care-free woman, in the prime of her life and her beauty.

Beatrice looked at her more kindly than she yet had done, and while she seated herself beside her, said almost affectionately:

"How well you look, Juanita, and how happy! I am so glad if you really love my kind, good uncle."

"*The Grandare Hotel.*"

"I shall make him happy, do not be afraid, Trix; although, confess you have been horribly frightened," laughed Mrs. Charlton; and Beatrice, vexed at feeling the blood burn guiltily in her cheeks, could not reply.

Mrs. Charlton pursued the subject no further, but occupied herself in arranging her draperies for some moments. Then she said abruptly:

"Yes, Beatrice, I have a message for you, and a package, and I promised Mr. Monckton that I would tell you something."

"Mr. Monckton!" echoed Beatrice.

"Yes; he came to see me after you refused him."

"Did he tell you that?" interrupted Beatrice.

"No, dear, not precisely; but I inferred it from what he said, and he did not attempt to deny it."

"You should not have tried to surprise me into acknowledging your inference, however," said Beatrice indignantly.

"Do you think so? Well, he came to see me, and was inclined to revenge the affront he had received from you upon me, because he said the annoyance you experienced, in finding that he and I kept a secret from you, was the primary cause of a quarrel, or a misunderstanding rather, which had separated you. Then he said that he was going abroad directly. The fact is, my dear, the man has a perpetual motion inside him somewhere, and nothing would have kept him long; but he said that he was going, and might never return—should not for a very long time, at any rate; and he thought I owed it to him to set him right with you after he was gone—on the principle of '*De mortuis nil nisi bonum*,' you know—and after a while I consented. But, Beatrice, you must promise me, upon your sacred word of honor, that you will never repeat what I am going to tell you to any living soul."

"It is not necessary to promise so solemnly —I am no tale-bearer," said Beatrice rather contemptuously.

"We none of us know what we are until we are tempted. A remark trite perhaps, but none the less true," said Mrs. Charlton sententiously. "And what I am going to tell you is, as somebody said of his head, not valuable to the world at large, but very important to the owner. So, promise."

"Very well. I promise not to betray your confidence," said Beatrice coldly.

And Juanita looked at her with a malicious smile as she replied:

"Remember, you have promised, and I hold you to it through every thing—so here is my story:

"While Mr. Charlton lived, I met my first love."

"Excuse me. You mean to say that Mr. Charlton was your first love?" asked Beatrice, a little perplexed.

"Not at all," replied her companion with admirable coolness. "What I mean to say is, that about six months after I became Mrs. Charlton I met Major Strangford, an officer in the United States army, and that he was my first love. Now, Beatrice, it is by no wish of my own that I am telling you this story. Had you been a confiding, simple-hearted woman, who would have accepted Mr. Monckton's assurance that the mystery between him and myself was nothing to you, I should have been spared the necessity of telling and you of hearing any thing farther; but since your own suspicions and Mr. Monckton's doctrine of compensation have forced this issue upon us both, let us accept it manfully, and with as few womanish complications of deceit, spite, and malice as possible; which episodical piece of advice please take in reply to the contemptuous smile and look of indignant virtue with which you have already favored me, and which I beg may not be repeated."

"I can turn my face away if its expression annoys you," said Beatrice quietly.

"Try, instead, to cultivate a wider scope of moral vision, and look beyond the blue laws in which you have been bred," retorted Mrs. Charlton. "However, the story is to be told, and I shall fulfil my compact with Mr. Monckton, however you receive the communication: Major Strangford and I then fell in love at first sight, if you will pardon the platitude—which in this case, however, was any thing but a platitude, for in both our hearts throbbed the fiery blood of the South, and both our temperaments were of the vivid and sympathetic order which recognizes destiny at a glance, and follows its dictates with blind confidence. But crime is a stupidity, and loss of social position is worse than annihilation. We recognized this truth, and separated. A few months later, he married; his heart of fire and brain of quicksilver were incapable of quiet inaction, and he could not wait. A year later, I was a widow. He heard of it, and travelled a thousand miles from his distant frontier post to see me. Fancy that meeting! No, you cannot fancy it; it is not in you to imagine the fury of remorse, despair, hopelessness, which raged in both our hearts. That one short day eat the pith out of my life and killed him, although we neither of us felt then the full force of the ruin that had come upon us. We parted once more, but now more hopefully than the first time, for we both believed that the volcano force of our passion must conquer every obstacle, and that could we but wait, fate would once more grant us the possibility of bliss."

"That is to say, that Major Strangford's

wife might die, as Mr. Charlton had already died," said Beatrice, her face resolutely turned from her companion.

"Yes, if you choose to put it so coarsely. Too restless to remain at his post, the Major resigned his commission, and went abroad with the woman he had married. She had always been delicate in health, and now showed symptoms of a decline. The Major was a man of high-toned Southern honor, and he omitted no measure for her recovery ——"

"She probably had discovered his relations with you," suggested Beatrice in the same resolutely calm voice.

"Very possibly," replied Mrs. Charlton with composure. "At any rate, she sickened, and the Major's constant letters to me spoke always of her failing health. They went to the East, and after that I knew nothing, for his letters failed to reach me. I became desperate with anxiety; and the necessity of concealing my anxiety—for it was this very last winter, while I was here with you—and the appearance of gayety, at least, must be kept up, or I did not earn the home your uncle was giving me.

"Then came the night when you found Mr. Monckton speaking to me, and your mad jealousy forced on this explanation. He brought me a package and a letter—just a few lines, but oh! what wealth would buy them from me? For, in the interior of Persia, his wife had died; he had buried her, and was hastening home to me, when a sudden fatal sickness seized him. He knew it was fatal from the first, and he wrote with his dying hand these lines to me, and another note to Mr. Monckton, an old friend, or rather travelling companion, who knew all our sad story, although a stranger to me. He sent him the amulet which I had hung around his neck at our last parting, and the letter, bidding him break the news to me gently, and to shield me from observation and suspicion. He would not send to me directly, because he feared to compromise me. You saw Monckton hang the amulet around my neck, and thought it was a love token—so it was, so it is, and shall go with me to my grave; but it is a token of a love in which neither he nor you have any part—a love that defies death, as it has already defied life, and exists to-day in all the fervor, all the omnipotence of its earliest maturity."

" And you have engaged to marry my uncle!" exclaimed Beatrice, turning her horror-stricken and indignant face full upon the speaker.

Mrs. Charlton shrugged her shoulders.

" Why not?" asked she. " I give him all he asks or can appreciate—my society, my beauty, my social position ; he does not expect love, and I shall not fail in the duty and attention of a wife toward him. It is his right by purchase."

" Have you, or will you tell him this story?"

" Did you ever know me to commit a stupidity?"

" If you do not, I will."

" You promised me that you would not, if you will take the trouble to remember."

" Oh ! but this is infamous ! You cannot do it !"

" We shall see. But what do you mean, after all ? Where is the infamy ?" asked Mrs. Charlton patiently.

" Where ? Why in marrying one man with your heart filled with love for another ; in deceiving and insulting so grossly a generous heart that has given itself to you, believing that it received yours in return."

And Beatrice, trembling, pale, almost choking with emotion, fixed her clear eyes upon Mrs. Charlton's unflinching face.

The latter smiled disdainfully.

" Your argument is apt. Mr. Barstow has paid the price of a heart—and has a right to expect a heart—for that is the law of trade, and he is a trader. But I am no defrauder ; Mr Barstow will receive at my hands all, and more than all that he has bargained for. I have told him that the fire and passion of love were not to be expected from him to me, or me to him ; I have promised him the affection, duty, and respect of a wife, and I will give them to him. What right have you or any one to interfere ?"

" No right, perhaps, and yet I must speak. How can I see this go on, and keep silence ?" exclaimed Beatrice in great agitation. Mrs. Charlton looked at her unmoved.

" Again, I say, I do not understand your horror, or your desire to annoy and bore your uncle with this story," said she. " Major Strangford is dead, and the memory I retain of him lies too far below the surface to be reached by any plummet in Mr. Barstow's hand. Let it sink out of your sight also, and forget what I have said to-day, as I shall certainly appear to forget it myself."

Beatrice looked at her doubtfully.

" Do you still wear this amulet he sent you ?" asked she.

" Certainly."

" And will continue to do so after you are married ?"

" Until I die."

" That in itself is enough to condemn you, for it shows that you intend to perpetuate the memory you affect to bury. Can you retain the gift, and forget the giver ?"

" I never announced the slightest intention of forgetting the giver," said Mrs. Charlton coldly. " I only said that his memory would remain buried in my heart."

" With his epitaph blazoned upon your bosom," said Beatrice bitterly.

" You become epigrammatic, which shows that you are losing your temper," said Mrs. Charlton.

Beatrice looked at her in astonishment. " How can a woman speak of a life-long love, and yet be utterly heartless ?" asked she, half aloud.

" Love is a passion, and what you call heart is emotion, prejudice, weakness. The two are seldom united," said Juanita, in precisely the tone of good-humored patience with which she had hitherto instructed Beatrice in the science of society. But this conversation, and perhaps her own experience of the last week, had changed the neophyte to an adept, and she answered coldly :

" Our theories differ so essentially upon most points, that it is not best for either to try to convert the other. The only question we have to solve at present is, what action you will adopt toward my uncle."

" I have already solved that question," said Mrs. Charlton in the same tone. " I shall marry your uncle, and I shall behave toward him with kindness and propriety. He will be very happy, and never miss what he never had, or expected to have, or could comprehend, if it were given him. The revelation you would make to him, in the way you would make it, would nearly destroy his present happiness, and give him no other. As for the rest, ' let the dead past bury its dead,' and let you and I be good friends, and harmonious companions, as it is our mutual interest to be. And, above all things, Beatrice, never refer by word or look, or silence, to this conversation between us two. Close the chamber I have shown you, lock the door and let the ivy grow over it—or, if you like it better, hide it behind the French flowers, the spangles, the gaslight, and drop-curtain of society. At any rate, forget it."

"Why did you ever show me this chamber?"

"I promised Mr. Monckton that I would do so!"

"How did he extort this promise?"

"Extort?"

"Excuse me. How did he persuade you to make it?"

"Excuse me in turn, but I never promised that I would tell that, and I do not intend to do so."

"It is not my affair, certainly," said Beatrice, pulling the check-rein, and through the speaking-tube giving James directions to return to the Grandare Hotel.

"But here is something which is your affair," said Mrs. Charlton, drawing from beneath her muff and placing in Beatrice's hand a packet, closely sealed, and addressed to herself.

"Mr. Monckton left it with me to give you after this conversation," said she. "And now tell me if this chilly spring weather is not detestable?"

Beatrice bowed her head, and Mrs. Charlton kept up a cheerful monologue, until, at the door of her hotel, she alighted with the remark that she had enjoyed her drive exceedingly.

<hr>

CHAPTER XXXIII.

A GRAND CLIMAX.

So soon as she was alone, Beatrice opened with some curiosity and a little apprehension the package Mrs. Charlton had left in her hands. Beneath the closely-sealed envelope of wrapping-paper appeared a box of ebony, inlaid with gold, in a rich arabesque pattern. A little golden key lay upon the top, and Beatrice, hastily applying it to the lock, raised the cover, and sat appalled at the sight before her. Upon a cushion of white satin lay a set of Oriental turquoise enriched with pearls, a crescent and band for the hair, a chain of stars for the neck, and bracelets of the same device, with golden pendants wrought in various cabalistic forms.

"Oh! I cannot take them!" exclaimed Beatrice aloud; and just then perceived a little folded slip of paper among the jewels. Opening it, she read:

"I know that you will feel remorseful, because, even without fault of your own, you have done me an injustice by your suspicions; and, later on, have dealt me a blow whose wound will endure for years. To natures like yours, there is no comfort like reparation and atonement. I offer you the opportunity for both in this set of trinkets, brought from India by me for the unknown lady of my love. If you will take them and wear them, I shall feel that we are friends once more, and that you have forgiven yourself and me for the injury that friendship has sustained. Do not refuse me this amends; and believe me always while I live,

"Yours, most faithfully,
"REGINALD MONCKTON."

"Mine, most faithfully," murmured Beatrice; "and the man whom I loved so well that I sacrificed pride, delicacy, resolve to him, was faithful half a year, and then took comfort in another woman! I wish I had loved Reginald Monckton as I did Marston Brent."

And then—for such is woman—she examined the jewels, appreciating their beauty, recognizing the rare purity of the pearls, the deep color of the turquoise, and the unique style of the setting.

Monckton, wily even in his sincerest display of emotion, had struck the right chord in the manner of offering his gift. Had it been laid at her feet as a tribute to her charms, or as the memorial of an absent and despairing lover, Beatrice would have refused it without question or regret; but Monckton bid her accept and wear the jewels in token that she repented the involuntary injustice she had done him, and she frankly complied with his request, feeling, as he intended, that the obligation was from her to him.

But when she reached home, Beatrice laid aside both gift and giver, and sought painfully and eagerly for her own path of duty in the matter of Mrs. Charlton's marriage with her uncle. True, her promise bound her from repeating the secret she had learned; but could she allow the marriage to go on without opposition? Could she see her single-hearted, generous, confiding uncle blindly walk into the snare this woman, disappointed in her love, had laid for him, or rather for his worldly advantages?

These were questions that Beatrice found herself unable to answer, and she still sat pondering there in the early twilight when a slow step ascended the stairs, and Mr. Chappelleford appeared at the door of the drawing-room. Beatrice rose to meet him with some embarrassment, for in her thoughts she had unconsciously linked him with his niece, and felt as if her unfavorable opinion must be written upon her face.

The cynic was in his least cynical mood; and the first greetings over, began a conversation upon the topics of the day, in which, while affecting to despise them, he always contrived to be well informed.

But Beatrice, although polite and cordial, found it impossible to interest herself in what he was saying—a fact soon perceived by Chappelleford, who closed his account of a recent political pageant with the remark:

"You offer poor encouragement, Miss Wansted, for me to assume cap and bells in your behalf. You remind me of some story I have read, where Rowena, or Ermengarde, or Yolande says to the zany who tries to charm away her love-sick melancholy: 'Go to, fool! Thy jesting is sadder than a sermon, and I will have thee whipped for a false fool, who knows not even folly!'"

"Your mediæval beauty was unreasonable; but you say she was suffering from a disease I never yet experienced. Perhaps that was one of the symptoms," said Beatrice, a little vexed at the suggestion.

"What! love-sickness? No, I did not suppose you were love-sick," said Mr. Chappelleford with composure.

"Thank you; I should be very sorry if you had."

"No, your complaint is an ocular one," pursued the philosopher.

"What do you mean, Mr. Chappelleford?"

"Why, like a young kitten, you are just getting your eyes open, and the operation is a painful one."

"I suppose I must accept the kitten, since you just compared yourself to a fool," said Beatrice, smiling languidly.

"I am sorry for you, but it is what we all go through, sooner or later; and when it is once over, you have no idea how comfortable you will find yourself."

"Please tell me, without metaphor, exactly what you mean, and I then will answer you."

"What I mean? Why, that you are a good deal shocked to find that Juanita Charlton has decided to sell herself to your uncle, and that he is idiot enough to pay his hard-won treasure for so damaged a piece of goods. You are also shocked at the sudden downfall of the fine cloud-palace of friendship in which you had elected to dwell with Mr. Monckton, and you are a little desolate in losing the stimulus of

his presence. Also, you are dissatisfied with your own prospects, as a supernumerary in the houses of Mrs. Israel Barstow and Mrs. Wyman Bliss. Finally, there is the old grievance of the faithless lover, whom you believe you no longer love, but whom you do not forget. Now, every one of these disappointments and annoyances would have been foreseen and prevented had your eyes been open wide enough to see their approach. I could have warned you of several of them."

"Which?" asked Beatrice faintly.

"Why, Mrs. Charlton's designs upon Mr. Barstow, and the termination of your friendship with Mr. Monckton."

"Why did you not warn me?"

"Twenty years ago, I should probably have done so, and have made enemies of four persons with whom I do not wish to enter into such intimate relations as enmity. Now I am wiser."

"A selfish wisdom, it seems to me, that prevents your saving the man for whom you profess friendship."

Beatrice paused, perceiving to what discourtesy her impulsive remark was leading. Mr. Chappelleford grimly smiled.

"Saving him from my niece, you were about to add," said he. "The remark is frank and youthful. But, in the first place, I profess friendship for no man; and in the next, I am by no means certain that it is a bad thing for Mr. Barstow to marry Mrs. Charlton. He gives money and a settled position in exchange for beauty, wit, and a facility in society, which he mistakes for talent. Nobody says any thing about love, faith, or sincerity—the myths upon which your theories of marriage are based. The parties to the bargain are content—why should you or I grumble?"

"If the matter is fairly understood by both, perhaps we should not," said Beatrice, hesitatingly. "But I fear that my uncle is deceived."

"In the matter of Mr. Monckton's communication from Major Strangford?" asked Chappelleford coolly; and then, as Beatrice, coloring scarlet with surprise, sat blankly looking at him, he added, with a laugh:

"Oh! yes, I know it all. I knew of the affair from its commencement, and warned Juanita that I should not permit her to make a family scandal, even if she chose to throw away the worldly position, which is the only thing in the world for which she cares. Then, when you took her confidences with Monckton to heart, I compelled her to repeat them to me. She is always submissive in my hands, because I neither admire nor love her, and do understand her thoroughly. She told me the whole, and had already promised me to set you right upon the matter when Monckton returned from his fruitless visit to Milvor, and she was shrewd enough to make a separate bargain with him. He used a bribe, and I a threat, and she was equally open to both. Neither would have succeeded with you, but hers is a meaner nature."

"Is it right that you should tell me what the bribe and the threat were?" asked Beatrice.

"Why not? I threatened to lay the matter before both Mr. Barstow and you, and Monckton gave her a set of jewels. The provident fellow came home from the heart of India, resolved to find a wife, and not knowing whether she would be blonde or brown, brought a set of turquoise and a set of garnet as his betrothal present. You disappointed his hopes, and Juanita failed to secure him, but he gave you two his two gifts, and has gone away fancying himself heart-broken. That is the way the plans men lay are apt to terminate."

"How do you know every thing?" asked Beatrice, looking in terror at the cold, impassive face of this man, who, without emotion, sympathy, or curiosity, succeeded in reading the lives of those about him like an open book.

"How do I? Oh! my eyes were opened a good many years ago, as yours are opening to-day. After the process is complete, you also will see what is about you."

"I do not wish to, if, like you, I am to find deceit, selfishness, and folly upon every side," said Beatrice sadly. "What do you leave me to found any confidence upon?"

"Not men, certainly, nor yet women," replied the cynic. "Put them out of the question once for all, and turn your mind to more important matters. Read Hugh Miller, and found your confidence upon the 'Old Red Sandstone;' read Ruskin, and expand your imaginative powers in following out his theories; read Hegel, and strengthen your thinking powers by trying to follow his; and then go to Nature, and you will find sympathy and healing in her manifold forms of beauty. The trees will not deceive you; the sky and water profess no constancy; the stars ask not your secrets, nor reveal their own. These are the only safe friends, and to these you yet will turn for comfort."

He spoke with an earnestness that carried conviction, and Beatrice raised her melancholy eyes appealingly to his.

"These are your friends, I see it," said she, "Bring me to them, teach me how to know them. It is so desolate to set forth all alone upon a new path. O Mr. Chappelleford! if you would say that you were my friend, I would believe you."

"Foolish child! Have I not this moment finished telling you that human friendship is naught, and less than naught? and for answer you beg me to help you cheat yourself yet once more. Have you not just tried the experiment with this man Monckton, and failed most signally? There is no such thing as friendship between man and woman—either it is companionship founded on mutual interests, or it is mere acquaintanceship, or it is a Jesuitical love—sure, sooner or later, to throw off the mask and claim its reward. Monckton's was of this nature, and I knew it from the first. No, Miss Wansted, I will not pretend to be your friend, for it would be a pretence without rational foundation; but I will, if you wish it, be your tutor, your adviser, your companion. I will introduce you to those friends of mine of whom I spoke but now, and teach you how to know them. I will give you fruit of the tree of knowledge, instead of the husks upon which you so far have fed, and I will help you climb the heights of thought and reason, where alone peace dwells serene. Shall I do this?"

"Yes, yes!" cried Beatrice, with feverish eagerness. "All that I thought to find in life has failed me: love, friendship, the world—they are all alike hollow and deceitful. Give me knowledge, teach me philosophy, lead me to those cold heights where you find peace—all else I leave behind."

"Come, then, poor, ruffled, storm-beat bird—poor, lost child, come and be my pupil, my charge, and at least I will never deceive you," said Chappelleford, with a most unwonted tenderness shining in his eyes, ordinarily so sad and so severe. "But, Beatrice, to make this companionship practicable, you must become my wife. I shall not continue to visit familiarly in this house after my niece becomes its mistress, nor could I see you elsewhere. You must come to me in the only manner in which man and woman are allowed to live together."

"Marry you, Mr. Chappelleford!" exclaimed Beatrice in dismay. "But I do not love you —I cannot!"

"Have I asked you to love me? Have I professed to love you? Have I ever alluded to any such weak and stupid delusion upon either side? Is not the very foundation of the education I propose for you an emancipation from all such romantic credulity as you now evince? What I wish is to make a rational being out of a woman; and, to do this, the woman must be directly and constantly under my influence, and this can only be effected by making her my wife. This is my motive, and yours is immunity from deception, increased knowledge, and a content—or at least a calm —infinitely superior to what you call happiness. You see I do not deceive you. What is your answer?"

"I will marry you, Mr. Chappelleford, just as, under other circumstances, I would enter a convent."

"Yes, either course is the refuge of a sick heart—the one dictated by reason, the other by superstition," said Mr. Chappelleford.

Beatrice made no reply; and so, in the deepening twilight sat the betrothed pair— she, her head bent upon her breast, her hands idly folded in her lap, gazing drearily into the glowing coals—he, shading his eyes with his hand as he leaned upon the chimney-piece, and steadfastly regarded her.

So passed a half hour, and then Mr. Barstow entered, to whom spoke Vezey Chappelleford half kindly, half in disdain of himself and all men:

"Mr. Barstow, I have given you my niece in marriage, and now compensate myself by taking yours. Miss Wansted kindly promises to become my wife."

"Why, why, Trix! this isn't true, surely! Have you promised to marry Chappelleford, Trix?"

"Yes, uncle, and shall keep the promise," said Miss Wansted in a voice of icy calm; and rising, she left the room before another word was spoken.

CHAPTER XXXIV.
THE OMEN IN THE AIR.

High above the crests of the hemlocks hung the June sky, deep, clear, and soft; the heat of noon-day brought out the balsamic odors

of fir and spruce; just within reach of eye and ear the full-bosomed Sachawissa sang her song of life and love, as she hastened to her marriage with the sea; all sights and sounds spoke harmoniously of free and joyous existence, and of fullest content in being; and man, God's last and greatest work, might well be joyous when all beneath him was so glad.

So thought Marston Brent, standing with bowed head beneath the arches of the wood, and feeling a new life stirring in the heart that so long had lain cold and dead within him.

"When all else feels God's beneficent kindness, why should we two be miserable?" said he aloud. "In some way, we shall yet be brought together, and without falsehood to each other or to ourselves. Then comes happiness, which shall compensate a hundred-fold for all these weary months, or even years. I feel it in the air to-day that I am to receive good news of my darling—none the less mine that her mistaken will divides us for the present. In all the manifold and unexpected developments of life, one is approaching which shall bring us again together—— "

"Mr. Brent!"

"What, Comfort, is that you? Here am I."

Down the long arches of the wood came running a light girlish figure, a bright and blooming face, two eager eyes searching for him, and a voice breathless with delight and haste.

"O Mr. Brent! Richard has come home, and he got you a newspaper, and I knew you would be so glad, for you were wishing this morning you had told him to try and get one, and none of us supposed he would. So I ran right out to find you, and bring it."

"Thanks, my little Comfort. You are always ready to run when you think you can do me a service," said Brent kindly, and Ruth, looking frankly up into his face, said with a smile:

"Of course I am glad to do a little for you who do so much for me."

"Nonsense, child, and nonsense again. Aren't you my Comfort?" said Brent, half jestingly, half tenderly, and seating himself upon a felled hemlock-trunk beside the path, he opened his week-old newspaper with the hungry haste of a man who has been too long divided from the world, whose affairs are still his own.

Ruth—if this blithe, rosy, smiling maiden,

whose every motion spoke health and light-heartsl content, could indeed be the Ruth whom we last saw a pallid and tremulous fugitive from a horrible accusation—Ruth went singing through the wood, stopping now to pluck a berry or a flower, now to mimic the strains of linnet or blackbird in the tree-tops, now to drink in the beauty of the day and scene. At last, when she thought he might be ready to speak to her, she returned to Brent. He still was sitting as she had left him upon the hemlock-log, the paper hanging idly from one hand, the other supporting his chin, while his eyes were fixed upon the ground with such a look of white despair as Ruth had never seen in her life before.

"*He was sitting on the hemlock log.*"

Half terrified, half eager to console her friend, the girl drew near and stood beside him. He neither moved nor spoke.

"Mr. Brent!" said she softly.

No answer, for, indeed, he had not heard her; and the child, growing bold in her alarm, seated herself beside him, and laid a hand upon his arm.

"Please tell me what has happened," said she tremulously. Brent started, and raised such wild, fierce eyes to hers that she shrunk from his side, and then crept yet closer to it.

"Something has happened! Oh! tell me what it is, dear, dear Mr. Brent," moaned she.

"Something! Well, yes; it might be called something here in the woods, although in the world, I suppose, it would be called nothing," replied Brent huskily; and then he snatched the paper from the ground, laid his finger upon a paragraph, and thrust it before Ruth's tearful eyes.

"Read that!"

She meekly obeyed. It was this:

"On Wednesday last, Vezey Chappelleford, Esq., the distinguished antiquarian, philologist, and historian, was united in marriage to Miss Beatrice Wansted, niece of our respected fellow-citizen, Israel Barstow, Esq., at whose house the strictly private ceremony took place. The happy pair, after a breakfast proportioned rather to the means of the host than the number of the guests, went directly on board the Ethiopia, and sailed within the hour for Europe, and still more distant points. It is to be hoped that Mr. Chappelleford will enrich the public mind with the fruit of his travels, either through the press, or from the rostrum, soon after his return, and that all foreigners not yet converted to faith in the preëminent loveliness of American ladies may have an opportunity of seeing this fair bride, and judging from her as a specimen."

Ruth read this paragraph attentively, and laid the paper down with a puzzled face.

"Did you know Mr. or Mrs. Chappelleford?" asked she.

"Did I know her? Child! I had no more doubt that she and I should stand together hand in hand before God's throne, if not before His earthly altar, than I had that we both breathed. I never once dreamed that she could do this thing. O Beatrice! How little one life seems in comparison with the eternity I had hoped to pass with you, and now, now—— O my God! I cannot think!"

And starting to his feet, Brent raised to Heaven a face so wild, so ghastly, so despairing, that the tender girl watching him hid her own in terror, while he, glaring about him for a moment as doubtful where to turn for refuge, dashed away into the wood, and was presently lost to sight and hearing.

Ruth watched him so long as she could follow his course, and then taking the crumpled paper from the ground, she folded it carefully, and hid it in her pocket.

"He will come back after a while, and I will wait for him," said she softly, and sat patiently until he slowly approached through the forest, his bent figure, painful steps, and haggard face showing the work that years should not have done.

He came straight toward the place where

she sat, and yet had so forgotten her presence there, that he started back in recognizing it.

"I was looking—— I left a paper here," said he in a low voice.

Ruth handed it to him, glancing sadly, yet not inquiringly, into his face as she did so.

"I thought you would come to look for it here, and I waited to give it to you," said she.

"Thank you. Oh! yes; I remember you were here."

And Brent was turning away when a new idea crossed his mind, and he returned.

"Comfort!"

"Yes, sir."

"You like to help me, to make me happy, do you not?"

"You know that I do, sir. I like it better than any thing."

"That is the reason I call you Comfort. Well, dear little girl, remember that you never can do half so much to help me in any other way as you can by keeping this secret—what you know of it."

"I will keep it, sir, and I should have kept it, if you had not spoken."

"I do not doubt you would, Comfort, I do not doubt it, if you saw that it was a secret, but I did not know that you understood. I cannot tell you any thing more than you saw for yourself; but I dare say you guess the whole. It is not a thing of which I shall ever speak after this moment, and it is a thing I shall never forget. But we will appear to forget it, both of us, and perhaps you will—it is nothing to you, but to me——"

And he wandered down the path muttering to himself—the broken tone, the uneven gait, the crushed look of the whole proud figure, more like those of some luckless fugitive from a torture-chamber than the free, noble bearing of Marston Brent.

Ruth rose, and slowly followed until she saw him close beside the shanty, and then she turned back a few paces into the wood.

"O Beatrice Wansted, Beatrice Chappelleford, how I hate and detest you?" cried she, clenching her slender hands, and shaking them in the air.

"What are you, or any woman in the world, compared with such a man as this! And he said it was nothing to me, and that I should soon forget it, and he told me not to betray his secret! How little he knows me, after all! But I hope that hateful woman will have to suffer yet, two pains for every one she has given him to-day! I hope she will, and if I could give them to her, I would."

And then Ruth, her mind slightly relieved of its burning anger and grief, returned slowly to the house, where Zilpah had long since prepared a reprimand for her.

CHAPTER XXXV.
ALMOST A DEATH-BLOW.

THE next morning, Ruth watched for Brent's appearance with an anxiety almost impossible to conceal, but to her infinite relief, the night had brought him at least the semblance of peace, and although a little paler, a little brighter eyed, and graver than his wont, there was nothing in his looks or his demeanor that would have attracted the attention of an observer.

Breakfast over, he followed his men out of doors.

"You will finish that clump at the east side of the hill where you were yesterday," said he, "and I will come along too."

"That's right, Cap'n. The fellers work just twice as smart when you're 'round," said Richard aside; and Ruth, creeping up at the other hand, softly asked:

"May I go too?"

"What, into the woods, Comfort? Why, yes, if you like, and Zilpah will spare you," said Brent, looking kindly down at the girl, who darted back into the house.

"I am going out for a little while, Zilpah—Mr. Brent said that I might—and I will do my work when I come back; you can leave it all for me," said she, snatching her hat from the wooden peg where it hung, and hurrying away before the old woman could remonstrate.

"Well, I declare!" exclaimed she, following as far as the door, and standing there with arms akimbo, to watch the procession of oxen and drags—accompanied by the lumberers in the picturesque costume of the woods, and followed by Brent's stately form, with Ruth tripping lightly beside him—as it would slowly in among the trees, which presently hid all but now the glimpse of a scarlet shirt, now the glint of an axe-blade, or the polished balls upon the oxen's horns, now Brent's towering head, or his Comfort's floating skirts.

"Well, I declare!" repeated Zilpah. "Trapseing off to the woods again, and leaving me with all the work to do! And Marston won't let any one say a word to her, more than if she was a feather and would blow away in the wind. I don't see what Paul Freeman's thinking on, if he cale'lates to have the charge of her, to let her be following round after Brent this fashion. Any way, I didn't stretch it much, only just a leetle mite, when I wrote Nancy that they was going to be married some time, for I shouldn't be took aback any day to hear that it was so. She's most fifteen, and my aunt Polly Jane's sister was married when she was sixteen. All I hope is, them stuck-up Barstow folks and Beatrice Wansted heard of it. That's all I want."

So Zilpah went back to the dishes, and the procession, winding through the wood, fresh

"*Brent's stately form, with Ruth tripping beside him.*"

with the cool purity of the summer morning, came at last to the hillside, already half stripped of timber, where the day's work had been appointed. The ground above was strewn with felled timber, chips, branches, and sheets of bark, left as the men had abandoned them upon the previous evening; and while a certain number of choppers attacked fresh trees, others applied themselves to peeling those already felled, cutting them into lengths, and hauling away the logs to be piled beside the principal road of the forest, there to lie until

the next winter's snow afforded facility for sledding them to the river.

Ruth watched all these operations with interest—always, however, keeping close to Brent, who superintended every thing with a sharp decision of manner which induced from Richard the remark :

"Tell you what, Paul, the old man's wide awake to-day. There a'n't no chance for shirking, I can tell you."

"I don't know as any one wants to shirk," replied Paul rather sullenly. "I don't, for one ; nor I don't want to be drove round as if I was a nigger, neither."

"Seems to me you got out o' bed wrong foot foremost, young one," replied Richard good-naturedly ; and shouldering his axe, he walked from the tree he had just felled to the next one, a monster hemlock, three feet in diameter and at least two hundred in height.

"Four, maybe five market-logs in you, old fellow, if there's an inch," remarked Richard, softly whistling as he measured the giant with his eye, and calculated its contents.

"Here, Jebson," continued he, calling to his especial mate, who was still busy with the last tree. "You come and peel a section of bark off this thumper, while I fix a bed for him to tumble into."

Jebson, obedient to the call, approached, silently measured the tree as the other had done, and then shortening his keen axe in his hand, cut a ring through the bark of the hemlock close to its roots, and another four feet above it ; the next movement was to connect these by a perpendicular line ; and then throwing down his axe, Jebson took up a spud, an instrument resembling a chisel, but curved to fit the boll of a tree, and proceeded to loosen the bark, which he did so nicely that it presently fell, an entire sheet, beside the tree, and was carefully removed to a pile of similar sheets close at hand.

Richard meantime had felled and laid side by side a couple of middling-sized birch-trees, growing near the hemlock, and now so disposed as to receive it in its fall and prevent its imbedding itself in the earth, as it otherwise would have done.

"All ready now Jebson," said Richard briefly, and swinging his axe high above his head, he buried it in the bared trunk of the hemlock ; as he withdrew it, Jebson's fell ; and so with swift alternation, the murderers, as Ruth mentally styled them, pursued their work until the slender tip of the hemlock, lying like a finger upon the sky, trembled visibly, and a shiver ran through the stately trunk to its remotest plumy branch.

"Hold on, Jebson! She wants trimming a little; we aren't falling her square on the bed," said Richard, pausing to wipe his streaming brow and glance anxiously aloft. Then while Jebson waited, the experter woodsman cut deeper into the heart of the tree in the desired direction, hesitated, looked aloft, and then dropping his axe-head to the ground, stood leaning upon the handle, attentively regarding the tree, whose topmost branches, still thrilling as if with their death-agony, slowly began to describe upon the cloudless sky the first line of the great arc in which they were to sweep earthward; at the same moment, the sharp sound of rending the fibres knit by years of deliberate growth became audible, and its heart-strings snapped at last, the great tree came plunging and crashing to the earth, tearing through the branches of such smaller growth as stood in its path, and falling fairly at the last upon the bed prepared for it.

"A good stick of timber that, Cap'n; five good markets if there's one, as I said before I struck it," said Richard, viewing his work complacently, while Ruth, hardly yet able to draw a full breath after the emotion of the scene, came timidly forward, and looked at the great stump with its fresh-cut wounds.

"Poor tree! It had been so long growing, and maybe knew that it was growing, and now it is nothing but wood for burning," said she in a low voice.

"Not wood for burning, Ruthie," said Paul Freeman, who, with a spud in one hand and an axe in the other, was approaching the tree on the same side with herself. "These hemlocks are cut full as much for the bark as any thing else; they use it at the tannery, you know, and the logs are floated down the river and sawed into boards. It wouldn't pay to cut such timber as this for firewood."

"And what part do you do, Paul?" asked the girl, feeling with a little remorse that she had not been as attentive of late to her old friend as he had a right to expect.

"I'm a peeler. First come the fellers—that's the ones that cut down the tree, you know—and then the peelers cut the bark into lengths and peel it off, just as Jebson did before he and Richard felled this tree; and then the hewers cut the trunk into logs about fifteen foot long; and then the teamsters carry off logs and bark, and skid them up, ready to be skaled off next winter."

"Yes, I have seen almost all those things done this morning," said Ruth, "and I always wanted to come out with the men before, but Zilpah never would let me. I only come now because I asked Mr. Brent first."

"You might have come with me most any time," said Paul jealously, and just then Brent approached the spot, saying:

"Comfort, I am going to look at the new skids the men are laying up on the road to the river; do you want to come? It is about half a mile from here."

"Oh! yes, sir," said Ruth hastily; and Paul, looking after her as she followed Brent with glad alacrity, threw down his tools, and snatched the goad from the hand of a teamster just guiding his oxen with the faintly traced path the drags had worn.

"Here, Jim," said he hurriedly. "You help those fellows get their loads aboard, and I'll team this to the skids for you. You said you didn't want to walk on that sore foot."

"All right, mate, no more I don't," said the man, a little astonished, but well content; and resigning his place to Paul, he picked up an iron bar and turned to help his comrades roll the logs prepared for transportation upon their drags.

"I don't know as you'll be able to help up these logs, Freeman; it's man's work, I can tell you," said the brawny fellow who slouched along at the other side of the drag.

"I've rolled logs before to-day," said Paul, rather contemptuously, as he hurried the oxen down the road Brent and Ruth had taken.

"Yes, but there a'n't much roll to these, I can tell you. They've got to be h'isted up on top of the pile. I tell you, we've got a hansome skid, me and my mate have, about twenty logs, and these will just top it off pooty. It's the biggest one in the job, I reckon."

"I heard the Cap'n say he didn't like these great skids, and wouldn't have them," said Paul. "It does make awful hard work, getting the logs on and off."

"Yes, there's some lift in it, I tell you, and I reckon you'd better go back now, and send Jim along. I'm dog sure you can't handle 'em."

"You see," replied Paul briefly; and the other, sinking his hands deeper into the waist-band of his trowsers, and whistling softly as he went, slouched along without farther remark.

Through the forest-path, flecked here and there with sunshine, but for the most part lying in the heavy shadow of the hemlocks, through the clearing whence one might look far over valley and stream to the majestic mountains upon the horizon, wound the wood-path, until, near the brow of the hill, where the road descended to the valley, Paul halted his oxen beside a pile of great logs laid across a platform of small sticks, technically called skids, and designed to raise the logs above the deep snow, in which they would otherwise be hidden. Some twenty logs already were piled upon these skids, and the four now to be added would, as Paul's companion remarked, just make up two dozen, which was "a pooty lot to see together."

"Now, I tell you what, boy," continued the woodsman, taking his hands out of his waist-band, and suddenly awakening to full activity and energy, "we've got to fly round and get these logs h'isted to the top of the pile before the Cap'n comes along. He took the other road by the brook, and will go to the lower skids first, and if we're spry, we'll finish and be off before he reaches here. If we don't, he'll let out the worst kind at us for building so big a skid."

"Let him. I a'n't afraid of what he'll say," replied Paul, whose temper was in its worst condition this morning.

"Yes, but he's boss, and there a'n't any getting away from it, he means to stay boss," said the other, whose name was Bevis.

Without reply, Paul backed his oxen a step, so that the sled lay immediately beneath the towering pile of logs, and seizing one of the iron bars or handspikes, lashed upon the top of the load, placed the point of it beneath the upper stick, and signed to Bevis to imitate his example. Bevis obeyed as silently, and the two men, with prodigious effort, much skill, and a judicious use of the principle of leverage, succeeded presently in elevating the great log inch by inch to the top of the pile, and rolling it to the farther side of the platform made by the tier below.

"Now the next," exclaimed Paul, leaping down the instant this object was effected.

"Don't you want to catch your breath?" asked Bevis, panting a little.

"No. He'll be along," said Paul doggedly;

and Bevis resumed the handspike he had just thrown down. The second log was larger than the first, and the men less able to manage it, through need of the moment of rest they had omitted to take; so that, although it reached the top of the pile, it was by efforts that both felt were too severe for prudence.

"Tell you what, boy," panted Bevis, sinking down upon the top of the pile. "This sort of thing don't pay. You and me a'n't stout enough to handle such logs as these on such a skid. We'll have to go fetch Jim."

"There's Brent," replied Paul in a low voice, and both men, looking from their elevation, saw the tall form of the master coming up the path, with Ruth beside him.

"What is this? Why, men, what under the sun are you about here?" commenced he sharply. "Haven't I said, time and again, that I won't have these immense wood-piles laid up in place of decent skids? And, Paul Freeman, what are you doing here? Your business is peeling, and I won't have you mixing up in this way. Bevis, how came you to lay up these logs in this fashion, after what I have said?"

"Well, I don't know, Cap'n," replied Bevis slowly. "Jim and me, we're two-fisted fellers, we are, and we just liked to see what we could do."

"Well, I should just like to see what you can do toward minding what I say," replied Brent angrily. "You two get those logs off again in a hurry, and load them on to your drag. Then haul them a dozen feet further on, lay some new skids, and begin a new pile. Freeman, since you like to meddle with another man's work, let me see if you can undo as well as do."

"I wish't I could undo one job that I was a fool for doing," said Paul sullenly; and seizing his handspike without waiting for Bevis, he lifted the end of the log nearest to him, and sent it crashing down upon the load below, with such force that it rebounded several feet, and the smaller end springing outward, struck Brent a heavy blow upon the breast, felling him to the ground, and toppling over beside him, but fortunately not upon him.

"O Paul! You wicked, wicked monster. You have killed him! You have killed my darling friend!" cried Ruth, throwing herself down beside Brent, who, to the astonishment of all, was already struggling into a sitting posture. The girl, throwing her arms about him, with some wild idea of supporting or raising him, would have poured forth a torrent of questions, ejaculations, sympathy ; but Brent, with one hand laid heavily upon her shoulder, silenced her with the one word "Hush!" and then in a strange, hoarse voice, hardly louder than a whisper, briefly ordered :

"Get that log upon the drag, then roll down the other, and do as I told you. If it isn't done in half an hour, you'll both leave Wahtahree to-night."

Without a word, and with white, awe-stricken faces, the men obeyed ; and Brent, without moving from his position, relaxing his hold of Ruth's shoulder, or again essaying to speak, watched their movements with glittering eyes, set in a face paler than death, until in less than the prescribed time his orders were obeyed to the full. Then, while Bevis turned the oxen into the path, Paul Freeman approached his wounded employer.

"Mr. Brent," said he, "I am very sorry you are hurt. I never meant to do it. Can't we carry you home on the drag, or won't you let me help you?"

"Go back to your work, and remember that you are a peeler, and not a teamster." whispered Brent, waving his hand so imperiously toward the road, that Freeman obeyed without another word.

CHAPTER XXXVI.

FIGHTING FOR LIFE.

"AND now, Comfort," whispered Brent, as the retreating footsteps of the men died away, "now we will see what is left for me in this world. I think that was my death-blow, but I was resolved those men should see that I was master while I lived. Can you stand firm, poor child, and let me raise myself by you?"

"Let me raise you! Oh! dear, dear master, let me help you in any way," cried the girl, unheeded tears streaming down her face, and her whole puny strength exerted in the effort to raise the stalwart figure of the injured man in her arms.

"Stop, stop, child!" gasped Brent in agony. "You will injure yourself, and you torture me. Wait a moment and I can raise myself."

"Cling round my waist then—I am very strong, you have no idea how strong—and pull yourself up that way," said Ruth, bracing herself like a young birch emulating an oak.

Brent smiled faintly, and adopting the plan she suggested, succeeded in raising himself to his feet, stood for a moment, his arm about her shoulders, his form swaying backward and forward in a vain attempt to gain its equilibrium, his face growing more ghastly in its pallor, his eyes rolling wildly upon an earth and heaven that seemed to have broke their bonds and joined in chaos, and then he fell prone to earth, the blood gushing in a torrent from his lips.

Ruth, too utterly terror-stricken for any action, sank down beside him, and presently summoned courage to raise his head and lay it upon her lap, all ghastly and gory as it was, and so they remained for moments that grew to hours—the man stricken down in the splendor of his strength, more helpless and more defenceless than the feeble child who watched him, and who thought him dead or dying.

But at last Brent opened his eyes.

"Darling! No, you are not mine now.— What is it? What did they tell me?— Beatrice—— Oh! it is you, little Comfort. Where are we?—So cold. Why is it so cold?"

"Oh! you are not dead, dear, dear Mr. Brent! I am so glad!"

And Ruth's tears fell hot and fast, dripping upon the white face in her lap.

"No, I am not dead," repeated Brent dreamily. "Why do you cry, Comfort? Because I am not dead?—I remember those logs. When did I see them before? Ah! now I have it! Yes, yes! Those men and the great log, and the whirl of the woods and sky! Yes, I have it now. And you have been sitting here to hold me, Comfort, and never thought of deserting me for a moment? Well, it is a Comfort truly named. Now let us try again. Stand up and let me cling to you. So—that is it, that is brave! Now walk on, slowly, softly— do not hurry. Can you pick up one of those sticks and give me? Here, I can cling to this tree while you stoop. Now then, let us get on!"

"O Mr. Brent! let me run and call some of the men to help you home. You will certainly fall—you will kill yourself doing so much. They can carry you in their arms!" exclaimed Ruth, watching the faltering steps and uncertain, swaying motions of her charge with tremulous anxiety.

"No, Comfort, no," muttered Brent, leaning yet more heavily upon his stick and conquering the growing faintness that seized him by an effort of his resistless will. "I will not have

7

the men—they shall not see me in this fashion—I must be master of myself, or I cannot be their master. No; we are getting on toward home, and you and Zilpah will take care of me. We won't have the men."

So muttering at intervals, leaning now upon his staff, now upon the shoulders of the girl who watched his every step with such agonized solicitude, Brent struggled on, with many a pause, many an alternation of deadly faintness and heroic effort, many a whispered word of encouragement and apology to his Comfort, who replied not a syllable, her whole soul being absorbed in sustaining those faltering steps which promised each one to be the last possible before exhausted nature failed.

But at last came the clearing, the open sky, the shanty, with Zilpah at the door, feeding the poultry she had with infinite pains established in her new home. Zilpah, seeing at a glance the position of affairs, rushed forward, eager, clamorous, inquisitive, and yet most efficient and eager to be of use.

Ruth told the story in brief, tremulous words, and between them they led Brent to his own room and laid him upon the bed. Then, while Ruth ran for water, cloths, restoratives of various sorts, the old woman tenderly undressed him and examined the frightful bruise upon his chest.

"Do you think there's any ribs broke, dear?" asked she tenderly. "Or is it an in'ard hurt? I wish 't I had some sage to make you a tea, though there's nothing like sparmecity-candles scraped in merlasses for an in'ard bruise. Yes; you can come right in, Ruthie. There now, Marsie sonny, let me wash your face—same as I used to. Lor, it seems as if we'd gone clear back to the day you clim' the big nut tree to shake it for Beatrice Wansted, and tumbled down, and was took up for dead. That was the year afore your ma died, and she was so scared at seeing you all white and bloody—just as you are now—that it gave her a turn, and I don't think she ever got over it. Yes; it seems as if you was no more than that same boy over again. There, you look a little better; and now you drink some of this hot whiskey and sugar to keep up your strength; and, Ruth, you come here to the door."

Ruth obeyed in the same dazed way in which she had moved and spoken ever since the terrible shock of seeing Brent fall lifeless at her feet.

"Wake up, child! Wake up, and think what you're about!" said Zilpah, shaking her by one shoulder somewhat impatiently. "It a'n't going to help him any to act that way. There's got to be a doctor sent for right away; it's too big a hurt for me to handle all alone—though I know as much as any woman you'll fetch about roots and yarbs and seeh stuff, but of course that a'n't like a doctor. Now, Ruth, you know where the men be, and you slip out quiet, and find Richard, or maybe Paul Freeman would do, and tell 'em to take the Cap'n's horse and ride for the doctor, lickety-split. Maybe five minutes will be the saving of his life, for I don't know but he's bleeding in'ardly, and I don't know how to stop that. Run, now!"

But there was no need to bid her hasten. So soon as she comprehended the service required of her, the wind could hardly have outstripped her speed to perform it; and almost before Zilpah knew that she was gone she was out of sight, and fifteen minutes later stood breathless, pallid, and excited in the path of the men, who were returning homeward for their dinner.

"Richard, come here quick, I want to speak to you," called she impatiently; and as Paul also darted forward, she waved him imperiously back.

"No, Paul Freeman, I don't want you," said she, turning her back upon him, while she whispered to Richard:

"Mr. Brent is dreadfully hurt—dreadfully; and Zilpah says we must have the doctor just as soon as we can get him. She says take Kitty and ride down to the Ford, and tell him to hurry all he can. Oh! do hurry, Richard, do!"

"How'd he get hurt?" asked Richard, already hastening toward the stable, while the other men, except Paul, turned toward the shanty.

"A log rolled down and struck him; but oh! do, do hurry!" said Ruth, following the man for a short distance, and then standing, with clasped hands and white face, breathlessly watching his movements.

As she thus stood, a slow and reluctant step approached her from behind.

"Ruthie!"

"What do you want, Paul Freeman?"

"Why do you speak so short, Ruthie? and why won't you look at me? You don't think I meant to roll the log down on him, do you?"

"I hope you didn't, for your own sake as much as any thing, Paul," said the girl, never moving her eyes from Richard, who was rapidly saddling the sure-footed mountain nag Brent had selected for his own use over roads where a horse accustomed to travelling a settled country would probably have broken his own legs and his master's neck in the first day.

"Is he much hurt?" asked Paul in a low voice.

"Killed, maybe."

"O Ruthie! don't say that."

Arrival of the doctor.

"Well, it's true. And what killed him?"

"Not I, Ruth. I solemnly swear to you that when I gave that h'ist to the log I had no more idea of hitting him than you with it. Don't you believe me?"

"Yes; if you say so, I believe it, Paul. But if Mr. Brent dies, I never can bear to look at you, or speak to you, or hear your voice or your name again."

"Even when I didn't mean to hurt him?"

"Yes; even then, because you did hurt him if you didn't mean it."

"Then you care a great deal about Mr. Brent, Ruthie?"

"A great deal! I shouldn't think you'd ask such a question, Paul."

"More than you do about me, Ruthie?"

"Why, of course I do. More than I do about any body," said Ruth impatiently.

And Paul turned away without another word.

CHAPTER XXXVII.
DOCTORS DISAGREE.

"WELL, doctor, what do you think about him?" asked Zilpah impatiently, as the doctor finished the ample dinner with which the housekeeper had hospitably provided him before she asked any questions.

"Well, ma'am, if you want my candid, outright, and downright opinion about Mr. Brent——"

"Yes, what is it?"

"Well, ma'am, it is that he is a dead man!" And the doctor, adjusting his spectacles to his nose, tilted his chair against the wall, thrust his hands in his pockets, and steadily regarded the little junta composed of Zilpah, Richard, Paul Freeman, and Ruth, who breathlessly waited for his words.

As they met her ear, Ruth turned, and hiding her face upon Zilpah's bosom, burst into hysterical sobs; and the old woman, with tears streaming down her withered cheeks, found no word of comfort to whisper to her. Paul Freeman turned miserably toward the open door, yet lingered, hoping for some alleviating word to this terrible sentence; and Richard pursed up his lips as if to whistle; then glanced uneasily at the women, and doubtfully at the doctor, while he slowly said:

"Sho! it a'n't so bad as all that, I guess."

"It couldn't well be worse," replied the doctor dogmatically. "The man is injured very bad inwardly, and there's no way of getting at an inward wound to see what it is. There's a couple of ribs broken, too, but they'll heal of themselves in a week or so. It was walking with them ribs playing against the vital organs inside of him that did the mischief, I expect. They sort of tore him all to pieces, and I don't see how he's going to get mended."

"You can't do any thing more about it?" asked Richard, still whistling softly as he eyed the doctor with increasing disfavor.

"I don't see as I can, young man, really. I have no objection to coming into the woods again—say day after to-morrow ; but its pretty hard on a horse, and I really don't see what I can do."

"Well, now, doctor, I'm an ignorant sort of man alongside of you ; but it's my opinion that the boss is going to get over it, and I'll tell you what he'd ought to take to help him over."

"Well, sir, what ?" asked the doctor, much in the tone ordinarily assumed by the master of the ring toward the clown at a circus.

"French brandy and loaf-sugar," replied Richard undauntedly, and meeting the doctor's sneering laugh with good-humored indifference.

"Well, that's a new cure for broken bones," said the man of science at last.

"It a'n't broken bones—you said they'd heal of themselves in a week or two," replied Richard sententiously.

"Well, what's your brandy and loaf-sugar going to do anyhow ?"

"Why, the brandy keeps the blood a-circulating lively, so that the bruised parts won't die before they heal, and the loaf-sugar makes 'em heal."

"Sugar's dreadful healing, every body knows," said Zilpah corroboratively.

"Now, doctor, you think I'm a fool, but you just hear what I've seen in my day," pursued Richard, rising and marching up and down the room, pausing now and then to confront the doctor with some sentence more emphatic than the rest, and speaking with the eloquence of conviction, and an earnest purpose.

"Three years ago, I was on a job with a man named Sparks. It was down in the State of Maine, where the lumbering is carried on a little different from what it is here, but is full as dangerous. This man was a great fellow for taking hold of every thing himself, though he was the boss ; and in the spring, when it came to rafting the lumber down the river, he was here, there, and everywhere. The end of it was that, one day, there was a jam just above the rapids, and not a fellow on hand man enough to go out on the raft and break the lock, till Sparks himself seized up an axe, tossed off his jacket and boots, and just waiting to have a rope tied round his waist, sprung out on the logs that were bobbing up and down, piling one over another, and grinding away like as they were alive, and in a hurry to chaw him all up. Out he went, found the

lock, hit right and left, knocked out the key-log, and then sprung for it like a man that feels the devil close on his heels, and the church-door open all ready for him. We fellers hurrahed and cheered him on, and pulled away at the line, keeping it just taut and not pulling a bit ; and well was it for him that we did, for, just at the church-door as it were, the devil caught up with him, and over he went, down among the dead men, we all thought and said ; but while there's life there's hope, and we hauled away at the line, and after five minutes or so, up he came, looking more like the pieces of a man than a whole one, and hanging to the end of the rope with no more force about him than a dish-cloth.

"We got him ashore, and carried him up to the shanty, which wasn't far from the river. The only one to take care of him was an old Indian squaw we had picked up to help cook and wash for us while we stayed in that camp, and with her we left him, while we went back to the logs ; for the man we worked for wouldn't have thought it much of an excuse if we'd let all his lumber slide just because one man got killed.

"When we got home at night, the first thing we said was :

"'Is the boss gone under ?' and the old squaw up and made answer :

"'He no go under, never ; me makey well.' And sure enough, there was Sparks lying on his bed, as happy as a lord, and alongside of him a cupful of white sugar just wet with brandy, while he had a bottle of it for medicine, though it hadn't never been opened till that day, and the white sugar he'd fetched up when the man that owned the job came to spend a day or two on it.

"Well, where that old woman got her idee, or how she knew the brandy and sugar was in the shanty, is more than I can tell ; but she seemed so sartain sure she was right that we just let her go ahead, and when the brandy was gone, one of us fellers went all the way to Bangor to get some more.

"Well, sir, that was all there was to it. The cup of brandy and sugar didn't never get empty ; and about once in five minutes, either Sparks for himself, or some body else for him, would tuck a spoonful into his mouth. It kept him about half drunk, I do suppose, and he slept right straight along, day and night, most all the time. When he got a little better, we used to carry him out on a sort of bed we made for him, and set him in the sun a little while; and when it came midsummer, we laid him where he'd get the good smell of the spruces and fir-balsams. Then we fed him on thin slices of raw pork, sprinkled with red pepper; and the amount of it was that by early fall he was a well man, and it was brandy and sugar that cured him."

"Brandy and sugar, and the smell of pine-woods, and raw pork and red pepper!" repeated the doctor contemptuously. "Well, young man, if you think you're competent to manage this case on those principles, I am quite ready to leave it in your hands, for I confess that I don't understand that style of treatment."

"Nor no other that'll haul Brent through, do you?" asked Richard, much in the same tone.

"No, I can't say I do. A man that's injured as he's injured had ought to die, and I don't doubt he will die," said the doctor, allowing his chair to resume its quadrupedal position, while rising to his own feet, he buttoned his coat, finished packing and strapping his saddle-bags, and showed symptoms of a dignified departure.

"All right, doctor. You say he'll die, and you can't help it, and I say he shan't die, not if we can hender it; shall he, Ma'am Zilpah?"

"No, Richard, he shan't; and I don't doubt but what we can hender it, if all you say is true," replied the old woman, jerking her chin into the air, with a defiant glance at the doctor.

"Very well, then, I leave the case in your hands—only mind and don't you blame me when the man dies," said that worthy practitioner, putting on his hat and approaching the door.

"No, we won't; but maybe you'll tell me if you've got any first-rate French brandy among your physic down to the Ford?" said Richard, accompanying him.

"Yes, I've got some worth eighteen dollars a gallon, if that is good enough," said the doctor with a grim smile.

"Who cares for the price if the stuff is first-rate! I'll buy a bottle anyhow out of my own pocket."

"And I'll go down with the doctor and bring it back," said Paul eagerly, looking toward Ruth for approval; but she was whispering to Zilpah:

"Let us go back to Mr. Brent now."

"You go, and I'll come as soon as I put these dishes together," said the old woman kindly; and the girl, waiting for no further permission, flew back to the post beside Marston's pillow, which she had unwillingly quitted half an hour before, at Zilpah's call.

CHAPTER XXXVIII.

A GHOST.

"Mr. Monckton! Is it possible? This is indeed a delightful surprise."

"I may echo the delight, but not the surprise, for that would have been in finding Mrs. Barstow less charming than I left Mrs. Charlton," said the traveller, touching the finger-tips extended to him, and bowing profoundly.

"Still a courtier," said the lady, lightly laughing as she glanced toward a chair and resumed her own.

"No satire, pray. Remember that I am but just off a journey, and more than usually powerless in your hands."

"You have but just arrived in town?"

"Or in the country either. I landed upon republican soil just four days ago."

"After an absence of— how long?"

"Four years."

"And you have explored during that time how large a proportion of the habitable globe?"

"Ah! one's ideas of habitable become so vague in the course of extended travel that I cannot answer your question, especially in comparing this apartment with the hut of my friend Eric Jakell, the Icelander, where I spent a week last summer."

And Mr. Monckton suffered his eyes to wander admiringly through the elegant drawing-room, its charms, like those of its mistress, heightened by the softened and tinted light alone suffered to enter the heavily shaded windows.

Mrs. Barstow noted the glance, and felt an added kindliness toward so delicate an appreciator of the taste displayed in her surroundings.

"It is a pity you should waste four years upon the Eric Jakells of the world when so many of your more civilized friends are wishing for your society," said she, with a smile so becoming that Mr. Monckton, doing a little sum in mental arithmetic, decided that eight and thirty must be the grand climacteric of woman's beauty.

"I did not spend all my time in Iceland," said he slowly. "I travelled in various quarters of the globe beside, and met many persons whom I knew."

"The Chappellefords, for instance," said Mrs. Barstow with a slightly malicious smile. "Beatrice told me that they met you in London, quite by accident."

"Yes," said Monckton gravely. "But a very happy accident for me, as I enjoyed their society exceedingly during the few days I was able to remain with them."

The reserve of his manner checked the jest Mrs. Barstow wished to utter upon the subject of Beatrice, and she asked instead:

"Did you share Mr. Chappelleford's triumphs among the English *savans?*"

"Not at all. The Oriental Club were hospitable enough to give me a chair, and I belong to the Travellers', but otherwise I saw nothing of society. I was only passing through London on my way to Scotland. But Mrs. Chappelleford's success was even greater than her husband's."

"Indeed—in what direction?" asked Mrs. Barstow coldly.

"As a *belle esprit*, almost a *bas b'en*. In fact, had she been less beautiful, less elegant, older, and more stereotyped, she might have been consigned to the ranks of learned women, and lost to the general society which eagerly claimed her."

"Indeed! I did not know she had become such a paragon. I shall be quite afraid of her when I find time to appreciate her."

'Pray, do not delay that period, for I assure you that you are losing a great deal," said Mr. Monckton, smiling ever so little. "You have not seen much of your friends then since their return?" added he directly.

"No; they only came in the last steamer, the one just before yours, by the way, and I have hardly found time for a call, and to see them once at dinner. They will be here tomorrow evening, however, at a little gathering in their honor, and I trust we shall have the pleasure of welcoming Mr. Monckton also. Mr. Barstow will be most happy to call upon you in the morning, although, you know, society is not his favorite occupation."

"Thanks—I shall be most happy. Mr. Barstow is quite well, I hope."

"Oh! quite, and just as devoted to business as ever. I hardly see him except at dinner, for he is not fond of going out, and I am unable to avoid so many engagements that they quite absorb me."

She raised her eyes with such an air of pathetic protest against her fate, that Monckton would certainly have laughed had he not been absorbed at the moment in contriving an opening for the one thing he had entered that house to say.

"I dare say you are thinking that Mrs. Monckton shall be more domestic," continued the lady with an arch smile; and the traveller replied in the same tone:

"'Bachelors' wives,' you know, are perfect, and I am afraid I never shall have any other. But you were asking of my travels, Mrs. Barstow. Among other places, I visited Persia again."

"Indeed!" and Mrs. Barstow turned pale beneath the *nuance* of rouge upon her cheek; but recovering herself by a rapid and violent effort, she boldly picked up the gage which she imagined thrown down to her.

"Then I dare say you heard further news of an old friend, Major Strangford," said she carelessly.

"Yes, Mrs. Barstow, very singular, very startling news," said Monckton earnestly.

"What is it, pray? He was always original."

"This time extremely so, for after dispatching a letter and parcel which I transmitted to you four years ago, he recovered from the fever supposed to be fatal, and in the course of several months resumed the use both of his body and mind, which, as I understand, had been nearly equally affected by his illness."

"He recovered!" gasped Mrs. Barstow, too deeply agitated now for concealment.

"Yes, and was about to proceed upon his journey homeward, when, in looking over a file of American newspapers at some consulate upon the route, he met with the announcement of your marriage. It was a great shock to him, as he had formed his own plans with regard to your future. You will excuse this freedom, I trust, as both you and Major Strangford have honored me with your confidence in times past."

"Yes, yes; go on, please!"

"The Major was, as I have said, much shocked, and also very angry, and in the first heat of his emotions, he did a very foolish thing."

"Shot himself?"

"Oh! no, much worse than that: married

himself to a woman for whom he never pretended to care, and whose devotion to him only serves to render his indifference more apparent. She was an English widow, very rich and very vulgar; he met her somewhere in Italy—Naples, I think—and they were married in ten days from their first introduction."

"I thought you said you met him in Persia."

"No; I only mentioned Persia by way of introducing this subject. I met them in Paris."

Mr. Monckton paused, and Mrs. Barstow sat for a moment, her face covered with her hand, then raised it, pale and haughty, to say:

"Your account of my former friend is interesting, Mr. Monckton, for one never ceases to feel an interest in the fate of one's intimate associates, but as I shall probably never meet or hear again of either Major or Mrs. Strangford, the news is hardly as important as you seem to think."

"Pardon, madam," said the traveller coldly. "It is precisely because it is important that I have intruded it upon you. Major and Mrs. Strangford were passengers with me in the Phœnix, and I know that it is his intention to call upon you to-morrow—which is New-Year's day, you will remember—in hopes of giving you as painful a shock as he experienced in hearing of your marriage. I know this, for he told me."

"And you came here to warn me! That is real kindness, real friendship, Mr. Monckton," and Mrs. Barstow, rising, offered her white and jewelled hand to her guest with more sincerity of feeling than she had experienced before in many years.

"You repay my slight service a hundredfold," said Monckton, returning the cordial pressure of the hand he held. "But you will remember you did me a service long ago, and although I never have thanked you, I felt none the less grateful."

"That was simple justice," said Mrs. Barstow with a very becoming air of proud rectitude, and a convenient oblivion of the garnets. "And although the confession caused a breach between Mrs. Chappelleford and myself, not yet healed, I have never regretted making it."

"Thank you. And you will be ready for Major Strangford?"

"I shall be ready, and will even ask him to waive all ceremony and bring his wife to me

to-morrow evening," said Mrs. Barstow with a smile of honeyed malice.

"Ah! I see that forewarned is forearmed in this case, and I need interfere no further," said Mr. Monckton, taking his leave.

Going down the stairs, he proposed to himself this little problem, and left it unsolved:

"Which is meaner, for a man to stand by and see a woman ill used, or to turn traitor to another man?"

CHAPTER XXXIX.

A COUNCIL OF WAR.

"MADAME begs that you will come up to her dressing room, if it is not too much fatigue," said the *soubrette*; and Mrs. Chappelleford, with a silent inclination of the head, followed to the suite of apartments that had once been her own, and were now Mrs. Barstow's. That lady, standing *en grande toilette* between two mirrors, watched a little anxiously the first expression of her guest's face in entering the room, and felt a thrill of satisfaction at its cordial approval.

"You look magnificently, Juanita. Nothing can be better for you than black velvet and diamonds."

"I am so glad you think me properly dressed. Fresh from Paris as you are, we all must look to you as an authority."

"I pray that you will do no such thing, for I am the least reliable of women in such matters. I have such a habit of altering and adapting every thing, that I am no guide at all in the way of fashion."

And Mrs. Chappelleford, suffering the loose fur-lined wrap she wore to drop into the hands of Pauline, stood forth the living personification of one of those rich, dusky old pictures before which we stand for hours, silently praying the mocking lips to open, the fathomless eyes to return our imploring gaze, the dead canvas to give up the story and the passion it half reveals, yet half conceals.

Such a picture, full of the romance and mystery of the past, mingled with the gracious and graceful womanhood of to-day, looked Beatrice, standing so serenely unconscious in her quaintly fashioned robe of violet silk, soft and lustreless, the ivory whiteness of her neck and arms heightened by the yellow hue of the old point-lace shading them, her beautiful hair coiffed in a style all her own and Titian's, and ornamented with sapphires of inestimable value, for they had been wrought in the unremembered years to deck perhaps an empress, perhaps some simpler yet nobler woman, and then had returned to the bosom of the earth to wait through centuries, until they again should see the light of day, and again serve as beauty's foil.

Mrs. Barstow looked at her guest with envy and dismay, thinly veiled by admiration.

"My dearest Beatrice! How odd, and how thoroughly charming! Where did you get that dress?"

"I bought the silk in Constantinople, and it was made in Naples. Do you like it?" asked Beatrice simply.

"It is lovely. But the fashion is so odd! Are they wearing those square necks in Paris now?"

"I don't know, I am sure. It is a fashion I am fond of, and I have all my evening dresses made in that way. I believe I was guilty of a little plagiarism in this, and gave the *modiste* a sketch to work by, which I had taken from a picture in the Pitti. Don't expose my presumption, will you?"

"I shall be very good if I refrain, for everything and everybody in my rooms will be thrown into the shadow by that toilette and that wearer," said Mrs. Barstow with a constrained smile.

"How sorry I should be to believe you, for it is so vulgar to be conspicuous," said Beatrice with unaffected dismay. "And I have been away so long that I dare say I may have grown too *bizarre* in my style. Shall I throw a shawl over this dress?"

"Nonsense, my dear. No, indeed," said the hostess with a magnanimous effort greatly to her credit. "Is it your fault that you are charming? But now, sit down a moment, please, I have something to say to you, something very serious."

With a look of some surprise, Beatrice took the offered chair, and fixed her clear eyes upon the face of her hostess, who continued with some embarrassment:

"It is a subject upon which we spoke once before, and did not agree very well, but I know you will be willing to help me, when I really need help."

"Certainly, Juanita, if I can."

"Mr. Monckton was with me yesterday," pursued Mrs. Barstow with a visible effort, "and he told me very strange news. You remember Major Strangford, Beatrice?"

"I remember what you told me of him just before your marriage with my uncle."

"Well, my dear, do but fancy that this man is not dead, that he recovered from his fever, heard of my marriage, and took it so to heart that he actually married again for spite, and now has absolutely come home, is in town at this moment, and intends calling here to-day."

"Intends calling here?"

"Exactly, and with the avowed purpose of annoying and confusing me. He confessed as much to Monckton, who with real kindness came to warn me. Now, Beatrice, what can I do?"

"It is a very painful situation, certainly," said Beatrice gravely. "And I do not see anything that you can do except to assert your position as a wife and a matron with quiet dignity, and by showing Major Strangford that the past is really past to you; make it impossible for him to annoy you by bringing it up."

"Ah! but, Beatrice, suppose it is not really past," exclaimed Juanita, clasping her hands in an agitated manner, while her very lips turned white.

"I do not understand you," said Beatrice, raising her eyes to the other's face with a look of shame and surprise. "You cannot mean that you still cherish any feeling of love for this man, and are afraid of betraying it?"

"But remember, Beatrice, all that he has been to me; remember how much he has suffered on my account; remember the weakness of a woman's heart."

"I remember only, Mrs. Barstow, that you are my uncle's trusted wife, that you assumed that position quite of your own wish—I may say, by your own effort, and that the only tolerable excuse you found at that time for not revealing the whole truth to your future husband was that it was a matter of the past altogether, and that with Major Strangford had died all possibility of your swerving from the affection you professed for my uncle. But if you intend to say that, in finding this man alive, you find that you still love him, and dread to see him on that account, and are asking me to help and shield you in this disgraceful position, all I can say is, that I am very much surprised at your selection of a confidante, and that I shall return immediately home."

She rose as she spoke, and stood upright

before the cowed and trembling woman, who, looking up at her majestic figure, and face severe and beautiful as that of an offended Diana, felt a sudden sickening at the heart, in recognizing a height to which she might never hope to climb, which she had never even imagined until that moment.

She caught at the soft, shining drapery flowing around the stately figure, and fell upon her knees before it.

"O Beatrice, Beatrice! I am a poor, weak, simple woman! Help me, save me while there is yet time."

Beatrice stooped in an instant, and took both the clinging hands in hers, a great pity softening the disdainful lines of her face, and her eyes filling with tears.

"Don't do that, Juanita," said she in a low voice. "Get up, I implore you. Indeed, I will help you, if I can—or rather I will help you to help yourself, for it is you who must do the work, after all. There, let us sit quietly down again, and consider the matter. Major Strangford is coming here to-day professedly to annoy and embarrass you. That proves him no gentleman to begin with, and proves, too, that his feeling toward you is more one of enmity than good-will. It seems to me that you are not called upon to treat such a person with much ceremony. Why do you not tell the servant to refuse you to him?"

"That would be almost impossible on New-Year's Day, when gentlemen come in such numbers, and altogether as it were. They do not give their names very often."

"Well, then, if we cannot keep him out, let us consider how to deal with him after he is in," said Beatrice almost gayly; for, like most proud and sensitive persons, she felt the humiliation she had inflicted more keenly than even the sufferer herself.

"And, after all," continued she, "it is better that you should see this person once, to convince yourself how indifferent you have become to him. We all change so rapidly that it is very seldom we find ourselves in the same position to any other person after a separation of years. We have to begin actually a new acquaintance, if we wish to renew broken ties, and it is ten chances to one but we find our new friend entirely a different person from our old one, and altogether uncongenial to our new selves. But one can avoid this shock by refraining from remaking the acquaintance, and just laying away the

past memory in one's cabinet of curious antiques, properly numbered and classified; and, after all, a cabinet of minerals or shells, or even butterflies, is better worth collecting."

"You are talking to yourself now, instead of to me," said Juanita, half petulantly, and Beatrice colored to the waves of her shining hair.

"That is true," said she frankly. "I too married from unworthy motives, and I too had memories to subdue, but I replaced them so thoroughly with other and better things that they soon ceased to trouble me, and it is now far beyond the power of man to revive them."

"And you would not be afraid to meet that old lover of yours, ever so suddenly, or ever so unreservedly?" asked Juanita curiously.

"I could not meet him so suddenly as to make me forget our mutual position, and as for unreserve, it seems to me that every wife should live in an atmosphere of reserve, within which no man can penetrate," said Beatrice so gravely that Juanita could not pursue the subject.

"Well, what are we to do in this matter?" asked she, after a moment of awkward silence.

"Why, since you are prepared for the attack, it seems to me to have lost all its danger," replied Beatrice. "You will, I suppose, receive Major Strangford precisely as you would any other gentleman; forget, if you can, that you ever knew him more intimately than you do to-day, and let him perceive that you acknowledge no secret understanding whatever between you."

"I shall turn him over to you, Beatrice. You can make him understand better than I that he is not welcome here. I am, after all, the hostess, and must not be rude, you know."

"There is not the slightest occasion for rudeness," said Beatrice a little impatiently. "Your proper manner toward this man is polite formality, verging on indifference. Rudeness would be almost as objectionable as emotion. Let him see that you have no feeling of any sort toward him. Nothing will discourage him like that."

"But if you have an opportunity, I wish you would let him see that you know all about him, and that you mean to stand between me and harm."

"O Juanita! it is you who must feel and show that such harm as this cannot come near you. You must not depend upon me or any one, or you will certainly be disappointed in the end."

"Hark! There is the bell. We must go down," exclaimed Mrs. Barstow, giving one slow, comprehensive glance at her figure in the mirror, and then sweeping out of the room, sadly followed by Beatrice.

CHAPTER XL.
ALL THE WORLD.

"I MADE eighty-two calls yesterday, between eleven o'clock in the morning and eleven at night, sir," said Mr. Laforét upon the second of January in the year of which we write, "and I give you my honor, sir, that I did not find a handsomer drawing-room, or two women any thing near as handsome as at Israel Barstow's. I give you my honor, Mrs. Chappelleford, since her return, is enough to take the breath right out of a man ; and Mrs. Barstow, when she gets herself up in black velvet, with just a touch of rouge, and the right shade under her eyelids, and sits with her back to the light, I tell you she is stunning. As for the spread, it was perfect—just enough, and nothing too much: sherry and sweet wines, but no champagne, no punch-bowl—nothing loud. No occasion for fellows to carry olives in their pockets to that house, or to come out of it noisy—just the best house in town, sir, I give you my honor."

And having the opinion of such an authority as Mr. Laforét, we need not doubt that Mrs. Barstow's New-Year's at home was perfectly successful, or go farther into the details of the occasion.

The day wore on until about five o'clock in the afternoon, and Mrs. Barstow had just smiled acceptance of Mr. Monckton's compliments, when Beatrice saw a slight, nervous tremor run through her figure, and at once turned her own eyes toward the door.

A gentleman stood just within it, looking with peculiar earnestness toward the hostess—a gentleman in middle life, of military figure and bearing, and with a face once singularly handsome, but now wasted and haggard with a life of fatigue, exposure, and unrestrained passions.

"A volcano almost burned out," thought Beatrice, as she watched the new-comer advancing slowly up the room, his eyes still intently fixed upon his hostess, who, pretending not to observe him, jested flippantly with Mr. Monckton.

"Juanita!" said Beatrice in a low voice, and full of meaning.

Mrs. Barstow turned her head, smiled with a very tolerable imitation of indifferent surprise, and said :

"Is it possible, Major Strangford! Did you drop from the heavens among us?"

"No, I have come 'up from the under world,' as your favorite Tennyson has it. You see, I remember your tastes, Mrs. Barstow."

"So good of you. But then you have been out of the world, and so have had time for the pleasures of memory. We of the town are too busy for that luxury," said Mrs. Barstow with admirable *sangfroid*.

"Beatrice, allow me to present Major Strangford, a gentleman I used to see in New Orleans. Mrs. Chappelleford, Major Strangford; Mr. Monckton, I believe, you know."

"Your servant, Mrs. Chappelleford. How are you, Monckton," said the Major, acknowledging the presence of those whom he addressed with brief courtesy, and turning again to Juanita with a malicious smile.

"Yes, Mrs. Barstow, I have just arrived in town, and my wife has hardly recovered from her journey ; but when she does I hope she will see you among her first visitors. You and she should be good friends."

"You are married, then? You forget that we have all been ignorant of your movements, your very existence, I may say, for so long, that we hardly know where to place you. There was even a rumor of your death some time ago. Did you not tell me so, Mr. Monckton?"

"Yes, several years ago, before I went abroad."

"So I was thinking ; but one lives so fast in these days," said Mrs. Barstow, with a little sigh of protest against the heartlessness of the age.

"And one's dearest friends are soon forgotten," said Major Strangford bitterly.

"Is that your experience, Major? Well, now, I don't find it so. Delusions and fancies pass away, but I don't find that real friendships do. How is it with you, Beatrice?"

"One certainly sees more clearly as one gets on in life," said Beatrice quietly. "And the certainty that things are at last reduced to their true limits is a consolation in seeing them lose the magnificent proportions with which we first invested them."

"Some things reduced to their true limits become so insignificant as to disappear altogether," replied Major Strangford with a sneer. "Lovers' vows, for instance."

"Or mean revenge," added Beatrice coolly. "Yes, most small and false matters become extinct with time. The world has only room for truth and nobility of purpose."

"What a peculiar world you must live in, Mrs. Chappelleford," said Major Strangford, turning to stare her almost rudely in the face. "And what a delightful sympathy must exist between Mrs. Barstow and yourself!"

"Such an one should exist, since we are kinswomen, or at least close connections," said Beatrice, unmoved by look or tone.

"Indeed! May I ask how?'

"Mrs. Barstow married my uncle, and I hers; so we are naturally much together."

"I see; and you are educating your niece in your own way of thinking, are you not?"

"Juanita, will not the gentleman take some refreshments?" asked Beatrice as quietly as if she had not heard the taunting question: and Mrs. Barstow, aroused to a memory of her duties, hastily replied :

"Oh! certainly. Mr. Monckton, will you do the honors of the dining room to Major Strangford?"

Both gentlemen rose, and the entrance of another party most opportunely offered cover for a retreat, which might otherwise have become very awkward: but Mrs. Barstow, smiling and bowing welcome to Messieurs Rein and Grahame, could smile and bow adieu to Messieurs Monckton and Strangford in the same breath and with precisely the same manner.

An hour later, the ladies withdrew to rest for a short period before dinner, and had to prepare for the fatigues of the evening, which was to be celebrated by a " little gathering " of Mrs. Barstow's dear five hundred friends.

"That will do, Pauline ; you may go now," said Mrs. Barstow impatiently, as the maid lingered after inspecting and repairing the fabric of her mistress's toilet.

"O my dear, dear Beatrice!" continued she as the door closed. "I am so obliged to you, and how splendidly you stood by me !"

"I am sure I do not see how," replied Beatrice with a smile. "You treated Major Strangford as a lady should treat a gentle-

man, and he treated both of us as a boor treats women of whom he is not afraid. That is all there is to say."

"Well, he is a boor, although I used to think him the most polished gentleman of my acquaintance," said Mrs. Barstow reflectively. "But I was entirely disappointed in him—entirely shocked, I may say. Did you notice how broken and ugly his teeth are?"

"I noticed how false and malicious his eyes are, and how tremulous and dissipated his hands," said Beatrice with lofty scorn.

CHAPTER XLI.

A LEAP FROM MRS. CHAPPELLEFORD'S DIARY.

" *April 15th.*—This is my twenty-fifth birthday, speaking after Babbage—my thousandth, judging by my own consciousness, for it seems to me that the days when I was what I remember to have been float backward faster than the other current carries me forward, so that youth retreats while age does not advance ; for I am not old yet, I suppose. And yet, if life is a condition of progress, what is left for me to learn ? I mean, of course, personally ; for of intellectual growth and attainment, there is no end. But without wishing to be weak or sentimental, I cannot but wonder if science and metaphysics, mathematics and philosophy, are the highest aims of our being. Suppose we heap our individual mound of sand a few grains higher than that of our brother-ant next door, what then ? Is it large enough to hold us, after all? Or, on the other hand, is it worth while to heap so toilfully a mound beneath which to bury ourselves? Cheops always seemed to me a victim of Almighty irony. He erected the Pyramid, and his atom of mummy was lost in the immensity of his memorial.

" The pyramid of acquirement these men about me are piling for themselves will not last as long as the stones, and it is so much harder to build it.

" Well, then, what do we live for ? To learn, is the best answer, and that is but poor. Five years ago, I should have said, to love ; but what puerile trash that all becomes as one gets on a little ! To be happy ? It is only another form of the same childish dream. How can a rational, thinking being, with a mind and reasoning powers properly developed, talk of being happy, when the very fundamental principle of existence is disappointment? The child enters life with hopes amounting to certainties, with ardent friendships, loves, theories. He travels on and sees them drop away, or, remaining, change like fairy gold to worthless rubbish in his hands, until, at the last, he stands beggared of all but the experience he has bought, the knowledge he has won. But is this experience the end of life? Is the means also the result? Must we give the price of the candle and play the game through, however little worth we find it?

"And then? What comes next? Mr. Chappelleford tells me, resolution into the elements, and reproduction in other forms; but what a trivial idea that seems as the grand motive of creation! Like the games of everlasting I used to play with grandmamma, when we always put the cards we gained at the back of those in our hands, and so never came to the end. Is eternity one grand game of everlasting, with the same stupid kings, and simpering queens, and contemptible knaves, always recurring without variation or amendment? But my grandfather and the rest of his genus tell me that after life and death come heaven and hell, and so describe a sort of vaporous, gaseous existence for the good, and a Mumbojumbo punishment for the wicked; the one too tedious, the other too absurd for belief. Pious people of more modern education promulgate various theories—some tolerably interesting, others tedious, none of them vital—at least to me. It may be that it is this "me" that is wrong, and yet how? To return to the pleasant places where these people dwell would be like returning to bread and milk, the Arabian Nights, and my belief that heaven was to be scaled from the top of Moloch Mountain. I cannot go back, and to go on looks inexpressibly dreary and tedious.

"I will study Sanscrit, and help Mr. Chappelleford in his new work upon the mother of languages. But that is only a way of passing time; and how idle to invent ways of passing time when we are waiting for nothing!

"I never talked of these matters with Marston Brent. I wonder what convictions he has arrived at, for he will not fail to have wrought some answer to the eternal problem? I should like to see that man again, and study him as a specimen of human nature. I hope he, like me, has forgotten all that foolish past, and either has married the girl of whom they told me or contented himself with marrying

no one. I am glad I married. Mr. Chappelleford has fulfilled his promises to the letter. He has taught me much that is worth knowing, and untaught me more that was best abandoned. He says now that I am more personal than womanly, and he congratulates himself and me upon the improvement. Well, I suppose it is one; but I sometimes envy Juanita with her milliners, and upholsterers, and cosmetics, and Laforêts. There is no danger of her exhausting her world, or asking herself ' Cui bono?' Well, I will study Sanscrit——"

The opening door made Beatrice glance round, and the sentence was not finished, for Mr. Chappelleford entered with an open letter in his hand.

"My good child, prepare for sad news," said he kindly. "I have here a letter from Dr. Bliss, who tells me that your grandfather —you know, Beatrice, that he has been failing for months——"

"And he is dead?" asked Beatrice calmly.

"Yes, my dear. He died yesterday about noon, quietly, and without suffering, Bliss says. You will wish to go to Milvor, I suppose."

"Certainly, at once."

"I have already ordered a carriage and some lunch, for you must eat before we set out."

"We?"

"Of course, I shall go with you; I am your husband."

"True, I had forgotten."

And Beatrice locked her desk, and left the room quietly, and without a tear. Mr. Chappelleford looked after her thoughtfully.

"I am glad of this," said he at last. "She has lived upon the heights long enough for once. A little human emotion will be a relief, and she will return by and by with fresh ardor to the region of abstractions. The atmosphere is too thin for a woman to breathe without occasional relief. After this, we will go to the West to make those mound explorations."

CHAPTER XLII.

CHILDISH.

"YOU'RE welcome home, Beatrice, though you've grown such a stranger," said Mrs. Bliss, embracing her niece with a sort of reproachful fondness. "You've only been down once since you got back from Europe."

"I know it, aunt. I should have come oftener," said Beatrice wearily.

Mrs. Bliss looked sharply into her face a moment, then laying both hands upon her shoulders, as she had often done when charging her with some childish sin, she said interrogatively:

"You're not happy, Trix?"

Beatrice winced.

"Don't call me Trix, please, aunt. Or, no, why should I not like it? But it belongs to the old times, you know, and I have changed so much that——"

"That what, Beatrice? Are you happy?"

"I suppose so, aunt. But grandpapa——"

"Yes; you shall see him in a moment. That is, unless you had rather wait."

"I—I do not think I want to see him," stammered Beatrice, turning very pale.

"Not see him at all! Why Beatrice Wansted!" exclaimed Mrs. Bliss with such genuine horror and surprise that Beatrice hastened to add:

"That is, not to-night, aunt. I feel rather tired and faint after my journey, and you know I never saw any thing of that sort, and——"

"'Thing of that sort!'" interrupted Rachel, more and more displeased. "What are you talking of, Beatrice? Because your grandfather has died, and his spirit gone to eternal glory and happiness, has his body become something to be afraid of and disgusted at? Just fancy that he's asleep instead of dead—and in point of fact, it's nothing more; for he is asleep, and will wake up at the last day just as good as new."

"I will see him by-and-by, Aunt Rachel," said Beatrice, putting by with dignity the argument she felt hopeless of supporting. "How is grandmamma?"

"Poor, dear old lady, she is in a very distressing condition, too," said Mrs. Bliss, shaking her head hopelessly. "She is quite childish now—has been for a month or more, and she don't understand any thing about father's being dead. She thinks he's away somewhere, and she keeps mourning for him the whole time. We showed her the body, and all, but it didn't seem to convince her. She looked at it, and then hushed us with her finger, and tiptoed out of the room for fear of waking him up. But the next minute she began moaning again just the same way. She'd forgotten, you see. Hush! she's coming up-stairs now!"

And Mrs. Bliss, followed by her niece, hastened out into the passage to meet the widowed mother, who stood clinging to the railing beside the stairs, looking about her in a bewildered manner.

"O Rachel! is that you? And who else is up here?"

"Only Beatrice, mother — our Trix, you know. We were just coming down to see you," said Rachel very gently.

"Beatrice—oh! yes—Beatrice. Where is Alice?"

"Why, mother, she is dead long ago. She

"She seated herself at her grandmother's feet."

died when Beatrice was born; don't you remember?"

"And Arthur—no, Arthur was married to you—he didn't die, did he?"

"Yes, mother," said Rachel softly.

"Dear grandmamma, you remember me, don't you?" asked Beatrice, tenderly leading the bewildered woman into the chamber they had just quitted, and seating her in the great square easy chair before the fire. "I will stay here and talk with her a little while, aunt; and you can go and see after the others," said Mrs. Chappelleford aside; and as Rachel softly left the room, she seated herself upon a low stool at her grandmother's feet.

"You remember me, dear, don't you?" asked she again.

And the old lady laid a tremulous hand upon her bright head, and stooped to look into her face with the anxious scrutiny of failing sight.

"Why, of course I remember you, Alice. What should ail me not to know my own child?" said she presently, with a little crackling laugh. "And my favoright child, too; though the deacon he always said there shouldn't be any favorights in families. But then, Alice, you always was so winning and pretty, how could we help it? And though I know Rachel was disappointed, I couldn't blame Arthur not one mite, not one mite; and then, again, Rachel married—let me see, she married—well, I forget his name; but she was married some time before she died. Have you seen father, Alice?"

"No, dear grandmamma. My father is in heaven, they say. Where is heaven, grandmother?"

"Heaven? Why, Alice Barstow, a great girl like you ask such a simple question! Heaven is where the whole air is made up of love, and nothing to hinder or harm love. God loves men; but somehow we're so far off down here that we don't always seem to feel the love; and then again, there's so much going on in the world that half the time we forget to love each other with all our might, same as we're told we ought to. Well, now, in heaven, you see, close up to God, we shall breathe in His love, just as we do the common air here, and so we shall act it out to each other just as here we act out nater', because love will be nater' then, don't you see?"

But Beatrice, with her head bowed between her hands, did not reply, and the old woman went on:

"Now, there's father and me. When we were young I don't suppose there ever were two sweethearts set more by each other than we did. He'd have given up all the world for me, and I'd—well, I'd be afraid to say what I'd have given up for him. And so it was along for a while after we got married. But then came the children, and the farm, and a whole grist of work and trouble and care, and then he and me sort of fell off, not from loving, but from talking about it and showing it out. And then we got old; and old folks they get sort of crusted over—like Rachel's preserves, I think. The sweet's all

there just the same, only it can't get through the snell, and any one that didn't know would think 'twas sp'ilt. That's the way it is with old folks like father and me. But, Alice, when once we get into that heaven full of love I was telling you of, the crust will melt right off in the fire of God's love for us both, and we shall know that we're just the same to each other that we were in those young days. Just the same? No! a thousand times better, and dearer, and worthier; for then we shall be angels instead of men. I wonder if father thinks about that? I forgot to say any thing to him about it. I'll go talk with him now a little."

And the old lady rose from her chair almost with the vigor of youth, stood a moment looking about her in a bewildered way, then turned to Beatrice, while over her face, but now clear and bright as with the reflection of heavenly light, dropped a sudden veil of human infirmity and decrepitude.

"Rachel! No—Alice, where's father? I want father. Where has he gone?" said she piteously.

"Let us go and see, dear grandmother. Lean upon me, for I know you are tired. Won't you come and lie down for a little while before we look for him?" asked Beatrice soothingly; and passing her arm around her grandmother's waist, she led her gently down stairs.

"Maybe he's lying down. He has been rather poorly along back. I'm afraid he hurt himself haying. Reuben and Israel were both away, and the heft of the work came upon the deacon. I guess he's lying down a spell."

So maundering, she allowed herself to be gently led to her bedroom, and persuaded to lie down and rest a little while waiting for the object of her ceaseless questioning to appear.

Beatrice sat beside her, pale, sad, and thoughtful. Once she raised the poor, wasted hand she held to her lips, and murmured:

"O mother! make me believe as you believe."

But in the other room Mrs. Bliss was saying to her brother, who had come without his wife to attend his father's funeral:

"Poor mother! She is perfectly childish now. You cannot rely upon a word she says."

"She's been a good mother to us, Rachel.

She made a happy home and a good one for us when we were growing up," said Israel Barstow a little reprovingly.

And Rachel mournfully assented.

"You're right, brother. She's been the best of mothers to us, and now that she's old and childish, she shall want for nothing that I can do for her."

Mr. Barstow was silent. His sister's tone jarred unpleasantly upon some hidden chord, but just where or what, he could not tell. Perhaps the successful merchant, the admiring husband, the respected citizen had found nothing since so sweet or so dear as his mother's love and pride in him. Perhaps this mother-love, confined in some hearts to a narrow cell, had been forced by the emptiness of the other chambers in Israel Barstow's heart to expand beyond its usual dimensions. However it may have been, it hurt him sorely to hear his sister speak, even as kindly and protectingly as she did, of their mother's state of second childhood, and he presently stole away to the bedroom where she lay, dozing lightly, her hand in that of Beatrice's.

Nodding to his niece, he seated himself beside her, his strong, broad hand lightly laid upon his mother's dress; and so they sat together, silent, and each absorbed in thought, while the soft April twilight stole into the room, and the last ray of sunlight quivered like a glory upon the white hair of the sleeper, as she murmured in her dream of "Father, dear!"

CHAPTER XLIII.
HUSBAND AND WIFE.

PRESENTLY, when Mrs. Bliss came to prepare her mother for tea, and then for bed, Beatrice glided quietly away, and, after lingering a moment at the door, entered the great parlor, where she knew that her grandfather was lying.

She had not been in the room since that time—now four years gone past—when she heard that Marston Brent had forgotten her, and when Monckton had vainly striven to comfort her despair. As she closed the door, she remembered it, and stood for a moment with vacant eyes looking back into the past, and pitying the Beatrice who had so suffered in that almost forgotten time.

"It was her death agony. She cannot suffer any more, poor thing!" whispered she at last, with a smile sadder than any tears; and then she went softly forward, and stood beside the quiet figure, stretched, as yet uncoffined, upon a table in the centre of the room.

Dressed as she had often seen him, with his shapely hands folded upon his breast—a placid smile upon his lips, and his eyes naturally closed, he looked as if indeed he slept, and should presently awake refreshed and glad. Or so Beatrice thought at first; but when she had stood for many moments beside that motionless form, had, as it were, gathered into her inmost consciousness the awful calm, the utter silence of that presence, had tried and failed to comprehend the suggestions of vastness, of immeasurable distance, which seemed to pervade the icy atmosphere of the chamber—when she touched that brow, so serene in its white calm, so unlike any thing human in its feeling—then, for the first time, the shadow of death fell upon Beatrice Chappelleford's life—then, for the first time, she knew how puny, how idle, how impious were the theories and actions by which she and her teachers had tried to measure eternity.

Sinking upon her knees, as if crushed by the weight of that mighty conviction, she hid her face between her trembling hands, and murmured:

"O God! I acknowledge thee in death!—teach me to know thee in life."

It was the only prayer she had breathed for years; and the heart she had thought dead stirred in its slumber as the holy words re-echoed through its silent chambers.

She still knelt, wrapped in strange yet sweetly familiar reverie, when the door opened softly, and her aunt's hushed voice summoned her forth.

"He looks natural, don't he?" whispered she, as Beatrice silently passed her. "I wonder how much of him is left in that body, after all. It don't seem as if he and it could become strangers all at once, does it?"

"O Aunt Rachel! I dare not think or speak of such matters," moaned Beatrice, gliding past her aunt and hiding from herself in the lighted, warmed, and human eastern room.

In the gray twilight of the next morning, Mrs. Bliss stood beside her niece and laid a hand upon her shoulder.

"Beatrice! do you know where your grandmother has gone?" said she in a frightened voice.

"Gone! No, indeed. Has she gone?" exclaimed Beatrice, rising hastily.

"Yes. I slept with her because she seemed so restless and queer, I was afraid she was going to be sick; and when I woke just now she was gone. My first thought was that she might have come up to see you, because she seemed so pleased yesterday."

"No, she has not been here. Let us go and look for her. Can she have gone out of the house?"

"It may be. Why, where is your husband, Beatrice?"

"He sleeps upon the couch in the dressing-room. Come, aunt."

And Beatrice hastily left the room, followed by Mrs. Bliss, in whose breast anxiety for her mother struggled with a curiosity almost as strong.

The house was hastily searched—the outside doors tried and found fast, and the rest of the family roused and alarmed; but still the childish, bereaved old mother was not found.

At last, Beatrice laid her hand upon the door of the great parlor.

"We have not looked here," said she.

"That door is locked all the time; and before I went to bed, I took out the key and put it in my pocket," said Rachel positively.

"Is it there now?"

"I suppose so." And Mrs. Bliss thrust her hand into her pocket, withdrew it, and turned very pale.

"No, it is not there. Try the door."

"It is fastened, but I think only by the button inside. It is not locked," said Beatrice in a low voice.

"Let us try." And Mrs. Bliss, raising the latch, applied a strong and steady pressure to the only slightly resisting door, which presently yielded with a low, rending sound.

The two women passed through and stood beside the dead, over whose form and face his daughter had reverently spread a fair linen sheet before leaving him to his silent watch. This she now turned down, and stood stricken dumb at the piteous yet beautiful sight before her.

The loving wife had found her husband—the childish mother had passed to wisdom and knowledge unutterable — the failing, faded form lay cold and silent there, yet glorified even to outward sense by the majesty and holiness of the life to which its soul had passed.

She had crept close to her husband's side, laid her head upon his breast, and her arm around his neck, and so had fallen asleep with a serene smile upon her lips, and a look of sweet content upon her face, which seemed to glorify it like that of a saint. Looking down at her with loving awe, Beatrice remembered her words of the day before:

"And then we shall know that we're just the same to each other that we were in those young days."

"They know it now," murmured she, reverently smoothing away the silver tress of the

"*The little green churchyard.*"

wife's hair which fell across the husband's lips.

"They know it now, and more than that."

And so, the next day, a double funeral went out from the Old Garrison House; and they who had been lovely in their lives were not divided in their death, and sleep to-day side by side in the little green churchyard, beneath the shadow of Moloch.

They sleep? Oh! no, not they, but the perishing forms that held them here; for they wake eternally in a life to which this is but death.

CHAPTER XLIV.

A STONE FOR BREAD.

"AND now, Beatrice," said Mr. Chappelleford one day in May, "my preparations are complete; and as soon as you are ready, we will begin our Western journey."

"I am ready at any time," said Beatrice, without raising her eyes from the book upon her lap, although she had not read a word in it for at least an hour.

Mr. Chappelleford looked at her speculatively.

"My objection to most things has been," said he at length, "that you come to the end of them before they make an end of you. I was in hopes that you would not prove so transitory. Are you going to disappoint me?"

"What do you mean?" asked Beatrice, raising her heavy eyes.

"I found you five years ago, young, inexperienced, with a mind framed for powerful exertion, and at that time utterly empty and untrained. What little of life you had seen had disappointed and outraged your preconceived notions, for you had no *ideas* worthy of the name, and you were just in the mood to turn to something new, larger, and higher than you had yet found. I gave you this new pabulum in the form of knowledge, and through the door of science led you into a new and inexhaustible region of discovery and attainment. You followed me with the docility and naïve delight of a child, accepted all that I offered with unhesitating faith, and avowed yourself overjoyed in the exchange you had made from the old routine existence of most women—yes, and of most men, too—to this higher plane, where only man, at his farthest remove from the monkey, can hope to dwell. Do you follow me, and do I speak the truth?"

"Perfectly. And how do I now disappoint you?" asked Beatrice faintly.

"By coming to the end of your growth, and beginning the retrogressive process which, in man, follows maturity. You have been to me a fellow-thinker—you threaten to become only a woman. I thought you were past the mourning for lost lives; the speculating upon future existence; the pondering of creeds and dogmas, which have absorbed you during the last month. You could and would have pursued this course at twenty. After five years of growth, I expected higher results."

"How do you know my thoughts? I have not expressed them," asked Beatrice, flushing scarlet; but Mr. Chappelleford replied only by a contemptuous gesture.

"Womanish, womanish!" muttered he, turning away.

"Well, but now that you have found me out, give me at least some counsel, if you can—some comfort," cried Beatrice bitterly. "I have met with a loss, with a grief, none the less keen because inevitable. My parents have passed from my sight, full of faith and hope in a life beyond the grave. Your philosophy and your science refuse to recognize the validity of such hope; they coldly ask for proof, and there is no proof. But can I believe those holy lives ended in the six feet of earth where the venerable bodies were laid? And if not, where have they gone—where are we going—what conditions await us—how shall we prepare for them? Are not we wandering blindly in the dark with the light behind us? Have not we too soon despised the simple faith of unlearned minds, and substituted the pride of human intellect for the voice of God within our hearts? O Mr. Chappelleford! you are wiser and far more learned than I, but are you sure that you are not the blind leading the blind toward the verge of a terrible precipice?"

The philosopher shaded his eyes with his hand, and from beneath that screen, regarded with attentive scrutiny the beautiful face of his wife, pale, haggard, and almost ghastly with emotion.

"I have not sufficiently considered your youth," said he at last. "All this must come, and I suppose no theorizing can take the place of actual experience. But it passes, as every thing passes, great and small—every thing but the eternal laws of Nature—and who is to say that Nature itself has no limit? Perhaps the colophon of what we call the Book of Nature is Annihilation."

"You do not answer me."

"How can I? When a child comes to me, crying for the stars, what am I to do with him? Put him off for a while; and when he is calm, explain to him what the stars really are. I know of no better course."

"But I am no child."

"You talk like one."

"Well, then, instruct me, educate me, answer as gravely as I ask them, these questions which torment my soul."

8

"How can I answer rationally questions which every reflecting mind answers to itself, and in its own fashion? I can give you my ideas, but I do not ask you to adopt them as yours. Very wise men have been devotees—even bigots; others as wise have been infidels, as they are called. Take your own course; but if you follow me, you will arrive at my conclusions. I look about me, using first my own eyes, my own brain, and afterward the eyes and brains of other people. I see a vast system called Nature—self sustaining, immutable, unsympathetic, irresponsible. It governs men and things—creates, sustains, destroys, not from motives of benevolence or of malevolence, not to reward or to punish, but simply because birth, death, life are its fundamental principles. The acorn drops upon the earth, and is covered by leaves and moss; it sprouts and grows up into a promising tree; comes the north wind and twists it off at the root; it dies and becomes mould, wherein sprout other acorns. Do the surrounding oaks cry: 'Glory Hallelujah! A miracle! a special dispensation! a gift from Heaven!' when the oakling sprouts; or do they abase themselves in the dust when it dies, and demand of each other why this terrible thing has happened, and how they are to guard themselves against the same fate? Nor do they waste time in inquiring where the sap dried out of that dead trunk has gone, or whether there may exist some unknown limbo whither it has fled, and become the ghost of its former self. The oaks recognize and submit to the inevitable law, simply because it is inevitable. Cannot you be as wise?"

"But man is different from an oak. He is the chief and crown of creation. All this system operates for his use and benefit."

"If he goes along with it, it does; if he goes contrary to it, he gets run over and smashed. Make a ship, and the ocean will float it and the wind propel it; throw yourself into the water bodily, and the sea will drown you; go up in a balloon, and the wind will carry you to the Mountains of the Moon, and dash you to pieces there. People talk of governing Nature, and they talk rubbish; the most they can do is to submit to her laws, and preserve their own devices subject to those laws—never forgetting that one of the principal of them is ultimate transmutation of every form of material in her laboratory, man among the rest."

"But what is the end? For what purpose is all this vast machinery put in motion? Who created Nature, and for what, and what is the grand result?' asked Beatrice wearily.

"Asking for the stars again? Your questions are too childish, but I will try to answer them. The end? There is none, but the necessity of some form of existence. The purpose? Nature knows no purpose, but simply superadds effect upon cause because such sequence is inevitable under her laws. Who created her and her laws? She herself is Creator and Eternal. And the grand result? The perfect unison of man with Nature. Through the ages, he is learning to understand and co-operate with her more and more, to 'flash the lightnings, weigh the sun,' as some one of these rhymsters has it, to work with her, and in measuring his wishes by her will, gain her powerful assistance instead of her fatal antagonism. The grand result, as I fancy, will be an earth where man is at last supreme, where he will create and destroy life, rule the seasons, sway the elements, command all the forces of Nature—but always, mind you, subject to her laws—and where, indeed, he shall at last deserve the name of a god. You see, child, I too indulge in dreams sometimes, although I do not often expose the weakness."

"But in that millennium will the souls and hearts of men also rise to the godlike level of their minds? Will perfect happiness reign then upon the earth?"

"I thought you had abandoned that senseless cry. Happiness? It is the content of fools. A wise man finding himself at the highest attainable point of knowledge and power, sees beyond him a thousand yet inaccessible summits, and understands that effort, like attainment, is limitless and eternal. No man ever in the past has said, no man in the future shall say: 'I have conquered, I have finished!' And until then I cannot conceive of what you call happiness."

"And there is no world beyond this, you think?"

"Wait, my dear, until this one has been thoroughly explained before you invite me to another. When some one has verified Speke's discovery of the Nile, and brought home Franklin's remains from the North Pole, and thoroughly surveyed the region about the Southern one, then we will climb the Mountains of the Moon, and so up to Paradise."

"I ask for bread, and you give me a stone,"

murmured Beatrice, her head drooping upon her breast.

"I try to give you common-sense, but——" and Mr. Chappelleford constrained himself to finish the sentence by nothing more uncourteous than a smile. Presently, however, he resumed in his ordinary tone:

"As I was saying, Beatrice, I am now ready to go to the West, and think you will enjoy going with me. Certainly your assistance will be most valuable to me, and important to the report I am to make. You know you entered into those matters in France and Switzerland *con amore*, and fairly silenced the Parisian *savans*, who could not hold their own at all in the arguments they tried to sustain against you."

Beatrice smiled faintly, and raised her head with an air of interest.

"If I can help you, I am very glad to go to the West," said she.

"You can help me very much. Bassthwaite was telling me a few days ago of some fossil remains found in a coal-bed somewhere in the western part of Pennsylvania, which I am sure will interest you. By the way, the mine is owned and carried on by a man named Brent, who I believe to be your old lover. Do you know whether he lives in that part of the country?"

"No; I have no idea. I have not heard of him since our marriage," replied Beatrice unmoved.

"I asked your uncle, who was present, and he thought that this was the man. Marston Brent, I think he is called."

"The Mr. Brent I knew was called Marston."

"No doubt the same. Your uncle said that some one in Milvor had been inquiring this Brent's present abiding-place and circumstances of Mrs. Bliss, and the result was to ascertain that he lived in Pennsylvania, and was engaged in coal-mining."

"I dare say. I wonder if he really married."

"That I did not hear, but I shall certainly go to him for information and assistance in this fossil business. Would you like to go there with me, or have you any sentimental objections to meeting him?"

"Not any at all. On the contrary, I have a curiosity to see Marston Brent again, and find whether he has changed as much as I."

And Beatrice drooped her head again with a weary sigh.

Her husband looked keenly at her.

"Come then," said he. "Even a relapse into sentiment will be better than this maudlin condition. We will go to visit Marston Brent, and his coal-mine and his wife."

CHAPTER XLV.

TWICE WARNED.

HALF way up the mountain, one of the precipitous wooded mountains of Western Pennsylvania, nature had fashioned a sunny plateau, open to the south, with glimpses of mountain scenery at the east and west, and ample shelter at the north. Here Marston Brent had built his simple home, and here lived, with no thought of further change, a grave, silent man, attentive to the business which was pouring unmeasured wealth into his coffers, a benefactor to the army of laborers with their families in his employ, a kind and indulgent head to his little household, and in all else as much a hermit as if he had lived alone in the cave, a thousand feet nearer to the crest of the mountain. Of himself, he never spoke, and that must have been a hardy explorer who had ventured to intrude upon the privacy so strictly guarded, so vigilantly maintained.

Even Ruth, who had so tenderly nursed him through that long illness of crushed body and wounded heart, who had seen him in those desperate and unguarded moments when the voice of nature, tried beyond endurance, forced the barriers of pride and reserve, and made itself audible in the anguished cries so terrible when extorted from a strong man's agony—even Ruth dared not now ask whether those wounds had healed, whether the past was forgotten, whether the timid flower of hope yet survived the storm that had prostrated so much of what was best and sweetest in the life of the man she reverenced and admired beyond all men.

It was of this very point that she was thinking, seated in a favorite niche in the mountain-side, with the bright waters of the creek shining far beneath, and a magnificent country of wood and mountain water, and distant reaches of fertile intervale, outspread before her. And here, breaking upon her reverie, came Paul Freeman, now a stalwart and handsome young man, and well to do in the world, as Mr. Brent's foreman and overseer well might be.

Here he came, seeking Ruth, and here he found her. Throwing himself upon the turf at her feet, he looked out for a moment upon the landscape, glorious in a sunset of unbroken gold, and then he turned and looked yet more admiringly into the beautiful face of the young girl.

"Ruthie!"

"Well, Paul?"

"You promised me an answer to-night."

"I know it, and I came out here to find it, Paul, but I cannot."

"Cannot tell whether you hate me who have loved you all your life?"

"*A favorite niche in the mountain-side.*"

"I know I do not hate you—but——"

"But you are not sure that you love me?"

"No, not sure in the way you mean."

"Look at here, Ruth, I know what it all means, even better than you do. You love some one else better."

"Some one else, Paul?" asked the young girl, crimsoning all over her pale face.

"Yes, some one whom you have always admired and looked up to, and believed in, so that you cannot at this moment fairly tell whether there is room for any one else in your heart or not. And all the while, you

know that he does not care for you, or any woman in the way of love and marriage, and perhaps never will again. You know it, Ruth, and yet you turn away from an honest love that has always been faithful to you since you were a poor little runaway child——"

"Paul, Paul!"

"Why, Ruthie, I don't think any the worse of you for that, nor I don't mean to throw it in your face; only that was what first drew me close to you, and I always remember it when I get to thinking of how much I love you. And though you never have told, and I never have known, the right of that matter, I never have seen the minute yet when I doubted that you were as innocent as of any blame whatever, from the first to the last of it."

"Oh! I wish I knew, I wish I knew——" murmured Ruth bitterly, as she hid her face in her hands and bowed it upon her lap.

"Wish you knew what, Ruthie?" asked Paul tenderly.

"Whether Mr. Brent would say as much as that for me."

"Oh!" And Paul withdrew the hand he had tenderly laid upon that bowed head, and sat looking moodily out upon the sunset.

A hasty step approached, and Brent's voice was heard from the path below, calling:

"Ruth! Are you there?"

"Yes, sir." And springing to her feet, the girl hastily obeyed the summons, followed more slowly by Paul.

They found Brent awaiting them, and looking pale and anxious, as he had not looked in years. He held a letter in his hand, and nervously folded it while he spoke:

"Ruth, we are to have company, and you must make preparation. Mr. Chappelleford and his wife wish to visit the Northern Mine, and will stay with us some days. They will be here—perhaps to-morrow morning—perhaps not till afternoon. You can arrange with Matilda about accommodation, I suppose."

"Yes, sir, I suppose so," said Ruth in a stifled voice, and, after a moment's hesitation, she passed Brent, and rapidly descended the path toward the house.

Brent, about to follow, was detained by Paul: "May I speak to you a moment, sir?"

"What is it, Freeman?"

"I want to ask you a plain question, sir, and I want a plain answer—not as from employer to employé, but as from man to man. Shall I have it?"

"You shall have it, Freeman." And Mr. Brent, thrusting the letter into his breast-pocket, folded his arms, and leaning against the boulder beside him, turned an attentive face toward his companion. The last rays of the setting sun lighted the scene, and threw into bold relief the faces and forms of the two men, each a type of his class, each striking in appearance, each worthy of attention, perhaps of admiration.

Brent represented the Saxon element, almost unmingled with other blood. Tall, deep-chested, broad shouldered, stalwart in every proportion, with a round and somewhat massive head, well set back, a proud and dignified bearing, a steadfast and perhaps immobile expression of face, crisp curling hair and beard of reddish brown, keen blue eyes, and a mouth affectionate or stern, as occasion warranted.

So stood Marston Brent, and confronting him, the slighter, more flexible, more elegant form of his workman and rival, from whose passionate, swarthy face, glowing dark eyes, and stormy mien, the sunlight seemed to glance off repelled, leaving the shadows deepened, and the lights untouched. No man's son was Paul Freeman, and from no distinct race had he sprung, but yet he was a representative man, for embodied in his sinewy frame was the haughty, progressive, ambitious spirit of the new world, the element of conquest and of encroachment, the ardor to pursue, the determination to possess, the will to retain.

Such men as he to cross the ocean and discover the new continent, and wrest its gold and jewels from hapless savages; such men as Brent to follow with their household goods, and reclaim the wilderness, and endure the hardships of the pioneer, forcing the savage to the wall—not by sudden raids and ruthless torture, but by steady, persistent, and unrelenting effort, the sword in one hand, and the law in the other, until the land lay at his feet—not desolated, scattered, and affrighted, but a happy, peaceful home for him and his, with a church on every hill, and a school house at every corner. But Brent is saying:

"You shall have your answer, Freeman. What is the question?"

"Just this: Do you want to marry Ruth?"

"I marry Ruth! The idea has never crossed my mind."

"That is not the answer you promised me,

sir. If you have not thought of it before, will you be so kind as to think now? I can wait."

And Freeman walked away a few steps and seated himself deliberately. Brent looked at him with troubled eyes, which presently wandered to the wide landscape beyond, while a sombre and introspective expression settled upon his face. At last he spoke.

"Paul, I cannot give you the answer you ask, to-night. You must explain yourself also to some extent. Why should you mention my marrying Ruth?"

"Because, sir, if you don't mean to, it would be no more than fair to others that you should let her understand so."

"To others? To you?"

"Well, yes; I love her, and I know my own mind, as I have known it for years, about wanting to marry her."

"Why don't you do it then?" asked Brent bluntly.

"Because, sir, if you must be told it plainly, she loves another man, and that man is you."

"Did she say so, Freeman?"

"Certainly not, sir—what girl would say such a thing? But I know it, and have known it for long. I know too, sir, that you have always loved another woman, and though she's married and out of your reach, I don't know why that should make you want my poor little Ruth. It seems hard enough, Mr. Brent, that you should have for nothing, and without even wanting it, what I would give ten years of my life to gain, and can't."

"Poor boy! His ewe-lamb," muttered Brent, casting a friendly and compassionate glance upon his rival, who returned it with one of almost defiance.

"If you do not want her, sir, it would be easy enough to show it, and a kindness in the end, even to her."

"But if your supposition is correct, and she loves me, Paul, she cannot love you at any rate; and I think she is too much a woman to marry one man, loving another."

"Leave that to her and to me, sir, if you please. Only say that you do not wish or intend to marry her," said Freeman, in so hard and defiant a manner that Brent replied coldly:

"This is hardly the tone for a discussion between us two, Paul Freeman. Let the question rest for a few days until I have time to consider it, and I will answer you definitely.

Perhaps I shall first speak to Ruth upon the subject."

"And perhaps to Mrs. Chappelleford," muttered Freeman, turning away, and rapidly ascending the hill.

The words reached Brent's ear, and with a quick flush of anger mounting to his face, he made a step in pursuit, but then restrained himself, and turned in the opposite direction.

"He is smarting under a great disappointment, and it may be overlooked," muttered he, striding down the path. "But if Ruth loves me—it might be well to speak to her to-night before——coward that I am, shall I need to defend myself behind any other shield than honor, from love of another man's wife? And yet, Beatrice, Beatrice, you should not have consented to try me thus!"

Entering the house, he was met by Zilpah, whose duties in these days had become merely nominal, but her privileges very positive.

"What's this, Mr. Marston? Ruth says, Beatrice Wansted that was is coming to see you. Is it so?"

"Yes, Zilpah. Her husband, Mr. Chappelleford, is coming, and she accompanies him. They are going to the West upon some scientific errand."

"What sort of an errand? But never mind what name she puts to it. Marston Brent, be warned in time, for the devil has laid a trap for you. Go in there, and comfort Ruth, who is crying her heart out for love of you. Go!"

"You too!" muttered Brent, but instead of entering the house, he turned away, and plunged into the darkening forest.

CHAPTER XLVI.

ASLEEP OR DEAD?

THE next day, in the golden glory of such another sunset, Marston Brent, with uncovered head and grave, courteous face, stood beside a carriage which had just toiled up the mountain road to the plateau where stood his house.

"Mrs. Chappelleford! I am very glad to see you," said he, extending his hand to the elegant woman, who threw back her veil and looked scrutinizingly into his face as she replied:

"And I you, Mr. Brent. You are scarcely changed in all these years. Let me present my husband, Mr. Chappelleford."

The host made courteous recognition of the introduction, and the guest replied:

"Thank you, Mr. Brent; and before entering your house I should apologize for taking it by storm in this manner. Nothing but my anxiety to see the curious remains of which I wrote, and Mrs. Chappelleford's desire to meet an old friend, can excuse us."

"No excuse is needed, sir. In this new country, hospitality is more an indulgence than a duty. It is I who am obliged to you and Mrs. Chappelleford for the honor you do me."

"And what a glorious situation you have found here, Mr. Brent," said the lady, lingering upon the little porch, and glancing admiringly over the wide view glittering and smiling in the sunset light. "Such scenery makes ours at home seem very tame."

"Yes, Ironstone Mountain is somewhat brighter than Moloch," said Brent simply.

"And somewhat more valuable," said Mr. Chappelleford smiling.

"To one's pocket—yes," replied Brent.

"What, have you the mal-du-pays, and do you regret New-England and Milvor?" asked Beatrice a little incredulously.

"I regret nothing that I have left behind me, Mrs. Chappelleford. The life of a pioneer must not be retrospective, if he is to retain energy and interest."

"Well spoken, Mr. Brent," said the philosopher heartily. "I like to see a man not only possess the qualifications for his place, but understand them, and cling to them voluntarily."

"And all regrets, all hopes are so idle," said the lady softly, as she turned to enter the house.

In the parlor, beside the prettily-laid tea-table, stood a slender, fair-faced girl, whom Brent simply introduced as Ruth, and whom the guests consequently could greet only as Miss Ruth, quietly wondering the while what her position in the house could be, and if she possessed no name, or relationship to Brent, by which he could have designated her.

"It cannot be his wife," thought Beatrice, as the object of her wonder took the head of the table. "And yet——"

"Will you have tea or chocolate, Mrs. Chappelleford?" asked the hostess.

And Beatrice, quick at distinguishing semitones of expression, felt that through this sweet, low voice sharply vibrated something of pain, something of enmity to herself. She wondered and waited, sipping her tea meantime, and listening to the clear, forcible language in which Brent replied to Mr. Chappelleford's scientific inquiries, and the keen apothegms which the cynical philosopher never long restrained.

The next morning, Brent took Mr. Chappelleford about his property, and into the great smelting-house in the valley where the iron mined by him was prepared for market.

Beatrice, weary with her journey, preferred remaining in the house, and drawing a deep-cushioned chair to the window, sat looking admiringly over the landscape, and trying to calculate its influences upon a man like Brent.

The door softly opened and closed, admitting Ruth, who, with her little work-basket in her hand, came to entertain, as a duty, the guest of the house left in her charge.

Mrs. Chappelleford looked at her smilingly.

"I am admiring this view, Miss Ruth; I suppose it is very familiar to you."

"Yes, ma'am. We have lived here now more than three years."

"You came then with Mr. Brent? I thought perhaps you had grown up among these mountains."

"No, ma'am. I came with Mr. Brent," said Ruth, coloring slightly, and bending over her work.

"Probably you can tell me, then, whether there was any truth in the report of Mr. Brent's marriage some years since. I did not like to ask him, thinking perhaps Mrs. Brent might have died, or ——"

"She never lived; he was never married," exclaimed Ruth almost indignantly, and then, with a great throb of pity, wonder, terror, she hastily asked: "O Mrs. Chappelleford! did you believe that?"

"Believe Mr. Brent to be married? Yes, I hoped that he was," said Beatrice, sweeping one keen, bright glance over the girl's glowing face.

"Hoped? Why, how could ——"

And Ruth suddenly paused, and bent her head lower and lower, until the calm, proud eyes so fixedly watching her saw only the soft brown hair coiled in rich masses at the top of the head.

"And he was never married at all then? But he was engaged?" asked Mrs. Chappelleford at length.

"No, ma'am, never," replied the girl without looking up.

"That is strange. We all heard so at Milvor," said Beatrice meditatively, but with so little emotion that Ruth forgot her own imprudence and looked wonderingly up. Beatrice read the look and smiled.

"My dear," said she, "you know something of my early history, I perceive, and perhaps some day I will explain what puzzles you so sorely. Tell me now, what do you think of Mr. Brent, yourself?"

"I think, ma'am, that he is—that I should —that—that—I think, ma'am, he is a very, very nice gentleman."

"Yes, and so do I," replied Mrs. Chappelleford without a smile. "And how long have you known him?"

"About six years, ma'am."

"It is about six years since he left Milvor," said Beatrice quietly.

"Yes, ma'am. I came with him and Paul Freeman from a town near Milvor, and have been with him ever since."

"And cannot you at all understand the report that Mr. Brent was about to be married?" asked Beatrice, smiling a little sarcastically.

"No, ma'am. There never has been any woman in the family but old Zilpah and Matilda Jennings, since we came here, and me."

"And you, did you say?" pursued Mrs. Chappelleford, presuming a little, as she felt with shame, upon her position and self-command, to draw this child's secret from her lips. But she had her reward, for Ruth, raising a quivering glowing face to hers, cried in a tone of genuine alarm and surprise:

"Me, madam! Oh! no, he never thought of me; how could he? Don't say such a thing to him."

"Certainly not, my dear. But why should he not think of it? I wish he would."

"You wish he would! Why, Mrs. Chappelleford, he never has forgotten you, and how could he love any one like me afterward?"

"Forgotten me! Why do you say that, Ruth? Are you Mr. Brent's confidante then?" asked Mrs. Chappelleford very coldly.

"No, indeed, ma'am, he is not the man to tell such things to any one," replied Ruth indignantly. "He has never spoken your name to me more than half a dozen times in his life, and then only when he was so desperate at the news of your marriage that he had to speak or go crazy, or kill himself, and then when he got crushed with the tree, and one night thought that he was dying, he gave me a message for you, but afterward he told me to forget it."

"And you forgot it?"

"No, ma'am, I could not forget it, but I will never repeat it."

"I do not ask you to do so, Ruth. But what are those events of which you speak? When did Mr. Brent hear of my marriage, and when was he crushed by a tree, and so near to death, as you say?"

"Why, did you never hear of that, ma'am?" And then Ruth, her hands clasped upon her knee, her eyes downcast, as if she read the story from a visible page, repeated the events we know already—describing even better than she, in her innocence, could understand Brent's terrible anguish in learning of the unfaithfulness of the woman to whom his whole life clung, in spite of their estrangement—his reckless behavior upon that day, the accident which had so nearly cost him his life, and the lingering illness which ensued, through which only the devotion of his nurse and constant attendant had brought him alive.

Mrs. Chappelleford, leaning back in the cushioned chair, her eyes riveted upon the far horizon line, one white hand supporting her chin, the other toying idly with her watch-chain, listened to all this recital in the profoundest silence. When it was finished, she said in her soft, sonorous tones:

"Thank you very much. Your story interests me extremely, and it is something to be interested for half an hour."

Ruth turned and stared into the face of her auditor with undisguised amazement. A feeling of delicacy had hitherto restrained her from even a glance.

"O Mrs. Chappelleford! Don't you care at all, then?" exclaimed she with quite involuntary horror.

Beatrice smiled sadly.

"You think me very heartless, do you not? But, Ruth, it is so long since I left all this behind me, all this heart-break and repining and emotion of every sort, that your story cannot even rouse their echoes. Love is the occupation of very young, or very thoughtless, or very unintellectual persons. Mr. Brent himself, I dare say, would smile to-day at these sorrows which to you seem still so real. I am interested in the story, as I said, for Mr. Brent was once a very dear friend of mine,

and I like to know what agencies have helped to build up his character. It was all necessary, I dare say, to develop his best qualities. He would not regret it, nor should we."

"And you don't care a bit for him, nor think that he cares for you?" asked Ruth, all amazement.

Mrs. Chappelleford answered only by a superb smile of self-reliance, of compassion for the inexperience of her companion, of dismissal, and Ruth, murmuring some excuse, rose and left the room, half indignant, half bewildered.

Beatrice sat still, her eyes fixed upon the distant mountains, glittering now with noon-day sunshine.

"So it was all a mistake," said she at last. "Well, what matter now? Fate so willed it. Mr. Chappelleford would tell me, and we poor puppets could not resist. I wonder what view Marston would take of it?"

CHAPTER XLVII.

THE BLUEBEARD CLOSET.

THE fossil remains of Ironstone Mountain proved even more interesting to Mr. Chappelleford than he had expected, and as Brent's coöperation in his researches and his hospitality to both his guests were evidently a great pleasure to himself as well as to them, the period of their visit was extended day after day, until it had reached nearly three weeks. Mr. Chappelleford was now busily engaged in making casts of some of the most curious of the antediluvian relics which he had discovered, and kept both himself and the workmen Brent had placed at his disposal actively employed. Brent helped him when necessary, and when he found that the savant preferred solitude, or the companionship only of the laborers, he devoted himself to entertaining Mrs. Chappelleford, who, either upon foot or mounted upon Ruth's active little pony, amused herself by exploring the mountain-passes, points of view, and curious freaks of nature, with which the region abounded. In some of these excursions, she was escorted by her husband—sometimes, when he and Brent were engaged, by Paul Freeman, with whom she liked to talk of old Milvor days, and sometimes by her host only.

In the beginning of this intimate association, Beatrice had vigilantly, although most guardedly, watched every look, word, or intimation of feeling in her companion, determined to repress all sentiment, or even allusion, to the past, with unsparing scorn. But she soon found she had no occasion for her armor. Brent—always courteous, always frank and cheerful, but never familiar, never retrospective, never even silent and preoccupied—appeared so little like a despondent lover, so little like the despairing and desperate man whom Ruth had pictured, that Mrs. Chappelleford herself fell more and more often into reverie in his presence, recalling the old tender scenes that had passed between

"The crest of Ironstone."

them, recalling the constancy, the tenderness of his nature as she had known him, wondering if indeed he could have so completely changed, or if this were only acting, until at length the desire to penetrate beneath that calm and debonair exterior, to the Bluebeard chamber far within became almost irresistible, and from dreading all allusion to the past, avoiding all questions of sentiment or personality, she came to seeking eagerly for the opportunity of introducing them, and of leading the conversation, when alone with Brent, to a confidential turn.

But here, to her amazement and mortification, she found herself foiled so quietly, and apparently so unconsciously, that at first she attributed her discomfiture to accident than to want of comprehension, and finally to a too fastidious honor. But in proportion to the difficulty of discovering the secret feelings of this heart she had so dreaded to still find her own, Beatrice felt a growing desire to penetrate this smooth but impervious veil, to force at least confession of something hidden, and satisfy herself that she had not been dreaming when she believed that Brent had once loved her truly.

"Only let me once know what he really feels, and I am satisfied forever," said she to herself, and began to search for the key to that locked door.

"Ruth was telling me of that terrible injury you sustained in the woods," said she one day, as the two slowly climbed the crest of Ironstone, and paused to look at the wonderful panorama below.

"Yes, it was rather severe at the time. Do you see that blue ribbon glittering among the hills, Mrs. Chappelleford? That is the Alleghany."

"Indeed. Yes, I see it quite plainly. But tell me of that time in the woods, Marston. Ruth says you were near dying, and very low in spirits, too."

"Did she tell you how I was cured?"

"By her tender care, I should think, from her artless story."

"By that certainly; but also by brandy, sugar, and salt-pork. I must tell you about it."

And Beatrice found herself obliged to listen with polite attention to a minute account of the novel medical treatment prescribed by Richard, with the doctor's indignation, and old Zilpah's incredulity.

When the story was ended, Beatrice sat silent and a little offended. Reserve was very well, but this was rudeness. At last she said:

"I find you very much changed, Mr. Brent."

"That is natural, considering the laborious and exposed life I have led here and in the woods. Why, Mrs. Chappelleford, I have not been idle, when I was able to work, so many hours in five years as I have in the last three weeks."

"And do you regret the occasion?" asked Beatrice, turning her head, "with eyes of sumptuous expectation fixt" upon the face of her sometime lover, who promptly answered:

"No, indeed. It has been a great treat to me to meet once more persons of cultivation and——"

"Marston Brent, why do you perpetually evade me thus?" cried Beatrice, with a touch of her old petulant humor. "It is no compliment to me to avoid so persistently a subject upon which I am willing to speak. Are you afraid for yourself or me?"

"For neither, Mrs. Chappelleford," said Brent in a low voice, while the expression of his face changed so suddenly that Beatrice felt her heart leap for joy. At last she had conquered—at last he must speak, and she would be satisfied once for all.

"Then why do you so pointedly avoid the past?" asked she, more graciously. "That it is quite past we neither of us doubt, and why should we not discuss it as we would the story of Hero and Leander, or Romeo and Juliet?"

"We will, if you wish it," replied Brent, and his mouth grew white, and his eyes resolute, as if he had just signified his assent to the torture, resolving all the while that not its fiercest extremity should extort confession or complaint from his lips.

Beatrice, a little startled at her own success, sat silent for a moment, but finally found voice to say:

"I have one confession to make, Marston. It was I who sent you the paper with the announcement of my marriage."

"Why do you call it a confession? Did you mean to wound me?"

"Yes, I am afraid I did. Can you forgive me?"

"Yes, I forgive you freely."

"Could you have forgiven me before the wound was quite healed?"

"I never felt resentment."

The answer did not satisfy her, and she put the question in a different form:

"You are content now, Marston?"

"I am content—yes."

"And happy? You no longer remember me?"

"I have not so many new friends that I should forget the old ones very easily."

"O Marston! you do not tell me what I want to know. Why will you not speak out for once?"

"What do you wish to know?"

"Do you—Marston, do you remember—do you—love me still?"

She had asked it, and sat aghast. The silence that befell seemed to her filled with accusing voices — the air with scornful eyes. She covered her face with her hands, and sat ashamed and silent.

At last he spoke, in a voice so low and stern that she hardly recognized it.

"Mrs. Chappelleford, that is a question you have no right to ask, or I to answer. Let us forget it."

"You find it very easy to forget," said Beatrice bitterly, and without raising her head.

"So be it," replied Brent in the same tone.

"But, Marston, before we leave the subject, I wish to tell you that I heard you were about to marry. I never should have been married myself if I had not thought——"

"Hush, Beatrice — hush! Whatever may be now, you once were my ideal of womanhood. Do not profane the sacred memories which alone are left to me by representing yourself as marrying from other motive than the highest, or as bearing toward your husband to-day less than an entire love and confidence. You have made this inquiry into my life, past and present, partly from the kind interest of an old friendship—partly in a spirit of psychological research. Here let it rest."

"But, O Marston! help me, advise me, comfort me! I thought I was content, and I find myself most miserable. I thought my heart was dead; and already the new life coursing through it stings me with anguish intolerable. Marston, I have slept through these five long years, and now I begin to waken. What shall I do? How shall I comfort myself in my despair?"

She covered her face, and wept passionately. Brent, pale and agitated, looked at her lovingly for a moment; then turning half away, said solemnly:

"You cannot comfort yourself, nor can I comfort you. There is one Comforter, and but one — His name is Christ: go to Him. Forgive me for yielding so rashly and so weakly to your request for open speech upon this subject. I should have been strong for both of us. It is my fault—only mine. Come, we will go home."

And without another word, he led the way swiftly and steadily down the mountain-path, where already slept the purple shadows of the night, the misty wraith of the departed day.

CHAPTER XLVIII.

RUTH'S OGRE.

SHE had never heard of Œnone, this poor little Ruth, "mournful Œnone wandering forlorn" upon the hills, nor could she so melodiously phrase her grief, and yet the burden of her song in those weary days, that sad, sad song without words, sung in her secret heart, was like the nymph's lament ·

"My eyes are full of tears, my heart of love,
My heart is breaking, and my eyes are dim,
And I am all aweary of my life."

For Brent, who, if never a lover, had always been the kindest of friends and companions, ever ready to sympathize, instruct, or counsel, now found but little time even to notice the poor child, giving all his leisure to his guests, and employing himself for the remainder with almost desperate energy about his business. And Paul, too, held aloof—Paul, whose devotion, hardly valued while it was so freely and constantly bestowed, became of sudden importance now that it was withdrawn.

"Nobody loves me, nobody cares for me, and why should I want to live? I will throw myself down the old pit-hole, and make an end of it," moaned Ruth, and crept stealthily out of the house and into the woods, until she came to the deserted shaft. Several times, in her rapid flight, she thought she heard foot-steps behind her, but looking round could see no one; and when she paused in the lonely glade beside the pit-hole, it seemed to her that she must be the only living thing in all the world, so intense was the stillness surrounding her. But the black shadows of the fir-trees fell across the mouth of the pit, and the water oozing through the stones at the side fell with a melancholy plash into the pool at the bottom, and the blackberry-vines clinging about the verge were red as if the blood of a murdered man had fallen there; and Ruth, chilled out of her desperate meaning, stood shivering and looking about her, feeling that, although life might be forlorn, death was terrible, when a rustling footfall close behind made her start and turn in sudden fright.

Parting the underbrush away where he stood, a man peered out at her, his face most discordantly framed by the tender green branches of the birches, and his stooping figure dimly discernible behind them.

At first sight of face and figure, the girl shrank back with no more than natural terror, but presently the glance of terror turned to one of horror, which slowly froze upon the delicate features until they resembled a marble mask of some Gorgon-victim, and step by step the girl drew nearer to the mouth of the pit, resolute to seek shelter there, if no better might be found, from the awful doom which menaced her.

But help was at hand; the sound of foot-steps and voices approached along the path, and the head among the birches suddenly disappeared, while Ruth, relieved from the horrible fascination of those eyes, turned with a stifled scream, and fled, passing Mr. and Mrs. Chappelleford without a word, nor pausing until she was securely hidden in her own chamber at home.

"Why, what is the matter with the young woman? It is too late for March madness," exclaimed Mr. Chappelleford, turning to look after the retreating figure.

"I am sure I cannot tell. Perhaps she saw some wild animal, or fancied a ghost among the trees," replied Beatrice, whose pale face and nervous manner ill-supported the careless tone she forced herself to assume. Presently she resumed:

"Then you cannot go to-morrow?"

"No, I tell you, nor the next day. My workmen are just preparing to take the most important casts we have obtained yet, and I think I shall discover something worth more than all the rest before to-night. I have said nothing yet to Brent, nor even set the men at work, but I think that I have a distinct impression of a gigantic ichthyosaurus in a bed of slate just below a loose deposit of shale, which I am picking away myself. I don't want to say any thing until I am certain, but if my supposition proves correct, I shall have conferred a lasting benefit upon my country and the Historical Society by my Western journey. We have not such an impression—in fact, I never have seen such an impression in any part of the world as this. It is really marvellous. You must come and look at it."

"Where is it?" asked Beatrice faintly.

"In a side-cutting of this old mine. My men are at work in the main tunnel, and I wandered away with my lantern yesterday to see what discoveries I could make. This is about half a mile from where they are at work. By the way, Beatrice, you amused yourself once by calling me Diogenes——"

"How did you know it? I never said so," exclaimed Beatrice, a little confused.

"I knew it; my eyes and ears are tolerably keen, and my mental perceptions not especially dull. But what I was about to say was, that, after Diogenes, I have taken to carrying a lantern in the daylight, and I have discovered what he did not—an honest man."

"Indeed!"

"Yes. It is your friend Brent. I don't know when I have come so near liking any one as I do him. It is very fortunate you did not marry him, madam."

"Why do you say so?"

"Because you would have been in love with him, and that would have been the end of you. Now you are something better than an affectionate, sympathizing woman—you are a companion for men, and a worthy friend and helpmate for a seeker after knowledge. Beatrice, I am glad you decided as you did that evening in Barstow's drawing-room."

"Are you, Mr. Chappelleford?"

"Well, what is it? Your eyes are full of unspoken words, and your lips tremble with repressed emotion. Speak it out, honestly and fearlessly. Perhaps I can fancy half the story beforehand."

"I wish that we could leave this place to-morrow. It is very hard for me to stay," murmured Beatrice, shrinking beneath the keen glances shot at her from under the philosopher's shaggy eyebrows.

"Well, go on. Speak it out."

"There is nothing to speak. I want to leave this place."

"And Marston Brent? You find that the old folly rises too vividly to memory, and shames the calmer and wiser present? You dislike to recall the stupidities you have outlived? Is that it?"

"No. I dread to discover that I have not outlived them," said Beatrice desperately. "I wish to leave this place before I add the crime of living, present love to the anguish—folly, if you will—of that which I believed dead and buried."

They had by this time reached the entrance of the horizontal shaft of the deserted mine, and Mr. Chappelleford paused, leaning against the gray rocks, with an air of profound discomfiture, while before him stood his wife, her hands clasped together, her head drooping, her whole attitude that of a criminal awaiting sentence.

It came at last, sentence and punishment in one :

"I once knew a man," said the philosopher slowly, "an ardent Darwinian, who undertook the education of a very promising monkey, hoping to develop in him the intelligence of a man. The work went on, with varying success, until one day, as the master was giving a lesson in the alphabet, and the monkey attending to it with the most promising gravity of demeanor, a mischievous boy rolled an apple across the floor, at which sight, the monkey, uttering a cry of delight, dropped upon all fours, pursued and seized the prey, and when his master would have snatched it from him, dealt him a blow upon the head with his own ruler, which nearly knocked him down. As he recovered his balance, he saw the monkey scuttling away across some sheds, holding fast to the apple, and uttering wild cries of brutish defiance and terror. My friend looked after him a moment, then slowly shook his fist in dismissal, crying: 'Go! It is I that was a fool in trying to make a man out of a monkey.' Mrs. Chappelleford, amuse yourself with whatever toys suit you best ; but do not concern yourself farther about my History of the Saurian or Treatise upon Philology. I release you from all such labors and interests."

He turned as he spoke, and entered the cave, leaving Beatrice to slowly and sadly retrace her steps.

"To lose even the respect and friendship of my husband! To feel myself shut out from the pursuits that have been my life since I lost all other hope! What will become of me next? What is left——"

And Beatrice raised her sad and wistful eyes to the trees, the sky, to nature, whom her teacher had set for her in place of God. But where was comfort?

"Could I speak with you a minute, lady?" said a hoarse voice at her side, and Mrs. Chappelleford turned to find herself face to face with a rough and ragged man, whose pale face and shaking limbs told of disease, as plainly as his coward eyes and shrinking manner did of guilt. A man whom a timid woman would have feared to meet, alone and unprotected ; but Mrs. Chappelleford was not timid at any time, and just now was too deeply absorbed in her own unhappiness to care much for danger from without.

"You wish to speak to me?" asked she coldly.

"Yes, ma'am. I think I've seen you before. You was at Milvor, at old Deacon Barstow's funeral, wa'n't you? You're she that was Beatrice Wansted?"

"Very well. What then?"

"Well, ma'am, it's a long story, and a pretty hard one for me to tell, but I've come all the way here on purpose, and I'll do it, if I can see my way clear to get away afterward. You're stopping at Mr. Brent's, a'n't you?"

"Yes."

"And he's a justice, a'n't he?"

"Yes."

"And there's a girl there, about eighteen or so. What do they call her?"

"Ruth."

"What other name?"

"I do not know."

"Well, ma'am, I've got something to tell that girl, or to tell a justice before her, and Square Brent would do better than any one; but I dasn't go anigh him, without somebody to go surety that he won't touch me."

"Touch you for what?"

"Why, there's something in my story that would lay me in jail if it was acted on, but I've got to tell it all out, or I can't settle to nothing, and I don't know as I could die if I set out to—not die comf'table anyhow. And I want to tell it, but I want the Square's promise, solemn, that he won't touch me for it. Couldn't you get it for me, ma'am?"

"Perhaps. But why do you select Mr. Brent as the most suitable person to hear your deposition?"

"Because, ma'am, he's a sort of gardeen to the girl, this Ruth. It's about her the story is."

"Something to her advantage, or to her hurt?"

"Well, pretty consid'able to her advantage, I should say."

"Very well; I will speak to Mr. Brent, and if he chooses to hear you, and to give you safe conduct, he can send here for you. You had better wait near that old well I just passed."

"And how'll I be sure, when I see some one come after me, that it a'n't a trap?" asked the man with a look of mingled cunning and terror.

"You will have to leave that to me," replied Mrs. Chappelleford disdainfully. "I shall not be likely to betray a person who has trusted himself to me; but I can give you no proof other than my word."

"Very well, ma'am, I'll trust you, and I'll wait by the old well. I was there this morning, and saw Ruth herself, but she run as soon as she saw me, and no wonder either."

CHAPTER XLIX

THE MARK OF CAIN.

FINDING Brent among his workmen at the forge, Mrs. Chappelleford called him aside, and in a few clear phrases told her errand. He listened attentively, and when she had finished said:

"Thank you very much. I can guess who this man must be, and, I hope, his errand. Certainly I will give him a safe conduct if his confession is what I think, and I will go myself to assure him of it. Ruth must be present at the examination; and if it is not asking too much of you, I should be glad that you should give her the support of your presence."

"Certainly. Arrange the whole as you think best, and I will do whatever you desire," said Beatrice humbly, for since their conversation upon the mountain-top she felt herself bitterly humiliated in presence of this man, and while ardently desiring to escape from it, found somewhat of comfort in submission and deference to him in all minor matters—thus asserting, as it were, that he was not only her superior in moral strength and worth, but the superior of all men in all things, and, consequently, that to be conquered by him was not so much of a defeat as a necessity. Brent, whose habit of thought was not analytical, and who himself felt sorely hurt and troubled by the conversation into which he had been betrayed, noticed this manner with annoyance, and did not seek to fathom its cause. He felt, however, that renewed intercourse had done harm both to Beatrice and himself, and he earnestly wished that it might terminate before either found deeper cause to regret it. Perhaps, although he would not think it, he felt in his inmost heart that the struggle between his deepest and truest convictions of right and the natural impulses of a strong and loving nature was becoming too nearly equal for safety, and he feared to lose self-respect as well as peace should the contest continue longer. "At any rate," he murmured, striding along the woodland path toward the old shaft, "I will tell Ruthie every thing, and if she can love me then, we will be married."

And then he sighed, or more nearly groaned, and frowned and clenched his strong right hand, muttering:

"Well, Brent, are you a villain or a fool?"

Deep in thought still, he reached the shaft, and looked about him blankly. Then remembered his errand, and called aloud:

"Joachim Brewster, where are you?'

At sound of that name, a stir became perceptible in the bushes beyond the pit, and presently the haggard face of the man appeared, as it had done to Ruth, but now wearing an expression of anxious distrust.

"Hallo, Square! How d'ye know my name?"

"Guessed it from your errand. Come out."

"She said she'd promise for you that I shouldn't be touched. D'ye agree, Square?"

"Yes, I promise you safe conduct as soon as you like to depart. That is, if your confession is worth any thing."

"It's worth that girl Ruth's neck to her anyway, and I reckon that makes it worth something to you, Square, if what they say is so."

"Follow me to my house, and I will hear what you have to say in the presence of witnesses," said Brent, staring a moment at the speaker, and then turning upon his heel and striding down the path.

Timidly as a wild animal leaving its lair for the open country, the miserable man to whom he spoke crept from his shelter and followed, muttering:

"She said I shouldn't be touched, she did."

Arrived at the house, Mr. Brent led the way to a small room set apart as a study, or rather office for the transaction of both private and public business, and leaving his somewhat reluctant guest seated there, went himself to summon Mrs. Chappelleford, Ruth, and Paul Freeman to meet him. Entering the room rather suddenly, the guest was found softly raising the window and looking to see what lay beneath.

"You need not trouble yourself to contrive a way to escape, Mr. Brewster," said Brent coldly. "The door is free for you at any time you choose to use it. You requested this interview yourself."

"Yes, yes, Square, I know it. I was only

looking out to see what sort of a place you'd got. The lady there said I shouldn't be touched, and I allow she knew your mind as well as her own."

"You are perfectly safe," replied Brent contemptuously. "What have you to say?"

"Where's Ruth? Oh! there she is. Don't look so scared of me, girl. I a'n't going to touch you now—and, in fact, I've come all this way to clear you and set you in your right place. You can have the farm and all, if you've a mind to go and get it."

Ruth, shivering with terror, and crouching upon a low stool almost behind Mrs. Chappelleford, made no reply, and Brent, seating himself at his desk with pen and paper, somewhat sternly said:

"Now, Mr. Brewster, if you have a deposition to make, I am ready to take it, and wish it given regularly and in order. You, of course, are willing to swear to its truth, and set your name, properly witnessed, at the foot."

"On conditions, Square—on conditions that I a'n't a going to be touched for it. I'm a sick man, Square—I won't say but what I'm a dying man, and all I ask is to go off and lose myself somewheres and die in peace. If so be you can't promise that, why I'd rather not put my name to nothing that's going to be used agin me, maybe."

"I shall take no proceedings against you, as I have repeatedly promised you; and although I shall use your confession to clear Ruth's character of the horrible stain you have thrown upon it, you will have ample time to escape, and, if you are at all wise, to hide yourself so well that you will never be heard from again east of the Rocky Mountains at least."

"Well, Square, it a'n't just as I meant to have it, but I'm about tired out, and I a'n't a well man, nor a cheerful man, and I don't know as I care how it turns out. I'll go ahead and do the right thing anyway. So this is what I've got to say, and you can take it down as fast as you've a mind to:

"Me and Peleg Brewster were brothers, but after he married Semanthy the brother part on't seemed to die out. I a'n't a going to tell all about it now, for it don't matter much one way or t'other, but I don't deny that Peleg had his trials, and like enough we didn't do jest right by him, me and Semanthy didn't. And then Semanthy hated the child, Ruth there—oh! how Semanthy did hate her—and treated her bad most every way that she could think of. The worst was, setting her father against her; but she did that for a reason she had—two reasons, in fact. One was that Ruth saw and told things that went on while Peleg was away—that made him awful mad with us; and another was that when Mary—that was his first wife, you know—died, he made a will and left all the money to Ruth—farm, house, stuff, and every thing—and he hadn't never changed that will, though Semanthy had asked him often enough. But at last one night there was an awful row in the house—no matter what it was now—but Ruth she up and told something to her father, and Semanthy said she lied, and she told her own story, that put all the blame onto Ruth, and I helped her out in it, for Peleg had a knife in his hand, and would have put it into me quicker'n a flash if Semanthy and me hadn't stood it out that Ruth was the liar and something worse."

"Oh! it was so cruel, so cruel to make my own father believe such things of me; and he died, and never knew ——" burst out Ruth; and then hiding her face upon Beatrice's lap, she fell into a passion of sobs and tears.

"Go on, Brewster," said Brent sternly, and never glancing toward the corner where the women sat.

"Well, Peleg was awful mad, and the worst of it to him was that he didn't know who to believe or what to think, and finally he fixed it that we was all banded together against him, and that Ruth was jealous of Semanthy, and so complained against her; for Semanthy made it out that the girl, young as she was, liked me most too well, and Ruth didn't know enough about it to lay her in a lie, as she might have easy enough. So, Peleg settled it that we were a bad lot, the whole of us, and he swore he would just quit for good and all, sell out the farm, put Ruth to service, take Semanthy home to her mother, and let me shirk for myself. That was at night, and in the morning, sure enough, Semanthy saw him get the will he'd made out of his old secretary and put it in his pocket with a lot of other papers—the deeds of the homestead, and such like, they turned out to be. Then he got up the horse and harnessed him, and called Ruth to come along.

"It was while he was sitting in the wagon a waiting for her that he tied the rope round his own neck, for he told Semanthy that he was going to Bloom, or Milverhaven, I most forget which, for to sell the farm and all the stock just as it stood, and that neither she nor me nor Ruth was to have the money, if he had to throw it away to keep it from us. And he told her he'd carry her home next day, and tell her folks the reason why; and he said a lot of other things, some to her and some to me, that was dreadful irritating, and dangerous too, if he did as he said—and Peleg was a man that was dreadful apt to hold to one mind for quite a long spell.

"So he drove away from the door, and Semanthy she stood ever so long looking at me

Joachim Brewster waiting for his brother.

with the awfullest look that ever you see on her face, and at last she said sort of quiet:

"'Joe Brewster, if that man gets to Haven alive, it's all up with you and me.'

"'Maybe 'tis, but how am I going to help it?' says I, feeling the goose flesh rising up all over me as she spoke, it was so sort of solemn. Then she smiled, and that was worse than all, and she said, pointing to my gun:

"'A'n't you going shooting to-day, Joe?'

"'O Lord! Semanthy,' says I, 'you don't mean that, do you?'

"And she says just in the same way:

" ' If you don't, I'll drown myself in the well before that 'ere sun sets—I swear I will.'

" And she'd ha' done it—I know she would.

" So I cut across the wood-lot, and I waited just where the road turns sudden and runs by Blackbrier pond, and—and there I done it "

And with the first touch of feeling he had yet shown, the miserable man wiped his clammy forehead, moistened his lips, and glared about him as if he dreaded to see the hangman approaching.

" Be more specific. What did you do ?" demanded Brent, fixing his eyes upon the wretch before him with undisguised abhorrence.

" I shot him in the back from behind a tree, and then I jumped into the wagon and held a knife at the child's throat, and told her that she'd killed her father, and I see her do it, and I'd carry her straight on to Bloom and put her in jail, and she'd be hung. The poor little fool was so scared she didn't know at first but what she had done it, and didn't hardly know what to say, and then I made her get down on her knees and swear solemn that she never would say a word to man, woman, nor child about the matter, nor answer any questions, nor even say yes or no if she was asked if she'd done it.

" She took the oath, and she was just the child that I knew would keep it if you skinned her alive to get the story out of her ; but for all that I was calculating to take her right off to the city and put her in an orphan asylum, or lose her in the street, or some way get rid of her. That was Semanthy's planning, mind you, not mine, for I always liked the child first-rate. I was always good to you, Ruth, wasn't I now ?"

The fawning, wheedling tone of the last words was even more odious than the callous brutality of the first part of the narrative, and while Ruth shrank silently into her corner, Brent peremptorily said :

" Go on with your story, Brewster, and address yourself only to me."

" Well, Square, there a'n't much more to tell. When I'd got the gal's promise, I left her and took the body and pitched it over into the pool, thinking folks would say it had fell there, and maybe it wouldn't be found at all. I hardly seem to remember now how we did plan it. Semanthy was to the head on't all, and I only did as she told me. You see, Square, I wa'n't nigh so much to blame as she all along."

" Go on with your story, Brewster."

" Well, as I was saying, I hove the body into the pool, and I fired off the gun, as Semanthy told me—that is, Peleg's gun, for I had my own beside—and I give the horses a good cut, and set 'em off down the road—that nigh one was always skittish enough, and I knew it wouldn't be a trifle that would stop him—and then I turned round to look after the child, and she was gone. Look high and look low, not a sign of her was to be seen, and, Square, I wisht you'd just ask her yourself, sence you won't let me speak to her, where did she go that time ?"

" Do you want to tell him, Ruth ?"

" I crawled into a great hollow tree and waited until he was gone, and then I came out and ran ever so far, and fell down. I don't know what happened afterward—I think I was sort of crazy for a while ; and the next I knew Paul Freeman was with me, and crying as hard as he could cry, and then he hid me in a barn, and next day took me over to Bloom and dressed me like a boy, and kept me at the tavern till you were ready to go West."

" You hear ? Brewster," said Mr. Brent, to whom this hurried narrative was as new as to any other of its auditors.

" Yes, Square, I hear ; and it does beat all what hindered me from looking into that holler tree. Seems curious that I didn't," replied Joachim with an air of meditative regret.

CHAPTER L.

AND HIS CURSE.

"Is that all ?" demanded Brent, as the miserable wretch before him seemed indisposed to resume his narrative, but sat wiping his forehead, furtively glancing at every member of the little company in turn, and moving uneasily upon his chair.

" Well, yes, Square, I b'lieve that's all."

" And now, what is the purpose of this confession, Brewster ? Why do you make it, and what do you wish done with it ?"

" That's the very pith of the whole, Square," replied Brewster, his face lighting with more expression than it yet had displayed. " It does seem a simple sort of thing for a man to do, to go and run his head right square into a noose when he is well out of it—now don't it ? But the fact is, Square, I was drove to it."

" By what ?"

" By suthin' inside of me, Square. I don't

justly know what," replied the murderer in an awe-stricken and mysterious voice. "It's been a working most ever sence I did it. Semanthy felt it, too, and it made her awful—right down awful. I declare for't, Square, I was afraid to stop in the house with her, and use to clear out whole days to a time. But then if I went off alone, it was as bad, for I seemed to see Peleg glimpsing out at me from every tree in the wood-lot, and from behind every stone in the fields; and then the child, I expected she'd made way with herself, and I was always looking out for her bones, and maybe her natural face a-staring up out of the ground at me. I *have* heerd of such things, Square. And then if I went amongst folks, there it was agen: I didn't darst to open my mouth for fear the secret would jump out of it, unbeknownst to me, like. It seemed to me sometimes as if I'd got to holler right out: 'I did it! I did it! 'Twas me killed my brother, Peleg Brewster, and hove him in Blackbrier Pool!'

"I declare for't, Square, I was clean afraid to trust myself amongst folks, and I was scaart to death of being alone; and to stop along o' Semanthy was worst of the whole. What sort o' thoughts or what sort o' sperits ha'n't that woman I don't know; but there's a look on her face—'specially deep down in her eyes—that makes a feller's flesh creep on his bones to meet. It's been a-growing there all these five year, and when she dies, it will be the look she'll carry to her grave. I wouldn't be the man to screw down her coffin-led, not for no money—she'll look so awful when she's dead. Along at first we used to talk about it, and she'd sort o' set me up, telling how ugly Peleg was to both of us, and how he was going to turn me out upon the world and disgrace her, and she'd laugh—though it wasn't never a good laugh—and say we'd got the best on't now, and pass it off as though she was happy; but—O Lord! Then we got further along, and left off talking about it, or, in fact, about much of any thing. The neighbors wouldn't come to see us, nor the women wouldn't speak to Semanthy at meetin', or sewing-circles, or such, and she left off going, and then the look in her eyes began to grow.

"There was one thing I kept from her, and I don't hardly know why, but I did. That was the will leaving every thing to Ruth. I told her it was gone, and that most likely Peleg had torn it up; but I kept it, and hid it

in the barn, and she never knew. It used to work her dreadfully at first, because the estate couldn't be settled for want of a will or knowing about Ruth; and finally we got some bones — well, we got 'em out of the church-yard, and dressed 'em in Ruth's clothes, and put 'em in the water nigh where Peleg was found, and then I fixed it so they was diskivered, and we swore to the clothes, and nobody cared much, any way, and so the property was made over to me and Semanthy had her thirds; but, by that time, we didn't neither of us care for the property, nor nothing else. I didn't do much about the farm, and it sort o' run out, and Semanthy grew dreadful slack about the house, and took to setting all day in a chair, drawed up close in a corner of the room, so as nothing couldn't get behind her, and watching, watching all day, with that strange, awful look a-growing on her face, and seeming to come up into her eyes from way down somewhere. I can't justly tell you what I mean, Square, but I've stood outside and peeked in the winder at that woman till it seemed as if I looked out of her eyes, and seen the devil a-coming, ready to catch her any minute.

"Bimeby we got dreadful poor, and I took to drink; but that was no better, for I darsn't drink in company, and when I was alone, I had the horrors so bad I wonder I didn't shoot myself. I should ha' done it time and agen, only it seemed just as if Peleg was waiting to catch me in the dark just as soon as I got out o' life, and I darsn't meet him.

"Then at last it come inter my head that if I was to find Ruth, supposing she was alive, and clear up the charge agin her, and give back the property, what's left of it, that Peleg would be kind o' pacified, and I might get rest. What set me thinking on't was hearing that Marston Brent—that's you, Square, you know—had got a gal he was going to marry, and she was a sister to Paul Freeman, and her name was Ruth. All that come out through Zilpah Stone's folks; but nobody in Milvor seemed to mistrust any thing. You see they all swallered the story of them bones being Ruth, and then forgot all about her. But I knew better, and I knew, too, that Paul Freeman hadn't got no sister, but he was always mighty partial to our Ruth; so putting every thing together, and working over it nights and day-times—when I set one side of the fire and Semanthy the other, and neither of us speaking for hours at a time—I began to see my way out of it pooty clear. So then I went kind o' quiet and sold out the last of the bank-stock that Peleg left, and crep' away one night, leaving Semanthy setting up with the fire all out, and the candle jest guttering down, and the wind a-howling in the chimbly like folks. I couldn't stand it no longer, and she'd got sort of used to it, I s'pose, so I left her.

"I'd inquired round some, of Dr. Bliss's folks and the Stones', and I'd found out pretty nigh where you was located, Square, and so came right along; but when I got here, I kind o' hung off till I found out how the land lay First, I see Ruth in the wood; but as soon as she got sight of me she run—I expect remembering who it was, and thinking I was going to serve her same as she see me serve Peleg; and then pretty soon I see the other woman and spoke to her, and she promised for you, Square, that I shouldn't be touched; and so I came."

"And what are your future plans?" asked Brent in a repressed voice, as he finished writing.

"All I ask, Square, is a chance to die quiet —that's all I want—so help me God," replied the man, with desperate earnestness in his voice, and turning his haggard face and bloodshot eyes from side to side of the room like some maimed reptile seeking a crevice wherein to hide and die.

"Let him go, Marston," said Beatrice in a low voice, as her eyes followed the motions of the criminal with a look of mingled aversion and contempt. "Let him creep away and die."

"He has my promise," replied Brent in the same tone; "although I do not know how far the law would justify my action after this confession. Still, he has my promise, and he is safe.

"Joachim Brewster, sign your name to this paper in presence of these witnesses; give up the will of which you speak, and depart, remembering that, should you ever reappear, your confession will be used against you without hesitation, and that though you now escape the justice of man, the justice of God still pursues, and will yet overtake you."

"That's most too bad of you, Square, when I'm a-doing all I can to set things straight agen," whimpered Joachim, signing his name in a character so shaking and so crabbed as

hardly to be legible. "Don't you believe that Peleg will be pacified with this day's work, Square?"

"It is not your brother that you have to dread," said Brent in a low voice. "It is God who will demand him at your hand, as He demanded Abel of Cain."

"O Lord! O Lord! a'n't there no getting away from it nohow?" gasped the man, sinking upon his knees, while the sweat of mortal agony gathered upon his sordid brow, and his eyes, filled with abject terror, wandered from

"O Uncle! there is a God."

Brent's firm, unsympathizing face to meet the look of satisfied hatred upon that of Paul Freeman, and at last sought with piteous appeal the two women, who had risen, and stood looking down upon him—Mrs. Chappelleford with close scrutiny, Ruth with terrible but mingled emotion.

That look demanded words, and Beatrice replied to it:

"It would be happier for you to believe that there is no God," said she calmly.

"That were to cast away the small remnant of hope left possible. Do not counsel him thus," said Brent sternly; and then Ruth, fluttering forward, fell upon her knees beside her father's murderer and her own cruel enemy, and taking his poor, trembling hands in hers, cried, while the tears ran down her face:

"O uncle! there is a God, and there is no escaping from Him or deceiving Him; but He is the God of Love and Pardon as well as of Justice, and He will forgive you if you truly, truly repent—I know He will, for he puts it in my heart to forgive you, and to promise you that father will forgive you, too, if only you will use every minute that is left of your life in repenting and doing right."

"Is that so, Ruth? Do you feel as if you'd got a right to tell me that? O Ruthie! don't you cheat your poor old uncle that's most killed a'ready with what he's got to bear."

"It is true, uncle—it is true! Oh! I am just as sure as sure can be!" sobbed the girl, her pale face glorified with the earnestness of her faith. "It was a terrible sin; but nothing is too bad to be forgiven if only you are sorry enough, and do all you can to make up for it in this world."

"I'm glad I come here, Ruth. I thought it were for your sake I was a-doing it, but it were for my own. Ruth, you've give me the first word of comfort I've felt in five long year. I wish't you'd come along o' me and teach me the way to repent; seems as if I could keep up to it easier if I had you clos't by."

But Ruth shrank back at this proposal, and Brent spoke sharply and decidedly:

"That is out of the question. There lies the door, Joachim Brewster. Go! and God grant that His pardon may indeed reach you."

Without a word, the broken man whom he addressed rose to his feet, cast one tremulous glance of gratitude and appeal upon his niece, who could not meet it, and then slunk out of the house and down the road, glancing behind him and around him at every step, as one who feels himself pursued by unseen avengers, and so passed from their sight forever.

CHAPTER LI.

THE ICHTHYOSAURUS.

But Beatrice stayed not to watch the departure of the God stricken sinner, nor to discuss the story he had told with those who remained behind. The few words of stern reproof with which Brent had met her attempt to soothe the culprit's terrors by suggesting a doubt as to their foundation had smitten her sorely, and while the attention of every one was absorbed in Brewster's movements, she stole softly from the room and the house.

"O Marston! if I have lost faith, and hope, and all Christian graces, it is your fault, only yours," murmured she, gliding along the wood-path where the shades of evening already lay. "If you had but held me in your keeping, you might have made of me what you would. But cold reason, unwarmed by love, yields only bitter fruit. Why should I believe in a God who has denied me every thing?"

And then as if terrified at her own question, she stood still, glancing timidly into the dusky coverts of the wood, and hesitating whether to venture farther from the human companionship which was at once an accusation and a protection.

While she stood thus hesitating, the miners employed by her husband, under Brent's permission, came trooping along the path, laughing and singing with the boisterous mirth of rude health and animal spirits. Any thing so tangible restored the poise of Mrs. Chappelleford's mind at once, and she moved slowly forward to meet them. The foreman stopped to speak to her.

"Good-evening, ma'am. Has Mr. Chappelleford come out of the mine?"

"I have not seen him. Have not you been with him?"

"No, ma'am. He said he didn't want any one to come anigh him unless he called, and as we didn't hear any thing, we concluded he'd come out, and gone home. Was you going up there, ma'am?"

"No—yes, I think I will go and meet him. He is in the path to the right of the entrance, is he not?"

"Yes, ma'am. Some ways in, I judge, though he didn't want to be followed, and I don't know justly where he is. Maybe you'd like to have me go with you, ma'am, as it's getting kind of latish for the mines."

"No, thank you, I am not at all afraid; and Mr. Chappelleford, you say, asked you not to come?"

"Yes, ma'am, he said so; but, any way, you had better take my lantern. It's dark as Egypt after you get in a piece; long before you'll see his light you will lose the daylight, every glimpse of it."

"Thank you, I will take the lantern," said Beatrice, with the courteous smile that won for her the hearts of such men as this—too far beneath her to feel the scorn and satire with which she too often visited the faults and foibles of her equals.

"Say, Mike," asked the foreman of one of his companions, as they passed on, "don't the Queen you're so fond of talking about look something like that?"

"Only she a'n't so purty nor so ginteel in her figger. This un 'ould make the better queen of the two if she had the luck," replied the Irishman.

But Beatrice, moving swiftly on toward the deserted mine, was thinking:

"Yes; I will go to him and ask him to pity and help me; for what else have I left in heaven or earth? His teachings have deprived me of any faith in the love of God, and my own folly has cut me off from the love of man. What is left to me but the cold intellectual companionship he has so far given me? I cannot lose that too." And hastily, as one who fears to feel her purpose fail before it is accomplished, she glided along the darkening path beneath the rustling shadow of the firtrees, past the broken well where the murderer had lain that morning concealed, and up the steep and stony hill, until, breathless and with palpitating heart, she stood in the entrance of the mine, the daylight all behind her, and impenetrably dark before.

Listening eagerly, she heard no sound except the slow dripping of water oozing through the loose slatestone and plashing upon the floor beneath.

"Mr. Chappelleford!" called she timidly, and an echo far within the arched passage returned the cry in a strange, mocking tone, like that of the demon of the mine daring her to enter.

"Oh! I cannot go in," whispered Beatrice, shrinking back, and trembling nervously, and then the bitter thought of a few moments before returned upon her.

"He is my husband—he is all I have left for this life or another. I must not shrink from following where he leads; I must make my peace with him before the sun sets."

And with trembling fingers she lighted her lantern, and with desperate courage pushed forward into the dismal darkness and mocking echoes of the mine. A hundred rods and she had lost the daylight, and felt as if miles of darkness and desolation separated her from her fellow-men. Holding her breath with terror, guarding her steps that they should make no sound, glancing now at this side, now at that, catching reflections of the light she carried from the glittering surface of quartz or mica, or from the brilliant eyes of some bloated toad squatted beside her path, shrinking from the spectral flight of bats and nightbirds haunting the place, she hurried on, feeling as if she was moving in a dream, in a dismal nightmare which presently must culminate in some fantastic horror never yet imagined or experienced by human mind.

On, and on, and on, until her limbs shook with weariness, and her swimming brain threatened to give way beneath the pressure it sustained; and as she paused, leaning against the slimy rock for support, and dimly wondering, if she were to die there, what Marston Brent would feel in finding her, her straining ears caught a faint sound, and she fancied a yet fainter gleam of light far down the noisome tunnel she was traversing.

"Thank God, I have reached him!" was the cry of the desolate woman's whole heart, and then she hurried on, running now, and never heeding the echoes that mocked and the shadows which came crowding after her, never heeding bruises, or soil, or fatigue, for every moment the far light grew nearer and more certain, and every moment Beatrice expected to catch sight of her husband at his work or coming toward her.

But the journey was over, the friendly beacon reached, and still she could not see him; only just opposite the light which stood upon a projecting shelf of slate lay a great mass of rock almost filling the passage, while above it a corresponding chasm in the wall of the gallery showed whence it had fallen.

Beatrice stood for a moment viewing this scene in wonder and dismay, and then a sudden horror seized upon her, and she called sharply:

"Mr. Chappelleford! Oh! speak, if you are here!"

"Who is it?" asked a voice dim with anguish—a voice that seemed to come from beneath the huge mass of rock, and to feel its weight in every tone.

Her muscles tense with horror, her eyes wild with dread of what they must behold, Beatrice passed between the rock and the side of the gallery, and came upon a sight that had well-nigh killed her as she stood. Her husband lay beneath that crushing weight, only his head, his right arm, and a small portion of his chest visible—the rest of his body mercifully hidden, save that a slow stream of blood trickled out from beneath the rock, and stagnated in a ghastly pool beside her feet.

Unable to stand, unable to speak, Beatrice sank down beside that livid head, and felt that the horror which had led her so far had culminated here, and that the worst was upon her.

"Is it you, Beatrice?" whispered the white lips of the dying man.

"Yes. I must go for help. But what help can move this rock?"

"None. Do not go. I should be dead long before you could return. Sit quietly there, and see me off. I have been thinking of you. I am glad you came."

"But something must be done— we must at all events try," gasped Beatrice, wringing her hands and looking piteously at the tons of torture piled upon that poor crushed body.

"Nothing can be done. Do not speak of that again. It is the ichthyosaurus. He is on this surface next me, and he is lost. The roof is too low to admit of turning the rock, and they cannot blast without burying it, besides they will never take the trouble. I wish you could have seen it, and then you could describe it in the work upon Saurians. I want you to finish that book, Beatrice. I am afraid you could not manage the philology, although you would have helped me amazingly. You may give the papers collected for that to Arnold, and let him see what he can do. I won't play dog in the manger. It is getting very cold here. Beatrice, I am sorry I told the story of the monkey—it was not courteous, and your manner toward me has always been perfect——"

"Oh! sir, I wished my heart had been more so," sighed Beatrice, and she stooped to press her cold lips upon the colder forehead of the dying man.

"Nonsense. Your heart, child—it is a muscle, nothing more. You have been all to me that I wished or asked. I was vexed at you to-day, because I thought you were past such follies as you hinted, and when I am dead, I suppose you will relapse completely, and marry this man, and prattle of love and moonshine, as you did at seventeen. Well, the time grows short—finish the Saurians first. Promise me that Beatrice."

"I will finish it—I promise you."

"Before you marry Brent?"

"I shall never marry again."

"Pho! nonsense. And perhaps, after all, Beatrice, perhaps it is as well for you women. I thought I could place you above your sex, and I have; but it is an isolation—love, kisses, dress, cooking, babies, they are your natural delights, and you miss them. It was an experiment, and I shall make no more."

"Dear friend and teacher! Forgive me that I have not better rewarded your care—forgive me that I have not held myself steadfast in your path! But this is not the moment to think of me. Tell me, have you no message, no trust to confide to me?"

"None. My worldly affairs are in order, and you know all my plans. If not what other men call wife, you have been a dear and valued comrade to me, Beatrice. I have not cared to say how dear——"

"And, O my friend! how desolate you are leaving me!" cried Beatrice, made selfish by despair. "Oh! that I too were dying, that I might follow you to that other world, as I have through this."

"Other world—do you believe it, dear? I am sorry I uprooted that simple faith of yours, for now I want it. Beatrice, is there no God?"

"Oh! sir, do you ask me?"

"And you dare not answer! It is my own work, my own work, and it turns upon me now. Woman, it is for you to hold your faith steadfast and shining while man gropes blindly through the labyrinth of reason. It is my doing, but it is your disgrace that you have not a word of comfort for me now. Oh! if I could hear my mother praying beside me as I heard her once when I was a child, and as she thought dying. She begged my life of God that night so piteously, so passionately, that He gave it her. If she were here, she would beg my soul's life even more fervently."

"But you do not believe—you derided my faith—you reasoned away my hope—you rooted out all the pious teaching of my youth," moaned Beatrice, writhing beneath the sense of her own powerlessness in this extremity.

"To reason, and deride, and uproot were my gifts; yours should have been to cling fast to your faith. If only I had my mother here— my mother—how her eyes shone as she lifted them heavenward! Where is she now? Do you believe, do I believe, that saintly woman is mere dust and daisies? O Beatrice, Beatrice! speak a word of hope—tell me that dear mother lives, and I shall see her—tell me I am not going to annihilation—what, lose all that I have learned so painfully!—this mind, this memory, these heaped thoughts, all going to oblivion in one brief hour! O woman! argue with me, force belief upon me—at the least, pray for me—pray—pray—call upon God to shine in upon the black despair which overwhelms me! O woman! if you are a woman indeed, like those who lay the night through at the foot of the cross, say one word of prayer to God, for I—I dare not!"

And kneeling there, her head humbly down-dropt, her voice choked with anguish and terror for his soul and for her own, Beatrice faintly murmured the words that she had learned, an innocent child, long years before, and had never spoken since her marriage.

"Amen!" whispered the white lips of the dying man, and then death laid his finger upon them, and they spoke no more.

CHAPTER LII.

RUTH'S BETROTHAL.

SHE knew that he was dead, and yet she sat there dumb and motionless, her face white and still as his, her eyes fixed, her mind wandering through time and eternity, she knew not whither.

Through all the chaos into which her life seemed of a sudden fallen, one thought alone rose definite and undeniable. He, that dead man there, the man toward whom she had assumed such solemn and unending duties, he had asked her for comfort in his dying moments, for a word of faith, or promise, or supplication, and she had none to give him, not one. No comfort for him, none for herself were she too dying—not even the poor cry of unreasoning belief. And this was the result then of life, this the end toward which she had so arduously toiled, this the grand result of philosophy, and intellect, and intelligent theory as opposed to blind faith. He, her teacher, and the most learned man she had ever known, the profoundest thinker, the clearest reasoner, the most fearless theorist and analyzer, he had died longing to hear his mother's voice interceding with God for the soul of her unbelieving child. Was this the end of such men? Must such an end be hers ere long?

So she sat, while the minutes and the hours went by, and the twilight gave place to night, and the toad and bat and slimy creeping

things came softly up to glide about her feet, and stare at the glittering pool of blood, and flash their moist skins and evil eyes in the dim light, and creep in beneath the stone which had crushed out that life but now so full of power and thought.

And she, never seeing them, sat motionless beside her dead, and learned from his dumb lips such teaching as, living, he never had been capable of giving.

They found her there as the night wore on, Marston Brent and the rest, and gathered about her with broken exclamations of pity and dismay. Brent it was who raised her in his arms and carried her forth to the living world once more. He did not speak, and she said only :

"Bring me to your Ruth."

And in Ruth's arms he left her.

With infinite labor they raised the great stone, and drew the poor broken body from beneath it, then let it fall, and shudderingly left it, the imprint of the antediluvian monster soaked in the blood of the man of latest science who had sought to steal his secret. The monster had conquered, and he lies there to-day even more secure from molestation than when the dead man first discovered him.

They bore the body forth, and the next day buried it with the Christian ordinances which the philosopher, despising in life, had clung to in death, and let us hope that the sleep to which they laid him shall end in the light of clearest day.

A week passed away, and then Brent asked an audience of his guest, who had never yet left the room whither he had carried her from the mine.

He found her calm, pale, and silent, receiving such words of sympathy as he could offer almost without reply, and seeming to half forget his presence even while he spoke.

At last he said :

"I trust you will not doubt my pleasure in retaining you beneath my roof, or my desire to leave you time to recover from this great shock before you are troubled with outward matters, but I think it right to tell you that I am about to journey to Milvor with Ruth, that her affairs there may be permanently settled, and if you think best to go with us——"

"Yes, I will go. I wish to go to Milvor," interrupted Beatrice, catching at the name.

"I thought it likely, and perhaps you will suffer less in the journey now than after a while. The first effect of such a blow is apathy, the anguish comes later."

"How do you know, Marston Brent? You never have suffered 'such a blow,'" exclaimed Beatrice almost fiercely.

"My life has not been desolated by death, but I have suffered," said Brent quietly, and without waiting for a reply, he recounted the preparations he had made for the journey, and mentioned the day and hour in which he proposed to set forth.

Beatrice listened to all without raising her heavy eyes or making any remark. When he had done, she only said:

"Do as you think best. All I wish is to be at Milvor, and hidden from the world."

"In another week you will be there, and may you find the rest you seek. Poor Beatrice!" said Brent softly, and so left her to the solitude she seemed to crave.

In the passage he met Ruth, who hesitatingly said:

"Can I speak with you a moment, sir?"

"Certainly. Come into the office," said Brent; and when the door was closed: "Well, Ruthie?"

"I thought it best to tell you myself, sir, that I have about concluded to marry Paul," said Ruth, turning very pale, and leaning against the corner of the heavy table in the centre of the room,

"Indeed! Why, Ruth, I thought—he told me, in fact, that you had refused him, or nearly so," said Brent in sudden bewilderment, for out of Paul Freeman's bitter revealings and Ruth's own artless confessions, and the desperate need of his own heart, he had built a shadowy scheme for the future, hardly confessed as yet even to himself, but growing every day more clear and certain.

"I thought you did not love Paul, Ruthie," said he again as the girl stood mute and white before him.

"He loves me very much indeed, sir, and perhaps that is better than for me to love him, and he not care any thing about me," said Ruth, with hidden fire.

"Why, yes, I suppose so: and yet, Ruth, if you do not love him, or if you could love some one else now, do not be in such haste. Wait a little, and——"

"No, sir, I don't want to wait—that's just what I had rather not do," replied the girl, so vehemently that even Brent suspected a hidden meaning in her words, and after a moment's thought took her hand, saying:

"Ruth, my dear, you must explain this. What has happened to make you angry and doubtful of me? What has Paul been saying to you?"

"He says, sir, that you were going to—to take pity on me — because — because — you thought I liked you, and that now you will be sorry, but you will keep to the promise you have made yourself because you are so strict in keeping your word; but—but I'd rather a great deal that you should not, sir."

"Paul has done very wrong, and has shown himself dishonorable in putting such ideas in your head," said Brent in much displeasure. "If I have for a moment dreamed of asking you to be my wife, it was hoping to receive as much happiness as I could give, but I have never put the idea in words to Paul or to myself, and——"

"And please don't do it now, sir, for indeed I had rather not," hastily interposed Ruth, her cheeks aflame.

"Then I will not; but tell me why not now as well as some weeks ago, when I spoke of this matter with Paul?"

"Because, sir, Mrs. Chappelleford is a widow now, and though you might ask me to marry you, and try to feel contented, you never would forget the chance you lost for me, and I should know it, and I should suffer more than—than—and I had rather marry Paul, who loves me truly and wholly, and never has loved any one else."

She turned toward the door, and laid her hand upon the latch, yet lingered with downcast eyes and quick-throbbing heart, lingered for his reply. It came:

"Ruth, can you believe that never until this moment have I connected the thought of Mrs. Chappelleford's widowhood with any possible advantage to myself, never until you yourself suggested it? And, Ruth, had you accepted the offer I was about to make to you I never should have associated the two ideas, for having once given my faith to you, I humbly trust that there is nothing in my nature so base that I could have broken it, even in thought. I say, Ruth, had I been your promised husband, those words of yours would have been of no effect. But now——"

"But now that I have suggested it, you see that you love her, and only her," cried Ruth in a sharp, passionate voice.

"No. I have so long and so resolutely disconnected Beatrice Chappelleford, wife of another man, from Beatrice Wansted, whom I loved devotedly, that I may boldly say I do not love her now, and had her husband lived, or had I bound myself to you or another woman, I never should have loved her, other than as the angels love. But now, Ruth, were I to become your husband, I cannot promise, I cannot be sure that I should never remember her. I do not wish to speak to her of love, but the thought of her might come between me and other love. I cannot be certain—I dare not bind myself."

"And you shall not to me, Mr. Brent. My mind is quite made up, and I am going to give Paul Freeman his answer this minute. I am so sorry that you fancied I cared, for though I am very, very grateful for all your kindness, I never thought, I am sure——"

"There, child, there! Say no more. We understand each other now, and for all our lives you are my dear sister, friend, daughter, in one. Perhaps all that I shall ever find of woman's love is what Paul will spare to me from the treasure you will bring him."

And Ruth without reply, without turning her face toward him, left the room, and finding Paul, threw herself into his arms, sobbing:

"There, take me, Paul, take me and comfort me."

CHAPTER LIII.

A LITTLE CREEPING FLAME.

NIGHT fell sombre and starless—one of the dark, breathless nights of summer, when the perfume of the flowers seems to cling close to the earth, too languid, too oppressed by its own sweetness to rise heavenward; when the straining eyes find themselves unable to penetrate the dense blackness of the atmosphere, and the ears, growing preternaturally acute, seem to discover a strange and mysterious meaning in the cries of insect and night-bird—seem to listen to a half-revealed secret in every sigh of the fitful wind, every whisper among the invisible foliage of the trees; nights filled with melancholy and with electricity, when a sadness, equally without explanation and without remedy, weighs upon the spirit, and wakes in its profoundest depths vague memories, regrets, longings, but half understood, half believed, and yet more real than the grossest realism of daylight, for they are the voice of the soul struggling to assert itself without the limitations of mind and body; they are the utterances of the life that lies hidden deep within the recesses of every man's existence—hint of the life hereafter to be developed from this germ which every one of us carries within him, and yet so seldom recognizes.

Sombre and starless fell the night, and the dense shadow of Moloch Mountain, stretching across the valley and the wood, touched the distant hill-side and the lonely grave where Mary Brewster lay asleep, with her murdered husband at her side—that hill-side upon whose green slope the farewell glance of that husband had dwelt, as he rode forth from his own door, and went to meet his doom; and then the shadow crept on and clung about the old house beyond, wrapping it close and fatally as the veil is wrapped about the head and shoulders of the doomed slave led from her luxurious harem to her cold bed beneath the Bosphorus. The old house, dreary and lonely in its best estate, and in these latter days showing a desolation and a doom in its every faltering line, every unshuttered and staring window, in the atmosphere that seemed to cling like a visible curse about it. Within, sat the wife of Joachim Brewster, deserted now of him as of all mankind, and left alone in that melancholy house—alone, yet never alone, for the memories of the past and the terrors of the future were there, and never left her—sitting beside her at hearth or board, lying down with her upon the haunted couch, waking her remorselessly to the dawning of a new day of torment. She had not seen her thirtieth birthday, this woman, and yet her hair was white, her skin cadaverous, her limbs faltering and distorted. She had lived fast with these constant companions of hers, and the life was telling upon her. But chief among her torments was a shadowy horror—intangible, yet none the less real; forever near, yet never within her reach; never seen, yet never to be eluded—a presence at her side, although neither eye nor hand discovered other than empty air—a something waiting just behind each door she opened in the dreary house, lurking in every shadow, waiting for her in her chamber as she crept stealthily up stairs to bed, sitting close beside her in the darkness of the night, mingling with the shadows of the dawn when the weary night was through—a something tormenting her with a sense of being just beyond her range of vision, seeming, however sharply she might turn upon it, to be just gone from the spot at which she looked, just visible at some point behind or beside her, if she could but reach it soon enough; for here was the horrible fascination of this horror—while dreading nothing so much as to encounter it, she yet must spend her whole life in its pursuit, waiting, watching, with bated breath and staring eyes, now wandering from room to room, now sitting motionless—struggling, as a drowning man struggles for breath, to overcome this forever receding and invisible barrier behind which her tormentor hid. So she sat sometimes the whole night through, sleepless and vigilant, her ears alive to the dim, uncertain sounds that filled the remoter chambers of the empty house, her unresting eyes following with fierce and hungry glances that formless presence forever eluding their pursuit.

So she sat, while the night fell sombre and starless, while the shadow of the mountain stretched across the valley and the wood laid a finger upon the hill-side graves, and then crept on, spreading itself like a black pall around and above the doomed house, and stealing shade by shade through the room where she, the woman sat, crouched in the farthest corner, watching and waiting, her white face and gleaming eyes showing in ghastly contrast upon the sombre background of the wall.

A sullen fire was dying upon the hearth, the last charred stick flickering and blackening above the gray ashes of the rest, then breaking in the centre, and falling, over half extinguished by the fall, the other rolling across the hearth, and resting upon the edge of the boards beyond. Opposite the fireplace stood the old brass-bound secretary where Peleg Brewster had kept the will that his wife had so often urged him to destroy, the picture of his wife Mary, with the letters that she had written him before their marriage. So often she had seen him sit there, his head upon his hand, his eyes fixed upon the little drawer where she knew these treasures lay—his sorrowful, introspective eyes, that never had met her own with love, so often with reproof. The picture and the letters were there still—she never had dared look at them but once—and the other things too lay just as he had left them. She would almost as soon have opened his coffin as open that secretary, for it still was his, his very own.

His? Whose? That shadow's that flitted over and past it, now seeming to sink through the solid wood, now swiftly gliding aside or upward, to lose itself in the obscure corners of the room? What was it? Not a shadow, for the night had fallen, and the room was black-dark, save for a creeping bluish tongue of flame fastening upon the floor where it joined the hearth, and a strange light that seemed to her to float about the old secretary—the secretary, as much Peleg Brewster's own possession still as was the coffin wherein his murdered body mouldered. Was this light then the thing that so long had troubled her? Was it the light or something which it presently would disclose? Was that a form just disappearing behind the end of the secretary—no, at the other side—where? Gone? No, but coming, growing within that light, taking form and shape, and then disappearing when she turned to watch it. Disappearing and again appearing, as it had always done through all these weary years, the years since—well, since what? She did not know now, but it was no matter, for that thing was just about to disclose itself—surely, surely it was about to confront her at last, and what would it be? Those sorrowful, stern eyes? Did they look at her out of that shadow—nay, that light? Well, light or shadow, what matter? Why must even that remain a bewildering doubt, vexing her with its unending question? Light or shadow, IT was there, more nearly visible than ever it had been before; and now she could grapple with it, demand its meaning, deny its accusations, retort its reproaches. But no, no, it was gone again, hiding in the farthest corner of the room, creeping along the walls, brooding above her head, wrapped in this cloud of hot, stifling smoke, crouching behind her. Behind her? Why, how could that be, when she was pressing back against the wall with all her might? for it must not get behind her, she could not endure that—and, no, it was not near her now, but flashing angry glances from behind this cloud which wrapped it and the secretary, and the room, and crowded down so fiercely upon her breath, almost stifling her beneath its awful pressure. Such red, fiery glances, such consuming and withering wrath as they flashed upon her! Was it coming at last then, coming in visible presence to seize upon her, helpless and unheard, with no chance to struggle or retort? And what were those words the minister said the last time she ventured within the church? Something about the " worm that never dies, and the fire which is not quenched." The fire which is not quenched, is this it—this scorching and devouring flame which creeps along the floor, and climbs the walls, and reaches out its long tongues toward her? And now it sinks, and now it rises, and she, huddled there in the farthest corner, sits glaring at it, and drawing her garments closer about her, and cowering to the wall which shuts her in, yet opens to shut out that Thing, which haunts her even in the flames, until, as one long serpent-tongue sweeps out and fastens upon her clothes, she breaks into maddest frenzy, shouting, laughing, screaming, rushing recklessly forward to meet and defy the foe she thinks to have found at last, and who wraps her about in his fiery mantle, and scorches the breath upon her lips, the blood within her veins !

When morning dawned, and old Moloch, drawing toward himself the shadow that had wrapped the scene, looked across valley and forest to the grave upon the hill-side, he saw beyond them a heap of smoking and smouldering ruins which no human being had yet approached, although the scene was not without its mourners, for a gaunt hound sat beside the blackened doorsteps, howling dismally, and upon the blasted pine behind the house hung, flapping and croaking, a pair of carrion-crows.

CHAPTER LIV.
PENANCE.

To Beatrice, sheltered in her childhood's home, safe and quiet in the guardianship of her aunt, who, if she did not understand, at least did not interfere with her, came after a time her uncle's wife, with not insincere expressions of sympathy and affection, and an urgent request that Mrs. Chappelleford should return with her to town, and accept a home beneath her uncle's roof. But Beatrice shook her head, smiling sadly :

"Thank you very much, Juanita, and thank my dear uncle, too, but I cannot come at present; I am busy here."

"Busy, my dear child?" asked Mrs. Bar-

stow, glancing around the quiet chamber with incredulous surprise.

"Yes, busy in settling my life."

"But that is just what we want to do for you—to settle your life. Come to us, and that will settle it."

"I don't mean that sort of life," said Beatrice quietly. "I am trying to understand—but no matter now."

As her voice drearily died away, and her eyes sought the distant hills where the sunshine lay brightly, although the country between was all in shadow, Mrs. Barstow looked at her with quiet worldly scrutiny.

"My dear," said she, "I would not do it."

"Do what?"

"Either of the two things you have in mind—either marry Marston Brent or become devout. Neither will suit you as well as the role of belle esprit you have so successfully played since your marriage with my uncle Chappelleford. You are too young, too handsome, and too brilliant for a dévote; and as for Mr. Brent —— That reminds me to thank you, Trix, for saving me from an awful stupidity. If you had not been with me when Major Strangford came home, I might have gone into some sentimental nonsense with him—it was quite on the cards. But you helped me over the first danger, and after that I reflected—why really it would have been very foolish—and I found, on a second look, that he had gone off immensely, quite broken up, and passé indeed. And, that danger over, there was no chance of another; for a good house, as many carriages as I choose, and a husband with a hundred thousand a year, are ever so much better than moonlight and Tennyson, as I dare say you knew when you advised against the Major. And really Mr. Barstow and I am very comfortable together; he is a prince for generosity, and as indulgent as possible. He has never spoken a cross word since we were married, Beatrice."

"Dear, good uncle Israel ! And is he happy, Juanita?"

"I mean to make him so, and I think I do. I always consult him before ordering dinner, and never object to his inviting his stupid old merchants, and smoking in the library. And actually, my dear, I find that I am growing almost domestic in my tastes. Having no girls to bring out, I have not the ties to society that most married women have; and—now don't you laugh—I positively enjoy a game of whist occasionally, and even a 'hit at backgammon,' as Mr. Barstow calls it. And I make it a positive duty to give him a little music after dinner, almost every evening, and he likes going to the theatre with me. So, altogether, Trix, I count myself a model wife—quite a Grizelda in fact, and I think your uncle would tell you the same story."

" I am very glad, very glad indeed, Juanita, for I never knew a man who deserved better of his wife and his home than my uncle Israel," said Beatrice warmly.

And the elder matron, laughing slyly, inquired:

" Not even Marston Brent?"

" Don't, Juanita. I do not think of Mr. Brent, or he of me. My mind is filled with other matters, and he, I hope, will marry Ruth Brewster."

" Beatrice, I want to ask you a question; will you answer it truly?"

" Truly, if at all."

" Your old Jesuitical answer; but n'importe. When I told you that I was afraid to meet Major Strangford, because I fancied myself still in love with him, you almost crushed me with your virtuous indignation at the idea of a married woman being in love with any one but her husband, and, if I remember, you vowed it would be impossible for you to even imagine such a thing. Now, Trix, tell me, after you had stayed three weeks under the same roof with Marston Brent, did not you change your mind?"

And as Mrs. Barstow asked her searching question, she looked keenly into that pure, pale face so steadily set toward the distant hills, whose shining peace was reflected in the eyes that watched them. The face did not droop, the calm eyes did not quail, but a slow wave of color mounted through cheek and chin, even to the masses of bright hair coiled away from the white brow—mounted, and burned, and faded before Beatrice replied; then she said:

" I will answer you, Juanita, and truly, though to my own shame. The armor of which I so presumptuously boasted to you proved of no avail when the hour of trial came, nor would the worldly shield which saved you have proved sufficient for me. Even while I assured myself that there was no danger, the danger stood face to face with me, and all my defences of philosophy, and reason, and intellect dropped away like flax

within the fire, and left me simple, defenceless woman."

" Well, what then? What saved you?" asked Mrs. Barstow breathlessly.

" The honor, the conscience, the Christian principle of Marston Brent," said Beatrice with a sudden fervor in her voice. " I failed, and he upheld me: I was simple, and he rebuked me; I was despairing, and he, by the noble example of his own life, taught me how to live."

" Then you acknowledged to each other that you were still in love?"

" Certainly not."

" But you are, aren't you?"

" Juanita, you are profane. You grasp at matters of which you should not even speak."

" Mercy on me! Beatrice, I cannot understand you in the least," exclaimed Mrs. Barstow pettishly.

" I know it—I do not understand myself as yet, and I certainly should not have said what I have to you, but that ——"

" Well, what?"

" I considered it a fitting penance for my arrogance when I spoke to you before. I was right in my conclusions then, but all wrong in my reasoning, and more than wrong in my estimate of my own strength. Now, dear, let us speak of something else, and lay this aside forever."

" And you will not come to town with me?"

" No thank you, Juanita."

" Or join us in the winter?"

" No; I have done with life, such life as that, and I shall stay in Milvor until ——."

Juanita waited patiently, but the sentence was not finished, and she left the room.

CHAPTER LV.
REWARD.

THE summer waned, and in the bright autumnal days, Beatrice resumed the active out-of-doors life she had so much enjoyed during her girlhood. Many an hour she spent upon old Moloch, climbing his topmost crest to catch the first rays of sunrise, seeking new points of view whence to admire the well-remembered, well-beloved landscape, where sparkles of the distant sea seemed glimpses of another world, with promise of delights not known of this.

But best she loved, in the melancholy, golden light of afternoon—those autumn afternoons which murmur, in their sleep upon the hills, of the long, dreamless sleep waiting for them beneath the snows of winter—to sit beside the rushing mill-brook, half choked now with gold and scarlet and rich brown leaves whirled down upon it from the trees above; and sitting there, she dreamed—her wistful eyes fixed upon those distant sparkles of the ocean, or upon the sky stooping to meet it, almost as blue, almost as bright, and holding no less of promise, dared one accept it. These dreams? Sometimes they were of the lands beyond the sea, whither she had already wandered, and might some day return—sometimes of fairer possible worlds beyond that smiling sky—sometimes of her own life, which seemed, having rounded its circle of experience, to be finishing here where it began.

And then, with a stifled sigh, Beatrice would sometimes look about her, and remember the glow and glory of those early days, and the unreflecting gayety with which she had so often trod the mountain-paths, or sat here beside the mill-brook, and not alone.

"But that was spring, and this is autumn," whispered she one day, and fell to thinking of the two—spring, so full of promise and of growth; crude, raw, and untaught, but glowing with hope and possibilities that make amends for all—autumn, strong, brilliant, mature, bringing sheaves and fruit instead of buds and flowers, and yet with an inexpressible melancholy in its glory, tears beneath its smiles, the hint of approaching death in all its brilliant coloring.

' And this is autumn," repeated Beatrice, slowly rising and descending the hill, until in the cloudy glory of sunset she passed between the rows of box, holding her breath not to perceive their fragrance, and entered the gray old house which was now her home.

"Where have you been all the afternoon, Beatrice?" asked her aunt from her seat beside the fire in the eastern room. "We have had company. Marston Brent has been here, and waited until the last moment to see you. He came East on business, and ran down here for the afternoon. He was very sorry not to see you."

But Beatrice, with a sudden faintness upon her, sat suddenly down beside her aunt, and did not reply. Mrs. Bliss, busy with her story, and a troublesome stitch in her knitting, went on without looking up.

"He could not stay because he had to attend a directors' meeting in the city to-morrow

early, and was to start for home in the afternoon with some of the other directors. He has got a company to take his mine—sold it, I suppose; at any rate, he has made a great deal of money, and don't mean to stay in Pennsylvania always, he says; he thinks some of going abroad."

"Does he?" said Beatrice with an effort.

"Yes, as soon as he gets matters settled out there. I believe he thinks he shall stay there this winter. That Brewster girl and Paul Freeman are going to be married at Christmas."

"Did Mr. Brent say so?"

"Yes; and old Zilpah is dead. Marston was over at her brother's this morning to tell them about it, and arrange about some property Zilpah left them."

"Zilpah dead! Why did she?" asked Beatrice, over whose pallid face had come a sudden color.

"Why did she? What a queer question, Beatrice! Because she couldn't help it, I suppose; she had the lung-fever besides," said Mrs. Bliss dryly.

"Oh! yes, I dare say; but, aunt, I forgot to ask you to begin some knitting for me. Can you do it now?"

"I began this for you, child. You have grown amazingly industrious lately. You never did half so much work before you were married as you do now, and I am sure you didn't while you were married."

"I like to be doing something," said Beatrice with a brilliant smile, whose meaning her aunt could not define.

"Well, here it is then," said she, holding out the stupendous "tidy" she had commenced; but Beatrice murmuring, "One minute, aunty," left the room, and appeared no more until summoned from her chamber to the tea-table.

"Seems to me your rage for knitting was soon over this afternoon," said Mrs. Bliss, as she handed her a cup of tea.

"The knitting? Oh! dear me, aunty, I forgot all about it!" exclaimed Beatrice with such a laugh and such a blush as no one had seen upon her face for many a month—nay, year.

———

The autumn passed, and the winter, and the spring. Then came summer, and the garden of the Old Garrison House was gay with all its homely, heartsome bloom, and the willow beside the river had donned its fullest verdure, untouched as yet by dust, or worm, or decay, when Beatrice one morning thither betook herself and her book—a volume of sweet, rare old Herbert.

Her days of mourning were over, yet faintly remembered in her pure white dress, with a violet ribbon threading her golden hair, and knotted at her throat; and although there was no mourning in her face, its beauty had taken a pensive and thoughtful cast in this last year, not farther removed from the light-hearted grace of girlhood than from the cold and somewhat haughty expression most often seen upon the face of Vezey Chappelleford's wife.

So sitting—the unopened book upon her lap, her eyes fixed upon the shining, sunlit brook—she heard a step coming down the path—heard and knew it, and would not turn until Marston Brent stood close beside her—his hand outstretched—his frank eyes full upon her face, with a meaning other than ordinary greeting in their glance. Then she rose, gave her hand—both hands indeed—and while the words of courtesy died upon her lips, she gave him welcome with all her glowing face. At last, seated beside her upon the rustic bench, so carefully kept in repair because he had made it, Marston said

" Beatrice, we parted here six years ago."

" Yes."

" Parted forever, as we thought."

" Yes; you said so."

" I? But it was you who willed it!"

" I? No, you!"

" Oh! never, Beatrice!"

" Well, then, not you. But I wish I had known you thought so through all these years."

" Beatrice, we two have suffered——"

" So much!"

" And erred, both of us——"

" Not you."

" Yes, I; I might have yielded something in that old time."

" You could not, and remain true to yourself."

" You have not blamed me, then?"

" No—no, indeed."

And then he took her hand, and what would next have been, who can say, when the sparrow who all this time had watched these terrible interlopers upon her domain with round black eyes shining like little stars above the edge of her nest, fled with a sudden whirr of wings, which startled the lovers, and brought a laugh to relieve the somewhat stringent pressure of the moment.

" Beatrice, are 'any birds in last year's nest?'" asked Marston softly, as he glanced up into the tree.

" Yes, for they are singing in my heart at this moment," whispered she.

" And then——"

But as they went back through the garden, Beatrice paused beside the heart-shaped pansy-plot, and looking into her lover's face with a shy smile, said:

" There were two large purple pansies and one yellow one on the ground here, one morning, and now they are pressed between the leaves of a little Bible Beatrice Wansted used to keep upon her dressing-table."

" What! you found them and saved them, darling!" exclaimed Marston in pleased surprise. " I looked for them as I went back, but could not find them. The willow staff I cut that morning, however, is now a thriving tree beside the Sachawissa. I wanted to carry a cutting to Ironstone Mountain, but I dared not."

" You were always better than I," said Beatrice, smiling and blushing. " I kept the pansies through every thing, although I pretended to myself that I had forgotten them."

Marston returned her smile, but absently, and stood looking at her with all the love of his great truthful heart, so long and painfully repressed, shining in his eyes.

" I wonder if it is the summer sunshine or if it is you that lights up this old garden so!" said he at length. " Even the creeping shadow of old Moloch seems full of brightness and joy."

" We have lived in his shadow six long years, and it is time that it should turn to sunshine," whispered Beatrice tenderly; and so they passed on through the garden and into the dim and echoing old house, so full of memories, and now so full of hope.

CHAPTER LVI.
THE END.

MARSTON BRENT and his wife went abroad, and spent a happy year among scenes which Beatrice had visited indeed, but had never really seen until now, for inward happiness possesses a wonderful power of opening the eyes to all forms of outward beauty. She was pleased, too, to discover that, although Brent's life had been more one of action than of study, he had turned the enforced seclusion of his forest and mountain homes to good account, and was even better acquainted theoretically than she was practically with that Old World whose wondrous stories have been said and sung from the days of Herodotus to this, when books of travel seem to have superseded visiting-cards as announcements of the return of our friends and acquaintances from Outre-Mer.

But before she went abroad—nay, before she married Brent—Beatrice fulfilled in its widest spirit her promise to Mr. Chappelleford. The book of Saurians was published, and although no name but that of the philosopher appeared upon the title-page, it was whispered among the *savans* that at least half the credit of the minute research, elaborate collocation, and elegant and classic diction characterizing the work was due to the unnamed editor.

The papers relating to the philological treatise were also placed in the hands of the literary friend whom Mr. Chappelleford had designated, and we may yet expect a biography of the "Mother of Languages," which shall convert us all into her devotees, although Mrs. Brent's Sanscritian studies never have passed beyond their most elemental stages.

Somewhere abroad, the Brents encountered Monckton, who offered his congratulations, and lingered some weeks in their society with a friendly ease incompatible with bitterness if not with constancy. If he could not forget, he had certainly forgiven the keenest of all wounds with which a man's self-love can be wounded.

"All passeth but Goddis Will." Yes, all passeth, even the shadow; for although earthly journeyings may fail to bring us to the sunny places where other lives seem blooming without pain or care, the shining hills lie full in view beyond the shadow and beyond the flood, and no feet are so tender, no heart so weary, no strength so broken, that they may not hope to win safely through, and scale those glorious heights at last.